PARIS
2005

PARIS
2005

PARIS 2005

CARLO ZEZZA

M. EVANS AND

COMPANY, INC.

NEW YORK

Library of Congress Cataloging-in-Publication Data

Zezza, Carlo, [date]
Paris 2005 / Carlo Zezza
p.   cm.
ISBN 0-87131-588-2
I. Title.
PS3576.E95P3   1990   89-77265
813'.54—dc20

M. Evans and Company, Inc.
216 East 49 Street
New York, New York 10017

MANUFACTURED IN THE UNITED STATES OF AMERICA
2 4 6 8 9 7 5 3 1

PROLOGUE

NOVEMBER 3, 2002

Robert Landry listened to his boss, who was far away in Cleveland. In a few hours the president of the United States would announce the World Peace Agreement, and the chairman of Parallel Technologies wanted Landry to come home.

Landry spun his chair halfway around, so that he could look through the glass that formed one wall of his thirtieth floor office. Spread from his feet to the horizon, the city of Paris glistened gray and green in the afternoon light. He thought of the view from Parallel Technologies' building in Cleveland.

"You won't be able to travel," Landry's boss said. "There's going to be an international visa system. It's aimed at terrorists, but it applies to everyone."

"I don't need to travel," Landry said. "I can get a visa because the French government wants me to stay here."

"What about Helen? They won't give her a visa."

"She'll go. . . . You know the situation." The split in his marriage was no secret.

"Listen, Robert. Even without the World Peace Agreement, it's time for you to come back to the States. What's left for you in France? The machine works. We've made the big money on the project. Turn it over to your staff and get out of there."

"The machine works," Landry agreed, referring to the world's first national computer. "But it's only giving a quarter of its potential. I need another year, maybe two, and this will be a model for the world to copy."

"The Japanese are ready to copy it today. They want to buy your know-how, and we're talking about hundreds of millions of dollars."

"Our patents will protect us for years. The Japanese can wait a few months."

"You don't understand the economics." When the boss talked about economics, he meant profits for Parallel Technologies. "The Japanese are the future. Don't you get it, Robert? The World Peace Agreement has the Japanese behind it, it's an attack on Europe and Europe is going to lose."

"You'll have to explain what you mean," Landry replied.

"I can't spell it out on the telephone," his boss said. "I'm sending my plane over. I want you in my office tomorrow morning. That's an order."

THE live telecast of the president's speech began within minutes after Landry's two A.M. takeoff from Charles de Gaulle Airport in Paris. Even on the small TV screen in the Parallel Technologies jet, the president projected the triumph of making history.

Landry tried in vain to find ominous portents in the speech.

The key feature was destruction of all nuclear weapons, agreed and enforced by Russia and the United States.

"Peace for our children . . ." That brought a standing ovation from the joint session of Congress.

There was more: an end to interference in the sovereign affairs of nations, new covenants for international banking, trade, and travel. The World Peace Agreement would let people prosper while minding their own business.

Landry switched off the television. His leather seat reclined to make a bed, but he slept badly. At five in the morning, Cleveland time, the wheels of the jet squeaked down. He was home.

SHOWERED and shaved, wearing a fresh shirt, Landry presented himself at seven A.M. His boss was already at work, but he quickly got up from his desk, gave Landry a warm smile, and squeezed his hand in a hearty handshake.

"I watched the speech," Landry said. "It seemed good. What did I miss?"

"We can't talk here," his boss said, gesturing at the windows, computers, and communications hardware in his office. "It's not secure."

They went to a windowless room in the center of the building, bare except for a plain table and two steel-framed chairs. There was no telephone and the light on the table was powered by a battery, to avoid wires through the walls. The door sealed behind them with a hiss.

"The president didn't tell everything," Landry's boss said. "There's a secret part to the World Peace Agreement. It's this: no matter what happens, the United States will live up to its nonintervention agreement. Even if the Russians take over Europe."

"That isn't possible."

"The Russians have a three-to-one majority over the Europeans in conventional forces. Their frontier problems in Asia have calmed down, so all the Russians' military weight can be concentrated in the West. Listen Robert twenty years of internal reform and intelligent diplomacy have made the Russians strong. Compared to the West, they are twice as powerful now as they were at the peak of the cold war."

"But it doesn't make sense: they let their satellites in the East Bloc go free. . . . Why would they want all of Europe now?"

"They relaxed their grip on their satellites because they couldn't rebuild their own economy and also hold their neighbors in line. They've won on that strategy. Now they will take Europe for just one reason: there is nothing to stop them."

"But, are we all crazy? My French friends think the Russians are more peaceful than we are. What about us . . . would we just turn our back?"

"We have no choice. The Japanese forced us to make the deal; they threatened us in secret with an economic catastrophe. Japan won't pay any longer to protect Europe by financing our deficit. Europe has become Japan's main competitor. That speech you heard from our president was Japan killing their competition."

"I don't believe the Russians are greedy enough for such a risk."

"There's no risk. They won't need to fight, because the odds are so big in their favor. And that's the whole story, Robert. . . .

The Russians aren't better or worse than the rest of us. People take whatever they can get until something makes them stop; that's the first lesson of history. The Russians are being offered Western Europe on a platter, and they are going to take it. We would probably do the same thing."

Landry tried to imagine himself in a neutralized France, whose allegiance would be to Russia. Would he be able to continue his work?

His boss went on. "We won't pay you to stay in France."

"I can live. If what you say is true, I'm needed more than ever. The machine can't be managed by a bunch of apparatchiks."

"The new French government will agree with you. They will certainly lock you up, just to make sure you do what they want. And our government won't try very hard to get you back."

Landry thought about that. There were steps he could take to keep his freedom.

"I made a commitment to pioneer something, and I'm not finished," Landry said. "If France is going to be Finlandized, that doesn't let me out. No one is ready to replace me."

"This is false vanity, Robert," his boss argued. "You aren't indispensable. You're the best I know, but we have kids working here today who are equal to the Robert Landry of two years ago. Bury yourself in France, and they are going to pass you by."

"I wish them luck."

"The contract with the Japanese is a challenge. You would love the job."

"No."

His boss looked around the room, as though fearing to be overheard. He leaned forward and spoke in a confidential whisper.

"Listen, Robert, we have confidential sources in Japan. Top secret, and God help me if you ever tell anyone what I am telling you now, it would get some people hurt. When you leave this room you must erase what you're about to hear."

Landry nodded, staring at his boss.

"We're not talking about a political maneuver. The Russians are going to roll their tanks across Europe starting the week after Christmas. A military invasion. The Russians want to move fast, before the West Germans and the French start to get nervous about losing their nuclear umbrella and their ally across the Atlantic."

The concern in his boss's face said as much as the words. Landry was stunned, and then felt a rising flush of anger. Could it happen?

"Now will you come home?"

Landry knew he should obey, but anger made him shake his head. They had no right to seize France by force.

"Give me one reason," his boss insisted.

"France can still run better than any country in the world, because of me. That's what I want. Not to work for the Japanese."

Once he had said it, there was no more choice. Even when his boss shouted at him, Landry knew that there was no retreat.

Before Landry left for the airport, his boss promised him a job at Parallel Technologies whenever he asked to come back. But Landry hardly paid attention to the promise. He was furiously thinking about ways to resist the Russians if they came. It would be the biggest challenge of his life, and he had the machine.

FEBRUARY 26, 2005

1 **She** saw them at the end of the street, two hundred meters away, and she hesitated before going on. She knew they were plainclothes detectives; no one but a policeman would wear a black leather overcoat in Paris these days. It was a warm day for February in Paris, and the three policemen were soaking in the last low rays of the afternoon sunlight, looking toward the Champs-Élysées, their shadows cast long across the sidewalk.

She glanced at herself reflected in the window of the Café de la Poste. A shabby woolen coat, and a strand of hair floating loose from under her kerchief. Her eyes met her eyes in the rain-streaked glass.

Her papers, neatly stowed in a plastic folder at the bottom of her knit satchel, identified Chantal Senac: resident of the 13th, widow, born March 12th, 1970, and now approaching her 35th birthday, gray eyes and brown hair, 52 kilos and 1 meter 60 centimeters tall, assigned to night cleaning duties at the Fourth Section of the Ministry of Agriculture, around the corner from the Café de la Poste.

There was nothing to do about the police. They were everywhere, a low level menace, like idle barracuda in a warm sea. She pushed through the door of the café and exchanged a nod of greeting with Madame behind the cash register and Monsieur behind the bar.

At four in the afternoon, there were only two other patrons, elderly workers drinking beer together at the back of the café. Chantal went to a table in the corner, where the window met the wall and the winter sun could angle in over the roofline across the street. She waited for her tea.

In the two years that had passed since the Russians had come across the Rhine, cafés like the Poste had changed little except for the mandatory photographs. Comrade André Joux, president of the People's Democratic Republic of France, and Comrade Georges Paccard, prime minister and first secretary of the Communist party, stared down from the wall behind the cash register. The ornate cash register remained for tradition's sake, but its functions had been replaced by the cash-card reader, a squat black box that sat beside Madame's elbow. The photographs and the card reader were omnipresent now in France. In the Café de la Poste, they were only small reminders of the present.

She came three days each week to drink a cup of tea. It was her second luxury. Her first luxury was washing her hair on Sundays and Thursdays. The shampoo, with the extra charge for hot water in the tub, cost almost exactly the same as her three cups of tea. Together, these two pleasures cost exactly one half of one day's pay.

Monsieur brought the tea. In exchange, he took Chantal's cash card and carried it to Madame, who put the card in the reader, pressed buttons, and waited five seconds for a green light and a printed receipt.

Before Chantal returned the card to her knit satchel, she looked at the receipt to verify that she had been charged the counter price instead of the much higher table price. Since her fourth visit they had extended this favor, in defiance of the government's price code.

The tea's aroma caressed her. She liked tea better than coffee, which was a good thing because tea came from India, and a cup cost only half the price of coffee. Coffee came from the American half of the world, and only the rich could afford it.

Chantal sipped slowly. She thought about her son and wondered if he was ever given a cup of tea, or verveine or camomile, wherever he was. She wished he could be sitting beside her, enjoying a warm cup with her. If she were in the union and had a child to support, she would be paid an extra two days a week for each child. But she was not in the union, and she could not afford to pay for a child without both of them starving. Thinking about Noël made her eyes wet and her throat thick.

She was using the paper napkin to dry her eyes when she heard the door swing open, and she flinched, thinking it was the police coming in for an identity check. Instead, she saw a bearded man hobble through the doorway, supporting his weight with a cane. The man's beard was scruffy at the edges and his hair was matted, roughly trimmed just above the collar in a ragged line. There was an alertness in his manner that caught her attention. Their eyes met.

She started to turn her eyes away, but she could not. His eyes were a light color, as steady as a pair of stones. She stared at him, and then realized in horror that his blank gaze was reading her mind. She yanked her head away, shuddering inside.

He was limping toward her. Painfully, he sat down at the table next to hers. Monsieur came from behind the bar. The bearded man asked for a cup of coffee and a *croque-monsieur*.

Chantal pressed the warm cup of tea to her lips, fixing her eyes on the far wall, calling on herself to crawl back into her cleaning woman's shell, to hide behind her *tablier*. She thought about her hair and was glad that it was clean, and then she was glad that her clean hair was hidden under the kerchief. She thought about the wool socks that were keeping her feet warm. Wool socks. The Faubourg-St. Honoré was far away.

The bearded man spoke, without looking at her, in a quiet voice intended for her alone to hear, "Don't hold the cup like this, or the people will understand you too well."

He showed his thumb and forefinger held together, his little finger extended.

"We of the revolution hold our cups like this," he continued in the same soft tone, wrapping his whole hand around an imaginary cup.

She let the quiet voice ring in her ears. His way of speaking had vanished from her life, and it frightened her. Her heart was racing. She wrapped all the fingers of her hand around the cup and wet her lips with the tea. He was expressionless, watching Monsieur making coffee behind the bar. She knew, as surely as he was dressed in a blue smock and carried a cane, that he, also, was living in disguise.

She looked again at his face. His eyes were set deep under a sharply carved brow, and his high-bridged nose arched down to a square tip. His lips were thin and pale. It was an intelligent face that matched some echo in her memory. She thought that she could have known him. Somewhere, sometime, this man could have shared those strange lost times when she had had a husband, a child, money and friends. She felt a chill run down her back.

The café door opened and two leather-coated policemen came in. Through the window, Chantal saw the third policeman, also in a black leather overcoat, take up a position across the street, facing the door.

Fear pulled at her muscles and caught her breath.

The police in the café were both in their early twenties, carrying their authority with officious swagger. One was tall and thin, with a sallow complexion and a coarse black mustache. He remained by the cash register near the door. The smaller man took three steps into the center of the café and clapped his hands once. His face was pale, with a sparse blond mustache covering pimples.

"Silence, comrades," he commanded. "This is a formal control. Remain where you are. When I instruct you, give me your identity card and your account card."

The two workers in the back of the room had put down their beer steins. One of them reached for his wallet.

"Stop," the policeman said. His tone was sharp but confident. "Wait for my instructions."

The bearded man sat quietly, watching as the policeman with the blond mustache walked to the two workers, asked for their cards, and slowly examined them.

Chantal quickly rehearsed herself. She could tell the truth. She was perfectly ordinary, not worth taking time over. She worked from five in the afternoon until half past midnight, cleaning in the Ministry of Agriculture's offices nearby. She had stopped on her way to work to have a cup of tea.

The policeman was coming toward her now. He stopped two paces away and addressed them both. "You are together?"

The bearded man looked at Chantal, as if surprised to see her, and shook his head. "No," he said.

"Your identity card and cash card, comrade," the policeman said to the bearded man.

The two cards appeared from inside his blue smock. The examination was brief.

"What are your hours of work?" the policeman demanded.

"Twenty-four hours," the bearded man replied. "I lock up my warehouse when I go out to eat."

The policeman looked sharply at the man. He held the identity card up to his eyes, scanned the small print.

"From Luxembourg, comrade?"

"Many years ago."

"I can hear it in your speech."

The bearded man shrugged, a silent apology for his Luxembourgeois accent. The policeman acquiesced with a small nod.

It was her turn.

She retrieved the plastic folder from the bottom of her satchel, trying hard to keep her hand from shaking. She started to undo it, but the policeman motioned to her to give it to him. He unfolded the packet and took out the papers, glancing at her as he studied the documents.

"Tell me your identity number and your date of birth," the policeman said, fixing her with a hard look.

Chantal hesitated, not wanting to make a mistake. "Zero one five, five nine six seven A," she said.

The policeman waited.

"The twelfth of March, nineteen-seventy," Chantal concluded, her voice weak.

"Your occupation?"

"I am a cleaning woman assigned to the Ministry of Agriculture."

The policeman looked at the papers and back at her.

"Please come outside with me, comrade."

Her knees were like jelly, but she managed to get up. She took her coat and her satchel. For a fraction of a second she regretted the sip of tea left in the cup on the table.

"Has the comrade paid her bill?" the policeman asked Madame behind the cash register.

"She has paid."

The sunlight was failing fast, and headlights flashed at the bottom of the street where it ended at the Champs-Élysées. She snatched a glance at the glassed-in storefronts and, above them, the linked disharmony of moldings, ironwork, shutters, and peeling plaster that made every side-street building in Paris a cousin of every other. Was it to be her last view of freedom?

The policeman waiting across the street was older, plump, his expression severe.

He asked her name, her address, where she worked, and Chantal recited the answers, trying to gain control of her fear.

"Where are your parents?"

"They are dead."

"A pity. Where are they buried?"

She did not know.

"Amiens," she said.

"What was your father's occupation?"

"He worked in a factory."

"What did he do?"

"He did something with tools. I don't know very well what he did."

"He was an engineer?"

"No. A worker."

The younger policeman interjected, "What was the name of the factory?"

"My father worked for Saviot & Compagnie."

"Saviot? How is that spelled?"

She told him and watched him write in his notepad.

"Stay here," the older policeman said to Chantal. The two men walked ten steps away to confer. She tried to hear what they were saying. They looked again at her papers, and looked at her. The younger policeman made another entry in his notepad and stuffed it into his overcoat pocket.

He walked back to her, holding out her papers. "All in order," he said.

Chantal watched the backs of the long leather coats, the three of them disappearing toward the Champs-Élysées. She had only felt a pulse of wind from the passing wings of disaster. She could go to mop and dust in the quiet offices of the ministry. But her thighs and her back were clammy with sweat.

Looking through the café window, Chantal could see the back of the bearded man's head, motionless. Who was he? Not police, she thought. Could he be an agent of MSIE, the organization that guarded against *Menaces à la Sécurité Interne de l'État*? She pulled her coat tight around her back, her mind racing. What if they checked about her father? Of course she had lied, anyone could understand. But why should they care, she had told no lies to get her job, she had done nothing to escape assignment to a State Factory, nothing except to keep silent and be grateful for kind old Monsieur Sussoy. She started to walk to the ministry offices. She felt cold as the winter air found its way to her sweat-damp underwear.

As François Blanc, watchman, union member, he sipped his coffee, his eyes half shut, his gaze fixed on a patch of wall across the café.

He could not believe his weakness.

Two years of discipline, abandoned.

Because of a pretty face.

Not even so pretty. The image of Helen Landry came to him, her big, healthy body, her flashing smile, the heavy locks of ash blond hair swinging as she moved her head to laugh.

This cleaning woman was nothing compared to Helen. But . . .

She was not a cleaning woman. . . .

That made his stupidity worse.

He had seen the two policemen on the street, and still he had risked coming into the Poste when there were half a dozen other safe cafés five hundred meters farther away from the Champs-Élysées. And then, knowing that the police could come in for an identity control, he had become clever and wise for the benefit of this non-cleaning woman. It was the worst lapse since Robert Landry had disappeared. What if the woman had been an informer for MSIE?

She was not an informer. In the instant when their eyes met, he had felt her innocence and fear and had understood that she was another fugitive.

He finished his coffee and pushed the round table away, acknowledging the photographs of President Joux and First Secretary Paccard, the New State's leaders. They were his adversaries, if there could still be a contest for power; and they should be victims of justice, if there was a way to make them pay for their crimes. But he did not think he could make them suffer enough.

Landry limped into the street, trying to focus on his tasks for the night, wondering what had developed in the power game that the first secretary was playing with the minister of the economy. He pushed the woman out of his thoughts, but her image persisted.

Her number was zero one five, five nine six seven A, unless she had made a mistake. As the most elementary safety precaution, he would find out what the police had recorded of their encounter. The next time he saw that delicate round face, the sad eyes, the long narrow nose, he would know her name, her address, and every other recorded bit of information about her that existed in France.

In the first moment of her arrival, Chief Inspector Pierre Dupont did not recognize his brother's daughter. Tears had streaked mascara in gritty channels through the powder on her cheeks, and tears started to stream again when she saw him. Her breath came in great heaves that raised her generous breasts and shook the frills on her purple sweater. The sweater itself was too extravagant for his niece. It was the latest mode, at the outer limit of permissibility in the New State.

But it was not the tears or the sweater that delayed Pierre Dupont's recognition. He failed at first to recognize his niece because her nose was wrong. It was swollen and set to one side. A brown track of dried blood tied Mireille Dupont's nostrils to her upper lip like clown's paint.

Mireille was standing on high heels of bright metal, just visible under the overlong blue velvet pants that squeezed her legs. Someone else's cash card had dressed his niece, and Pierre Dupont wondered whose. He waved away the patrolman at the door, who was staring at her rump.

Mireille tried to wipe her tears with the back of her hand, and the pain of touching her deformed nose brought a wail of pain.

"Uncle Pierre," she sobbed, but he shook his head to silence her and turned his back. Fancy clothes that she could not have earned, a broken nose, in the middle of the afternoon . . . trouble.

Pierre Dupont rocked his bulk on the toes of his heavy polished shoes and looked out the window. In the dying light, he traced the bare limbs and splotched bark of the tree that grew behind the police station of Pontoise, the station where he had worked all his life as a patrolman and then had leaped to command immediately after the revolution. The police station of Pontoise was not the finest in France, but there was progress. His men were loyal, and none of them accepted gifts or favors, at least not in excess. The central heating was working now, for the first time in ten years. Paint was flaking from the window mullions and detaching itself in shards from the outside of the building, but Paris had promised to refurbish the entire building in the spring. The revolution had given him power in the town of Pontoise, and he was using it well. Only four months before, the Pontoise party journal had devoted a front page article to praise of his leadership. Among the hundred and fifty thousand inhabitants of this Paris suburb, thirty kilometers from the center of the city, Pierre Dupont commanded respect. He had not come so far to be dragged back by a brainless child.

As his eyes traced the branches of the tree outside his window, he realized that words were coming out of the noise behind him. His niece was talking. He turned to listen.

Bruno had hit her. With a bottle.

Who was Bruno?

She did not know, but she could find her way back to his apartment.

Why had he hit her?

He was drunk and angry, a crazy man.

What was she doing in his apartment?

The sobs stopped, like flies capped in a bottle.

What was she doing there?

She was there, he had invited her there. . . .

Why, to do what?

It was not important. It was a date, a date for a night with friends.

In the middle of the afternoon? In a whore's clothing, when there were no more whores in France?

The tears came back, and Pierre Dupont waited. He thought about calling his brother, Mireille's father, at the Mairie. That was no good, the matter should be kept inside the station until he understood better what to do.

When she started to talk again, Pierre Dupont learned that she had been delivering a parcel to Bruno, and that was the reason she had been in Bruno's apartment.

A parcel. What was in it?

Mireille shook her head.

Chocolates? Cigarettes?

She did not know. Truly, she did not know what was in the package, but when Bruno had opened it he had gone mad. He had screamed at her, and she had not been able to answer. He had hit her in the face.

So, how had she come to the police station?

In a car.

Whose car?

A friend's . . .

Was it, by chance, the same friend who had given her the package to deliver?

Pierre Dupont observed that this question provoked a look of panic that twisted over his niece's smashed face. Her eyes left him, searched the room for help, came to rest on the wall.

He followed her gaze to the wall and saw that she was looking at the photographs of the president and the first secretary.

Well then?

She shook her head, her eyes fixed on the photographs.

It was the president's car? . . . the first secretary's package?

"Leonid," she mumbled.

A hand reached into the cavern of Pierre Dupont's belly and seized his viscera.

"Leonid . . . Paccard?"

She nodded.

"Leonid . . . He got you these clothes? You are driving his car? The son of the first secretary of the Communist party? Leonid Paccard, secretary for youth, sports, and culture?"

"Yes."

"It was his package that you took to Bruno?"

"Yes."

"Then why did you come here?"

"I was scared. . . . You are the police, you are my uncle."

"Do you have his telephone number?"

"Leonid?"

"Leonid."

She nodded.

"Call him, tell him what happened, and let him tell you what to do."

"What if he is angry at me?"

"Then at least you will know."

He pointed her to the telephone, and she went to it like a virgin at a sacrifice.

"It is Mireille Dupont. Please let me speak to Comrade Leonid . . ."

"It's me, Mireille. I took the package to the address, and Bruno, he went crazy and . . ."

"Yes, I took it . . ."

"In the police station of Pontoise. My uncle is the chief, I am in his office."

"All right, I will . . . but he hurt me. I will never be beautiful . . ."

Tears swelled out of her eyes.

"All right . . ."

She held out the telephone to her uncle.

He tried hard to keep his hand from trembling as he pressed the receiver to his ear.

He spoke. "This is Chief Inspector Pierre Dupont, of the Pontoise police. Is this the secretary for youth, sports and culture?"

The voice was soft, blurred, not what Pierre Dupont had expected from the son of the first secretary. "I just told Mireille to go home and forget it. You should do the same. I will see to the man Bruno. You have it, Comrade Chief Inspector?"

"I have it," Pierre Dupont said, projecting his most formal voice. "But, comrade secretary, the girl must go to the hospital; her nose is broken. She will say that she fell down stairs, or some other story, but she must have a doctor's attention."

After a short silence, the soft voice returned. "Tell her to go home and wait there. I will arrange for medical attention. And say nothing of this, comrade. You have it?"

"You can be sure of it."

"Good . . ."

The telephone clicked, and Pierre Dupont stood for a moment, listening to the line tone, as though it might have some more information to give him.

He put the receiver gently in its socket, avoiding offense to the machine. "You should go home and wait for Comrade Paccard to send a doctor."

She was weeping softly, her hands holding her cheeks.

"Tell your mother that you fell down some stairs. I will confirm it if she asks me."

"I will not see her. I am not living at home."

"Where, then?"

"In an apartment, with a friend."

"Where is that?"

He wrote the address, a new building in the best area in Pontoise, and then the name of the friend, a girl named Viviane Labrett.

"Go, Mireille. I do not know what you are doing, and I do not want to know. Say nothing to anyone about this. Never come back to this police station, never in your life. Do you understand me? You can only bring trouble, here in Pontoise, for your father or for me."

He watched her leave. It was impossible to tell his brother; it would only cause more problems.

But his official conscience tugged at him. What had been in the package? Nothing that the state permitted, that was clear. Leonid Paccard was implicated in some kind of traffic. Besides Bruno, others might know. And if it was known that Mireille had come to the station, to him, and he had not reported the matter, what would happen then?

He had promised to use his eyes and ears for MSIE.

If he reported the matter, he was only doing his duty. He could say that he had reported before Leonid Paccard had told him to say nothing, if it came down to that.

He had memorized the number, which was not listed in any directory. The shaking in his hand would not go away, and he tapped the buttons on the telephone slowly to avoid making a mistake.

LEONID Paccard walked away from the desk, a frown creasing the high dome of his brow. He stopped at the sideboard to pour another glass of the champagne. Bruno's champagne.

The champagne was real, from Reims, ten cases sitting in the cellar, but what an ass Bruno was. Only problems, dealing with Bruno.

And the girl, an idiot with a pretty face and, incredible, an uncle who was chief of police in Pontoise. If she had ever told that small fact, she would still be living at home with some memories of one sweet night and a sniff of wealth and power.

"Who was it?" Marina asked. She was sitting on the couch in the living room of his home in Chantilly.

"Mireille Dupont," Leonid answered. "Little bitch. Bruno beat her up, and she went straight to her uncle. The chief of police of Pontoise."

"Jesus . . ."

Marina's shoulders sagged, and the corners of her lips, normally cocked up in a smile, turned down.

She was dressed in a pale blue cashmere sweater and a soft

blue-on-blue plaid skirt, a real kilt from Scotland before the revolution, with a big gold pin to hold it together. Real gold bracelets
graced her slender wrists, and a gold chain necklace hung around
the sweater's soft turtleneck.

Wide eyes looked up at Leonid and accused him of risking the
elegant picture that she had composed of herself on the sofa. She
tossed her head so that the blond strands of her hair floated up
into the air and down again onto her shoulders.

She followed him with her eyes as he walked away from her and
then came back. If only he would listen.

It was not enough for him to be his father's son, he needed to
take risks. And for what?

In advance payment for the packet, the first delivery of syn-
thetic cocaine from Italy, Leonid had received fifteen blank vacation vouchers, each worth two weeks in the south of France, and
ten cases of good champagne. The vacation vouchers were worth
a fortune in barter, the most negotiable of all merchandise in the
cashless trade that had grown up outside the cash-card system. All
for a small packet. And then Leonid had tried to multiply the
value of the shipment by withholding a third. Bruno had gone
crazy, and the girl had gone to her uncle. To the police.

"I could not send Alex," Leonid told her. Marina had told him
to send the package with Alex, the household bodyguard. "I know
he is making reports to my father."

"What will you do now?" she asked.

"It should be all right. The girl will go home. I will send her a
doctor, we can find a discreet doctor. The policeman will say
nothing, he sounded frightened. The girl will say nothing. Bruno,
well, Bruno will get the rest of the shipment, so he will be quiet.
And then everything will be all right."

"And then?"

"And then, well, we will be finished with this business. You
have it?"

Her eyes followed him as his soft hands waved in the air, waving trouble away. Half steps took him across the Persian carpet
and back again, to face her with that open, boyish smile that
pleased the photographers. The son of the prime minister and

first secretary of the Communist party of France, himself the secretary for youth, sports and culture, with thousands of people looking to him for leadership . . .

"No," she said. "I think you must tell your father."

"It is impossible. Impossible." He was at the far end of the room now, standing beneath the Motherwell painting, which he had taken down but had put back up when he found out how much it had cost the original owner.

"If you tell him you were only delivering the package, that it was not yours, that you were only returning a favor . . ."

Leonid would not look at her. "He will tear me apart. You do not know his rage when he is angry."

"If your father helps you now, then he will be engaged in the problem, and then it will be harder for him to abandon you if the story comes out later."

She watched him and let the thoughts sink in.

"I will call him," Leonid said. He waved his hands.

She nodded and nestled back into the red pillow, letting her long blond hair flow over her shoulders and onto the cushion, where it would contrast with the red needlepoint and the pale blue of her cashmere sweater.

2 The gray-painted warehouse doors opened on the rue Pouchkine, formerly rue Lord Byron. Landry did not understand why they had substituted a Russian poet courtier for an English poet lord. Pushkin would not have survived three days in the revolution. The street started from one of the grand avenues that stemmed out from the Arc de Triomphe, crossed two other narrow streets, and then curved to an end, an insignificant comma in the great book of Paris. A good place to hide.

He used an antique key to open the small door. A larger door, adjacent, was big enough for trucks, but that door was never opened. Nothing had moved in or out of Landry's warehouse for two years. Not since the revolution.

His warehouse was not much larger than a big garage. It contained blank computer forms that had been printed before the revolution for the Ministry of Finance. The forms had been rendered useless by the change in government and now reposed in hundreds of brown cardboard cartons, stacked to the ceiling. Some of the stacks had started to lean like trees in a wind-struck forest. Now and then, Landry would need to rescue a leaning tower of cartons before it tipped over. The place smelled of mildewing paper.

According to the government documents pertaining to the property, the warehouse was now under control of the sub-commissioner of the Closed Accounts Section of the Ministry of Finance. The sub-commissioner did not exist. Neither did the Closed Accounts Section of the Ministry of Finance.

Landry walked through the warehouse into the darkness at the rear, still limping. The limp belonged to François Blanc, but he kept it as a constant reminder of his alias, even when he was by himself.

He unlocked the door to his small sleeping room and pushed it open without stepping in. He reached around the jamb and switched on the light. As he had done daily for more than two years, he looked down at the looped strand of thread, untouched, on the doorsill.

The narrow room was in a corner at the back of the warehouse. A steel-framed bed stood against the wall at the far end. The carpet, threadbare in spots from the wear of long-departed furniture, covered all of the floor. It was too wide, and its edges had been curled under to fit. Against the long wall opposite the door was a refrigerator and a counter with a hot plate and set-in ceramic sink, flanked by a painted wooden table and a folding chair. A calendar for the year 2005 hung from a nail over the sink. The picture on the calendar was of the Arc de Triomphe, with the flag of the People's Democratic Republic of France under the arch. Hammer and sickle blazed against the white of the flag's tricolor. Photographs of First Secretary Paccard and President Joux were hung beside the calendar. To a stranger, these were evidence of loyalty to the revolution.

The removable linoleum panel in the floor was in front of the counter with the hot plate and sink, a place where the absence of dust would not be noticed. Steel pins held the panel down, reinforced by four layers of plywood to avoid any hollow sound under the feet of visitors.

Even going down the ladder, Landry limped. His feet echoed on the perforated metal rungs.

It was a long way down, one hundred and thirty meters. In the beginning he had worn a rope and had paid it out over a pulley at the top. With daily repetition the abyss had lost its terrors, and he had stopped using the rope. But still, the concentration required by his exposure to the void forced itself like a wedge between the world above and his private world below. The descent took eleven minutes.

A light bulb with a metal shade hung from a hook drilled into the rock, the bare bulb throwing hobgoblin shadows in the rough-hewn stone. The cave was three paces wide and six long, full of books stacked against the walls. Another light dangled from the roof at the back of the cave, where a metal folding chair faced a wooden table. On the table, a computer monitor's screen glowed softly, a pale ovoid blank waiting for him to begin. A tunnel, only big enough to crawl through, extended from the back of the cave, a narrow passage that led twenty meters straight back to a masonry wall. There, a small hole drilled through the wall, no bigger than the palm of a hand, passed a thick cable from the terminal in the cave to a large circuit board fixed on the other side. Dozens of conduits led from the circuit board to the computers in the vast, dimly lit room beyond.

That room, twenty meters from Landry's monitor, was the nerve center of France.

The computers were housed in twenty gray boxes, each as tall as a man and three meters square. Their hum was blanked out by the much louder sound of the air conditioning fans. It was always warm here, even in winter. The air conditioning ran twelve months a year.

The machines were maintenance free. Pairs of green lights glowed on the tops of the gray boxes, but no one was there to see them. Yet, thousands of men and women, operating thousands of devices throughout France, were linked to the billions of bits of information stored in this room.

When he had crystallized the first plans for the national computer, two years before the revolution, Landry had decided to locate the machines in vaults under the farmers' fields between Paris and Melun. The economics had been clear: one of the accountants from Parallel Technologies had described the decision as a "no brainer." But the last president of the Fifth Republic would not hear about Melun. The world's greatest national information system could only be put in one place, at the sentimental center of France, underneath the Étoile. The Étoile, the Star, was the hub of a wheel around the Arc de Triomphe, where twelve grand avenues met like spokes. Landry had yielded gracefully to the president of France.

A romantic gesture, adding billions of francs to the system's cost. The computers were buried under the Arc de Triomphe, and now, a cable's length away, so was Landry.

Everyone knew the computer was there, under the Étoile, and so the machine had gained its name: the Star.

The first time Landry had heard his machine called the Star, the term had seemed so familiar and approving that he had felt a glow of paternal pride. Those had been glory days, when success had been piled on success.

Now, two years after the Russians had come, the hammer and sickle were still blazoned in the center of the tricolor flag that hung in the arch, and Landry felt no pride at all.

He had never worked harder than now, and the more he achieved, the worse he felt. Each time he unravelled another mind-stopping problem, his self-esteem would decline another notch. Because his hope of good from the Star was gone. Now, he intended to hurt. He wanted revenge on the New State.

At the beginning, Landry had expected to assemble an underground resistance. His private list contained hundreds of names, people with the intelligence and conviction to fight back if the Russians came. He had men who could bring violent action, others who could plan and manage. Communications were ready to bring them together.

But even Landry, who was prepared for the revolution, had been taken by surprise. For the planners of the revolution had their own list, which included all Landry's people plus thousands more. Only two months after the Russian tanks had entered Paris, Landry realized that he was alone. He could not identify one living soul in France at liberty to fight back. The men and women of his hopes were imprisoned in State Factories if they were lucky, dead or brain damaged if they were not.

Among all the names on the list that he had prepared before January 1st, 2003, only one person had escaped, and he was a continuing enigma. Instead of sending Marcel Chabon to a State Factory, the Russians had made him a minister.

In that first year, when Landry had understood that resistance was impossible, he had started to prepare the Star for sabotage. The plan had grown in scope and subtlety. When he was ready, the government would lose control, but not all services would stop. The cash cards would often be useless, but not for everyone and not all the time. Some industries would be blighted, others spared. The Star would create new inequalities to upset the bureaucratic ladder and then shift them before anyone could adjust, so that France would learn how to live without its leaders, out of control. But the Star would never collapse outright, never create a void that might encourage developing a new system from scratch. Landry had worked two years. He thought it would take another four months of work to be ready.

And now there was the woman at the Café de la Poste, whose address and identity number were firm in his memory. Did it make a difference if there was another survivor like himself?

He put her out of his mind. He could not violate his routine.

His fingers started to tap the keys. The access procedure remained a pitfall-ridden series of commands to the computer. It was impossible to program a way through the ever-changing maze of passwords, and the smallest mistake meant hours of repair.

He accessed the secret files of MSIE and checked for a dossier on François Blanc, warehouse keeper. He performed the same operation for three other aliases. Nothing. All his faces were still invisible.

Then he went to MSIE's file for Robert Landry. The last entry was now months in the past. An identical entry had been made in Helen Landry's file, stating that the Landry search had been turned over to the Department of External Security, the DSE, because Robert and Helen Landry were presumed hiding in the United States.

The twin security services, MSIE and DSE, had worked hard to find him. They had quickly rounded up his colleagues in France. His friends had given up what they knew and then they had been discarded, alive or dead—it didn't make much difference after the chemicals used for interrogation.

But there was no new mention of Robert or Helen Landry in the files of the DSE either.

Landry moved on to review the morning's security meeting.

The barriers built into the Star were believed by the government to be more secure than written minutes, and so the verbatim records of the most secret proceedings were routinely entrusted to the machine. Landry appreciated this official confidence in his own earlier work—it made his present task much easier.

Words came up on Landry's screen. The machine's voice reader had transcribed the spoken words with total accuracy.

There were five in the meeting. Morand, the minister of the interior, who was also head of MSIE; Comrade Gousset for the National Police; and Comrade Ebert for the DSE. Two others with anonyms, Karel and Victor. Karel was in charge. Victor seemed to be Karel's aide.

There was nothing new about himself or Helen Landry, but there was a scandal to report.

—The chief inspector of the Pontoise police had called his MSIE contact in Pontoise about the comrade secretary for youth, sports and culture, Leonid Paccard.

—Leonid Paccard had given a parcel to the chief inspector's niece, to deliver to a man named Bruno. Bruno had assaulted the girl after opening the parcel.

—Chief Inspector Dupont had no idea what was in the parcel, but it was surely some kind of contraband.

—The man, Bruno, seemed to be a Bruno Mounier, employed as a truck driver by the National Transport System.

Landry reread the words on his screen.

A misdeed that involved the son of the first secretary. This was news. The New State had seemed, for all its faults, remarkably free of corruption.

He tapped a key, and the words scrolled up so that he could continue reading.

—Morand, as head of MSIE, had been instantly informed, because of the level of the problem.

—Had Morand informed Comrade First Secretary Paccard? Karel inquired.

—Of course not. The matter needed discussion before the first secretary could be involved.

Now, Landry mused, *that* was a revelation. Paccard had been held out in the cold until Karel could be consulted.

—We should send a man to investigate, Morand continued. But at this level, should it be a man of MSIE, or a man of Department 100?

Department 100 seemed to be Karel's own staff, an anonymous group working out of sight and sound, with unspecified functions.

—Not Department 100, Karel said. The matter was reported to MSIE, MSIE should investigate. Send the man out to Pontoise, and then tell Paccard. The matter could not be left unquestioned, just because Leonid Paccard was his father's son.

Landry mused. Was Karel supposed to keep the New State from corrupting itself? Landry was certain that Karel was the Russians' representative. It was not clear if he was French or Russian, but if he was Russian, his command of French was extraordinary.

The meeting ended. Landry sorted the scandal into his mind for future reference. Robert Landry, Helen Landry, had passed another day safely in the dark.

Marcel Chabon, minister of the economy, was next in Landry's daily routine.

When Landry had known Chabon, the man was a high civil servant, a rough, charming man with no political ambitions and a reputation for getting results. Their contacts had been brief, but they had quickly established a mutual respect. Chabon had been one of the first in the government to benefit from the Star's power.

Landry classed his former acquaintance with the enemy, but Chabon had many points in his favor. The hierarchy of party hacks hated him. He never mouthed the party line. And he was still getting results—France was ahead of the other countries that had been swept up by the Russians.

And now, Chabon was under attack. Three days before, the Star had found a reference to Chabon's name in the daily minutes of the communications minister: all future quotes from Minister of the Economy Marcel Chabon were to be cleared by the first secretary, Georges Paccard. Georges Paccard had put a muzzle on his colleague.

This came in the wake of a newspaper quote attributed to Chabon: "If they are working, they should eat like workers."

Chabon had made experimental changes in some State Factories—shorter hours and more food had earned their cost in better production. Similar changes were underway in all the State Factories, with the party grumbling that the revolution was turning soft.

Landry did not yet understand the infighting, but he found himself thinking more and more of the minister of the economy. Marcel Chabon was the only free man in France who could fully appreciate the genius of the Star. Was it only vanity, Landry asked himself, that made him hope Chabon was not going into eclipse?

Among the trillions of bits of information that the Star had stored in the past day, Landry's lightning search found Chabon's name in the minutes of a lengthy meeting, and in a signed decree. Then, in the most secret files of MSIE, he found a request from the first secretary asking for information on the past personal behavior of Minister Chabon. Scraping for dirt, Landry concluded. The request had been wait-listed for a reply.

Landry's routine was over. Now his self-control yielded to his pent-up curiosity. Two minutes later, Landry was reading the dossier of Chantal Taillard Senac.

The file was short. Her husband, Arnaud Senac, a senior civil servant in the Ministry of Finance, had been "redeployed" shortly after the Russians had seized control, and he had died four months later "of natural causes." That was a familiar story. A key number referenced Arnaud Senac's file. Landry committed the number to memory.

A Comrade Sussoy had intervened on behalf of Chantal Senac. At the time of the revolution, Comrade Sussoy was the communist mayor of the town of Doullens. A note in the file described his longtime friendship with Chantal's father, Fernand Taillard, a technician employed in the Saviot factory at Amiens, and his regret that Chantal had married outside her working class origins. Sussoy's letter even recommended that Chantal be admitted as a novice member of the union.

That was surely impossible, Landry thought. It was odd that Sussoy's intervention had been accepted at all.

For the New State, sentiment had no meaning. Without exceptions, the rich and privileged population of France had been redeployed.

Redeployment meant living as a prisoner and working in a State Factory. Families had been scattered, according to the needs of the different factories for individuals of one sex or the other, or for certain skills or physical strength, or according to the random whims of a blind and unfeeling government.

Anger filled Landry as he thought of the upheaval. Before the revolution, the Communist party had been laughably maladroit, a dwindling minority led by hacks. No one could have predicted the party's searing takeover, starting from the day the Russian troops had poured across the bridges on the Rhine.

Some French citizens had been more fortunate than others: doctors, scientists, individuals whose skills were needed outside the State Factories. Handpicked, these fortunates did not include one name that had figured on Landry's list, and they were still under the constant watch of MSIE. They made a large and active sector in the Star's security files.

Chantal Senac had no skills that were vital to the state. Despite Sussoy's letter, she should be working as a prisoner. Landry wondered.

He continued reading from his monitor.

She had a child. Noël, aged ten at the time of the revolution. Noël had been transported. Below the age of one, children of redeployed parents remained with their mothers. From one year to eight, they had been placed in foster homes in France. From eight to sixteen, they were transported to Russia or the other countries of the East. Over sixteen, they were put to work in the State Factories.

Chantal Senac had kept her freedom but had lost her husband and her son.

Landry had no children. At one time in his life he had wanted a child, and now he understood that God's denial was a mercy.

The perished husband, Arnaud Senac, had a well-documented career. He had been near the top of his class at the École Nationale d'Administration, the best preparation for a climb to the highest rungs of the civil service. He was assigned first to the Ministry of Culture and soon promoted to the Ministry of Finance. There, he had encountered a problem. Landry pondered the comment, "reprimanded for exceeding limits of authority," followed by a reference to an administrative proceeding. That had been twenty years ago, when Arnaud Senac was twenty-eight years old.

Shortly after his reprimand, Senac had been sent to work in the Prefecture in Lille. A demotion. He had worked out his penance in Lille for six years, and in that time he had met and married Chantal, who was thirteen years his junior.

Landry read on.

After his marriage, Senac was recalled to Paris, where he performed brilliantly in the Ministry of Agriculture. He was promoted to an obscure but influential job in the Ministry of the Interior; he managed liaison between the Armed Services and the SDECE, the French espionage and counterspy organization.

But the years wasted in Lille had cost him dearly. Senac was rejected for *Chef de Cabinet* of the Finance Ministry because he was too old. Instead, he lingered another year as the main link between the spies and the generals, and then was made undersecretary in the Ministry of Finance with responsibility for the treatment of great fortunes. In other words, for taxation of the rich. That had been early in 2002, the year that had ended with the revolution.

Landry probed his own memory. Had he not met Arnaud Senac? Senac was the age and had reached the level where he would have been visible. He was a more important figure than many on Landry's list.

It made no difference, the revolution had seized Senac as quickly as it had taken the people on Landry's list. Senac was redeployed to the once-abandoned coal mines at Longwy, to brave the rigors of forced labor, cold, and hunger, if he survived the collapsing mine shafts and explosive coal dust.

His fate was predictable, Landry thought, and again rage surged against the New State.

What was still surprising was that Comrade Sussoy had saved

Senac's wife. She would have been spared Longwy, the mines were for men, but certainly her marriage should have earned her a job in confinement.

Landry called up the file on Comrade Sussoy.

The file was a brief transliteration of the pre-revolutionary written dossier. Only the last lines were in the data processing format that had been set up for the Star. Comrade Sussoy had been mayor of Doullens for fifteen years. He had been a member of the party, but that did not mean much.

He had died at the age of seventy-eight, of cancer, on February 8, 2003, six weeks after the Russians crossed the Rhine. Sussoy's letter was dated January 23rd. A parting gift from his deathbed, Landry thought. Perhaps that had added importance to the letter.

Landry accessed the file of Chantal's father, Fernand Taillard. The file was even shorter than Sussoy's. Fernand Taillard had died of a heart attack in October, 2002, three months before the revolution, at the age of sixty-three. He had been employed throughout his life at a steel fabrication company named Saviot, in Amiens.

Something was wrong.

Landry's mental processing slowed to a crawl. The record of Taillard's death did not fit.

Landry tried to remember the events of that year. He had put the Star in service, with much fanfare, one full year before the revolution, on the 1st of January, 2002. After that, it had taken months to convert all of France from a collection of partly hand-written, partly computerized records to a single centralized data base.

Outside of the main metropolitan centers, the conversion of civil records had been delayed until late in the fall of 2002. Until that time, any birth, marriage, divorce, or death was keyed into the Star's memory without changing from the old format that had been used for decades. But the official record of Taillard's death was entered, like Sussoy's, in the form that had been devised for the Star. The date and the form of record did not match.

Landry invoked a program to examine the storage sector that contained Taillard's file. Twenty-five minutes later, he had pieced together the original record of Fernand Taillard's death from the magnetic debris in the file. Taillard had perished on March 18th, 2003, five months after the recorded date. By that time, every village and commune in France was entering records directly into the Star. The death notice of March 18th had been electronically written over, along with some other essential details of the life of Fernand Taillard.

Like Arnaud Senac, Fernand Taillard had died of "natural causes."

And, like Arnaud Senac, the reason was apparent. Chantal's father had been the owner and president of Saviot.

No one of the *patronat* had escaped the revolution's wrath.

Landry shook his head in disbelief. What divine hand had sheltered Chantal from redeployment? It was hard to believe that Comrade Sussoy, a village mayor, had been so persuasive.

Landry returned to her file. There was no trace of the civil servant who had given Chantal her work assignment. An anonymous state had provided her with papers and a job.

Landry closed his eyes, recalling the round, soft face, the frightened eyes locked to his gaze. He had known that she was no workingwoman. He had been more than right.

But what had he seen? The sadness of outliving a better life? Of losing a child? Whatever it was, it showed.

Landry felt that he was spending too much time now, but there was still a loose thread to tie up before he could leave Chantal Senac. He called up the dossier of her child.

Noël Senac's file consisted of his gender, location, date of birth, parents' identity, and one line: "Transported 3-3-2003. MAE Sec.10-255."

MAE was the Foreign Ministry. That would be a job to dig out. Landry decided that it would make no difference whether Noël was in Russia, Germany, or Czechoslovakia.

He had saved one last task before shutting down his link to the Star. Enough time had elapsed for the police to have reported the interrogation of Chantal Senac.

Landry entered the files of the Paris police. The security level was low, and the procedure was simple. It was easy to locate the daily records of the eighth arrondissement, transliterated by the Star from verbal reports.

Landry let the Star search for the word "Senac." Thirty seconds later he was reading the verbatim file.

>*Detective inspector GROUX detective LOUCHE detective JAVEL FOURTEENTH SECTION/LOUCHE REPORTS: sixteen thirty hours TWO FOUR rue arsène houssaye café de la poste woman interrogated suspicion absence from work, name SENAC first name CHANTAL born TAILLARD resident thirteenth verified night employment ministry of agriculture ONE ONE TWO av de friedland no further action.*

Landry guessed that Louche was the young one with the blond moustache. "Absence from work" was plausible, but Louche had been looking for something more interesting than a shirker.

Landry erased Louche's report, careful to destroy any electronic remnants. There would be no trace of the encounter. If Louche ever tried to find the report, he would blame the void on a malfunction in the Star. If anyone else tried to find the report, they would blame the void on Louche. The Star never malfunctioned.

Landry shut down.

He thought of Chantal Senac on his long climb up the ladder. Clump—climp. His weakness in speaking to her was compounded by his weakness in thinking of her face, of her thin arms, her feet encased in heavy wool socks.

Landry had channeled his sexual energy into the intensity of dealing with the Star, letting fatigue take over when the Star was done. His love for Helen had been broken long before the revolution, but it was still the only love he had had, and he thought of Helen when he thought of a woman. For him, there was no one like Helen left in France after the revolution, but there had been no woman like Helen before the revolution, in France or any other country. Without her, love was dead.

Climp—clump. Landry conjured up the image of his wife. He saw the two Landrys walking up to the customs gate, presenting their U.S. passports, the douaniers hardly looking at the documents when there was such a fine, healthy woman to look at, so obviously American in her size and her abundance of energy.

He had sent Helen home without regret. He had not wanted to worry about his fading marriage, had wanted solitude to organize a resistance as soon as the Russians came. His self-confidence had been so strong—he had expected to burn up his loneliness in the passion of his work. But now he felt his solitude, and his loneliness added to his rage against the New State.

He reached the top of the ladder, and instead of Helen, he pictured the face of Chantal Taillard Senac. For better or worse, he knew that he would need to meet her again.

CHANTAL Senac sat up in her bed at nine in the morning. She had not slept. Normally, she was not in bed before two o'clock in the morning, and a blanket was stapled over her single small window, to keep out the sunlight while she slept. This morning, she welcomed the morning light that glowed around the edges of the blanket. She had lain awake in the narrow bed waiting for day to come as questions raced over and over through her mind.

She had lied to the police on two verifiable matters, the location of her parents' burial, which she did not know, and the occupation of her father, which she knew only too well.

Everyone knew that MSIE could verify such details in a matter of seconds by using the Star, the giant computer located under the Arc de Triomphe.

The police report would be passed automatically to MSIE for verification, and she would be trapped.

They would come for her. She would be sent to work as a slave, if they did not kill her. Noël would be finally and forever an orphan.

She looked around her room. It had once been maid's quarters in a private house. Now it was a single-room apartment. Stained floral wallpaper was coming unstuck in the corners despite her efforts to glue it back. Her furnishings were gathered by chance, a mattress on an old innerspring, covered with a single sheet and an aging brown blanket, a square table with the veneer peeling off from the heat of the hot plate that rested on top, and a solitary chair. A rickety armoire stood at the narrow end of the room away from the bed, next to the door. The small sink had no mirror over it. The bathroom was twenty paces down the corridor. Warmth filled the room, a blessing owed to the hot water pipes in the wall and a manager with bad circulation in the basement, who kept the furnace on day and night.

She considered herself lucky to have a room of her own. None of the other single women who cleaned at the ministry could claim such privacy.

Chantal slipped out of her nightgown, a relic of the old days. Naked, she stretched up on tiptoes, then ran her fingertips across the corrugation of her ribs. She could not eat much on her budget, and she was careful what she ate. She felt herself thin and healthy. They would take her health from her if they put her in a factory: everyone knew about the conditions in the State Factories.

She would not wait for the police to come. She dressed, substituting an old wool skirt and cotton blouse for her cleaning woman's *tablier*.

She walked quickly from the stone house on the rue de l'Espérance, which now contained no less than seventeen apartments. After the revolution, newly privileged union workers had flooded into Paris from the outlying wasteland of public housing and gritty decay. The length of the rue de l'Espérance was lined with low houses that long predated the Russian takeover, but most of them had been divided into apartments to receive the influx.

It had been a gray street, she was sure, even before the revolution. The trees in the old days had been just as barren of leaves during the winter, and the sun had been just as low in the sky, hardly rising above the notched roofline of tile and tin.

But now, with the passage of two years since she had moved to this residential street, the difference was palpable. There were just as many cars, but they almost never moved—one old Fiat had not left its parking space since the preceding summer. The houses had started to blend into each other with a common lack of paint and care. The sidewalks were clean, absent the messes that dogs had made in the good old days, because the New State was hard on dogs and their owners. Passersby seemed preoccupied, closed to contact.

At the small circular *place* that marked the upper end of the street, the brasserie had suffered first a loss of trade and then a loss of tables and chairs, a phenomenon that Chantal remarked each time she passed by on her way to the *métro*. Had the proprietor bartered them away, or had they been taken into the surrounding apartments for lack of other furniture? Now there were only a half dozen chairs and three tables, their white paint turning brown, barely enough in number to fill out the sidewalk space under the red awning that proclaimed in faded gold letters, Bar Brasserie Éleuthère. At least they had not changed the name of the place like the café at the other end of the street, which now was called the *Lenine et Marx*.

She took the *métro* at Tolbiac, direct to Châtelet.

The *métro* police were everywhere, but they did not seem dangerous to her. They were surely the cousins and nephews and children or friends of the party faithful—passing their time while the New State put funds into their cash accounts.

She emerged in an area that had once glittered with shops, a part of the city that had been renewed in the sixties and seventies. The old buildings had been razed and replaced by new ones in metal and glass, or gutted and renovated, and occupied on the ground level with the brightest and most amusing shops, tiny restaurants, fast food in the American style, to say nothing of the boutiques with scandalously offensive photos displayed right at eye level, the overflow from a street that had once pandered to the base instincts of the rutting male. All this was dead now, a morgue where nothing moved. The signs were defaced, the shops closed. The New State had no room for such frivolity.

Across an open space lined with bare trees, she approached the huge block of a building that had been the Centre Pompidou and now was the People's Center. This strange construction, girded with red, blue, and yellow pipes and beams, like a man wearing his

nerves and his veins outside his skin, had once been much casti-
gated for intruding on its nineteenth century environs. The government, by some quirk of special interest or budgets, had kept
the paint on the building fresh, so it contrasted even more than
it had when it was built.

The *métro* was free to Chantal, as a worker with a card. So was
the Lenin Library, inside the People's Center. The library was her
haven, a way for her to leap out of time.

She had come here since her university days, to pore through
the library's original eighteenth century documents dealing with
the Chouans. As a vacationing schoolgirl in Brittany, she had
become fascinated by the folklore of these Breton nationalists,
royalists, ardent Catholics, who fought in vain against the French
revolution of 1789. At university, Chantal had done her history
thesis on the religious roots of the Chouans, and when Arnaud
had been transferred back to Paris, she had continued her
research. And now, by some omission of the new government, the
renamed library still offered the same freedom of access, the same
accommodations for scholars, the same peace, free to anyone
with a card.

The Chouans—her Chouans—had been disappointed, pur-
sued, and defeated by the revolutionary government in Paris, but
their faith and purpose had outlasted the revolutionary government. Their endurance gave Chantal comfort to endure the
French revolution of 2003.

Chantal spent three hours searching for details of the childhood of the Comte de Puisaye, a Norman who had appeared as
though by a miracle and taken command of the Chouan forces.

She returned to her apartment at three in the afternoon. There
was no sign of the police. She told herself that they would not
check her story and that they would not come, but the fear would
not release her.

Half a head of Spanish lettuce sat on the windowsill. She had
waited in line for two hours to buy it, along with the can of com-
pressed chicken that still contained a spoonful of chicken meat.
She knew that she should make her lunch with the lettuce while
it remained fresh and use up the canned chicken before it dried

out, but she could do no more than draw water from the tap to drink.

She rinsed out her glass, changed into her *tablier*, and went to the ministry to clean.

COMRADE Hubert Morand, minister of the interior, head of MSIE, put down his telephone and leaned back in his chair.

What did it mean?

He was a small, wiry man, with hair that plunged in cascades over his forehead and down the back of his neck: His thin lips were pursed, his eyebrows lifted out of sight under his forelock, and a deep vertical crease formed at the juncture of nose and brows.

As the KGB's most senior mole in the DST, the French internal security organization before the revolution, he had taken over the Ministry of the Interior with hardly a change of pace, but kept security as his first responsibility. He left all the other vast responsibilities of the ministry to subordinates. His office had changed from a cramped and windowless space in the back of the ministry to a spacious room looking out on a stone courtyard. He was surrounded by computer monitors, four in all, so that he could call up the sum and substance of all that was known by MSIE, which was to say, everything worth knowing about the citizens of France.

But there was nothing in the Star that could help with this problem.

He stood up and walked around the desk, his shoulders hunched as though straining against the effort of deciphering the news that he had just received from his agent in Pontoise.

As soon as he returned to his seat, he picked up the telephone and dialled a number.

"Red, blue, red," Morand said and hung up. He turned a small switch, so that the phone would ring busy to all inbound calls but one.

He waited, thinking.

The telephone rang.

"Morand . . ." he said, and without waiting for a response, he gave his report.

"Our agent has been in Pontoise. He went to the apartment of Mireille Dupont. She was not in the apartment, it was empty.

"He went to the family home of Mireille Dupont and spoke with the girl's mother. The mother did not know about her daughter's difficulties.

"At our agent's request, the mother called all three of the medical centers in Pontoise. Mireille did not go to any of them.

"Our agent then went to see Chief Inspector Dupont. Our man had great difficulty talking to the chief, because Comrade Dupont had already received another visitor."

Morand looked up at the ceiling and paused. He ran his free hand through his hair.

"About an hour before our man arrived, the chief had a visitor who showed MSIE documents. This was not surprising to the chief, because he had already reported to MSIE. The visitor told Comrade Dupont to keep total silence about the affair of his niece, or risk his whole family. The visitor was explicit about the risks, and his threats went far beyond anything that we would do. Of course, Comrade Dupont believed every word, so our man had to have Dupont's first MSIE contact call Dupont, to convince him that the first visitor was an impostor."

Morand paused and scratched his head.

"I am categorically sure that it was not one of our men. It was a heavy, muscular man, middle-aged. He was wearing a beret, but Dupont thought that he was completely bald. We have no one of that description in MSIE, no one bald to the ears."

Morand stopped to listen and grinned, his lips twisting. "I have not lost any hair until now, but this may be the beginning. I must speak soon to our comrade first secretary. What should I do . . . tell him that his son is corrupt? That Leonid employs a thug who is impersonating an MSIE agent? I should add one thing. Our agent reports that Chief Inspector Dupont is a hard man, experienced in police work, and yet this tough policeman was terrified by his visitor. Dupont thinks that Mireille has been kidnapped and killed."

The response was what Morand had wanted to hear.

"Thank you, Comrade Karel. I do not like to share my burdens, but it will help me if the labyrinth can deal with the first secretary. I will send more agents out to look for the girl, and I will have one of our women call Leonid Paccard's residence to ask for her there."

He listened again.

"Abruzzi? The Corsican? I never met him. He was supposed to be totally bald, and he would be the right age. Am I correct that they put him away before the revolution? Wait, please, it will only take a moment to know what happened to him."

He turned to one of the monitors and entered the name, Abruzzi, followed by a code.

"Do you remember his first name?"

Morand listened and tapped in "Ugo."

"He is not alive in France. Wait."

More code flowed from his fingers to the keys, and a scroll of names, places, and dates rolled onto the screen.

"He was put in a military prison near Valence, in the summer of 2001. We did not release him. He died in the prison a few weeks after the revolution, in February 2003."

Morand listened and nodded affirmation.

"Yes. It comes back to me. He was convicted for involuntary manslaughter after killing a detainee. His troubles began with a complaint in the National Assembly, and the national deputy who brought the complaint was none other than Jacques de Celigny. We thought it was an old grudge from the time when de Celigny was in the police and Abruzzi was in the Action Branch of SDECE, but de Celigny was right. Abruzzi was a brute. If the bald man in Pontoise had been Abruzzi, we would waste our time looking for the girl.

"Yes, I will look for witnesses to Abruzzi's death."

Morand was about to put the telephone down, but he hesitated as Karel asked a last question.

"De Celigny? No. We have his children where we can use them if he ever reappears, but we have never found him."

3 Chantal woke out of a deep sleep. During the night the fear had left her, after ruling her for three days. She felt like someone after a bout with the flu.

Her stomach growled empty. The last of the lettuce and the can of chicken had been planned to coincide with the end of February and the end of the cash in her account. Now, despite the passage of the first of March with its meagre monthly credit to her account, she had not yet summoned the will to go to the market and replenish her stores.

After the shoppers' rush on the first of the month, there would be no fresh vegetables for a few days. Flat on her bed, she thought of the market and asked herself if the freedom to eat was so important to her.

She accepted the worst. The police could still come for her. They could take her freedom. She could suffer anything after losing Noël.

She saw the government as the policeman with the pimples and the blond mustache, a willing slave of the Russians, or, if you believed the gossip among the cleaning women, of the Russian, singular, who sat at the center of a burrow under Paris called the labyrinth.

Fasting, she could last another day. She knew what she would do.

Chantal went to the schoolyard near the Place d'Italie.

The school was red brick, with cement sills on the windows and doors. It towered over the neighboring buildings.

The schoolyard was always full at midday.

A tall wire mesh fence separated the children from the sidewalk, but she could stand on the sidewalk and watch the children of the proletariat at play.

She looked for boys about twelve, Noël's age, but there were none as handsome as Noël. Still, she noticed one boy, nine or ten years old with neatly cropped blond hair and an attractive smile. He was playing soccer with a dozen other boys, and he was the best one. His hair bounced on his head when he ran, and his teeth flashed in a happy smile when he scored a goal. The similarity was near enough to provoke her tears. She stood next to the fence and thought of the mothers who saw their children every day.

She remained by the wire mesh fence for fifteen minutes before she turned and walked away. She walked with her back straight, her stride measured, full of hate for the men who had taken her child.

She thought of Noël on her way home, turning over and over the task of finding him, somewhere in Russia or one of the other Slavic countries. He would lose his identity and his language and forget where he came from. He would have no recollection of her by the time things changed enough to find him, if things ever changed so much.

But, she asked herself, if she felt the bond between mother and son so strongly, wouldn't he keep the same feeling? He *would* still love her, if she could ever find him.

It would take time, maybe years. She must be patient.

She walked down the tree-lined sidewalks of the thirteenth arrondissement to her apartment.

Three steps led up to the double door at the front of the house. A huge brass knob gleamed on the left panel, patined by decades of pushes and tugs. The door was painted green. Its fine thick wood had disappeared, along with the good old days, underneath the flaking paint.

Opening the heavy door required effort. A strong hand on the knob and a pull with some weight behind it. Chantal used both hands on the knob. Inside, in the shadow of the entryway, she saw the small, bent shape of Comrade Giroux, the elderly concierge. He was waiting for her.

He put a cautionary finger over his lips, which had sunk over absent teeth.

"There is someone," he whispered. He nodded toward the doorway on the right that led to the stairwell. The big house had been arranged so that the servants could reach their rooms on the top floor either by a stairwell to the right of the foyer, or from the kitchen at the back of the house. Now, the stairwell in front was used democratically by all the tenants of the house.

"Who?" she asked, fighting back the fear that seized her again.

"A man. He showed me a government paper, and he made me let him into your room."

"What paper?"

"I did not read it." Comrade Giroux shook his head.

She could flee, but there was no place to hide. She could go to work early, but that would only postpone the inevitable. She summoned back her hate in the form of courage and mounted the stairs, remembering an image of a moustached boy in a leather overcoat.

She opened the door to her room.

He was sitting on her bed, and he stood up when she opened the door, a young man still in his twenties, handsome and strong, with a brush of hair hanging in soft spikes. His suit was made of a brown worsted that recalled the suits her husband had worn, and his necktie had come from that other era when silk prints were manufactured and sold for real money. He did not smile, but he showed none of the arrogance of the policemen that she had met in the Café de la Poste.

"Forgive me, Comrade Senac," he said. "I am Inspector Theron."

He produced a leather document carrier from the left inside pocket of his worsted suit and opened it to show her his identification. She saw his name, neatly inked in block letters, and the police emblem. Like Monsieur Giroux, she did not read the paper.

She felt her fear grow, and forced it down as she made herself speak. "What can I do for you, Inspector Theron?"

"You were the subject of a police control, I believe, in the rue Balzac, at the Café de la Poste, on the twenty-sixth day of February."

She nodded.

"And the gentlemen of the police, they were respectful and courteous to you?"

"Yes."

"You have no objection or complaint in the handling of the matter?"

"No, of course not."

"Good," he said. He had been holding his document carrier, and now he folded it and returned it to his pocket. "It is over two years since the revolution. Your government wishes to restore a more normal relation between the authorities and the people. We are making checks such as this one, to be sure that all those in authority understand the change."

He smiled.

"This is, after all," he said, "a civilized country."

Be careful, she said to herself. He is looking for any word to betray you.

"Excuse me for this disturbance, comrade," he said. "You will understand that it is an expression of the government's good will to you and to all the people."

"Thank you," she said.

"Good day, comrade." He had brought a brown cloth raincoat, which he took from the bed and put over his arm. She was still standing just inside the doorway. He stepped around her.

He was three steps toward the head of the stairs, when she risked everything.

"Wait," she said. "Please. I have a question."

He stopped. "I hope that I will have an answer."

· She chose the words carefully.

"My son and I were separated in the days after the revolution. I wonder who I might speak to, to know where he is." As she spoke, she knew that the question could open up all the history that should have sent her into a factory.

The young man cocked his head. "That is not an easy matter," he replied. "Those days are a closed book, and it is better that they should be."

They looked at each other.

He asked, "What is your son's name?"

"Noël."

"What was his age at the time of the revolution?"

"He was ten."

"I will make an inquiry, madame, with all discretion of course. But, you would do well to forget any member of your family who was ... separated at that time. This is an honest answer, and I urge you to accept it."

"I understand," she said, feeling the wall of the government's indifference in his voice, but also feeling, against her will, that his response was at least civilized. He had said "madame" instead of the required "comrade."

"Goodbye, monsieur," she said.

"Goodbye, madame." He stopped. "You were a resident here, in the thirteenth?"

"No. We lived in the sixteenth. Rue de Civry."

"That will be helpful." He disappeared down the stairwell.

THE ministry office where Chantal worked had been an office building before the revolution. All of the main offices of the Ministry of Agriculture were still lodged on the other side of the Seine, close to the Matignon and the Russian Embassy, and Chantal's office on the Avenue de Friedland was only an outpost that had been taken over as part of the seizure of all private enterprise. The fine stone façade of the building was old, but the interior had been restored. Each of the six floors had been propped from below to straighten their centennial sag, the rabbit warren of walls had been opened up, and the spaces had been refinished in austere white planes and angles, relieved by glass partitions and carpeting. Until the revolution, the building had housed the Paris headquarters of a prosperous sugar beet cooperative.

Chantal never saw the daytime workers. No one ever worked late at 112 Avenue de Friedland.

Each evening, she went through the routine of registering her arrival on the time clock, signing for her bucket, mop, rags, and soap from a cheerful old woman who manned the back entrance, and taking the elevator to the fifth floor. She and one other woman, Comrade Pernoud, were assigned to that floor. Comrade Pernoud was a lady in her sixties, and she belonged to the union. Monsieur Pernoud had been in the CGT, the communist union, before the revolution, and that had earned his wife a place in the new union of all the workers. Chantal was not in the union, and the difference established a gap between them.

The front of the floor had the three comrade managers' offices, which except for the windows were easy to clean, and the men's toilets, which were not. The back had the ladies' toilets and more desks to vacuum around and trash baskets to empty, so that there was no clear preference for cleaning one section over the other. Chantal had suggested that they should change sections weekly, to relieve the monotony. Comrade Pernoud had rejected the suggestions out of hand and had chosen the front half for herself, since it was clear that she should be responsible for the managers' offices.

Chantal did not care. Sometimes she wished that she could share a floor with Comrade Jeanneau, who cleaned on the third floor. Comrade Jeanneau had a bright, lively smile for everyone, and talked constantly. It was Comrade Jeanneau who had first spun tales to her about the labyrinth, and the dour Russian who presided over the fate of France, like a spider immobile in its web. Comrade Pernoud spoke less but seemed to know more, and from time to time she also would speak about the Russian, and how he could help or destroy a young communist's career.

She said that it was the Russian in the labyrinth who had made the plan, the lists of names for the new government and for all the public services, and also the names of those who were to be redeployed, so that when the Russian tanks had come racing from Germany down the autoroutes into Paris, and the Russian troops had stormed through the streets picking up the members of the sitting government, the security teams were already at work, taking hundreds and then thousands and then tens of thousands into custody.

She said that this revolution was the final one, because there was no one left free who could ever think of upsetting it.

Chantal listened and thought of the Chouans, but she said only enough to be polite.

The desks were lined up in rows of four, in six ranks. A pale brown computer terminal occupied the center of each desk. Papers were few, and Chantal had no clear idea of the work that was done; she understood that all the information was managed through the Star, not so far away under the Arc de Triomphe. Many of the trash baskets would be empty at the end of the day, so Chantal appreciated the Star's labor-saving benefits.

On this evening, she looked at the symmetrical pattern of brown boxes and realized that they were connected to the machine that also held her past, and Noël's location.

If the police had not bothered to seek her past in the Star's memory, surely Inspector Theron was doing so now. Her future was in the hands of a functionary who called her "madame." She was resigned to treachery, she had no reason to expect anything more, but she still did not regret reaching out for this random strand that might lead her to Noël.

At twenty minutes past midnight, on schedule, Chantal finished mopping the ladies' toilet, put her mop in the bucket, and went to meet Comrade Pernoud at the elevator. They always rode down together when the work was done. Usually they did not speak until they had clocked out, and then they would exchange idle comments as they walked together to the *métro* station at L'Étoile. Chantal was glad to have company to ward off the chill feeling that someone might be watching or following in her path. She had such feelings from time to time, and sometimes she would turn to look. She never saw anyone or anything that she could say was unusual, nothing more than an occasional curious glance from a passerby. Of course, there was no danger now in Paris, even late at night.

Comrade Pernoud was in a good mood walking up the Avenue de Friedland to the *métro*. The government had reopened a supermarket near her apartment, with more food in stock than in most of the old stores. She talked about buying a turkey in partnership with her neighbor, and she offered Chantal a share in the purchase. Chantal's cash account could hardly pay even a small share, but it was good to be asked. She refused with thanks and asked to be remembered for the next opportunity. They walked briskly up the wide avenue, toward the looming silhouette of the Arc de Triomphe. They reached the vast round of pavement that surrounds the arch and turned the corner so that they could see down the Champs-Élysées.

The sight still shocked her.

The most dazzling spectacle in the city of lights, the Champs-Élysées had been a sea of nocturnal life and movement in the old times. Now it was somber, lit only by the double row of evenly spaced streetlamps that stretched away on each side of the thoroughfare to the Place de la Concorde, dark in the distance, and the arch at the Louvre beyond, a faint silhouette. The traffic signals had all been extinguished, unneeded to control the few lonely cars, not more than five or six as far as the eye could see. The glass faces of the buildings at street level were black except for the reflected dull light of the streetlamps. The Drugstore, with its jam of customers, was now an empty shell across the thoroughfare.

They had only a few minutes before the *métro* turnstiles closed at one A.M.

The train going home was always nearly deserted, except for a few night workers like themselves. At the Châtelet stop, Chantal said good night to Comrade Pernoud, changed trains, and took the line eight stops to Tolbiac.

The walk from the *métro* station to the house on the rue de l'Espérance was twelve minutes, and she never cared for it in the loneliness of a late night. Along the rue de Tolbiac the way was lit by streetlamps, but the rue de l'Espérance was dark. Her last steps were taken in dim halflight, the cold penumbra of a lamp in the entryway of the third house on the left. Chantal lived in the fourth house, where it was too dark for shadows.

She felt the man's presence before he spoke.

She stopped, poised to run back toward the rue de Tolbiac. She was keyed to act, to move, to shout, whatever she should do depending on what happened next. Ready.

He was ten meters away, standing in the dark doorway of the two-story house beside #20, where she lived.

He took one step, and she knew who it was. His limp could not be disguised.

"Don't run." His voice was quiet, but the words carried clearly through the quiet of the night. "My name is René Leveque. We have met."

"I know," she said. "In the Café de la Poste. You spoke to me, about holding my cup."

She stood still and waited for him to walk to her. It was too dark to see more than an outline of his bearded face.

"Excuse me for that business about the cup; it was foolish."

She tried to read the voice. She liked its sound, resonant without harshness.

"The police filed a *procès-verbal* concerning their meeting with you. The matter was concluded without further investigation."

Now she was wary. "You are the second man who has come today from the police to tell me that the matter is concluded."

She thought he drew back from her by a fraction of a centimeter, as though she had surprised him.

"I am not from the police," he said. "Who came to you? What did he say?"

"A polite young inspector came to my apartment at midday. He came to ask whether my treatment by the police had been correct. I told him that it had."

"That was his reason? To ask about your treatment?"

"Yes."

He spoke half to himself: "But the police want the people to fear them. It makes them more persuasive."

"This was not an inspector of the arrondissement. He wore a good suit, and he had good manners."

"Did he give you his name?"

"Theron."

He asked her to spell it. She did, trying to remember her glimpse of the identity document.

"What was his attachment?"

"I do not know."

"I am not a policeman, but I have knowledge of the police. Your inspector's visit is not normal."

She started to smile. "At one in the morning, your visit to this street is not normal, Monsieur Leveque."

He laughed. The sound was spontaneous, like a short bark. It had been so long since she had shared a joke that she suddenly felt good about this Monsieur Leveque. She tried to remember his face as she had seen it at the Café de la Poste, and she recalled steady eyes and a gentle expression. She wanted to trust him.

"I thought it would be easier to meet you like this, and safer," he said. "I wanted to bring you the report about the police control, and it seems it was not necessary. But in fact, I wanted to see you again. Forgive me."

"How can I know that you are not an agent of the police? Monsieur Leveque, you came from the same world that I did, it is in your voice as much as it must be in mine, but that does not mean that I can believe in you. I have heard about people who gave information for their freedom. How do you know my name, and where I live? What do you do? What is your interest in me?"

He did not answer immediately. Standing still in the cold night air, Chantal started to feel chilled.

"Affection," he said.

"What?"

"Affection. When I saw you it filled me with affection, and I came out with the stupid remark about the cup, in order to have something to say. What do two fugitives say to each other when they have each broken through the other's disguise? You can only believe me if you can believe without proof. There is nothing to prove what I do or who I am, because it is all a fiction, and it is safer if you don't even know the fiction. But let us see each other again, when the sun is up and we have time to talk. I will offer you a cup of tea to replace the cup you left half full at the Café de la Poste. You should meet me in two days, at noon, just inside the gates of the Jardin du Luxembourg, above the *métro* Luxembourg. If it rains, I will be inside the entrance."

She hesitated.

"Whatever you think I am," he continued, "you cannot harm your situation by coming to meet me."

Doubt stood as big as a house in the path of reason, but she yielded.

"I will come," she said.

She left him standing in the shadows. He watched her until the door closed behind her, and then limped up the rue de l'Espérance toward the place where his delivery van was parked.

THE sun was glorious, radiating warmth on the city of Paris. It seemed as if the rays had drawn all the dank of winter out of the streets, leaving the air clean and fresh. Chantal saw him waiting at the top of the steps as she climbed up from the *métro* station, and she felt a smile form on her lips.

Walking slowly side by side down the Boulevard St. Michel, like old friends, they went to a brasserie in the Place de la Sorbonne.

Light flooded through the wall of windows and the fringed pink lamps were frugally extinguished, so the tables near the front were much brighter than the ones in the rear. He chose a table beside the glass, where the sunlight threw his features in relief. She liked the way the corners of his eyelids were cast in softly etched wrinkles.

She asked for tea. He ordered coffee, but cheerfully asked for tea instead when the waiter told them that the coffee was finished for the week.

"I almost didn't come," he told her. "You have no reason to be free and employed, instead of working in some hell-hole of a factory. Your Inspector Theron doesn't exist. When I tried to trace Theron, I told myself that it would be madness to meet you here. If you have protectors in high places, you are more dangerous to me than a loaded gun."

She watched him speak, listening to his voice, hearing the words, but feeling the man's warmth. Arnaud had possessed the same force of intelligence. But this man was softer than Arnaud, and more direct. He spoke to her as if it was important for her to accept what he said.

"Well, if we are here together it is only my fault, so I am glad to see you, Chantal Senac. We make a pair, you and I. Even though you still wear your own name and I do not, we are both sheltering our past from the present. Let me tell you about René Leveque, a civil engineer, employed by the Department of Public Roads and Bridges. René Leveque's job takes him all over France, so he is absent from Paris for long periods. When you saw me in the Café de la Poste, I was someone else, and on other days, I can be other people. I have a very powerful friend in the government, who has allowed me to have a selection of identities. The same friend is able to learn almost everything that goes on in the government. That is how I was able to learn your name, and how I know that Inspector Theron does not exist as an inspector of the police. But my friend would not protect me if I am ever discovered and arrested."

"Your friend is against the revolution?"

He smiled wistfully. "My friend is too powerful to have passions."

She sensed that he wanted to tell her more. How had he come to trust her? She could destroy him with a word. But then her own refuge would be exposed, and maybe that was his protection.

Listening to him had killed the worms of suspicion in her mind.

The tea came.

He continued. "My friend could not tell me how you were protected, after losing your husband and your son."

"A kind old man helped me. He had some influence."

"Was it Monsieur le Maire Sussoy? What influence did he have?"

"Monsieur Sussoy was a member of the Communist party ever since he was in the FTP, the communist resistance in World War II."

René Leveque listened intently. A lifetime in the party was not enough influence, he told her. What else?

She did not know.

How had she learned that Monsieur Sussoy had intervened?

She shook her head. Her temples flushed with the sudden effort of fighting away the memory, and she felt a line of moist sweat at the edge of her hair.

"Please," she said. "This is very hard for me."

He waited. When it was clear that she would not speak again about Monsieur Sussoy, he asked her to recall the days of change after the revolution. She tried to remember, except for the terrible moment that she could not bear to remember. After the Russians invaded, Arnaud had talked about driving to the Swiss border in the Jura and trying to walk into Switzerland. On the fifth day, Arnaud had dressed in denim trousers and a soft shirt that he usually wore in the country and had gone to the bank to take out their money. They had seized him at the bank.

How had she been informed?

The bank manager was a friend. He had telephoned.

Who had arrested Arnaud—police in uniform, gendarmes, fiscal police in plain clothes, party members?

She did not know.

What was the bank? The manager's name?

She told him.

And Noël?

"I can't go on," she said.

When had Noël been taken?

A week later.

What time of day? Who had come?

She could not speak. Her mind would break if she brought that time back.

His voice was gentle. "There is a mystery about your son. He was sent to Czechoslovakia, and responsibility for him was transferred to the Foreign Ministry. But the Foreign Ministry knows nothing about Noël Senac. If you would like me to ask my powerful friend to find Noël, you must start at the beginning of his journey."

She put her hand on his. He had a big hand, with a strong muscle at the base of the thumb. She squeezed his hand for courage and brought the memory out of her mind.

What time of day?

They had come at night, late. She was asleep, and they had come in with a passkey or a pick, into her room, waking her up with the light.

Who had come?

A brutish block of a woman, about fifty, and three men, all about the same age, forty to fifty. They had told her to get out of bed, and then they told her that they had come for Noël.

Who were they? Names?

No names, no papers, they had just come to take her boy.

What were they wearing?

The woman had worn a dingy blue dress with a floral print, and the men had been wearing workmen's clothes.

And then?

The brutish woman had gone out of the room to look for Noël, and when Chantal had tried to follow, the men had held her. She had struggled and even broken free, but one of them had hit her in the face, his fist smashing into her right eye, and knocked her down. She had heard Noël calling for her, crying, and then she had heard the door and known that he was gone. She had tried again to follow, fighting them to let her go, but two of the men had held her arms and the third had hit her again. Her mouth was bleeding. That was when she had learned about Monsieur Sussoy, on the night that they took Noël. The man who hit her had spoken to her while his companions held her arms. She should have been taken with her son, he had said, but her friend in the party, Comrade Sussoy, had kept her out of the shit, and if she wanted to keep people from asking Comrade Sussoy what favors he had gotten from her in return, she would never speak of him to anyone. And if it was up to him, the man had said, she would be taken out and disposed of like the *ordure* that she was.

She relaxed her grip on his hand, exhausted with effort.

He was pensive. "Did you know that Sussoy is dead?"

"No."

"He died soon after he wrote a letter on your behalf."

"So, it is true that he saved me."

"It seems to be true."

"Do you think I am safe now?"

"Probably."

"And you can find Noël?"

"I don't know."

"I asked Inspector Theron to help me find Noël."

His eyes shut and his head rocked back, as the impact of this information registered. He turned his hand over and carefully closed his fingers over hers.

"I shouldn't have done it," she said. "I knew the risk, even when I asked him, but finding my boy is the only thing that counts in my life. I had not met you then, not to know you."

For a moment, she started to panic. What if this last news brought too much danger for him to support?

He smiled. "It's all right. Inspector Theron, who does not exist, and René Leveque, who also does not exist, are now both engaged in a race to find your son. Judging from his report to you about the police control, Inspector Theron is well-informed. He may win, whoever he is."

THEY shared the *métro* and parted underground, with a rendez-vous in three days at a restaurant near the Gare de Lyon. Landry needed the time.

Everything about Chantal Senac was wrong.

Someone had changed the record of her father's death.

A fictitious inspector had come to see her.

Her son had disappeared, not only in person, which was easy to comprehend, but in his documentary record, which was much more puzzling.

And somehow, she was free when she should have been rede-ployed.

If Chantal's cover should ever disintegrate, his own could crumble with it. She already knew too much about him. Landry asked if this madness was worth the danger.

To be safe with Chantal, he would need to understand who had protected her, and how it had been done within the government. The tampering with the death records in the Star was a clue, but not a good one: the records were easy to modify for anyone with a rudimentary knowledge of the programs. A file clerk could have changed the death record of Monsieur Taillard.

It could even have been done by telephone, by anyone with a superficial knowledge of the codes.

The loss of Noël's record was more difficult to explain. It was less likely an erasure than an omission, deliberate or accidental. If deliberate, the boy was probably dead and the people responsible had found it more convenient to let him disappear between Czechoslovakia and France than to record his death. If the omission was accidental, the boy would be hard to find, somewhere inside Czechoslovakia.

And who was Inspector Theron? He must have been sent to verify that she was resisting the pressures of solitude and fear. Her protectors had sent him.

There was no Theron in any branch of the government that could be remotely associated with the police of the eighth arrondissement, yet the man had known as clearly as the Star about Chantal's *procès-verbal*.

Like an astronomer speculating on the existence of conscient life in an unknown solar system, Landry felt that he was not alone. Someone else was working, as he was, in the shadows.

Who?

THE room was not large, but it spoke in every detail of the elegance that had once been the birthright of France. Between fluted columns in bas-relief, dark portraits of men in wigs and lace were hung on the walls. Elaborate carved moldings graced the intersection of walls and ceiling, and the ceiling itself was decorated with carvings that surrounded an oval painting of cherubs and farm maidens.

This room was one of the few belonging to the government of France that lacked the mandatory photographs of Comrades Joux and Paccard. The man known as "the Russian" had decided that photographs would spoil the decor, and the portraits had been omitted.

The polished oval oak table nearly filled the room. The chairs around the table were Louis XV antiques, freshly upholstered.

Morand, the minister of the interior, came in bouncing on his toes, his hair over his eyes. Ebert, the director of the DSE, an austere contrast to his colleague, was so stooped, silent, and slow that he seemed to be near death. Gousset, the head of police, gruff and direct, made a tour of the table, shaking hands with each of his comrades. Each of them was dressed in the solid gray wool-and-polyester suit produced now by the State Factories. Blank notepads and microphones were set out in geometric symmetry around the table, one for each seat. Telephones were placed at each end.

The Russian nodded as he entered. A younger man followed the Russian into the room and sat down immediately in front of one of the telephones.

The Russian chose a place three seats away, near the bulge at the center of the oval. He was stocky, square shouldered, of medium height, with a round balding head and a small double chin under powerful jaws. His movements were deliberate and assured, and his manner was polite; he greeted his colleagues with a smile and a short, formal bow of the head along with the hand-shake, as though to minimize the weight of his authority.

As soon as the Russian was seated, everyone still standing found a chair, and the young man at the Russian's side tapped his microphone to begin the meeting. Each of the participants iden-tified himself for his microphone, so that the Star's voice reader could match the ensuing dialogue with each individual's voice-print.

"Karel," the Russian intoned. His French was accentless.

"Morand."

"Victor," said the young aide. He was slender, with a chiseled profile and long blond swept-back hair.

"Gousset."

"Ebert."

The meeting had started.

"Tell us, Comrade Morand," the Russian began, "about your talk with the comrade first secretary."

"He is furious. He accuses me of disloyalty and you of treason."

"And what does he say about his son?"

"He refuses an interrogation for Leonid."

Victor interjected in a loud voice, "He refuses to do what Department 100 tells him to do? How can he refuse?"

A frown of concern passed like a shadow across the brow of the Russian.

Morand responded. "Comrade Paccard is the leader of the party, and he is the head of the government. Those are his reasons."

Victor started to speak, but the Russian cut him off. "Do you think Abruzzi is dead?" the Russian asked.

"I think he is alive," Morand answered. "The signature on his death certificate belongs to no one we can identify, and we cannot find any witnesses."

"Then it could have been Abruzzi who visited the police chief in Pontoise?"

Morand nodded. "We showed a picture of Abruzzi to the police chief. . . . He thinks it was the same man."

The Russian gave an explanation for the others. "Comrade Morand and myself remember a man who fits the description of the bald man who appeared in Pontoise claiming to be an MSIE agent. Ugo Abruzzi was an operative for the SDECE, until he was put in a military prison for questioning someone to death."

Ebert intervened. "This was the man in the SDECE who was denounced in the National Assembly? I remember the affair, it caused a furor in the intelligence services."

"The complaint was brought by a national deputy we are still looking for. Do you remember Jacques de Celigny, the policeman who turned his headlines into a political career?"

"We never found him?" Ebert asked.

"No. We presume he is dead."

Morand came in, "To the subject, if the bald man in Pontoise was Abruzzi, it makes me ask who sent him there? Leonid? Or someone more important, like his father?"

Gousset, the head of police, raised his hand. "These are dangerous speculations, comrade minister . . . if you think that the first secretary could have sent this man."

"A lightweight like Leonid Paccard could not handle Abruzzi," Morand said. "But Georges Paccard was personally responsible for the reorganization of the army, including the military prisons. Still, you are right that it is only speculation."

"So," the Russian said, "what should we do about Georges Paccard?"

"He should be interrogated, as well as Leonid," Victor said.

Silence followed as the Russian waited for other alternatives.

"My job is to preserve the government, not to change it," the Russian said. "We must eliminate corruption from within and prevent attacks from outside, but I am not here to challenge the first secretary's authority."

"We cannot bring Leonid in for questioning unless his father agrees," Morand said. "His father will not agree."

"Then," the Russian said, "tell his father to get Leonid out of France. I think we have problems in Gabon, the President of Gabon is stealing the food we send in relief. Let Leonid go to Gabon. I will not tolerate corruption inside France. You must be persuasive. Interrogation or exile."

Morand grimaced but did not reply.

"Thank you," the Russian said softly. "What is our next subject?"

"Marcel Chabon," Gousset said. "The comrade minister of the economy."

"How is he involved with the police?" the Russian asked.

"He is not," Gousset replied. "But we have received a request from the first secretary's office to know if Comrade Chabon has ever been arrested. . . ."

"So, they asked you as well," Morand interjected. "The same question came to me, and they also wanted to know if Comrade Chabon's bachelor status was a sign of aberration. I told them that I had no information."

"How should I respond?" Gousset asked the Russian.

"The truth will be sufficient," the Russian answered.

"Then I have nothing to tell them."

"Could it be related that the first secretary's office wants information about five different Americans?" The question came from Ebert, the head of the DSE. "The name of Minister Chabon was not mentioned, but each of the Americans had dealings with our Ministry of Economic Affairs before the revolution. They could have had contact with Marcel Chabon."

"What answer did you give?" the Russian asked.

"No answer. I relayed the request to our branch in Washington. I still wait for a response."

"Give the first secretary the information he wants as soon as it comes in," the Russian told Ebert. "But tell me what you tell him."

The Russian sat back in his chair. This was his meeting, and with it he made France turn.

Ten minutes later, when the meeting ended, the Russian hesitated.

"Go ahead," he said to Victor, his aide. "I will meet you in my office."

"My admiration, sir, for the way that you have managed this affair with the first secretary."

"Thank you," the Russian replied, but his mind was not on the compliment. He waited at the door after Victor had gone, and then he went to a telephone on the table. He dialled, waited, and dialled again, just two numbers.

"Are you occupied right now?" the Russian said into the telephone. "Can you get away, so that we can share a moment together?"

They met not far from the Gothic palace of the Ministry of Justice, where the point of the Île de la Cité splits the slow press of the Seine. A minute apart, they descended the stairway that leads down to the little triangle of park just above the water's edge. At the apex of the triangle there was a fine willow, the drooping strands naked now of leaves.

It was not so cold for a March day in Paris, but Max, the Russian's oldest friend and most trusted confidant, the head of Department 100's Action Branch, was bundled in an overcoat, a scarf pulled up to his ruddy cheeks and a fur hat pulled down over his temples.

A bench waited empty at the point of the part. It faced the river with a perfect tourist's view of Paris, monotone in gray on gray. On their right, the bulk of the Louvre filled the landscape like a wall. Ahead, an ironwork footbridge, a grace note in the stately parade of stone and masonry bridges that tied the banks of the

Seine. In the distance, before the river bent out of sight, the Pont de la Concorde joined the Place de la Concorde with the Assemblée Nationale, where the deputies of the Communist party played at government. The Russian liked the harmony of the river and bridges.

The two men sat side by side on the bench, where even a lip reader with a telescope would have had difficulty observing them. They did not mention their caution; for a long time they had shared the same discipline.

The only sound was the rustle of willow branches and the lap of the wavelets below as the Russian gathered his thoughts and his friend waited for him to speak.

"Morand will go to Paccard to carry my message," the Russian said. "Morand does not like being caught in the middle, but he will deliver the message. Leonid must leave France."

"No reasonable man could object, but are you sure that Comrade Paccard is a reasonable man?"

"I think he will be reasonable. I have arranged a call from the embassy. It is not a step that I welcome. I prefer to bother our brothers as little as possible. But they understand that for a big fish like the first secretary, they should be involved. And, of course, they agree. They would have taken harsher measures."

"So, it is already decided."

The Russian assented with a slow bob of his head and then rubbed his nose. His friend waited patiently.

"The first secretary is trying to cook a case against our minister of the economy."

"I suppose we could have expected Paccard to react. Many people are starting to notice Marcel Chabon's efficiency."

"I will tell you if there are developments." The Russian paused again before he continued. "But that is not why I asked to see you here. I am troubled by another matter. We are so few, we cannot afford to lose even one."

"Who . . . ?"

"My assistant."

"Not everyone can carry such responsibility."

"But he seemed perfect. Quick to learn, full of dynamism. You know, his Russian is absolutely correct; he never makes a mistake."

"The question is one of ripening . . . not every fruit ripens well."

"I gave him my trust, as I must, and he has never fully opened his heart to me in return."

Max did not respond. The Russian resumed.

"He asked me for a car. He said that he should have a car with a chauffeur so that he could save time working for me. Here is a man whose parents were immigrant Poles, living in the coal fields, asking me for a chauffeured limousine. And today, at the meeting . . . He knew that I had talked to the embassy, and he behaved with arrogance. With only a little more responsibility, he would make everyone angry."

"Do not say more. I know what I must do."

"I should do it myself, but I trust your hand better than my own, and for this there is no one else."

"It is done."

"Be careful, old friend. He is trained in the same ways that we are, and he is young and strong. It would grieve me beyond all loss if this action should bring harm to you."

"I will need a reason to be alone with him, in a suitable place."

"I did not refuse him the car. He would like a large Peugeot. You must help him select it. He will call you to make the arrangements."

THAT evening, Ignacz Gorosczki, code named Victor, stopped at the government officials' commissary and purchased a bottle of champagne, already chilled. Then he nearly ran to his apartment. He could not believe his good fortune. Such a beautiful, gleaming, powerful machine to show his authority and success. He had not dreamed that the Russian would agree. He could not wait to tell Josephine. In the morning he would start to interview for a chauffeur among the men in Action Branch suggested by Comrade Max. For the first time, he would have a man who reported only to him.

Comrade Max, now, there was an odd duck of a man. He seemed untouched by the weight of the responsibility in his hands, and yet his power was vast, almost as vast as the Russian's. Max had a round face with red cheeks, and the strength of his gaze was almost lost in the smile that wrinkled his eyelids. Max was a man who invited trust. Gorosczki wondered what clandestine history had brought him into the Russian's confidence, what experience had prepared him for his unique role.

There in Max's office inside the labyrinth, over a glass of *pastis*, Gorosczki had asked Max if he had been a mole for the Russians before the revolution. Max had grinned and told him that moles have no history and no future, just a small section of tunnel, and even that is dark.

Josephine squealed with delight when she saw the champagne and heard the news. Her enormous breasts quivered with excitement, and her lover could hardly keep his hands off her long enough to uncork the bottle. They drank, undressed, made violent love, and drank again until the bottle was finished. She lay naked on her back, her thin legs open, her blond hair stuck with sweat to her forehead, her eyes watching him with admiration.

He dropped beside her, nuzzling her great breasts. They slept.

In the morning, Josephine had to push Gorosczki off her in order to sit up. He was hard to move.

It took a full twenty seconds for her to understand that he was dead.

When the ambulance came, she could barely control her tears as she told the driver that her lover was a functionary in the Ministry of Justice, which she believed. The death was duly registered as a coronary arrest.

4 Two blue-jacketed guardsmen closed the heavy metal doors after Comrade Minister Morand had gone.

First Secretary Georges Paccard stood rigid against the floor-to-ceiling windows of the office in the Matignon Palace that had traditionally belonged to the prime minister.

His jaw's clenched outline made a ridge under the sagging skin on his jowls. His eyes were liquid slits, the wrinkled lids shuttered over his fury.

Incredible, how the Russian could manipulate his masters. The embassy had been on the telephone twenty minutes before Morand's visit, dictating his choice in bad French.

Exile, then, for his son.

What idiocy had Leonid gotten into? It was not the time to be caught in such stupidity, when everything was prepared to remove Marcel Chabon. Interrogation for Leonid was out of the question. But to abandon him to exile, where his name would mean nothing? Gabon! The conditions now in Gabon were supposed to be a living hell and getting worse.

It was even worse than losing a son. How to explain, within the party, Leonid's posting to Gabon? Leonid's departure would raise the kind of fevered buzz that runs through any organization when there is a shift of equilibrium. Was the first Secretary too weak to protect his son?

His hand floated over the grid of telephones, electronic read-outs, buttons, and toggles on the black onyx console inset into his desk. His index finger descended on a black button with a purple stripe.

He turned back to look at his garden, the longest private garden in

Paris. He was alone in his office with the Fables of Aesop, priceless Gobelin tapestries hanging between fluted white pilasters. His office was resolutely antique and French. The modern needlepoint on the Louis XV chairs was artfully designed to match the faded colors of the sixteenth-century tapestries. The only jar to the decor was a signed photograph, of a Russian in Moscow, and another of a German in Berlin. Paccard believed that they were the most powerful individuals in the world, now that the American president followed the dictates of the Japanese.

Still, it was not that Moscow Russian who was the problem, but the other, the man in the labyrinth, whom everyone called "the Russian."

Two minutes later, a small door opened between two of the white carved pilasters to his left, and a Parade Guard officer appeared. The officer saluted and approached the desk. His dress uniform glittered with polished steel plates that recalled the cuirassiers of the nineteenth century. On his black trousers, a narrow lavender stripe traced the line of his leg. His silver epaulets proclaimed his colonel's rank.

"You failed me. Abruzzi was too late." Paccard glared. "The policeman in Pontoise called MSIE."

The officer, a dark-complexioned man with a heavy scar on his left cheek and graying hair at his temples, stood more than a head taller than Paccard. He listened without a sign of hearing or a response, as steady as a post.

"If you fail me again, in the matter of Marcel Chabon . . ."

"The magistrate will act as soon as we deliver Comrade Chabon. We have presented the charges against him. This morning the accusation was inscribed in the magistrate's official dossier. We wait for some detail from the United States to provide more substance to the accusation."

"It must go fast with Chabon. We cannot give the Russians time to forbid us."

The officer waited, at attention.

Paccard continued. "If we submit Leonid to an interrogation, he will last five minutes before he tells them everything they want to know. And then, how could we announce the misdeeds of

Comrade Chabon? It would not work. . . . People would say that we had done it to steal attention from Leonid."

The right side of the officer's face moved, twisting to form the words. The left side of his face was paralyzed, the nerves severed. "Exactly . . . but instead they offer Leonid an exile in Gabon? You would send him to Gabon?"

"I have no choice."

Paccard turned his back and faced the garden again, staring at the low, gray February sky.

"I want to kill him," Paccard said. He turned back and faced his officer.

"Leonid?"

"No! Kill the Russian—and destroy Department 100. The labyrinth is an accident of the revolution. It should not exist at all."

"We cannot do that."

"They have menaced me. What is your responsibility? You exist to protect me, do you not? Now you are needed."

"Comrade First Secretary, your guardsmen are expected only to decorate events of state. We are conspicuous, it is hard to develop a secret capability for action. Our intelligence is not complete. We have found some ears in MSIE, but none at all in Department 100. Two of our men are giving false reports to Department 100 intelligence, but they get back nothing in return. We know nothing of the labyrinth, our men would die inside."

"What if we could bring their agents up to the surface, up for a fight? Could we win?"

"I think they have only a dozen, maybe fourteen men in their Action Branch. . . . We would win if we could take them one by one, outside the labyrinth."

"Then we must bring them out of the labyrinth. Let us find a way."

The officer bowed.

Paccard asked, "Should we take care of the policeman in Pontoise?"

"Kill the policeman? I think it would increase the pressure on Leonid. We should let him live . . . if you agree?"

"Agreed."

The officer gave a military salute, turned on his heel, and disappeared through the same small door.

Paccard waited until the door was closed and chose another button on the black onyx console.

"**WHAT** do you think the embassy would do?"

President Joux's words spiralled between the two men, uniting their fear. The question was as hard and central as a dam in a river.

A gray garden stretched out beyond the arched window. A high ceiling gave space to a broad desk. The sunken console, framing the grid of electronic controls, was made of green malachite from Zaire.

Solitary figures at the head of a great nation, the president and the first secretary were alone in the office of the president, but four Parade Guards in dress uniform stood outside the massive doors.

President Joux looked smaller and older than in his official photograph, and he had much less hair. His back was bent as he addressed Paccard.

"You can put Chabon out of the way, and they will let you if you move fast. But the Russian is their man. We cannot kill him. Even if they did not react at once, they would not forget. I must ask you a question."

Paccard was in no mood to hear objections from his colleague. Joux was a figurehead, a hangover from the old days to help legitimize the new government, a man to open hospitals and give empty speeches. Only one man ran the government, commanded the military, told the judges how to decide. One man, Georges Paccard, ruled France, except for interference from a man called "the Russian."

But Joux continued, "The problem begins with Leonid. . . ."

"This problem . . . yes."

"I respect your family devotion." Joux looked down at the polished surface of his desk and spoke in the distant tones of a head of state. "But would it not be easier if Leonid were . . . absent?"

"You do not mean exile. . . ."

"More permanently than exile."

"No. He is my son."

"Of course."

"You are a fool. The embassy would understand that we had murdered him."

"They might think it justice...."

"Listen to me, this is the first test. We must be strong."

Joux whined for relief from Paccard's anger. "We must be realists."

"The Russian will attack me for the slightest hint of corruption in the government."

"That is what the embassy expects him to do."

"I am caught in the middle," Paccard retorted. "The Russian wants my head, and Chabon has too many friends."

"You are going to take care of Chabon. There is nothing to make you fear Chabon, just because your son has gotten caught with shit in his hands. Listen, Georges, Chabon did not join the party until after he was made a minister. I know the Russians. They wanted someone to run the economy, but they cannot embrace a man who was independent until two years ago. They have tolerated him, nothing more. The Russian wants what his masters in Moscow want. He won't move to protect Chabon."

"Agreed. So, Chabon will be gone. And if we eliminate Department 100, then the embassy can only deal with us."

"Yes, yes. But we must be realists...."

"This is my intention ... I will agree in principle to Leonid's exile, but he is my son, he must stay in France. We will find reasons to delay. We will find a weakness in the labyrinth, and we will be ready."

Joux shrugged. "My friend, when you find a weakness in the labyrinth, I ask you to keep me out of it. I do not want to owe Moscow for the life of their man."

LANDRY read the report of the security meeting and marvelled. Karel could attack corruption, even by exiling the first secretary's son. Extraordinary.

If Morand's speculation was accurate, Paccard had a vicious thug working for him. Landry pondered the bald man who had gone to Pontoise to terrify the police chief. Had he then murdered Mireille Dupont as well as her roommate and the man named Bruno? A bad character, Ugo Abruzzi . . . Landry thought he could remember news reports of the accusation in the National Assembly.

Landry put the Star to work looking for the name "Abruzzi." There were several dozen Abruzzis alive in France, none of them named Ugo, but the death record was in the Star.

Landry daydreamed about setting up a conflict between Karel and the first secretary as he entered the string of commands that would let him examine Ugo Abruzzis military record.

Abruzzi's record was complimentary. He had been effective, but none of his superiors had described his performance in detail. The record ended with the complaint that the deputy had given from the floor of the National Assembly. Deputy Jacques de Celigny . . . who had never been found after the revolution.

Now Landry conjured up vague recollections of a policeman who had earned acclaim as a crime fighter and then had joined the majority party of the political right.

Landry tapped the keys that would look for "de Celigny."

The Star found Jacques de Celigny in the MSIE missing persons section.

On the day after the Russian tanks had crossed the Rhine, de Celigny had left his two children and his wife, Agnes, departing as usual to work in the Mairie of Marly-le-Roi. He had never arrived.

The New State had wanted him badly enough to interrogate his wife. She had not known where her husband had gone, but her ignorance had not saved her. The new masters used mind-destroying chemicals to speed their interviews, and she did not survive the interrogation. The children were retained in France for future use in the case of Jacques de Celigny, although both were at the age when they should have been transported to the East. They were in Brittany, placed with a loyal communist family.

Did de Celigny know the fate of his family?

Landry probed de Celigny's dossier, fascinated.

Jacques de Celigny had come from a family of the *noblesse,* had played rugby on the national team, and then had chosen a police career. Landry noted this as an eccentricity; a more natural path would have led him to the banks, business, or agriculture.

The documents in de Celigny's career file showed a successful career, sprinkled with headlines for his successes. He had killed in the line of duty more than once, but if he had a wish to kill, the instinct was masked. The press had recalled his rugby fame and the headlines had made him a hero. De Celigny had spoken out with candor, and the politicians of the right had taken him up as a symbol of public safety. He had been elected as mayor of Marly-le-Roi and as a deputy to the National Assembly. He was fiercely anticommunist.

De Celigny would have been doomed, with such a history, if he had not escaped.

Landry wondered if de Celigny had planned to go back for his wife and had underestimated the speed of the attack on the establishment? Did de Celigny blame himself for his wife's death? What rage must be burning in his heart?

Landry's mind started to race. Here was a man accustomed to weapons, a man who would have every reason to hate the New State, a man of shared purpose. If he was alive . . .

The hounds of MSIE had a cold trail, but Landry was sure that the Star could find him.

Five hours later, the Star had matched de Celigny's physique, hair color, and eye color with the recorded characteristics of all the men in France within five years of de Celigny's age. On the resulting list were 288,524 men, waiting to be sifted until only one was left.

The Star had been designed to aid the former government in the collection of taxes. The new government had ended all personal taxes in favor of direct remuneration, but the Star's capability remained. If one of these thousands of men was making transactions in two places at the same time, or was travelling in one place when he should have been working in another, the Star could know it.

Finding his way through the maze of information stored in the Star, Landry was suspended in a long, taut thread of concentration. Slowly, he assembled the steps in the right sequence.

More hours passed. Landry rubbed his eyes. He was hungry, his head hurt, and his eyes were starting to burn. He knew these symptoms, when the rhythms of the twenty-four-hour day lost their meaning and grappling with the Star carried him around the corner of night, far into the following day . . . time wrap.

At a few minutes before noon of the following day, the Star found the man who was surely Jacques de Celigny.

Under the alias of Albert Gola, he was working in an aluminum smelter in Ugine. Landry knew Ugine. It was south of Megève, tucked down at the end of an Alpine gorge, nothing more than an ugly turn-of-the-century factory, a traffic light, and a few shops huddled around a crossroads, and then a new rolling mill with open walls and a metal roof. And that was where Jacques de Celigny worked, in the rolling mill.

Albert Gola was recorded sick forty-two days in the current year. The Star had noted that fact because it was more than one and one-half times the average sick leave of the factory.

Also, Gola had spent over six thousand francs for railroad trips to odd places like Poitiers and Metz. An extraordinary sum for a worker, also noted by the Star. It was made possible because the man had another job, as a waiter in the neighboring town of Albertville. Theoretically, it was illegal to hold two jobs, but the practice was tolerated by the New State.

And finally, Albert Gola had not existed in any public record before the year 2003. The man's employment in Ugine had started two months after the revolution, and in Albertville, three months later.

All circumstantial evidence, but Landry was ninety percent sure. If Albert Gola was not Jacques de Celigny, then de Celigny was dead and another man much like him had miraculously appeared without any prior history. Now, despite the hours of work inside the Star, it seemed almost too easy. The hard part would be to make contact without betraying him or driving him to flight. And then to recruit him. And then . . . what?

Landry tapped a key, and the Star dutifully told him the date and the time. He had already taken so long, but he had not even finished the minutes of the security meeting.

He keyed his way back. The first secretary was asking for information about Marcel Chabon. What did that mean? Who were the five Americans who might have dealt with him?

Now, having Jacques de Celigny almost in reach as a man of action, Landry wanted Marcel Chabon to be an ally ... and maybe Chabon was better than he seemed, if Paccard wanted to hurt him.

Landry found his way into the DSE files and verified the request from the DSE in Paris to the Washington branch. Five American businessmen had indeed been in touch with Chabon before the revolution. The DSE asked for details of their businesses and any deals that they had made with Chabon.

Now Landry left the DSE record and started a general search in the Star for mentions of Chabon's name. Landry tried not to think of his fatigue while the search hurtled through billions of electronic bits to stop on the combination that spelled "Chabon."

Chabon's name appeared in a sector that belonged to the Ministry of Justice. A magistrate had received a dossier concerning the minister of the economy. Accusations: Chabon had passed secret information to the United States. Chabon had a bank account in Caracas, now amounting to over half a million dollars. What secrets? Landry asked himself. Payment for what? Landry told himself that the dossier was a transparent fraud, but the attack was real.

Karel should stop this perversion of justice, Landry thought, but then he wryly asked himself what good he should expect of Karel.

And if Paccard's attack was successful?

Chabon would be gone. Landry would have lost the last man from his list, just when he had found Jacques de Celigny.

Landry asked the Star again for the time. He had four hours to sleep, and then he would go to his rendezvous with Chantal Senac.

He slept, but the question never left him: what reasons did he have to protect a minister in the New State?

SHE was late.

His head still spinning with the discoveries of the preceding hours, Landry had come early to the apartment of René Leveque, perched halfway up the hill from Pigalle to Montmartre. It was a place he had found in the last month before the Russians came, at the top of a building that rose high on the downhill side and sat squat and low where the entry faced the street.

In those first days, when it was clear that the catastrophe was worse than all imagining and he had started to wonder about his decision to stay in France, he had come to the apartment, looked out on the master view of Paris, and told himself that this was still the most beautiful city in the world—as if that were justification.

But after learning about the suffering inflicted on his friends, the view of Paris had become unimportant next to his anger and despair. He had visited the apartment just four times in the past year, to sustain his identity as the tenant.

The windows in the sitting room, the bedroom, and even the bath overlooked the city from a vantage point fifty feet above the top of the adjacent building. A motley gray patchwork of rooftops spread from below, with the buttressed spine and towers of Notre Dame beyond and the dome of the Pantheon still further in the background.

The apartment was arranged to support his alias as René Leveque and to look more lived in than it was. A white-topped trestle table facing the windows was strewn with engineering drawings and project specifications, and the red-painted bookshelves were crammed with books about architecture, environment, and the history of French public works. A diploma shared the wall with photographs of bridges and concrete seawalls. The diploma proclaimed René Leveque a civil engineer in the People's Democratic Republic of France.

The apartment was on the fourth and top floor, disposed lengthwise along the south side of the ninety-year-old building.

Light flooded in, touching every corner, even in the cooking alcove.

He wanted Chantal to share the view of Paris before the sun rose so high that its light would wash out the chiaroscuro on the rooftops. He tried to imagine her face, but could picture nothing more than big haunted eyes and a small curved mouth, a thin body and brown hair. What he remembered was not her face but her intensity, the taut awareness of a field mouse under a wheeling hawk.

He wished that he could tell her about Jacques de Celigny and Marcel Chabon. He wished he could speak about Leonid Paccard's scandal. He yearned to share something more than the false details of his created identity.

The doorbell buzzed. He jumped to his feet, telling himself that he should not tell her, because she did not need to know. He opened the door.

She came in, flushed from the sharp outside air and the climb up the stairs, her eyes bright.

"I did as you said, and I am alone," she said, breathless from the four flights. "I left the café next to the Opéra by the back door and then took three trains in the *métro*."

She offered her cool cheek to be kissed in the way that ladies used to be kissed by friends in the good old days. He brushed her cheek with his lips, and then the other side as it was offered in turn. She was taut as a bowstring.

"I think I came alone," she said. "Sometimes I feel that people are watching me. . . ."

"Don't worry," Landry answered, "we are quite legitimate in this place."

But as he spoke the words, a shiver ran up his back. His Leveque alias was not as secure as he would like.

"So, you live here," she said.

"Would you like some tea?" he asked. "I went to the market and bought some tea for you. Also, let me think . . . I have smoked sturgeon from Russia, a cooked chicken from Bourg-en-Bresse, pâté de foie from Strasbourg, lemons, onions, pasta and olive oil from Italy, fresh bread, spices, even a bottle of orange juice from Spain."

"You have all that? You are rich," she said soberly.

They drank orange juice and ate the smoked sturgeon with lemon juice and onion on toasted bread, sitting at his trestle table.

The sturgeon tasted better than anything she had eaten in months, and the orange juice was a forgotten nectar in her mouth.

"Do you always have such a supply of wonders to eat?" she asked, wondering how he had obtained the food but not daring to ask.

"When I wish," he replied, and then answered her unspoken question. "My friend in the government lets me obtain some luxuries."

"It makes me sad for old times. Arnaud and I would feast on picnics like this," she said.

"Don't think about those days," he replied.

She wiped her lips and asked, "Are you married?"

"I was married. My wife may still be alive."

"Did they take her?"

"You must not ask about my life before the Russians came. To know my life can put us both in danger."

"Then tell me, at least, your pleasures and your hates."

"My pleasures are in the France that exists only in my mind . . . simple things stored in my memory. Except for now."

"Your hates . . . ?"

"They exist . . ." He thought of his hates and felt the heat of his anger rise. "We should not talk about them now; there will be other times for that."

"I loved my life," she said. "I adored my child. Just to look at him filled me with joy. Arnaud, my husband, was a rock for me, so strong and sure that I never feared the future. I expected to grow old with him. I worked, too. I am an amateur historian, specialized in the time of the French revolution, the first one. I still find happiness in my private knowledge of the Chouans. . . . They were mad, you know. They dared all for their poor counterrevolution. As a student, I did a thesis. Now, the library staff know me and let me stay with their books. As I study, the story grows, full of scoundrels and heroes, and plots that failed. I daydream of myself as a Chouan, battling the government of the Russians. I wish I could be as mad as they were."

He watched her, imagining the wounds in her mind, her solace in the balm of long-ago history. She was gazing at the rooftops, her closed lips curved in a small smile. After so long without a woman, he imagined her in bed, and the image stirred him—she would be sweet and open, a trusting and tender lover.

She spoke. "Nothing in my studies had prepared me for the day the Russians came."

The words tore Landry away from male desire. He felt a pang of guilt, because he had been prepared for the Russians.

"Do you remember?" she asked. "That day?"

"Of course. Who will ever forget?"

France had renounced its *force de frappe*, the nuclear arsenal that it had held independent from NATO since the stubborn times of Charles de Gaulle. Scrapping the warheads came from necessity—the same antinuclear sanctions that applied to China and Israel applied equally to every nation—but the disarmament had ended with a sigh of relief. In the prosperity of a newly united Europe and the good will of the World Peace Agreement, even the most conservative politicians were glad to eliminate weapons as a voting issue.

On the day the Russians came, December 28th, 2002, there was no warning, no fabricated provocation—nothing more than the logic of Marx and Lenin: the revolution of the proletariat was fulfilling its European destiny. As simple as that. They had started from the center of Germany at midnight. At dawn they were in Belgium and crossing the bridges of the Rhine. Under blue skies, on a crisp, clear day, columns of tanks and personnel carriers had come down the autoroutes that converged on Paris.

"I listened to the radio that morning," Chantal said. "When I heard that there were Russian tanks in France, I thought it was a hoax, some terrible prank of the students. And then the radio went off."

"The radio was their special target, they had a team already in place, just waiting to go across the Seine to seize the broadcast studios."

"I saw the tanks that evening," she continued. "They used the Parc des Princes to park their tanks."

"And the Place de la Concorde . . . I saw them, too."

"Why did we let them come? Why didn't we fight?"

"Our intelligence had been betrayed, and the surprise was complete. The government was not disposed to use force, in any case, and besides that, I think they were afraid. Did you ever hear about the garrison of Reims? When the colonel there heard on the public radio that the Russians were coming down the autoroute from Metz, he took his troops out to stop them, without waiting for orders. Those French soldiers were annihilated from the air, with not a single Russian casualty, and then the event itself was obliterated from the records. That was the last act of French heroism, and it will never be written in the history books."

She shook her head. It was so sad.

"But it was in Paris that the French revolution succeeded. Georges Paccard and his gang of party hacks were all assembled and ready to replace the government with a new one. The planning was perfect—precise down to the last detail. Names and jobs and places, all decided in advance . . . Paccard had a regiment of Russians behind and about three dozen French party members in front of him when he walked into the Chambre des Députés."

"And they killed all the ministers of the old government?"

"No, not at all, at least not then. Why do you think that?"

"Comrade Pernoud, at work . . . she said so."

"They were rounded up and sent off to the State Factories, just like thousands of others. It was not easy for them. I think some have died, like your husband."

"Tell me, it was never clear . . . what happened in Italy and England, in Belgium, Scandinavia? What made them fall to the Russians? Did the Russians invade there, too, with soldiers and tanks?"

"France, Holland, and Belgium were the first to fall. There was fighting in Switzerland, in Basel and Bern. For the rest, they just gave up. In England, the government fell, and there was an election that voted the Labor Party into power, and then they gave up."

"And the Americans . . ."

"They are in debt to the Japanese. And the Japanese are quite happy to have the Russians and Germans occupied here in Europe, so that the Europeans are out of competition."

"And now, there is no hope," Chantal said. "We are alone in the world, and my child will grow up as a communist."

He was about to speak, but she continued.

"The trouble is that all our friends, every soul in France who might be a Chouan against the communists, is dead or in a State Factory. I lost all of my friends."

"It is the same for me," Landry said, but he thought of Jacques de Celigny, and then he asked himself what he should do to warn Marcel Chabon.

She continued, "But you have your friend in the government. . . ."

"That is true, but he is no counterrevolutionary."

She put her hand on his. The contact gave her strength. It had been so long since she could speak to someone who could understand what she had lost.

"We had so many friends. Arnaud had an address book as thick as a dictionary. Our friends were always near us, to share good times and to fill my days when Arnaud was gone. He was often away because of his work, and he was a great hunter. He would take weekends and sometimes whole weeks to shoot and come home with cardboard boxes full of dead birds."

"He took his vacations without you?"

"In the fall and again in springtime. But we had wonderful times together at Christmas and Easter, when Noël was out of school. We went to ski, always at Courchevel for Christmas, and then in February to Alpe-d'Huez or Avoriaz or Val d'Isère, wherever our friends and we decided to go. And each summer we took a place by the sea, at Cap Benat or L'Ile d'Yeu, always with friends."

Landry knew these places and asked himself if he had ever met this woman or Arnaud, her husband. He must have known some of her friends.

She laughed. "We sailed and skied like all our friends, serious as children. All of us wanted to become more expert, but in those days we just fell in the water and fell on the snow and had fun together. We ate well on those vacations, always in big groups at lunch and dinner, twenty at the table. It was such a good time."

"I know," Landry said.

She put down the knife that she was using to slice some pâté de foie and laid her hand on his. "In the first minute that I saw you, in the café, I thought that somewhere, in our past, I had met you."

A whisper of fear traced down his back. He sensed the hawks wheeling over his own head.

She remembered the moment in the café and how she had thought he could be an informer. She decided to tell him. "When the police came into the café, in my paranoia I thought that you must work for MSIE. Or even the labyrinth."

As the words hung in the air, the hawks seemed to spiral closer. Landry thought carefully about his response.

"How do you know about the labyrinth?"

"I think that everybody knows. . . . It is gossip that I hear from the women who work with me."

"You heard about the labyrinth from the cleaning women at the ministry?"

"Yes."

Of course, he thought, the Star did not deal in folklore, only in official records. But Chantal Senac also had access to information, information denied to him in his grotto below the Étoile. He would need to be careful. If every man in the street knew about the labyrinth, then so should Engineer Leveque.

Chantal looked at him, waiting for a cue.

"Forgive me," he said. "My friend in the government assumes that the deepest secrets are secret, and I think I shared his mistake. Tell me about the labyrinth."

She answered carefully, not wanting a wrong word to panic him.

"I only know the stories that I have heard from two women, Comrade Jeanneau and Comrade Pernoud. I think they heard the stories from their husbands, or perhaps from friends. It is secret, as you say. It is a small organization that is controlled by a Russian. Comrade Jeanneau says that the labyrinth existed before the revolution. She says that it was the brain of the revolution. Comrade Pernoud speaks from time to time about the Russian and how he knows everything that there is to know in France."

Landry nodded. Karel, the Russian, was the brain of the revolution.

She turned her eyes to his bearded face. He looked away, at Paris, and she saw him in that moment as she had seen him before, clean shaven, the face coming clear out of the closets of her memory, and then she connected again. She had been with him not once, but twice.

"You did not have a beard."

"What?"

"You were with the American woman, the skier. She was so healthy and strong, and she was a friend of a friend of a woman I knew. We had dinner together in a big group at a restaurant in Val d'Isère, and you sat at the far end of the table. It was . . . two years before the revolution. And then I saw her again, that same year, in St. Tropez, and you were with her. But we never really spoke, and the second time neither of you remembered me from Val d'Isère. I never knew your name, but I remember hers. . . . Helen. She was blond, with fine thick hair. Everybody talked about how athletic and American she was."

He thought of denying it but there was not point. He had been caught from the moment he had decided to see her again.

"I'm sorry, Engineer Leveque," she said softly. "You would feel better if we had never met, I think."

"It is all right," he said.

"You were very handsome," she said. "You made a beautiful couple. I felt quite invisible when you were in the room. I remember thinking that I could never be as self-confident and attractive as Helen. . . . Your wife?"

He nodded confirmation.

"And you . . . you are not from Luxembourg? The touch of accent that I hear is from the United States?"

"I am American, but I have spent most of my life here. We were often in Val d'Isère. And I remember the trip to St. Tropez. But you are right, I don't have any recollection of meeting you. Was your husband there with you?"

"You might remember him. He had broad shoulders and a big chest and stomach. He was not so tall as you, only a few centimeters taller than I am, and he was losing some of his hair, but he made an impression. He was quite dynamic. Do you remember?"

"Perhaps. From St. Tropez. Did he have a big head and a square face, with a nose that looked as if it might have been in a fight."

"He was not a handsome man."

"He asked me what I did for a living."

"He loved to know about people. He would ask a few questions and then listen for hours."

"Even in those days it was impossible for me to discuss my work. As I remember it, I told him that I spent all my time protecting Helen from strange men. I think that didn't please him."

She smiled. "He did not like people to play with him. He was always serious, even when he was enjoying himself."

Landry now could vaguely remember the man. It had been at the beginning of Helen's affair with Guillaume, and they had gone to St. Tropez because Guillaume was having a show. There had been a dinner party at the house of a potential patron, and Helen had insisted that they go, to provide moral support for Guillaume. Arnaud Senac, if in fact it had been Arnaud Senac, had been polite but direct, like a busy man accustomed to authority. Landry remembered steady eyes with gray pouches underneath. The moment came back to him because he had answered Senac spontaneously and immediately afterward had asked himself why that response had come to mind; it had been too late to protect Helen from strange men. Senac had turned away like an old dog from a rude puppy, not suffering fools kindly.

Chantal, it was true, had been invisible, hidden in the chorus of the opera.

And now, she was the only person in France who could tie him to the past. He would have to trust her, and trust the armor of false identity that remained between Engineer Leveque and the Star.

He took the knife and started to spread the precious country pâté on a round of fresh bread.

Chantal felt as though she had walked by mistake into a stranger's house. She studied him for signs of fear or anger. When he finally smiled, she melted in relief.

When he spoke, it was as though reading her mind. "There is danger in your memories," he said. "But it's good to share my life with you. Be patient with me."

They talked about living with the revolution, about food, music, and propaganda, and the rewriting of recent history. He thought that he could invite her to his bed and that she would come, but it seemed too soon. He had waited so long; he could wait a little longer.

Before they parted, he told her that he had not forgotten the search for her child, and again she felt that he was reading her mind. She pictured Noël and imagined Engineer Leveque as Noël's foster father.

On the way home, she changed trains three times, backtracking to be sure she was not followed.

Landry waited half an hour, cleaning up the apartment and arranging it to suit Leveque's character and work. Her departure left him hungry for her, but without regret—the time would come and be better for waiting.

Half an hour later, he took the *métro* to his little van. He knew what he needed to do about Marcel Chabon.

MARCEL Chabon walked into his office through the open door, past his personal secretary who sat in the corridor outside. The ancient parquet floors squeaked with each step, loud in the corridor, muffled under the wall-to-wall carpet as he passed into his office.

Chabon worked in the Louvre, facing the other part of the

Louvre that housed the National Museum. His windows looked down on the glass pyramids, which had been symbols of new prosperity in the France of the eighties. With the passing of prosperity the glass panels had become dusky with soot. Chabon took off his suit jacket, a rumpled polyester and wool product of a State Factory that he had personally inspected only a month before. His step was short and quick, taking him from a coatrack in the corner to the wooden desk in the center of the room. His shoulders were narrow and round but his arms were heavy, and his hands were muscular. He looked like a worker, not like the professor and career bureaucrat that he had been all his life.

The monitor on his desk glowed, full of messages that his secretary had entered during the day. Chabon's eyes scanned down them, and he touched a key to go to the next screen. At the end of the list, a cryptic note: a friend from the United States.

Chabon buzzed his secretary.

She answered before he could ask. "He would not give me his name," she said. "I asked him. He spoke in English, and he would only say he was calling from the United States. He said he would call back."

A mystery . . . Chabon knew many people in the United States, as he did in Russia, China, and Japan, but most of them would be quick to give their name and title.

His secretary asked, "If he calls back, should I put him through?"

"Not unless he gives his name. And if he does call back, be sure to trace the call."

For a moment Chabon wondered if anyone was left in the United States who would still call him a friend, and then he reassured himself. If they could make a few dollars by dealing with him, he would be considered their friend again.

Half an hour later, the secretary buzzed, and Chabon picked up the phone.

"It's the man from the United States. Your friend. He gave me his name, Mr. Winn, W-I-N-N, from Caterpillar."

Strange that James Winn had not given his name on the first call, Chabon reflected as he picked up the phone.

"Hello, Jim," Chabon said in heavily accented English. "It has been a long time since we spoke. How are you?"

"It is not James Winn," the voice replied. "But I am a friend, Minister Chabon, and it is vital that I talk to you. Is this line secure?"

"Yes. Who is this?"

"To protect my source, I may not say. Minister Chabon, can you write down what I tell you?"

"You are on tape."

The American voice spelled out the name of the French magistrate and the number of the file that would give the government's case against Marcel Chabon.

"What is this about?" Chabon asked.

"The first secretary wishes to see you in prison, I believe."

"I see."

"Good-bye, Minister Chabon. Protect yourself."

The line went dead, and Chabon slowly put down the receiver. He doubted he would live to see a prison if he was arrested. He went to the window, looked down at the glass pyramids below, and weighed his choice of defenses.

His secretary came through the open door. "May I interrupt?"

Chabon turned away from the window.

"Your call came from the Western Hemisphere, patched from the satellite."

Chabon nodded and gave a smile of thanks. "Please get me Pyotr, at the Russian Embassy," he asked. "I need to talk to him."

THE little truck rocked from side to side as the bends in the road took it down into the valley. Laurent Bellot drove easily, cranking the wheel with measured effort at each hairpin, letting his own weight shift with the centrifugal force. He was filled with the satisfaction of a good day. The sun had set, but enough light lingered to outline the mountaintops against the sky. The truck ran like a train, repaying him for the hours that he had spent on it. He listened for valve clatter on the downshifts and asked himself if it would be worth another hour working on the lifters to eliminate the last trace of noise.

Laurent Bellot, *garagiste* of Conflans, was returning from a day off his job, driving down from the high mountains of the Vanoise. He had left Conflans the night before and had spent the night in the mountain village of Pralognan at the home of an old friend, had left his bed at two A.M. to climb up in the dark, to reach a high flank of the Aiguille de la Vanoise with the first rays of the rising sun.

And there, like a vision out of his youth, he watched a herd of chamois rooting out bits of grass from under the snow. He loved these little goatlike animals, and just seeing them brought a burst of nostalgia and joy. Only the noble ibex was capable of greater heights, but he had not seen an ibex in years. The chamois foraged on the edge of the abyss for wisps of nothing, climbed with gay nonchalance in precipitous snow and ice, played and rutted and carried their kids where a human could only creep on his toes and fingertips. They lived as a man should be able to live, free. Laurent had never applied reason to his feelings about the chamois, because he came only to hunt them, and why should one kill something so dear? If anyone had asked him, Laurent would have explained that death by a clean bullet was better than growing old and sick, but hunting the chamois was more than that to him. When his eye was steady on the sight, and his finger tightened on the cold metal of the trigger, that bullet racing between him and the animal was like a bond of the spirit that made him as free as the chamois.

The two chamois in the back of the truck had been dead since that first light in the morning. Another had stayed with his friend. Most of Laurent's day had been devoted to bringing the three dead chamois down to Pralognan and dressing them.

The rifle had been given him by his father, and it had never been registered. Laurent's defiance of the New State had extended his defiance of the old. He knew some other hunters who had owned unregistered weapons, and he supposed that some of those weapons were still in the hands of their owners, but it would not be discreet to ask. As far as he could say for certain, his rifle was the only one in France that was currently used for poaching.

He knew the chamois would be welcome at home. Henri Moreau, his brother-in-law, would open a bottle of the good Burgundy wine that he obtained in exchange for bread, from the manager of the national store in Albertville. Catherine, Laurent's sister, would use the wine to make a rich stew of the chamois, the gamey, dark flavor of the meat blending in triumph with the warm, burnt taste of cream over potatoes. The revolution had not taken every good thing from them.

When he thought of the revolution, Laurent thought of their guest, who had suffered so much. Well, Jacques de Celigny would enjoy eating the stew.

The hairpin descent ended. The road ran flat along a slow, flat stretch of the stream that had carved the valley, and then it crossed a bridge to descend again. Laurent turned on his headlights as the road dropped into a dark cleft with cliffs on either side.

Just then, headlights flooded the road ahead, and a red wand made hasty semicircles, waving him down.

He braked hard, coming to rest on the snow-covered gravel at the side of the road.

"Identification?" the gendarme asked. Two blue police trucks were parked, one on each side of the pavement. Five gendarmes, bundled against the cold in heavy coats, idly watched the gendarme at Laurent's window. Laurent dug his wallet out of his hip pocket and flipped it open to show his identity card.

"What is in the truck?"

"Game," Laurent said.

"Game?"

Laurent nodded.

"Show me."

Wearily, Laurent went to the back, opened the door, and stood aside for the gendarme to look. The narrow beam of the gendarme's flashlight searched the interior, sweeping from corner to corner. Sightless eyes reflected out of the darkness, the goat's vertical slits of pupils now glazed over with a dull film. A purple tongue curled, glistening. The chamois were spread on the floor, lashed to the sides of the truck to keep them from sliding when the truck took a bend in the road. Their coarse black-brown fur soaked up the light, framing the eyes and the glistening tongues in darkness.

"Where did you get these?"

"In Pralognan. . . ."

"From who?"

Laurent shrugged. "I was able to help a man with a bad engine in his car. I am a mechanic. He gave me these. . . ."

"Barter is in contravention."

"These beasts are not in commerce. It was a gift of friendship."

The gendarme swept the inside of the van with the wand of light, walked to the open door at the driver's side, and swept again. He looked under the driver's seat, then walked to the other side of the van and opened the door to continue his search.

He put the beam on Laurent's face. "You are a mechanic?"

"I am the mechanic of the Garage du Pétrole National, in Conflans."

"What repair did you make, to receive these dead animals?"

"Nothing so much. I tightened the fan belt so that the engine would not overheat, that is all."

"And for this you received such a gift?"

"Ah, but he had several more. . . . I think he is keeping something like a farm up there, to raise the chamois."

"Wait," the gendarme commanded.

Laurent waited while the team of gendarmes consulted, out of his hearing.

A sergeant took the flashlight and came to him. "You are in contravention, comrade. You should leave these with us, and we don't ask how you got them."

In the gendarme's voice, Laurent heard no trace of the rich Savoyard inflection. He was from somewhere else, north. In the New State, gendarmes normally worked far from their native region. These men would know nothing of chamois.

Laurent spoke. "You know how to cook these, do you? I do not want to be blamed if you die from eating them. They make you very sick if you do not cook them well. Worse than wild pig, these are. You know how to cook the wild pig, then? . . . For the chamois, it is even more important."

The sergeant stared at him, aiming the light from his face to the truck, and back to his face. Laurent smiled cheerfully.

"Wait here," the sergeant said. He padded away to confer with his colleagues.

The wind was picking up, carrying a chill that cut through the layers of flannel and nylon in Laurent's parka. He shifted from one foot to the other, his hands in his pockets, thinking that he would need his gloves if they kept him much longer.

After a short conversation with his colleagues, the sergeant simply shouted, "Go on, comrade. We are through with you."

Laurent went to close the doors at the rear of the van and slowly returned to the driver's seat. He turned the key and listened while the engine settled into the even cadence that he had worked so hard to achieve. As he passed the group of gendarmes, he waved. It was going to be a cold winter's night for city boys, but in the house of Henri and Catherine Moreau, there would be a fine feast.

Half an hour later, Laurent was in the town of his childhood, approaching the garage of the Pétrole National.

Laurent had inherited the garage. He had given it up to the New State, and now he earned a salary for servicing the vehicles that came for repair.

In fact, the revolution had not brought many changes in the town of Conflans. There were fewer tourists, and the tourists who came spent less, but the New State paid salaries whether or not the tourists brought business.

Conflans consisted of two parts, as different as stones from cream. The part of Conflans that was above, on a hill, was very old. There, the medieval buildings had been restored to attract a small vacation trade.

The house of Henri and Catherine Moreau was above, in the old town. Despite the fourteenth-century walls, the house, like the bakery that stood adjacent, was quite new inside. They had shared in the general renovation.

The garage was down on the riverbank, where you could see Albertville from the windows at the back. It was an ugly square building with metal walls that had turned black over the years.

Laurent drove the little truck through the garage door into a familiar chaos of tools and parts. As he went to close the door, another pair of headlights turned in from the main road. Laurent waited, recognizing the vehicle. It rolled inside, and Laurent closed the door behind it.

Philippe, the bakery driver, and Jacques de Celigny, their guest since the revolution, climbed out of the bakery truck.

"You are just in time," Laurent said. "I have two chamois to carry up the hill."

"You shot chamois?" de Celigny asked, grinning. "You have been killing the chamois of the New State?"

"I shot them, and I passed them through a roadblock. The gendarmes wanted to take them, but I told them they would get sick if they didn't know how to cook them."

"How did you explain the rifle?"

"They never saw the rifle. See, I keep it here." Laurent patted the underside of the truck body, where he had welded a long, narrow box, padded with foam. The box had sheltered his rifle since long before the revolution.

De Celigny was short, dark, wiry, a trim moustache setting off the sparkle in his eyes. He was half the size of Laurent Bellot, but energy spun off him. His smile still in place, he asked, "The gendarmes took your name?"

"Sure. Of course."

"And let you go?"

"You see me. With my chamois."

"You should be careful, my friend Laurent, that you should not bring the gendarmes with you."

"We are all careful here," Laurent replied.

De Celigny turned away, sensitive to his situation in Conflans. If care was needed, it was because of himself, not because of Laurent's poached chamois.

They carried the chamois up the steep hill and hung them in the cellar, just outside de Celigny's little room. De Celigny changed his clothes and went to his second job, with a promise from Catherine that a fair share of the stew would be on the stove, awaiting his return.

"He did not like it, our friend, that I had killed the chamois," Laurent told his sister. "It makes him nervous that I hunt. But life must go on, no? . . . Because he is here, should I not hunt?"

"You should be careful, Laurent. He has killed more than chamois; he has killed men, remember that. . . . He would kill again if he could face the men who took Agnes, and he would not stop to add up his chances."

They were standing together in the cellar, Catherine watching while Laurent deftly drew the skin off the chamois. She was a big woman, almost as tall as her brother, with long dark hair that flowed like water, straight down over her shoulders. She was a baker's wife, and she could knead and turn the dough as well as any man.

"He is a dangerous man, our friend," Catherine said. "We must be careful that he should never be . . . provoked."

"He can take care of himself, Jacques de Celigny," Laurent replied. "I like him very much; he is my friend, but . . ."

"You should not use his name like that. He is Albert Gola."

"You are correct; I must call him Albert Gola. But a man must hunt, no? We have the right, given from our father to his children, no . . . ?"

They heard a creaking of heavy footfalls above, and both turned their heads to watch Henri Moreau tramping down the wooden steps. He was very tall, and he stooped almost double to keep from grazing his head on the stones that arched over the stairwell.

His eyes brightened seeing the chamois cadavers hanging in the bright light of a naked light bulb.

"Good hunting, then . . ."

"Excellent," Laurent replied.

"And what is going on about our friend?"

Henri had overhead the end of the conversation.

"It is nothing," Laurent said. "I had to pass these through a road-block of gendarmerie, up on the road between Pralognan and

Moutiers. I should not have told our friend, it would have been better to say nothing about gendarmes. It made him a little nervous."

"You did not mention any roadblock to me," Catherine said.

"It was nothing serious."

"You, with a rifle and two dead chamois, and you think it was not serious?"

"They were just city boys from up north, they only wanted to feel important. Not like the gendarmes in the old days, then I would have been in a hard place explaining two dead chamois."

"Laurent . . ."

Laurent smiled, his mind at ease. He turned to the carcass of the largest chamois and started again with his knife. Over his shoulder, he said, "Come with me next month, Catherine, there are ibex in Italy, and I think we should go over to get one. It would be like the old days hunting with father."

Henri put a hand on his brother-in-law's shoulder and squeezed it. "Be careful, Laurent. The gendarmes may be younger and easier than in the old days, but the New State is not. If MSIE understands that you have a rifle, they will not stop by giving you a fine. And if they learn the true name of Albert Gola, then we are all finished. You understand, I think. . . ."

Laurent nodded.

"You live here," Henri continued. "They would search our house, if you were under suspicion."

"What would they find? Albert Gola has a perfect story, no? . . ."

"We should not take risks."

"A man must hunt. . . ."

"When the revolution is overthrown, when Jacques de Celigny can be himself in public, then hunt."

"Neither the Fifth Republic nor the New State could prevent me, but you tell me to stop hunting the chamois? . . ."

"And also the ibex."

Catherine came in as her husband's ally. "We beg you, Laurent . . ."

"Then, Catherine, you must make this stew a very good one, because I will want to remember it for a long time."

Laurent returned to work with his knife, concentrating, finished with the conversation.

Henri Moreau's eyes followed the knife paring the skin from the dead chamois, but his thoughts were on Jacques de Celigny. As a rugby teammate, Henri had suffered and triumphed at Jacques's side, and together the two had put away many barrels of beer. When rugby was only a memory, Jacques and Agnes de Celigny had stopped in Conflans each winter on their way to the ski stations. Catherine had become as much a friend to Agnes de Celigny as he was to Jacques. And now, as Albert Gola, Jacques had become the most important part of their lives.

How secure was the alias?

Henri did not know the whole story. Jacques had arrived from Paris with papers that had been taken from a Basque, Albert Golalquiaga. Jacques had told Henri that Albert Golalquiaga was dead, in a way that made Henri suppose Jacques had killed him. And then, when he found a job, Jacques had contrived to get the shortened form of the name, Gola, inscribed on his records. It should be a blind trail, if no one asked for proof.

Henri Moreau put his arm around Catherine's waist and held her close to his side. He admitted to himself that he was frightened by his old friend.

5 **This** was not the Paris of monuments and palaces, of fine vast spaces defined by boulevards. That was on the other side of Paris, centered on the Étoile, where L'Enfant had applied his genius and made the first plan for a great city. It was not even the clustered chaos of the Left Bank, where the eighteenth and nineteenth centuries had patched over the medieval origins of the city without burying any of the ghosts.

Here, buildings of all sorts had been constructed in the past dozen decades, each respecting the laws of economics and the laws of the city more than high art. The laws of economics had dictated brick or slab concrete, the laws of the city had ruled their height and a myriad of other details, and so the Avenue d'Italie was like any other city street with buildings on each side.

Chantal had gone out to walk and to buy bread on the Avenue d'Italie, only a few blocks from home. She stopped in front of a shop window and looked past her reflection at the bare rows of shelves. Three years ago, the window would have been filled with sweaters and skirts to entice the passing shoppers. A single long-sleeved cotton shirt was spread in the center, with a handwritten price tag: one thousand francs. It would wait a long time at that price, even in the midst of shortages. Strange that the shop was allowed by the state to set such a price. But she was not really window-shopping. She had stopped to study the reflection of the street behind her in the glass: she was looking for a person waiting on the other side of the street, for a truck paused in the roadway, for anyone or anything that might be there because of her. Now she looked briefly down the street behind her.

It was noon, and there were some people out, but no one

seemed to be waiting for her to continue on her way. I am alone, she thought, but she moved on to the next window and waited, gazing at posters of palm trees. When she looked up, she quickly scanned the street. All the people she had picked out before were gone or departing, and the people approaching were new. Or so she thought. It was hard, a memory game, to pin an identity on each person in the street and then remember where that person had been a minute earlier: a woman with a shopping basket, walking away—an old man in a blue smock, carrying a wicker basket, walking toward her—the tall man in the overcoat who had just walked into view from around the corner, with a portfolio under his arm and a long stride.

The trick was to remember the faces and shapes, so that if they passed and waited for her, she would recognize them later.

This is paranoia, she told herself. René Leveque had told her to take precautions coming from and going to the apartment below Montmartre, and that had added a new weight of fear onto the apprehension that she had already felt.

Who would follow her? In the months past, there had been moments when she had caught eyes looking at her. Always a man, never the same, but she had felt each time that it was more than an accidental crossing of glances or a man's curiosity for a woman. Today, though, there had been no one out of the ordinary. Yet deep in the pools of her subconscious, she was sure that there were watchers, watching her.

She walked on, south to the intersection of Tolbiac, and then west on Tolbiac toward the rue de l'Espérance.

As she walked, she heard a motor start on the street behind her. She noted the sound and tried to remember if any of the parked vehicles had been occupied. Gears engaged, and a small Citroën van passed her. She watched it continue ahead and then pull in to the curb—a delivery van. But no one got out to make a delivery. It was waiting.

She stopped, thought about turning back, but knew that was silly. If the van was waiting, it could also come back for her. It was all silly, she told herself. The driver was just taking a siesta.

As she came even with the van, the curbside door opened.

She refused to let her apprehension stop her.

"Chantal."

Every muscle in her body contracted.

"It's me, René."

A wave of relief swept through her, washing the adrenalin out of her veins.

She tried to smile. "You frightened me."

"It's all right, there is no one else," he said. He stayed in the van, sitting on the right side, beside the curb. "I have been following you, to be sure you were alone."

She looked at the van. She had not noticed it on her walk. "I felt that someone was watching me, but I never saw you."

"Thank you. I am still learning from the state's secret manual on surveillance, and this is a compliment."

He laughed, and she felt the fear rise again. How could she have missed him?

He spoke softly, "You will receive a notice that the post is holding a package for you. Take it home before you open it. Please save the wrapping, with the address label. I want you to bring the wrapping to my apartment on the following day, in the morning, at eleven. Can you do that for me?"

"Of course," she said. "But what is in the package?"

"A surprise," he replied. "It is a gift from the state, but it is not for you. You must keep it hidden in your apartment. We will need it later."

She nodded, and then understood that he was waiting for her to play back the instructions, to be sure they were straight in her mind.

"I will get the package, but not open it until I am at home. I will bring the wrapping to your apartment at eleven in the morning on the next day."

"Perfect. I love you."

Her body surprised her.

"I love you," she said without hesitation.

The van door rasped closed and latched with a clunk, and the motor started. The van made a U-turn in the Avenue Tolbiac. She continued on her way home.

She was in her apartment before she let herself admit that she could not wait to bring him the package from the post, to see him again.

DANIEL straightened his necktie as he glanced in the mirror. He saw a handsome man in an English tweed suit that sat snug on his shoulders, his blue eyes steady under sand-colored eyebrows. His short hair lay neatly over his forehead in soft spikes.

He heard a movement in the corridor behind him, and he turned to recognize the man he could speak of only as "Max," the man who had recruited him, a man who had worked for years to create the revolution, and who now worked at the heart of the New State.

"Good afternoon," Daniel said. "We are early."

"We can go in now," Max said. "How are you, Daniel?"

"I am well." Daniel tapped the entry code into the buttons on the door and stood square in front of the monitor's eye, to be identified. "Your turn," he said and stepped aside to let Max stand in front of the monitor.

They waited ten seconds, and the door swung open.

Daniel was never sure of his orientation in these deepest recesses of the labyrinth. They were far under the Île de la Cité, but he thought that the general trend of the maze of corridors led south, and they might very well be below the Seine, or even under the Left Bank. He understood that there were multiple access points and corridors, each with its own security system. The labyrinth had been designed to limit each individual's exposure to others in the organization.

Within these spaces, everything that happened in all of France was known, but nothing was known of what was going on in the adjacent rooms. Each individual was forbidden contact with anyone in any other section, excepting only the Russian and the Russian's personal staff.

They walked side by side down a long corridor, turned at an intersection, and continued to a door at the end.

"Do you know why we are here?" Max asked with a smile.

"No."

"The Russian has a strong liking for you. That is why."

Max paused for the door to open, actuated by a sensor in the walls.

The office was not large. The desk was a standard mid-level functionary's, with a laminated wood top and painted sides, but it was big enough to dominate the space, leaving scant room to pass between it and the file cabinets that ranged along the walls. Stacks of paper were neatly arranged on the desk top, butted against a computer monitor and keyboard. Another computer terminal sat on a low sideboard behind the desk. The walls were painted beige, and the rug was beige. There were no pictures on the walls or the cabinets, neither Lenin nor Marx, Paccard nor Joux, nor members of the Russian's family, and the stacks of paper seemed rather old-fashioned in a world of totally electronic information. The only effort at decoration was a small French flag, the old style tricolor without the hammer and sickle in the center, hanging on the wall behind the desk. Two simple chairs faced the desk.

The Russian, Karel, was sitting alone at his desk, facing them. Like everyone else, Daniel thought of him as the Russian, not as Karel, although, unlike everyone else, Daniel knew the man's real identity.

The Russian did not get up for the obligatory comradely handshake, but he smiled, and Daniel smiled in response.

Then Max and Daniel sat facing the Russian, and the Russian spoke.

"Victor terminated his employment here."

Daniel knew no one could terminate his own employment in Department 100. "May I ask the reason?"

The Russian nodded. "An excess of ambition, and desire to make a display of his status here."

Daniel felt a twinge of concern for his tailored suit and silk tie.

"We are looking for a replacement," Max said.

"We considered that you might be a good choice," the Russian said. "We have confidence in you."

"There is a problem," Max said. "We want you to understand it, because without it you would be the first choice."

"You speak English, Italian, and German," the Russian said.

Daniel nodded affirmation. The German was not as strong as the other two, but he could get along in all three.

"But no Russian." The Russian clasped his hands. "I need someone who can speak easily to our big brothers at the embassy."

Max spoke. "I also speak no Russian, Daniel, so you are not alone."

"You may be asking yourself why we should tell you this, my friend," the Russian continued. "The reason is that we have no ready solution within our group, and we are still looking for a candidate who can come in from outside. It is not easy."

"It is my responsibility to replace Victor," Max commented, "but it will take some time to find someone acceptable."

"We wish you to take the job while we look for Victor's permanent replacement," the Russian continued. "But it must be temporary."

The Russian and Max gazed at Daniel, expecting a response.

"With pleasure," Daniel said. "I understand about the language problem."

"We have the highest regard for you," the Russian said. "We would feel sorry if you were disappointed because the position could not be yours permanently."

Daniel's response was automatic, from the heart, "I can never be disappointed if I have the chance to work for you . . . in any job you choose."

The Russian smiled. "Let us hope that you are working for the revolution, not just for me. But I thank you, Daniel. In the meantime, you might start to learn some Russian. . . ."

Then Max broke into a broad grin and clapped him on the shoulder.

"You will meet everyone, the key people in every branch. And then you will revert to work again for me, in Action Branch. Think how much we trust you, to give you so much knowledge."

"I thank you for your trust."

The Russian looked down at a page of notes. "Max will work with you to transfer your present assignments. He will show you how to enter my staff complex and will introduce you to my three comrades working there. Please report to me at nine A.M. on the day after tomorrow and plan to meet with me at nine on each day after that."

Daniel rocked forward in his chair, ready to be excused.

"There is one other matter," the Russian said. He pulled a sheaf of papers toward him and thumbed through the pile, extracting a single sheet. He read the sheet and then looked up at Daniel.

"Have you learned anything more about this engineer with the limp? Leveque?"

"No," Daniel said. "He is in the housing record, but not in any of the population records, and he has no money account. It is a simple error, I believe, in the Star, but it is hard to track without putting an expert on the problem."

"We can always just pick him up and ask him who he is and what he does," Max said.

The Russian shook his head. "It is not worth the trouble. How often has Comrade Senac been to his apartment?"

"Only once that we know of," Daniel said. He added, knowing that the Russian knew it, "Our surveillance is not full time."

The Russian glanced at the sheet of paper. "It would be disruptive to have Daniel continue the surveillance while he is on temporary assignment to me. I do not want to transfer this task to anyone else. We should suspend the program until Daniel goes back to Action Branch."

"I can take it over personally," Max offered.

The Russian gazed at his friend and then shook his head. "No, it is not important, you have more important things to do. I have thought, in any case, of cancelling the program. It seems that all is well with Comrade Senac, and it is all for the best if she has found a man."

"As you wish," Max acknowledged, but his face betrayed his disagreement.

"Leveque bothers you?" the Russian asked.

Max nodded.

"We have bigger problems, my friend. Let it drop."

Daniel found his eyes locked into the cool gaze of the Russian, who had sacrificed his family to the revolution. What more could a man give?

"Thank you, Daniel," the Russian said. "Let me see you at nine A.M. in two days."

Max waited with his chief as the young man left.

"He is the best we have," Max said.

"Make him learn Russian."

"He is trying, but it is hard without living there. As much time as I spent in Russia, I could not learn."

The Russian shrugged and changed the subject. "What is going on with the comrade minister of the economy, Marcel Chabon?"

"He is with Russians day and night. A commercial delegation from the Russian Embassy. I should say that he is quite safe."

"Have you seen the accusation?"

"Oh, yes. The magistrate agreed that the accusations were unfounded, after we explained to him that he would be protected from the first secretary. We also explained that the Russian Embassy did not want the matter to continue. He understood."

"And the call to Chabon?"

"We do not understand it at all."

THE package was no larger than her hand, but heavy for its size. Even at the bottom of her knit satchel, she could sense its extra weight on her arm.

In her room, she took the parcel out of her satchel. Pasted on the wrapping, the white address label was clearly printed, Cde. Chantal Senac, 22 rue de l'Espérance, 75013 Paris. But she was puzzled by the return address on the label, a number and a postbox without further identification. The wrapping was heavy brown paper with a shiny overglaze, tucked in at the corners and sealed with dark brown tape. She found a sharp knife among the kitchen utensils and neatly cut the tape. She unfolded the wrapping, careful not to tear the paper.

At first she did not know what the metal object was, but then she recognized it. In her hand, greasy and heavy, was a bullet clip. It was made for a pistol or a rifle, she thought, remembering Arnaud's guns. Nine bullets. She felt frightened, but only one notch higher in the scale of fear that she lived with every day.

What to do with it?

She looked around her room. There was no good place to hide a clip of bullets.

She went out into the corridor. She waited, listening for someone coming up the stairs, and then quickly went to the window at the top of the stairs. She twisted the latch, overcoming the resistance of a pivot that had not worked since the summer before, opened the window, and put the clip on the ledge outside.

She shut the window with relief and went back to her room. It was time to go to work. Tomorrow morning, Engineer Leveque would explain.

GENTLY, with both hands, he took the brown paper wrapping from her. He studied the label. He glanced up at her, grinning, and looked back at the label. He laughed.

"It works! This is magnificent. A gift from the state!"

She could not help smiling at his happiness. "Explain, please."

"I can't."

In fact, it had been an elegant use of the Star. He had been concerned about the identification of the sender, but there was no "Armurerie de France" on the package to alert questions in the mind of a postal clerk, who could hardly know that the number code and the postbox belonged to the central stocking point and distribution center for all the Army's spare parts.

Through the Star, Landry had requisitioned the clip for a garrison of the French Army located between Mulhouse and Basel on the Swiss-German frontier. Such a requisition was routinely processed by the Star. The labels were glued on by machine, following a computer-entered address. The Star had simply made a correction in the address. On the brown paper wrapping, the label addressed to Chantal had been accurately superposed by machine, over a label that had carried the name and address of the frontier garrison.

"I should not explain how this was done," he said. "But I can tell you what it means. Until now, I have had information, but I have had no way to build a counterforce against the government. This is a beginning."

She took the wrapping paper from him and put it on the table. She held his hand and pulled it around her waist, curling herself against him, so that her head rested on his shoulder. She wanted to stay there, soft and warm against him, without mystery packages and armed forces.

He held her, calmly, his lips touching her hair. He kissed her cheek and gathered her into his arms. She came close to him, her arms around the back of his neck. She put her lips to his. Her mouth was soft, yielding and sweet, and he held her for a long time. He felt her waist very slender and supple in his arms, and a shiver of excitement ran up his back.

Chantal felt his warmth and the gentle pressure of his arms, and her questions had no more need for answers.

"Come," he said.

They undressed in clumsy stages on the way to his bed and melted into each other as they fell onto the mattress.

Chantal let herself follow him, drowning in the pleasant weight of his body over hers. He was slower and more passionate, so different from the husband she had slept with. She loved the feelings that swept over her in waves, washing away her uncertainty. And when it was over, she felt it was the first time she had ever been so content after making love.

They slept in each others' arms under a down coverlet. She woke first, sat up, and gazed out the window at the most beautiful city in the world, now a hazy golden gray. Her lover was smiling in his sleep, an arm cradling his head on the pillow. She ran her hand down his thigh, wondering which leg caused the limp and feeling for a break or an injury. Her fingers could detect nothing.

"Chantal," he said, opening his eyes.

She kissed his forehead.

He sat up, rubbing his face.

She put her hand on his cheek and guided his lips to hers. She could feel him stir in response, and then she felt a wonderful current of excitement run through her, from her ears to her toes. He smiled as he kissed her, and smiled again as she gently pulled him over her.

Later, they woke hungry, and he got up to open a big can of *confit* of duck from the region of Landes. While she pulled on her clothes, he drew the cork from a bottle of St. Emilion.

They sat at the table, looking out over the rooftops of Paris.

"Let's talk about Noël," he said. His tone was detached, as though he wanted to talk about the price of wine and not her son. "I am almost sure that Noël can be found. My friend in the government has already found a man like us, hiding from his old identity—a fugitive. The same method will work for Noël. It is only a matter of time."

But what then, she thought.

"There is a coincidence, about this fugitive that my friend found. His children were also taken, to be held as hostages in case their father should reappear and make trouble. I want their father to be free of threats to his children. My friend in the government knows where these children are. It may be possible to create a place for them to live with their father under a new identity, and if that can be done, Noël can share the same solution."

She was quiet, thoughts boiling inside her. What would she do if her lover could find her son? Would it help to have a pistol? Who would she shoot?

He waited, wanting her to have time to think. He put his hand over hers on the table and studied the distant skyline.

Chantal struggled to unwind her emotions and her confusion, to apply her historian's objective judgment. She needed to study the choices. She could live on with her sadness and her fears or go the way of the Chouans. She could deal in bullets and guns, rescue her son, challenge the government. For an instant she felt a deep, painful longing for the security she had felt with Arnaud, but the feeling as quickly went away.

"What can I do?" she asked.

"I would like you to take this clip to a man named Albert Gola.

I will need to prepare the trip. It will take some time—you will need another name, and a cash card with money behind it, and a few other things. At work, you should start to complain that you feel the flu coming on, so that they will not be surprised if you call in ill for a few days."

She did not know how it would end, but she agreed.

It was a warm day for March in Paris, but the scarf was wrapped up over his chin. The hat and sunglasses completed his shelter from light, wind, or the random scrutiny of anyone who might be interested in this nondescript figure of a man, striding into the ornate palace on the banks of the Seine. Max showed his police badge and walked past the uniformed guard into the ministry without logging in. Even the people in the Ministry of Foreign Affairs feared the police.

He went up three floors in the creaking antique elevator and then went right, down a corridor with white moldings on the walls. The parquet floor squeaked under his feet. White paint peeled from the round part of the moldings, and the Oriental runner was threadbare. The lack of maintenance had started to show. France no longer had much need for a Ministry of Foreign Affairs. The Russian Embassy was so close and so influential.

He passed a series of elegantly carved double doors, all closed. No one in sight, no sound, not even the clacking of a keyboard. At the last door, Max stopped and used a key to enter, closing and locking the door behind him.

Sunlight flooded through the floor-to-ceiling windows into the spacious room. This was an office almost fine enough for a minister, but it was dominated by a glass plate two meters high and three meters across, standing square across the middle of the room, between the door and the desk. The glass was tempered and bulletproof. He turned on the lights in the crystal chandelier and reassured himself that the reflection off the glass was far stronger than the light from the window. Sitting at the desk, silhouetted against the windows, he would be visible, but totally obscure, a body without a face. The desk was a fine old table with bowed legs and a red leather top. On it was a new telephone, its cord spiralling across the carpet to a wall plug. To his eye, the cord spoiled the eighteenth century decor even more than the glass plate. One chair, matching in style, was centered behind the desk, and two identical chairs faced it, on the other side of the glass. There was a bookcase filled with orderly rows of bound volumes, but there was none of the memorabilia that normally clutters the offices of important functionaries, and there was no monitor, no keyboard. It was an office for a very important and old-fashioned official, with a glass plate in the center.

Max put his worn leather briefcase on the desk and opened it. He pulled out three hinged leather frames containing family photographs and a small stack of magazines. He set the photographs conspicuously around the room, one on a cabinet, one on the table, and one on the small sideboard between the windows, making sure that they could be seen from beyond the glass. He paused a moment to look out at the Seine, swirling gray below him on the other side of the road, and at the gray glass hulk of the Grand Palais across the river. Two books came down from the bookshelf and joined the magazines, opened and facedown on the sideboard.

As a last measure, he sat down in one of the chairs that faced the desk, verified that the occupant could see next to nothing through the glass, and then stood to survey the room again.

He pulled a sheaf of papers out of his briefcase and carefully placed the briefcase flat on the bookshelf, its bottom pointed toward the vacant chair. He took the papers to the leather desktop, spread them out, and sat down. His watch told him that it was almost time.

His eyes moved from one paper to the next.

This candidate's credentials were better than Ignacz Gorosczki's: a grandfather in the communist resistance, parents in the militant wing of the CGT, schoolchild summers in the East Bloc, two years in Russia at the ages of nineteen and twenty, then three years as an organizer for World Youth . . . in Bulgaria, organizing an international youth meeting, at the time of the revolution in France. Fluent Russian.

The personal side of the dossier was almost blank. No reports of emotional attachments. Max pondered whether an abnormality, a potential weakness, might be indicated. At least Goroszcki had been normal in his sexual appetite. Max shrugged. The Russian was also without a partner, but in the Russian's case it seemed like a penance for abandoning his wife. That triggered a thought, and Max extracted a small note pad from the inside pocket of his jacket. He scribbled on the pad and then returned to the papers spread before him.

Maybe this candidate would be more ... compatible than Ignacz Goroszcki. Max smiled to himself and looked again at his watch. The second hand was ticking past the hour.

He heard the knock and waited. Would the candidate be bold and try to open the door ... persistent, and keep knocking ... or, lacking conviction, simply go away?

Another knock.

Max shuffled the papers together, squaring the edges.

The next knock was heavier, louder. With a closed fist. Some emotion, a little impatience, that was not bad. Max smiled, wondering if the door latch would turn. It did not.

"Wait, please," he called, loudly enough to penetrate the panelling. He pressed a buzzer under the tabletop and heard the latch click. Looking through the glass, he watched the door swing open.

The file had not prepared him for the candidate. He had expected a young woman in the mold of the Communist Youth: severely dressed, no makeup, dull hair needing a wash. This one had made herself attractive.

"Comrade Clavel?" he asked. "I was speaking on the telephone. Excuse me for not coming to the door. Please be seated."

She took in the glass plate, her eyes sweeping the room.

"Comrade Secretary Gaubert?" She fixed her gaze on his silhouette through the glass, sat down, crossed her legs, and smiled.

Such self-assurance, Max thought. She is not nervous, not curious, not withdrawn. He looked into her eyes and let her smile disarm him, while he asked himself what the smile could hide.

He noted that she seemed perfectly formed: good height, as tall as he was himself or maybe a little taller, slender calves, womanly enough in her hips and bosom to round out her strawberry wool suit. The suit was serious without being dull, which meant that it was unusual. Her hair flowed from pink ribbons at her temples, full and clean.

She was carrying a red leather portfolio instead of a purse, and she laid it on her lap, crossing her hands over it. Still. Waiting for him to begin.

"You have been recommended for a most important job," he said. "The highest recommendations."

She smiled again and modestly bowed her head. She had a big, finely chiseled nose, deep-set eyes under straight eyebrows that almost met, and a broad, smooth forehead. She was too young to be beautiful, he thought, but she would be beautiful in five years.

He asked her to start from the beginning and speak about herself. He told her to take all the time needed, her candidacy was too important to leave any questions unanswered.

She spoke for almost half an hour, without a pause.

Max had conducted such interviews before, and he was used to interrupting, to clarify, amplify, resolve ambiguities, but now he listened in silence, because Valerie Clavel's story was clear. The important events in her life developed in logical sequence. She had loved her parents and learned from them to be disgusted by the excesses of Western capitalism. She had been nine years old during the Gorbachev upheaval in Eastern Europe, and barely twelve when the Russian economy hit bottom and Germany had become one nation. She had grown up during the eight years it had taken for the East to recover from the Gorbachev catastrophe, and she had been in Russia when a real majority voted for a planned economy. She believed in the economics of reformed communism—there was enough to eat, everyone had a job, and everyone was equal.

She ended by describing her present work, in the Ministry of Education. She was creating a new curriculum of communist images and vocabulary for preschool children, which would carry them naturally into their first year political studies. She was happy, presenting the revolution as it should be to children who would someday be able to perfect it.

When she was through, she looked at him as though to say, "That's all, did you like it?"

"What do you think of our revolution here?" Max asked. He stood up and stepped back to the window, giving her time to think about her response. "Have we inspired the people of France?"

"I think we still have much to do," she said, and added with her eyes flashing at him, "but our revolution is still clean. We can make it grow into true communism."

It was as though the Russian had coached her. For a moment, Max wondered if there could be some sort of game in progress between the Russian and this girl, but that made no sense at all.

"Do you have a man in your life?"

"No."

"Have you ever?"

"Yes."

"Please tell me the circumstances, and tell me why the affair ended."

"We were together for two months in Kiev, and then we parted. He was Polish. He went back to Poland and I went to Moscow. He was married to a woman in Poland."

"What was his name?"

She gave the name and explained that he lived in Warsaw. Max made a note in his note pad.

"Have you had any other affairs, since then?"

"Once. It was not as good as my first affair, and I ended it."

"Where was that?"

"Russia."

Again, he asked for the name of her lover and wrote down her response.

"It was not as good, why was that?"

"He was less tender, more self-centered. He was very handsome, young and unmarried, well connected in his family, really perfect for me, and I tried to fall in love, but it did not work. He never aroused me."

"Since then?"

"I decided that I would fall in love again when I would fall in love again, and that I would never again try to make it happen. It has not happened, so there has been no one since."

"You do not wish to have a child?"

"I will want a child when France is good for him. I will work for that day."

A male child, Max noted.

"Who is your closest friend?"

She hesitated, and Max entered this first hesitation in his mental record of the interview. Then she gave a name, and he wrote it on his pad.

"Do you see her often?"

"I have not seen her in three years. We grew up together."

"Were you intimate with her?"

"We were very close friends. Not physically intimate."

Her tone was flat. The question had been phrased so that she could answer as a friend or as a lover, and she had answered both sides, anticipating his next question. So, not only was she well prepared, she was quick as well.

"Well then, today, who is your closest friend?"

Now she was back on track, and the reply came instantly. "I spend much time with my comrade director of preschool education. It is a friendship of common purpose. We get along very well."

"Your comrade director has given you much praise in her report. I have it here." He gestured at the papers.

"Yes."

They spent two hours discussing her job, her ambitions, going back over the details of her life, repeating her story from every angle.

Max was baffled. She was so young. Her gestures and her speech, the liveliness of her reactions, were all as fresh and natural as a sixteen-year-old's, but her life story held together as though in cement.

Would the Russian be able to take her seriously? There were only four or five years of age between her and Victor or Daniel, but it seemed more like ten, or a dozen. Would the Russian's staff, people who had earned their places with decades of devotion, be able to accept her?

He continued the interrogation, watching for signs of impatience or fatigue, but she matched him, playing her answers back in exactly the pitch and tone of his questions. Finally, he yielded to his growing conviction that all was as it should be, and that she was as strong as he.

"Enough," he said. "You seem well qualified. I compliment you. Now I must speak about the commitment you might be asked to give." He paused, wanting to emphasize his next words. "If you accept our offer, there is no way to get out. If you fail, you will have given your life for the revolution."

Through the glass, her eyes were steady on his. "I understand."

"I do not ask for an answer now. We must decide first if we want you. If I speak to you again, it will be to invite you to join us, at the center of the revolution. You may decline. This glass plate is here to protect you, not me, so that you will never recognize Comrade Secretary Gaubert if you should see him on the street, if you decide to decline. If you do not join us, I can still promise you a great future, with my support and the support of many others who have recommended you. You can achieve all that you wish, even if you decline. Do you understand?"

"It is clear, and fair. As the revolution must be."

"If I do not speak to you again, it will mean that we have found a better qualified candidate."

She nodded.

"Whichever, I wish you much happiness."

She rose to her feet. It was rapidly becoming dark.

He watched her walk to the door, admiring her figure.

When the door closed, he picked up the telephone and dialled.

"She is too young," he said. "We should wait a few years."

He listened, scratching his cheek with his free hand.

"Who knows how she may change as she matures," he said. "She may be less confident and less convinced when she starts to lose her looks and has no man. She may become vulnerable."

He listened again, his expression blank.

"All right," he said. "I will recommend her. Karel may refuse. I will do my best."

Max put the telephone down and gathered up his papers. He

checked his attaché case to be sure that both tapes were still running, the voice tape and the tape that had recorded changes in Valerie Clavel's body temperature with the tiny infrared sensor that had been focussed on her throughout the interview. He switched the machine off, then he picked up the leather binders with the family photographs and put them back in the briefcase with the magazines. He glided the books back into their spaces on the bookshelf, and then let himself out, locking the door behind him.

He sighed. To complete the dossier meant hours of dull work, reviewing the tapes, checking the details of her story, tracking down her boyfriend in Russia and the man in Poland, locating her old girlfriend and checking her, as well. It would take at least two weeks, and it was work he could not assign to someone else. He wondered how he could spare the time when there was so much else to do, so many people that he needed to see.

It would be a waste of time. His own lie detector worked better than any infrared device. She had come to the meeting with her story well prepared, but she had told him the truth.

VALERIE Clavel went straight home to the tiny apartment that she had secured for herself as a privilege of her work at the Ministry of Education.

It had gone well, better than she had expected. He was a remote man, but easier than she had expected. Who was it? The Russian himself?

She ran the water in her bathtub, testing to be sure it was as hot as she could stand.

Her preparation had been good. She had prepared herself for everything. No mistakes.

The ideological traps were easy to avoid. The revolution was not perfect, only a fool would say that it was.

It had been as easy to suppress the small details of truth that had no need to be in her story. He would never know that her lover in Moscow had shared her with a friend, and then with another friend, and he would never know who her lover was, or how they had met. That part of her life had a cover over it like armor plate bolted on a tank, impenetrable and secure.

It was not important for him to know that she had been too long without a man, and that the lack was starting to preoccupy her.

None of it was important. It was only important to be accepted. She had given up so much to come this far. They could not deny her.

She undressed and admired herself.

Then slowly, absorbing the heat of the water, Valerie Clavel lowered herself into the bath and let her body unwind in a lather of soap and shampoo.

CHANTAL went through the turnstile of the *métro*, walked three steps forward, and stopped, as though she had forgotten something. She fumbled in her satchel and looked up quickly at the turnstiles behind her.

She caught him squarely in the eyes, before he could look away. He was coming through the turnstile, hurrying, so as not to lose her on a departing train. He was dressed in workman's clothes, with a nondescript blue sweater pulled over his coveralls. She had never seen him before, but she was certain that he was following her.

Instantly, her rendezvous with René Leveque was cancelled in her mind.

She took the train only as far as Châtelet. Out in the fresh air, she walked the short distance to the Seine and then through the pet market on the side of the street that flanked the river. Nothing here had changed—rabbits and roosters, pigeons, ducks and great Belgian geese, and the backdrop of the Île de la Cité's Palais de Justice across the water. In the afternoon light, its ancient walls were a yellow and ochre counterpoint of turrets and buttresses.

She walked the rows of wood and wire cages, exchanging blank looks with the animals in their captivity. Then she went to the Beaubourg and visited the library.

On her way home, three hours later, she tried to convince herself that it was a false alarm; the man had been no more than a fellow passenger, idly observing her as he hurried for his train.

The small bar on the corner of Tolbiac and the rue de l'Espérance was normally half empty. She never went in, because it had changed its name to the *Lenine et Marx*

From the outside, she saw first the blue sweater and then the man, sitting at the bar, drinking a beer from a tall mug. His face was turned toward the street, and she was sure that his eyes followed her as she passed.

She was frightened once again. René would need to set another meeting.

She wished that René was there with her, and then was glad he was not. René was danger.

But she longed for him.

MAX was seated in front of the Russian's desk with Daniel at his side. The Russian waited, but Max was in no hurry to speak.

When his words came, they were soft. "We must speak about Madame Senac. It distressed me to leave her dossier unattended while Daniel was on assignment to you, so I continued the surveillance. There is something wrong. She is trying to escape our watchers. When she takes the *métro*, she changes to the opposite direction, and we have lost her on two occasions."

Daniel interjected, "She did that before . . . when she went to visit the apartment of Leveque. But we did not lose her. That is how we learned the identity of Leveque."

"I thought we agreed to drop the surveillance of Comrade Senac," the Russian said.

"I did not wish to leave loose strings untied."

The Russian gazed at his subordinate, his eyes flat.

Max ignored the unspoken reproach. "We have been in Leveque's apartment. His possessions are correct for a bachelor engineer, but his past and present life remain a mystery—no letters from home, no personal list of telephone numbers, no mementos, no reminders of things to do. His work records are correct, even distinguished, but the miscellaneous personal details are lacking. It is much too neat, not normal. He is travelling now on assignment from his department. I want to question him when he comes back."

The Russian's voice was level. "You are right, my friend. We can never take anything at face value, we must always question. By all means, let us verify Leveque's work. We should check his diploma and learn what we can about him from his superiors—our own intelligence in Department 100 can do that in just a few days. If everything seems normal, let us leave the engineer in peace."

"I will put in a requisition to Intelligence Branch," Max said.

"Would it make sense for Daniel to visit Comrade Senac, to ask about her new friend? At the same time, Daniel might reassure her that it is quite normal for her to have . . . such a relationship. I can spare Daniel's time for such a small mission."

Daniel responded, "I would need to give a reason for my visit, besides asking about Leveque."

"Perhaps you could tell her about Noël Senac—that he is safe in, for instance, Czechoslovakia."

"I could do that," Daniel answered.

"Good," the Russian confirmed. "Then, Max, tell me about your search for a Russian-speaker to replace Daniel as my assistant."

"I have a candidate whose qualifications are superb in all but a few respects. Better than Victor."

The Russian sat still, waiting for Max's reservations or doubts.

"The reasons against her appointment are that she is a woman, and worse, that she seems very young, in her manner as well as her age."

"How old is she?"

"Twenty-five."

"Victor was twenty-nine. It is not a great difference."

Max said, "But she is physically attractive. Too attractive for such a job. Women will feel jealous of her, and men will waste their time wondering if they can get into her pants, or if you are getting into her pants."

"But you recommend her."

"She is so much the best of all the candidates, and so exceptional in her way, I must recommend her."

The Russian took the file from the desk and opened it. He held up a photograph of the girl, a standard identification portrait, and gave it to Daniel.

"What do you think, Daniel, should we hold youth and good looks against her?"

"If she were ugly, we would think it was unfair to speak about her looks."

"But she is not."

"To be fair, we should not speak about her looks."

The Russian took back the photograph and put it, deliberately, facedown against the cover of the dossier.

He read each page in the file, while Daniel and Max waited, watching him. So much depended on this file and on Max's judgment.

The Russian selected a few papers.

"Her intelligence is extraordinary," he commented.

"You feel it in her expression of facts and ideas," Max said. "She responded perfectly to my questions, and sometimes it seemed that she anticipated my thoughts."

"Explain your interpretation of the infrared track."

"It is remarkable. I can't remember when I have interviewed someone whose response was so flat."

"Could she have been treated with some drug?"

"I would almost say so, except that each time I questioned her about her lovers, the Pole and the Russian, her temperature registered a jump on the track. It was normal, perfectly within the normal range of response for such questions, so there is no reason to doubt those responses. But because of that, I should say that she had not been chemically prepared for the interview. Also, she was lively and quick in all her reactions. She was not drugged."

The Russian looked at the papers in front of him. The Pole was married, as the girl had said, and was now living in Poznan. He had an undistinguished job as a party official, two children, and a mistress. He was forty-two, much older than the girl. The Russian boy was, on the other hand, only twenty-seven. His father was responsible for agriculture in the Ukraine, a big job, and the KGB's report noted that since the father had received his assignment, agricultural production in the Ukraine had increased each year—reassuring, both for the man himself and for his family. The boy had been a student at Moscow University at the time of his liaison with Valerie Clavel, and was now assigned to the Russian Foreign Ministry.

"What did her Russian friend study?"

"It wasn't noted."

"KGB?"

"There is no way to know. They would not tell us, if he was."

"Could the KGB have a wire tied to this girl?"

"It is possible, but I doubt it. I would have caught some hint in my talk with her."

The Russian looked back at the papers. If they had a wire to her, it might not be so bad. It might even be a help. He had thought, at times, that some of Victor's arrogance had come from a KGB connection, although no one at the embassy had objected when Victor was terminated.

"You explained that the assignment is irreversible?"

The question was rhetorical; the answer was in the file.

Max nodded. "She understands, and it will not deter her."

6 A telephone rang on a desktop in the back half of the fifth floor of the building at 112 Avenue de Friedland. Chantal listened to the shrill, insistent sound as she cleaned, trying to ignore it. Comrade Pernoud shouted at her from one of the front managers' offices to pick up and tell the caller that it was a wrong number. The telephone rang five more times as Chantal put down her mop and walked toward it.

"Hello," she answered. "This is the Ministry of Agriculture, Department Ten, and we are closed for the day."

"I miss you," René said. "Meet me tomorrow morning at the Jardin du Luxembourg—at the *métro* exit. Ten A.M. Is it all right?"

"Yes."

"Good. I have found your son and prepared your journey."

The line went dead. She slowly replaced the receiver, stunned—and chilled, knowing that the time of hoping was now over, and that a worse time would soon come, when she must try to reclaim her boy.

SHE felt torn between trust and panic as she dressed in clean clothes, checked to be sure that her identification and cash card were in her satchel, and stepped into the corridor outside her room. Locking the door behind her, she walked to the stairs, on her way to see her lover about her son.

She heard footsteps coming up the stairs, the steps of a man, confident, brisk.

Inspector Theron looked up from the landing.

"Hello," he said. "You are going out? Have you a moment to spare for me?"

"Of course," she replied. She hesitated, wanting to speak to him on the stairs, but then she turned and went back to her room.

He stood inside the door, at ease, while she composed herself, waiting for him to speak.

"I have some news about your son. He was part of a group of children who went to Czechoslovakia. Most of the children who went to Poland and Czechoslovakia were settled with farm families. It might be possible to correspond with him, when we learn where he is. I am waiting for further information."

"My God," she said. "That is incredible."

He smiled, his head slightly bowed.

"Is there any way that I can reach you?" she asked. "Don't you have some way for me to call you, to know what more news you may have?"

"No, I am sorry. It is not possible. I will tell you when I know more."

"But, he is well?"

"So far as I know, he is well. The farm life is good for children."

"This is wonderful. My child! How can I thank you?"

"It is not necessary." He turned to go, then stopped as if reminded of something.

"I understand you have a friend," he said. "A Comrade Engineer Leveque?"

She nearly fainted.

"No . . ." she started to reply. But he knew. She could only admit what he knew. ". . . yes. I am fond of him, but he travels always, he is never in Paris."

"No need to be embarrassed, Madame Senac, there is no harm in a widow finding friendship with a man." He laughed gently. "I think it must be quite a serious friendship, from your reaction. Could it come to marriage?"

She tried to smile back at him. "I don't know."

"Do you know what work he does?"

"Not really. He is designing roads and bridges, I think. That is why he is always travelling."

"It sounds like a serious position. Was he an engineer before the revolution?"

"I don't know. . . . We don't talk about that time."

"I understand. Were you on your way to work just now? Can I give you a ride in my car?"

"No, thank you, I need to get out and walk in the fresh air."

On the street, they shook hands like friends.

"I wish you happiness," he said. "I will be in touch when I know more."

She walked toward the *métro* station at the Place d'Italie, questions churning. They had followed her to René's apartment, despite all her precautions. Or, they were following him and had snared her. She decided that she could not see him, but then changed her mind. If they knew, then there would be no harm in another meeting with René. It would be more normal than a clean break. If she was going to see him again, why not immediately? If René had also found Noël, he might know the address, the name of the family in Czechoslovakia.

René was there when she arrived, waiting next to the great stone gates to the Jardin du Luxembourg. He was dressed in a dark coat that blended with the dark iron grillwork surrounding the garden.

She kissed him on the lips. She would be his lover for anyone who was watching, it was the best disguise because it was true.

"I am late for a reason," she said, putting her arm around his waist and turning to walk with him, close by his side. "I was delayed by Inspector Theron, who wanted to tell me that Noël is alive in Czechoslovakia!"

He nodded, looking straight ahead. His mind was turning, wondering how he could pin down this mystery inspector of the police, bearer of false news.

"Wait," he said. "Let's discuss your son when we are having tea."

They went to the tea room directly across from the gates of the Jardin du Luxembourg.

Landry queried her. "Did Theron say where Noël was located inside Czechoslovakia? An address?"

"He does not know. He is trying to find out."

"He lied to you. Your son is in France. He is with a woman named Isabelle Bazin, in Notre-Dame-de-Bellecombe, near Megève, in the mountains. Noël is now Noël Bazin, no longer Senac."

So, Theron had lied.

"Something very strange is going on," he said.

"I am thinking the same," she replied. "There is more. He asked me about you. By name. Comrade Engineer Leveque. He wanted to know if we planned to marry."

"Well," he said, mastering his surprise. "Do we?"

"I said that I did not know."

"If I had no wife, would you marry me?"

"You are too dangerous, René Leveque, you frighten me."

He smiled at her, sadly, and she felt a rush of affection for him, a yearning to hold him close.

"Today, we have time before you go to your work. I have much for you to memorize, so that you can travel safely. And then, let's go to the apartment. By this time, it is probably full of microphones. If they believe we are lovers, let's not disappoint them. It will be the last time for the apartment, and we should say good-bye there. Then, I must tell you, Engineer Leveque will go on a very long journey. There are too many holes in his recent history, if our friends start to check in detail."

He explained to her the details of the trip, and that she should return to her apartment afterward, go to work, wait for a signal from him. If anyone asked about René Leveque, she should say that René Leveque already had a wife and that she had decided to stop seeing him.

They found two tiny transmitters, one in the curtains in the living room window, the other under the bed. When they made love, she could not believe that she was deliberately sharing her passion with the watchers, but she willed it, and then it became more than pretense. She made love, not caring about the microphone, hungry to make the best of the last time, already missing him before he left her.

They parted on the street, two blocks away from the apartment.

She was surprised to see tears in his eyes. She touched the corner of his eye with her thumb, dabbing the dampness away.

"It will be weeks now, will it not?"

He nodded.

"You will not forget me?" she asked.

"Never."

"Then I will not forget you. I love you, with all my heart."

They stood neither touching nor apart, savoring their closeness.

"Go on," he said. "We must make the best of it."

She kissed him, embracing him with all her strength, and then, as her tears welled up, she touched her fingers a last time to his cheek and turned to walk away.

THE Russian entered the meeting room with the girl. He sensed immediately the difference in his colleagues' attention and reassured himself that she had not been a mistake. Max had been right, she was perfect. She was a joy.

"Please," he rumbled to her, "sit here. Look, there is a button there. You can feel it with your foot. When the meeting is in progress, you control the door with that button. Don't open it unless I tell you."

When it was his turn to identify himself at his microphone, he said, "Karel. I will introduce my new aide, who is sitting at my left. This is Comrade Gentiane, and she is the permanent replacement for Victor." Softly, he added for her benefit, "You must identify yourself, for the voiceprint in the Star."

"Gentiane," she said, her voice strong and sure as she repeated her code name.

The Russian read the agenda. The DSE had located a long-sought fugitive. MSIE had to report on troubles in Marseille, conflicts between the Moslems and their neighbors.

The DSE man's white fingers, knotted with arthritis, clutched a single sheet of paper. It was not often that the DSE, the external security service, had a matter of substance to report, and Ebert made an important matter out of it.

The wife of Robert Landry had been located in the United States. Helen... The Russian remembered her, an American woman, an athlete. They had met twice, once in Val d'Isère at the restaurant called Crech'ouna, and once in St. Tropez at the house of Madame Forgues. Helen Landry's husband was the biggest fish to slip through his net, a loss that had caused anxiety ever since. The DSE could not find him.

Landry had changed the way the nation lived, had made magic with the Star. If the wizard ever returned to blight his own work, if the Star should falter... then there would be chaos. There was no going back to the old hodgepodge of paper bureaucracy.

Landry was dangerous, wherever he was hiding.

The Star never malfunctioned, which was fortunate, because the Ministry of Communications could hardly restore a major failure. Their main defense was refusal to change anything—at least they were aware of their limitations.

Two operatives had seen Landry's wife and identified her from photographs.

Ebert concluded his speech. The DSE recommended a covert operation, to bring the woman inside the French Embassy in Washington for interrogation.

The sheet of paper was laid flat on the table and the white, knobby fingers tapped twice on it, ending the performance. Ebert looked at the Russian. "What are your instructions?"

"She is an American national. We need to be very careful. Do you have a good man there?"

"The best... Comrade Androuët. He is the agent who found the women."

"Please give my congratulations to Comrade Androuët. And send me a report. I would like to know how he did it."

Ebert made a note, his head bobbing. "It will be done."

"Please instruct Comrade Androuët to detain the woman. She should not be damaged. Is Comrade Androuët a skilled interrogator?"

"He is skilled."

"Tell him to take the soft approach."

"It will be done." Ebert's smile distorted his bony face into a grimace. "He is making his preparations now, expecting your approval. At the latest, he will be there tonight . . . early tomorrow, Paris time."

THE fields of rural France flashed past the train window. Chantal's eyes rested on the rolling hills of Burgundy. Planted squares of trees stood silhouetted on the hill crests, below puffs of white cumulus in a deep blue sky. It had been a long time since she had last left Paris.

She could not keep from thinking about the bullet clip, sewed into the bottom of her knit satchel. She touched the hard outline of the sewing scissors in her pocket.

The man seated next to her was preoccupied with a newspaper and had not spoken since leaving the Gare de Lyon. He was about fifty, dressed in a standard polyester blue suit, a jowly functionary with badly cropped hair and a blue stubble on his cheeks.

She rehearsed her new name and address, the names of her deceased mother and father, her youth in Amiens, her school, her job at the Banque Nationale, the hotel in Courchevel where she would spend her state-paid vacation. She tried to become Annie Beaumont.

Then, she went through the litany that she had memorized for her rendezvous. If she got the sequence out of order, she might be dead before she could correct the mistake. René had not been reassuring about that. The man had been used to violence. He would be like a fused bomb, ready to explode, and she would be a stranger, therefore dangerous.

She had been nervous when she used her new account card to pay for the ticket on the TGV and was relieved when it worked. The transaction confirmed her understanding that René Leveque could have all the money he wanted from the account system. In principle, he was the richest man in France.

The man beside her folded his newspaper, sighed, and lifted a black plastic briefcase from the floor onto his knees. Chantal noted from the corner of her eye that it contained a sandwich wrapped in waxed paper, tucked in above some papers. The sandwich put her at ease.

He unwrapped the sandwich, the waxed paper crinkling in his hand. His eye caught Chantal's

"This is more than I need," he said. "Can I give half to you?"

"No, thank you," she said, although she was hungry.

He nodded and bit a large chunk out of the sandwich. A thin piece of cheese was hidden between the half rounds of the bread.

He chewed and swallowed.

"On vacation?" he asked.

"Yes."

"South of France?"

"No, I am going to the mountains."

He glanced up at her bag on the rack over her head, and she realized that it should be bigger for a winter vacation, to hold warm clothes.

She looked out the window at the passing fields.

He finished the sandwich, pulled out a manila folder stuffed with computer printouts, and started to make notes with a ball-point pen.

At Lyon, Chantal changed trains and continued her trip to Albertville. There, she asked directions and walked to the Hôtel de la Gare, where she would spend the night. Her reservation in Courchevel began the following day. She would have liked to go to Courchevel for a day or two, but she would never arrive.

CHANTAL might die from his love. The thought tore at him as he tried to force the Star to explain what she had told him.

Landry studied the screen.

He could find no record of René Leveque in the Star. But René Leveque was known to Department 100. Where were the computer files of Department 100? Was there nothing in the Star to document this secret core of the government?

Landry tried to imagine how a new secret section could have been set up inside the Star. The convoluted access and warning systems were too complicated for any technician in the present government.

Or was the Russian working with files imbedded in some unused section of the Star, like a hermit crab in an abandoned snail shell?

If he did not gain access to the files of Department 100, the mystery of Chantal Senac would remain a mystery to him. Why had they followed her? Who was Inspector Theron?

The name of René Leveque would be the key. If it appeared in any file except where he himself had put it, then the Russian's staff had put it there. It might take a long time, but Landry could penetrate each part of the Star to find out if it contained the sequence of code that spelled René Leveque.

The DSE file and the daily security meeting could wait, Landry decided. It would be better to find the Russian's secret files.

He stood up and went to the reference book that listed all the Star's sections, arrayed by level of security. There were 2,157 sections, each one guarded with its own barriers of passwords and secret protocols. He would go to work, looking for the combination of characters that would spell "René Leveque."

DANIEL'S foot stamped flat on the accelerator, hard on the brake, back on the accelerator, shooting his Peugeot though the limping traffic of Paris. Max was right. René Leveque was a fraud, a total fantasy. The functionary who had signed Leveque's fitness reports and authorized his travel did not exist at the Department of Bridges and Roads. René Leveque did not exist, except as the lover of Chantal Senac and as the occupant of an apartment below Montmartre. Even that last was questionable: Leveque had been absent ever since the couple had been recorded making love.

Daniel had to reach Chantal at home before she went to work, had to question her again about the man she knew as René Leveque.

He sped down Tolbiac, slowed to look for the street sign, and accelerated in the turn.

Up the stairs, two at a time. Knock on the door. Silence inside. It was too early for work, she must have left for an errand.

Down to the concierge. A mouse of a man, Comrade Giroux. Back up with the key.

It took Daniel no more than thirty seconds to realize that she was gone. The room was too neat, and there was no toothpaste or toothbrush, no hairbrush or comb. So, she was not innocent.

To be certain, he would wait for her to appear at work, but he knew she would not.

It was beyond Department 100 now. Only MSIE had the manpower to find René Leveque and Chantal Senac. The Russian would agree.

Daniel gave the concierge a telephone number to call if Comrade Senac should return to her apartment, and he went out to the Peugeot. There, by the curb, he called the labyrinth.

The phone in the Peugeot crackled and spit, but the pushbutton code brought the voice of the new girl, the Russian's new assistant, Gentiane.

"Listening," she said.

"Please tell Karel that the subject appears to have gone on a trip. I am on my way back. I suggest we put our friends in the service on the subject if she does not go to work this evening."

"Understood," she said. "See you soon."

Gentiane . . . cheerful but controlled, icy competent. She had not yet made a mistake. Daniel was pleased that she had come into the labyrinth.

Haste was no longer needed. The Peugeot rolled with the traffic.

Three minutes after the Ministry of Agriculture reported Chantal absent from her cleaning duties, Daniel faced the Russian in his office, with the girl, Gentiane, at his side.

"What do you think it means?" the Russian asked. "Who is Leveque?"

"I can only guess," Daniel said. "A spy from the other side . . . Someone who slipped the net after the revolution . . . Someone who has found a way to live without working. Anything. It might not be sinister. I will call Morand. He should start MSIE looking for both René Leveque and Comrade Senac." He hesitated. "It would help if there was a photograph."

The Russian shook his head. Only Max and Daniel knew his relationship to Chantal Senac. A photograph of Chantal and Noël was buried in his personal effects, but it would tell too much to the others.

"Then," Daniel acknowledged, "we will use the identity portrait in the computer file."

HUBERT Morand, the minister of the interior, was not accustomed to doing his own work, but for the Russian he wanted to be sure there were no mistakes. He filled in the blanks of a standard MSIE search bulletin that formed a grid on the screen facing him. An adjacent screen showed the computer likeness that had generated René Leveque's I.D. card portrait. It was a poor picture. Above the beard, shadows for eyes, long hair. Not sufficient for identification, but it was all they had.

As soon as he had completed the written details, he made the computer paste the picture into the form.

He scrolled to the top and tapped in, *Flash, Flash, Flash,* then scrolled to the bottom and tapped in *Mandatory Acknowledgment.*

The bulletin was instantly registered in the electronic mailbox of every MSIE station in France. *Flash, Flash, Flash* sounded an audible alarm and started a light flashing on the duty officer's desk. The bulletins would get attention.

Morand called up Chantal Senac's I.D. portrait on the adjacent screen. It was a better picture, communicating a personality as well as a likeness. She was not bad looking, Chantal Senac. He wondered where they would find her. She would be found, that was certain. With the Star, no one could move without leaving a trace.

But it was not the Star that found Chantal Senac.

A corresponding agent—an informant—of the Lyon office called almost immediately after the bulletin went out. Positive identification . . . He had seen the woman on the train from Paris to Lyon. She had said she was going to the mountains on vacation.

Morand put two of his best women to work on the list of ticket holders for the train, and on the list of reservations for every hotel south of Paris.

Chantal Senac had not been on the train, and she had not reserved a hotel room.

New identity documents could not be forged, but stolen documents were available to someone with criminal connections.

They would have the Star match all the names between the passenger list and the hotels and then narrow the field from there.

The machine's response was almost instantaneous. There were seven single women who had taken the train and booked reservations in hotels. Four were too old. One was a teenager.

Of the two who remained, one had gone to Clermont-Ferrand, and the other to Albertville.

Morand's women called the hotels. In Clermont-Ferrand, the hotelkeeper knew the visitor, who came twice a year to see her aging grandmother.

In Albertville, Annie Beaumont had checked in an hour before, put her bags in her room, and gone out for a walk. She matched the description.

Annie Beaumont. Chantal Senac.

Morand picked up the phone and called Gentiane in Department 100.

"WE can pick her up in fifteen minutes if we send the local police," Daniel said. "In an hour if we send an MSIE operative from Chambéry."

The Russian let the words settle before he answered.

"They don't know her," he responded. "What if it is not her?"

"It must be her."

"The police are allowed mistakes. So is MSIE. But we are not the police or MSIE—Department 100 must be infallible. We cannot risk the embarrassment of a comedy, a mistaken identity in Albertville."

"The next train is tomorrow morning," Gentiane said. "But the last scheduled flight to Chambéry leaves in twenty minutes—we could hold it with a telephone call."

"That would be quicker than requisitioning a plane," the Russian said. "Do it. Then get a driver to take Daniel out to Karl Marx Airport."

Daniel felt the Russian's eyes on him.

"Be careful with her," the Russian said.

AFTER fifteen hours of work, Landry concluded that the Russian had another computer. There was not a trace of René Leveque in the Star, except for his own entries.

He was tired and disappointed.

It was time to sleep, but the daily routine remained unfinished. Wearily, he started the procedure to enter the DSE section, to look for news of Helen and Robert Landry.

Five minutes later, his fatigue was forgotten and his heart was pounding.

The DSE reported:

> *HELEN LANDRY LOCATED WITH POSITIVE IDENTIFICA-*
> *TION, UNDER NAME DORIS SPEDDING*
> *NO COMPANIONS*
> *395 MARINA CIRCLE, ANNAPOLIS, MARYLAND, TELE-*
> *PHONE 301-268-9907*
> *EMPLOYED AS SECRETARY GANNON SAIL LOFT*
> *200 FOREST DRIVE, ANNAPOLIS, MARYLAND, TELE-*
> *PHONE 301-263-1008*
> *SPECIAL AGENT ANDROUËT STANDING BY FOR*
> *INSTRUCTIONS.*

The report had come in by wire—Landry checked his watch—just thirty hours ago.

With all the speed that the complex procedure would allow, Landry keyed through to the record of the last security meeting.

He barely stopped to note the introduction of Gentiane, the

Russian's new aide. A woman, he registered. He scanned rapidly down through the transcript.

He read the words and his heart sank. Helen would be kidnapped and questioned, held hostage.

Landry stared at the monitor. How could he warn her? He was late, they would be moving by now.

He read to the end of the transcript, turning over the possibilities.

He could call Helen, but they might have set up an intercept for her number in the United States. Then a telephone call would tell them that the DSE was not secure, and that Helen had a friend in France. It was too dangerous. If they suspected that the Star was compromised and that Robert Landry was in France, they might easily put the two together.

But he could not let them take her.

Landry stood in a telephone kiosk, with a *métro* ticket in his pocket, a fresh cash card in his gloved hand. He dialled Helen's number. He was in the Gare du Nord, the main train station for the area north of Paris, and commuters were streaming around him from the inbound morning trains to the *métro* and the street outside. It would be two in the morning in Maryland, in the U.S.A. The telephone buzzed and clicked, and then he heard the number ring.

"Hello? . . ." Her voice was sleepy.

"Helen! . . . Run, you are discovered."

The interruption was a female voice, polite. "Your call has been suspended momentarily because of technical problems, stay on the line for your connection." The message was tape-recorded, but it meant that within fifteen seconds the call would be traced to its source.

Landry dropped the receiver and moved with the crowd, as fast as he could without drawing attention, to the *métro*. He had risked so much to call her, but he was certain that he had failed. She had been half asleep, the connection had lasted only seconds.

There had to be another way to spare Helen from suffering.

Landry emerged from the *métro* and went back to the Star. He needed to arrange a patch from the satellite that relayed telephone communications around the world. And then he needed Chabon's help.

THREE hours later, Landry was in another public telephone. He dialled a code, waited for a tone, and dialled the number of Marcel Chabon in Paris. The signal would be relayed back to France from the satellite.

"The office of the comrade minister of the economy," a woman's voice answered.

"This is the minister's old friend, James Winn," Landry said. "I am calling again from the United States. Is he there to speak to me?"

"He is in conference. Can he call you back?"

"No. It is urgent. Can you give him a message?"

"I will try."

"Tell him that I will call back in ten minutes, and ask him to arrange to take the call in private, on a secured line."

"I will try."

"Good-bye, then."

"Good-bye, Mr. Winn."

MARCEL Chabon looked at the note. He nodded to his secretary.

"I will take it in my office," he growled to her.

"Please excuse me," he said to the two Russian trade commissars who had flown in to Paris the night before.

Chabon walked to his office, sat down behind his desk, and waited. What new message would he get from the fake Mr. Winn? Another warning? Who was the American behind the voice?

The telephone rang, and Chabon picked it up.

"Chabon."

"Minister Chabon. My real name is Robert Landry. Does that mean anything to you?"

"Of course. The Star . . ."

"An agent of the DSE's Washington station has orders to seize

Helen, my wife. She does not know where I am or how to reach me. They are wasting their time."

"What do you expect me to do, Mr. Landry?"

"Tell the DSE that she does not know where to find me. They have no way to use her as a hostage, because there is no way to communicate with me."

"Why would they listen to me?"

"Because you have spoken with me. Listen, I called you once before with help."

"I thank you for that help."

"Now I ask you to help me."

"Where are you, Mr. Landry?"

"In the United States."

"Why do you not warn your wife?"

"I do not know where she is," Landry said. "I know only that an agent has orders to take her. Tell them not to take her, or if they have her, to let her go. Will you do it? Listen, Marcel Chabon, help me and I will try to help you again. Do what you can."

"All right, Mr. Landry. I will do what I can."

Incredulous, Chabon put down the phone. Landry! No question about following the man's request: Chabon himself pushed the buttons to connect with the DSE. His rank brought Director Ebert onto the line immediately.

"Comrade minister. How are you?"

"Director Ebert, I have just received a strange telephone call from the United States. The caller said he was Robert Landry, the man who created the Star. . . . I believe you are looking for him."

"That is true."

"Landry says that he has information from your Washington station. He says that you are about to pick up his wife."

Ebert hesitated while deciding whether he would acknowledge a leak.

"That is true," Ebert said.

"Landry says that his wife doesn't know where he is. He says that we have no way to talk to him, so that we waste our time to pick her up."

"We will have to test that idea, comrade minister. Our man left

Washington two hours ago on his way to Helen Landry. He should have completed his mission by now."

THE van had no radio, so Jacques de Celigny sang alone in a loud off-key baritone, a song that he had heard played over and over by the Italian station on the other side of the Alps. Philippe, the driver, wincing at de Celigny's errors of pitch, accelerated the bakery van, drowning out his rider with the roar of aging pistons in worn and oversized cylinder bores. If the motor broke again, as it surely would, Laurent would fix it. The van hurtled down the Route Nationale between Ugine and Albertville, returning from the last deliveries of the day, bringing Albert Gola home from his day at work in the Pechiney factory.

The van slowed, its motor still intact for another day, as they reached the outskirts of Albertville and turned to cross the river into Conflans.

They left the van in Laurent's garage and climbed the hill to the medieval town. Catherine was in her kitchen, standing beside a great pot of boiling water that bubbled on the black cast-iron stove. The stove, like the bakery ovens, was a wood-burning antique. Burning wood saved a fortune in their meagre account, and the ovens made better bread. Smile lines had squeezed deep creases into the corners of Catherine's eyes and her cheeks, and she was smiling now as she stirred the soup, making thick, round swirls in the creamy surface. She looked up, brushing back a heavy hank of her hair with the back of her hand as de Celigny came through the door.

"You received a package," she said, her eyes on him as he took off his anorak.

De Celigny cocked his head.

"Henri took it from the postman," she said. "Who knows that Albert Gola lives here?"

"Maybe it came from the factory," he replied. "Where is it?"

"Henri put it in your room."

De Celigny felt a flash of anxiety. For most of the world Albert Gola did not exist, and so a package in the mail was too strange to be safe. De Celigny leaned over the soup. An odor of saffron and mustard tickled his nose. "What is in the pot tonight?"

"Chicken. Go see what came in the mail. We are all curious." She was smiling from habit, but de Celigny felt her tension. She, too, was worried.

He went into the small living room and then down the stairs to the cellar. The chamois were gone, a savory memory. He switched on the dim overhead bulb in his room. The package had been put on the chair beside his bed. It was an oblong block in glistening brown paper.

He did not like this at all.

He knelt and put his head down, pressing his ear against the wrapping. He half expected the ticking of a clock or the slow grating of an unwinding spring, but the package was as silent as death itself. Carefully, he picked it up and rocked it in his hands. He smoothed the paper, trying to feel any mechanism that might be secured to the wrapping. He examined the label. Albert Gola, rue de l'Épine, Conflans. The number and the postbox of the sender meant nothing to him. There was no indication of the town it had come from.

He took his Opinel from his pocket and traced a slit around the label with the tip of the razor-sharp blade, thinking that the box was less likely to go *bang* where the label had been pressed on. The label came away clean. He continued to cut, slicing along the same lines, through the corrugated cardboard underneath the wrapping, until he could lift out the square of cardboard on the point of the knife. He saw folds of oily waxed paper and smelled the unmistakable odor of oil on metal. He knew what it was before he cut through the paper. Carefully, avoiding the ends of the box, he cut diagonals in the corrugated cardboard, back to each corner, and folded away the four sections that remained of the box top. Snug inside lay a Beretta pistol, his weapon of choice for all the years that he had served as a policeman.

He took the pistol out of the box, examining it. There was a paper underneath, a shipping note. The pistol had been sent from the Armurerie de France three days before, to Comrade Colonel Jacotin, stationed in the State Factory at St. Étienne.

De Celigny put the gun on his bed and picked up the label, turning it in his hands, observing that it seemed to cover another label underneath. He used the tip of the Opinel to pry up a corner, and then he tried to peel the top label away. It stuck and tore, resisting his efforts, but finally he could read enough fragments of the label underneath to see that the package had originally been addressed to the comrade colonel.

He picked up the pistol. From its weight in his hand, he knew that there were no bullets in the clip. He examined it, working the slide, the safety, finally pulling the trigger and feeling the sharp snap of the firing pin on the empty chamber.

A gift, he wondered, from a friend of Jacques de Celigny, who had no friends left in France except for the family living in this same house? It seemed hardly possible. And yet, it was his choice of pistol, as anyone could have known from reading the newspapers.

The most urgent question was whether the good colonel could track down his missing parcel. De Celigny sat on the bed. He knew that the Star had formidable powers to direct and track the mail. If the Star retained a record of the colonel's pistol coming to Albert Gola, then his goose was in the pot with Catherine's chicken.

But the pistol felt good in his hand.

He considered mailing it to the colonel. That was bad—it could be traced to the sender, and there would be an investigation and perilous questions to answer.

He could take the pistol to the post office, show them the shipping slip, and let them correct their mailing error. That was better, the logical act of a loyal comrade who had received a wrong delivery.

What should he say to Catherine and Henri?

Nothing. They would be frightened.

But they knew he had received a parcel, and he could not avoid telling them something. They were frightened, in any case, keeping him.

He went up the stairs with the gun in his hand, and he showed it to Catherine.

Her hand never stopped the smooth stirring motion, but her eyes followed the piece as it moved in his hands.

"It came to me by mistake," de Celigny said. "It was mailed to a colonel in the army, and somehow it was relabelled with my name. I will take it to the post, tell them there was a mistake, and send it to the colonel."

"We must talk to Henri. He is upstairs."

"I am here," Henri said. He came into the room, his great size shrinking the space. "What have you there?"

Henri took the pistol, turning it in his hands like an unfamiliar talisman. He knew nothing of pistols, and Jacques de Celigny found himself taking it back and explaining its operation. He enjoyed the oily smooth action of the parts as he moved them.

De Celigny put the gun on the kitchen table. The risks mounted in his mind. If he went to the post and the simple explanation was not accepted, if the truth was so improbable that it demanded questions, then what?

Albert Gola's false identity was not so secure, if someone pressed for a history.

Henri, Catherine, and Laurent had sworn to help him revenge the loss of his family, but they could not be responsible for the risk from a pistol delivered by mistake.

As though echoing his thoughts, Catherine spoke. "It is too dangerous for you to carry this to the post. No one will ever believe such a mistake."

"Then I should disappear. . . . If they come to look for the Albert Gola who received the colonel's pistol and did not send it back, then I should not be here."

"What if it is not a mistake?" Henri asked. "What if someone wanted you to have this gun?"

"A kind of joke? Without ammunition it is only a toy; it is only dangerous to me and to you."

"It is time for you to go to the Bar Express, my dear Albert," Catherine said. "You should not be late. We will talk about this again in the morning."

De Celigny took the pistol back to his room in the cellar, put it in the box with the torn address label, folded down the sides, and put the box in his pillow. He smoothed the cloth.

A half-hour later, he walked into the Bar Express, near the train station in Albertville. Under his anorak he wore a shiny black rayon shirt, unbuttoned to his stomach, with a gold chain around his neck. The effect was Corsican, as intended, to blend with the clientele of the Bar Express. Part Turk, part Italian, part Arab, a small part indigenous French, a few Portuguese, they came for drink, for refuge from their wives or from boredom or solitude, sometimes for a sweating *croque-monsieur* or a steak with fries to soak up the alcohol. The Bar Express was always full in the evening.

De Celigny's features were finer drawn and he was a degree older than the other waiters at the Bar Express, but most of the clientele never noticed him.

He had some friends among the other waiters and the regular customers. He had grown to know the daily patrons, and over time he could sense the balance shift in their attitude to him. He had done nothing but bring their beer and take their money cards to the cash-card reader. And yet, they started to treat him as a man of respect, much like Gaston the proprietor. This worried him. It was a weakness in his disguise.

He got along well with Gaston, who had been a crony of Laurent and Catherine's father. He had been presented as Albert Gola, a former rugby friend of Henri's from Bordeaux, and he had quickly earned approval as a waiter, fast and friendly, always on time, never taking food or drink unless he was invited to. Gaston had forgiven Albert Gola's occasional absences, and if Gaston found anything unusual in Gola's lack of past references, he had never said anything.

De Celigny went to work, but his mind was on the pistol. It had felt like an old friend in his hand. Would the colonel have ordered clips of bullets as well, which might be sent in the mail?

Noise, smoke, the smell of beer, and a press of bodies filled the bar. The corpulent Gaston reposed, immobile, on a raised platform beside the cash-card reader, where he could survey his clients and sense pending trouble in time to make adjustments. He beckoned to de Celigny.

"This is for you," the old man told him, palming over a scrap of paper that had been folded several times onto itself and inscribed, "Albert Gola."

De Celigny looked at his boss, who gestured with his head toward a table in the corner. She was unmistakable, a lady, a dove in the wrong pigeon coop.

The hair came up on the back of de Celigny's neck. Slowly, he turned to survey the other patrons, looking for the lady's partner, who would be waiting to see what lucky fellow would get the note and therefore be identified as Albert Gola. Only old Floquet was looking toward the bar. He waved. De Celigny smiled at him.

"When did she come in?"

"Not long ago. Fifteen minutes. She bought tea, maybe she would like another cup. Aren't you going to read the note?"

De Celigny winked at the old man. "Not everyone was my friend when I left Bordeaux. I think I should go slow."

"I read the note. She is a cousin of a friend of yours."

De Celigny nodded. "What friend?"

Gaston squinted, his eyes disappearing in a mass of wrinkles. "Beretta. Pierre Beretta."

De Celigny gave back the note without unfolding it. His response was out of his mouth even before the name sank in. "He's no friend, he's a gambler. I owe him money. Throw this out."

"I didn't know you played."

"I quit forever," de Celigny replied. "Do me a favor, don't let her know who I am. If she asks, tell her I didn't come in. When she leaves, let me follow her out, to see if she came with friends. Is that all right?"

"Sure, Albert. I'm sorry, I shouldn't have told her you worked here."

"She knew anyway. I'll ask her if she wants more tea."

Gaston pursed his lips, a sign of assent, and resumed his stance as the proprietor of the Bar Express.

She glanced up at de Celigny, expectant, and the disappointment was clear on her face as de Celigny asked her, in his polite waiter's manner, if she would like another cup. She agreed, gave her cash card, and picked up her empty cup and saucer for him to take away.

He was baffled. He could read the woman instantly, from all the others he had known—Agnes's friends, and the friends and cousins and schoolmates of friends—but they had all been swept away. And was this woman supposed to be the cousin of the well-known Monsieur Beretta, whose namesake was lying snug in his pillow in Conflans? Incredible.

She reminded him of his wife.

It was clear that she was tied to the pistol. The note was intended to tell him that. So, she was a messenger.

Did he want to receive a message?

He wanted the pistol.

There was time to wait, to observe. He brought the second cup of tea, and she thanked him seriously, drawing the cup close to her. She was quite beautiful, he thought, but not in the way that attracts attention. Her features were perfect. Ingres or Boucher would have painted her portrait.

There was not much to her body, he decided, and again he thought of Agnes. He missed his wife, more than his children, as much as he missed them.

A big party of Algerians came in, and de Celigny was busy for a while bringing them beer.

When he checked, the woman was still at her table, holding the teacup to her lips with both hands.

Half an hour later, she accepted another cup.

Later, she asked him for the way to the toilets. He felt badly about the condition of the toilets, but there was nothing to do except send her.

It was after eleven when she took her fourth cup of tea.

At one A.M. she went again to the toilets.

She refused another cup of tea. She sat still, holding the empty cup in her hands.

At two o'clock, there were only two Turks at the bar. The woman approached Gaston, who listened to her without the slightest movement of his huge body. Almost imperceptibly, he shook his head, and the wrinkles above his eyes expressed regret.

Just as imperceptibly, Gaston nodded to de Celigny as the woman went out the door.

De Celigny moved swiftly, his anorak on his arm, out the back door and around to the front, identifying the woman in the light from the window of the bar as she walked away. The streetlamps had been extinguished at midnight and the street was dark. She was going to the Hôtel de la Gare, across the street, where a faint incandescence marked the entrance to the lobby.

De Celigny walked slowly along the opposite side of the street and took a position in the shadows. He waited. It did not take long. The lights went on in the windows of her room. Second floor above the ground, on the right.

He crossed the street and inspected the wall of the hotel. The outside was possible, if the inside proved too difficult. He walked down the passage between the hotel and the adjacent building and then around the back . . . nothing to worry about, no car or truck with a registration from far away. The back door of the hotel was locked.

The front door was open. There was no desk clerk: after midnight the man would be asleep somewhere.

Her light was still on, a slit of brightness at the sill, when he arrived in front of her door, Room 7. He heard water running and listened for voices in the room. She seemed to be alone.

He waited.

The light went out.

He went downstairs and found the desk clerk sound asleep on a cot in the small breakfast kitchen, far from the lobby. De Celigny went back to the lobby, picked up the phone, and plugged in the wire for her room.

On the third ring, she answered. "Hello, who is it?"

"This is the reception desk, madame. A gentleman is here named Albert Gola. He wishes to know if you would like to come down to meet him."

Silence. Then, "Tell him to wait. I will come."

De Celigny raced for the stairs. He was breathing hard as he reached the second floor, but he moved quietly to her door. The instant the key snapped the lock open and the doorknob turned, he was through the door and she was down, his hand tight over her mouth.

"Quiet," he whispered, and he released his grip a centimeter to see if she would try to scream. She was motionless, shivering under him, and he could tell, by the feel of her, that she would obey him.

He stood up, swung the door shut, and turned out the light. Kneeling beside her, he found her arms and lifted her, putting her on her feet. He guided her in the dark to the bed and pushed her down onto her back.

"Speak to me," de Celigny said. "Quietly. Tell me about Monsieur Beretta. Where is he?"

"I can't tell you where he is."

"How do you know my name?"

"Pierre Beretta gave me your name. He sent me with a gift for you, and a message."

"Give me the message. Then I'll tell you if I want the gift."

"I am supposed to give you the gift first. It will help you to believe the message."

"Where is it?"

"In my bag." Her voice was clear, and the words were measured. She was in control of herself, and de Celigny relaxed a fraction.

"I'll get it." De Celigny's eyes were becoming used to the darkness, and he was able to pick out objects in the half-light from the streetlamps outside.

"On the chair."

He rummaged through the satchel, feeling the compact weight of the clip and knowing instantly what it was.

"Thank you for the gift," he said. "What is the message?"

"There are three parts."

"Go ahead."

"The pistol is yours. Colonel Jacotin knows nothing about it; he never asked for it. It can never be traced to you."

"Good."

"That is the first part. The second is this: if you want more weapons, they can be obtained, and if there is any man in France who you wish to find, alive or dead, we can locate him for you."

"Go ahead."

"I must have a response. Do you wish more weapons or do you wish to find anyone?"

Instantly, "Yes."

"Listen carefully. I will tell you how to communicate your wishes."

"Tell me. I am listening."

"Send a letter to Comrade Beretta, capital B, e-r-e-t-t-a, at 999 rue de Macon, 69907 Lyon. The letter will not arrive at that address, any more than your pistol arrived at Colonel Jacotin's address. But the letter must be posted from Faverge. Only from Faverge."

"Go ahead."

"Repeat the address and the instructions."

"Comrade P. Beretta, 999 rue de Macon, 69907 Lyon, and the letter must be posted from Faverge."

"No. You have the name wrong. It is Comrade Beretta, not Comrade P. Beretta."

"Comrade Beretta, 999 rue de Macon, 69907 Lyon, always from Faverge."

"Good. Let me give you the third part."

"Go ahead."

"Your wife is dead. She died without pain. I'm sorry. I worried for three months before I learned that I lost my husband, so I understand it is better to know."

He had given himself a day to get Agnes out, and it had not been enough. They had been so fast ... so accurate in their response. He had known she was dead, but the confirmation was like ice on his heart.

"Your children ..."

"Wait," he interrupted. "How do you know about my wife's death? What do you know about how she died?"

"I am only carrying a message. I don't know the source. I was told to tell you, if you asked me, that she was taken by the police on the afternoon of your disappearance. They wanted to locate you. They used chemical means to interrogate her, and she died without regaining consciousness."

It was what he had thought.

"Your children are alive, living with a family in France. When the time is right, we can try to recover them. Until then, they are hostages. If the state thinks that you can be reached, they will use the children. At all costs, for the children, you must keep Albert Gola apart from your former person. You will not be truly free until your children are out of their hands."

"I understand."

"I also have a child, somewhere in France. I would like my child to be with me again, if I can find him. We have the same interest."

He could see her now, lying on the bed, her hands palm down on her thighs.

"I believe you," he said. "Forgive me for my caution."

"I understand your caution," she answered. "There is nothing for us between fear and madness, except caution."

"You are brave."

"I don't feel brave at all."

"Where do you go from here?"

"Back to Paris. I have a ticket on the first train."

"Until we meet again, then. Good-night."

He put his hand over hers and gave a gentle squeeze. "Thank you."

His hand was on the doorknob. "Tell me," he asked. "What does your friend want of me?"

"He has not told me. I can only guess, but I think he intends that you should attack the government. . . ."

"Tell him he is a dreamer, but maybe he has the right man."

"I will tell him."

"You should lock the door behind me."

The door opened and he was gone.

7

Jacques de Celigny heard the key turn in the lock, and he paused outside the door. The clip of bullets lay heavy in his hand, the metal warm from contact with his palm. The clip was real. The woman on the other side of the door was real—frightened, brave, convincing. The pistol in the Moreau house was real. He hesitated on the landing. It was so improbable. He needed more substance, corroborating details, proof that these wild shreds of reality were not part of a larger dream.

Who was she? Who was her friend, the fictive Pierre Beretta? Who was the target?

To live again as a hunter . . . The target was surely in the new government, where killing was due and overdue.

Breaking the silence, a male voice floated up the stairwell, confident, interrogatory . . . then a response, less confident—the words not intelligible. Someone had come in and woken the night clerk. Light suddenly bathed the landing, a pale yellow glow from a single bulb, switched on from below. De Celigny surveyed the space, looking for a place to hide.

The stairway occupied the center of the landing. There were four numbered doors to the rooms, two facing the front of the hotel, two facing the back. Between them, on the landing, were two doors, one marked *bain*, the other W.C.—it was an old hotel. There was a big window below the landing, on the bend of the stairway. That would open onto the passage between the buildings.

The *bain* and the W.C. were both locked.

Footsteps were coming up the stairs. Only one pair of feet, which meant that the night clerk was not coming with his guest. . . . It was better, the night clerk might be a client of the Bar

Express, might recognize the waiter from the bar and ask himself a question.

Back into the woman's room? Impossible, she had just locked the door. There was no time.

De Celigny moved as his plan crystallized. It was easy. He would go up, then come down, a late departure from a nocturnal rendezvous, nothing to remark, as long as he was not loitering on the landing.

The stairs creaked under his feet with only the softest protest. His tread was lighter than the mounting footsteps in the stairwell below. The clip went into the open pocket of his anorak.

On the landing above, de Celigny turned and started down, letting each foot fall with a thud as he descended the steps.

A tall figure in a long city overcoat was coming up to the woman's landing, his eyes scanning the numbers on the doors. He glanced up at de Celigny.

"*Bon soir, comrade,*" de Celigny said.

They passed each other.

"*Bon soir, comrade,*"

The man was young, well groomed. Not the type for a small, cheap hotel. De Celigny rounded the landing onto the next flight down. The man had found the door he sought, and he was raising his hand, empty; there was no key. He was going to knock. . . .

On the woman's door.

De Celigny stopped.

The man looked at him.

De Celigny grimaced. "I forgot my car keys."

De Celigny turned to go back up and put his hand on the clip in his pocket.

The man's eyes went back to the door.

The clip swung in de Celigny's fist, true and deadly, to the man's temple, smashing skin, tissue, bone.

The man's knees buckled, as de Celigny knew they would. He toppled into de Celigny's arms.

De Celigny yielded under the weight of the body, braced himself to lift, and then started up the stairs. It was hard to pull a man upstairs in silence—the feet dragged and thumped on each step.

But if the woman heard anything, she would not know what she had heard.

On the turn of the stairs, two landings above, de Celigny laid the body on the steps and dove a hand into the folds of the man's overcoat. The soft, thick cloth caressed the back of his hand; it was better than anything made in France.

A shoulder holster. De Celigny checked that the Smith & Wesson .38 was loaded, snapped off the safety, and pocketed the weapon.

A small wallet, containing only two cards. The first was a cash card that showed a number but no name—that was unheard of for common folk. The other was a party membership card, also numbered, also without a name.

Then, a thin leather case from the opposite breast pocket. As de Celigny opened the case, a folded sheet of paper fell out and fluttered onto the man's chest.

De Celigny read the man's identity. *Theron, Claude-Maurice, Inspector of the Police of Paris, Special Investigations.* No address. The issuing authority was the Commissioner of Police, but no name was offered over the illegible scrawl, and the issue date was blank. A statement in fine print begged the full cooperation of every citizen. An imprinted seal . . .

It looked official, but de Celigny had never seen a police identification so bare of information.

He took the fallen paper and unfolded it. It was a warrant for the arrest of Comrade Chantal Senac, alias Annie Beaumont. The authorizing signature was a telephone number and a four-letter code.

His last doubt was gone. The inspector had come to arrest the woman, had seen Jacques de Celigny close up.

Without thinking further, de Celigny used his thumbs to close the arteries in the man's neck, and waited for his breathing to stop. Then he waited some more.

He opened the window and lifted Inspector Theron's corpse by the armpits, pushed the inert torso head first over the sill.

A quick look into the vacant passageway below, a dark slot between the buildings. There were no windows in the wall opposite. De Celigny took the body's legs by the knees and heaved them up, until the weight of the trunk took control and ripped the legs out of his hands. The landing echoed between the walls, but the sound did not carry. De Celigny closed the window and went down the stairs.

He passed Chantal's door, and questions leaped at him—she knew too much about Albert Gola, but she should be safe until morning. He needed to move, to make the inspector's body disappear before the good folk of Albertville came out into the streets.

Before reaching the ground floor, he stopped to be sure the front desk was vacant. The night clerk had gone back to his cot.

The last bar had closed for the night, and the street outside the hotel was nearly pitch black. The only break in the darkness came from the faint light in the hotel lobby. The rumble of an automobile's idling motor drew his nerves taut. It was parked on the far side of the street, opposite the hotel. The outline of a man's head, a mere suggestion of shape in the driver's seat—the inspector's chauffeur, waiting.

De Celigny walked across the street, directly to the car. He rapped on the driver's window and stood beside it as the glass descended. The face inside turned to him—dark eyebrows, darker eyes, a moustache. A good policeman, the chauffeur did not speak, but waited for de Celigny to explain himself.

"The man inside wants you to go in. He told me to come out for you."

The chauffeur nodded.

The door of the car opened, and the chauffeur got out, a pistol glinting in his hand. Jacques de Celigny held the door for him, closed it. As the chauffeur took his first step toward the hotel, de Celigny shot him in the head with the inspector's Smith & Wesson.

The crack of the shot was deafening. Echoes came back from the surrounding walls. De Celigny feared that the night clerk would wake up and come to the door, that someone would look out a window and detect the fallen body in the dark street. He pulled the body by the legs to the back of the car, pushed it half under the rear bumper.

The trunk was open. He wrestled the body up over the ledge of the trunk and dropped it in.

In the hotel lobby nothing moved. The night clerk was a good sleeper. No lights came on in any of the windows up and down the street. People were not curious in the New State—or they slept well.

De Celigny found the chauffeur's pistol by its shine, a dull reflection from the light in the hotel.

The car was a big Peugeot. He eased himself into the driver's seat, turned across the street to park next to the hotel, and got out to go for the inspector.

In the passageway, he took the inspector's beautiful cloth overcoat off before he dragged the body to the Peugeot.

Ten minutes later, the Peugeot was departing Albertville, with one corpse in its trunk and another in the back seat, on the main road that runs down the west bank of the Isère River to Chambéry. He searched for a flat narrow stretch of bank that he remembered, where the road was close to the water. It would be a good place to lose the car in the river. But if it was too far away from Albertville, he would have a very long walk back, to collect the woman. What to do with her then? If the woman was ever interrogated, the Moreau ménage would be exterminated soon after, along with Albert Gola.

The sky was dark with clouds, absent the least light from moon or stars. Only the headlight gave shape to the road and its borders. The river was an invisible companion, a few meters to the left.

The place came up as he remembered it but farther from Albertville than he remembered. He continued past. The car should leave tracks from Chambéry, should be found aimed at Albertville if it could not be completely submerged. Slow, then, looking for a wide place to turn.

He returned slowly, to be sure of the place.

A sign signalled caution for an intersection five hundred meters ahead. It made a good take-off point.

De Celigny stopped the Peugeot, wrapped the clip, the inspector's Smith & Wesson, and the chauffeur's FN automatic in the inspector's overcoat and left the bundle by the base of the sign.

He walked the few meters between the road and the river's edge—a solid bank, no risk of burying a wheel. The water below was invisible but audible, a violent presence with a roar that spoke of force and speed.

He knelt and reached down over the edge of the embankment, feeling for irregularities and crevices that would allow a grip. The water would be cold; he would die with his victims if he took too long to get out. The bank seemed climbable, a blend of mud, grass, and embedded rocks. At least the air was not too cold, it was above freezing, and still.

Inside the Peugeot, he lowered the driver's side window. He moved the car's papers from the glove compartment to the hinge of the door, to keep it from jamming shut on impact. He backed the car onto the road, then down the road far enough to reach take-off speed on the return. He latched the seat belt, unlatched it to be sure of the action, and latched it again. Ready to fly.

Then he planted his foot on the accelerator, let the speedometer stabilize at fifty kilometers, and veered at the sign.

The wheels crunched on the shoulder, and the car dropped off the edge. Weightless in his seat, de Celigny flexed taut against the impact. The water hit hard, slamming him against the seat belt. For an instant the car floated, the first shock of cold water biting his ankles as he released himself. He forced his shoulder against the door, and the water met him like an icy wall. He gasped, pushed, and struggled free. The numbing current took him and he started to swim, disoriented, unable to locate the river's edge.

He swam with big, vigorous strokes, kicking his feet, fighting the cold, tumbling in the eddies. His feet scraped bottom, and the drag told him instantly where to find the bank, but then he was bounced into the deep and rolled away in a wave of turbulence. When he surfaced, he sensed the embankment beside him, struggled to it, grabbed for the mud and rock, but was torn away by the river's force.

Again he scraped bottom, and the river carried him off. The cold was like a clamp on his muscles, robbing his strength.

His hip grounded on sand. Blind in the blackness, he groped for the bank, but stopped when his steps took him down off the bar. He was going the wrong direction.

He staggered the other way, and this time he waded into the bank. He groped for handholds and climbed, pulling himself up. A shiver seized him so heavily it was like a convulsion, but he forced himself over and fell on the flat.

Will pulled him to his knees, pushed him upright. Distant consciousness told him that he needed to hurry to the warm coat by the sign, to run, to generate heat in his soaked and frozen body.

Two steps and a cramp seized his right thigh. He stumbled and fell, crying in pain as the muscle contracted rock hard, a victim of the cold. He lay on the ground, immobilized, while life returned to his leg. The seconds ticked past as he massaged the cramp, rubbing the pain away. At last he could flex his knee again, and he rolled to his feet. His feet were glacial blocks, without feeling, the road an abstract somewhere below his ankles. He managed to shuffle on his way. How far had the river carried him?

The movement brought blood into his feet and his fingers, and now an ache began that felt as though his bones were cracking. At last the road sign appeared, with the bundle on the ground beside it. His tortured fingers fumbled with the cloth, let the clip and the weapons fall free, wrapped the dry coat around him.

He stuffed the pistols and the Beretta clip into the pockets of the overcoat.

He picked his steps along the river's edge, over rocks and holes, as far as possible from the road. At the first glow of headlights he would hide at the edge of the riverbank. But no one came.

The first buildings of Albertville loomed dark ahead. But so much time had passed, he feared the dawn, the first light that would bring early workers into the street, expose his passage. It was still dark, as black and quiet as only a provincial town in communist France could be. He hugged the walls, making his way from the river across the checkerboard of streets to the Hôtel de la Gare.

At the front door, he hesitated, looking for the night clerk. The lobby was empty. He went through, up the stairs, as fast as he could move in silence.

He tried the knob on the door of Room 7. It turned, and the door opened. Inside, he closed the door, and then risked the light switch.

The room was empty.

Too late. Wherever she was, she was at the mercy of fortune and her own preparations, and so was he.

Jacques de Celigny made his way in silence down the stairs, let himself out, and walked through vacant streets to the river. On the bridge to Conflans, he transferred the weapons from the overcoat to his anorak pockets, and threw the coat into the churning water below.

The first streaks of impending sunrise were shimmering behind the mountains to the east when he reached the Moreau house on the hill. He would have only an hour to rest—who could think of sleep—before going to work at the rolling mill. And go to work he must. No one had seen him in the entire night's odyssey. The events would never have happened, as soon as he slipped back into the pattern of his life.

If Chantal Senac, alias Annie Beaumont, could somehow escape arrest in France.

CHANTAL sat on a bench in a corner of the train station, waiting for the first train to Lyon, eradicating the memory of Annie Beaumont, reciting to herself her new identity, Corinne Delonnet, on her way back to Paris. Annie Beaumont's return ticket was booked for a week hence, after the ski holiday in Courchevel. Corinne Delonnet was more serious, attached to the Ministry of Education, returning from a seminar in Megève. Chantal prepared Corinne Delonnet for eventual questions.

But the memory of the shot interrupted her rehearsal. It came back each time she lost her concentration, like a rap on the windowpane of her memory. Someone had fired a gun in the street outside the hotel. She knew very well, from those rare times when Arnaud had taken her hunting, the sound of a gun.

Right after Albert Gola had left her room, there had been footsteps, at least one other person outside her door. A friend of Gola's, a bodyguard? Then, quiet.

Then, a few minutes later, the shot. She had knelt by the window, seen movement in the street below, the automobile coming across the road and parking where her line of sight was blocked. The car had gone with hardly a sound, and she had sat for an hour on her bed before she decided that she would rather wait in the station for her train. If anyone asked, she could say that a friend had dropped her early on the way from Megève to Grenoble.

She had slipped out the hotel door without waking the night clerk. Her cash card—or, Annie Beaumont's—had already surrendered payment for the night, and her account number was still in the hotel's machine for eventual late charges.

The train came in at five fifty-five, on schedule from its early morning start in Moûtiers, higher up in the valley of the Isère.

She climbed on board. Most of the compartments were empty, and she chose one in the center of the center car. At two minutes before six, she was on her way to Paris.

She thought of Albert Gola . . . intense, volatile, a man on the edge. She had done her part, delivered the bullets and the message. She thought that if he was alive, he had already killed someone.

THE head of Department 100's Intelligence Branch, whose code name was "Eyes," faced Valerie, Max, and the Russian in the Russian's office. The plump, bespectacled soothsayer of the labyrinth, Eyes wore a perpetual expression of doubt, as though he was sceptical of everything, even his own report. He was reading from notes, and he was careful to say that the information came from Ebert, the director of the external security service.

The Russian listened, grim, to Eyes' story.

Helen Landry was dead. Shot, trying to escape, by the DSE's agent.

"The DSE man, Androuët, must be disciplined," the Russian said.

Max spoke. "The telephone call was truly from Landry. Who else would have gone to the trouble? It means that there is a leak in the DSE's Washington office."

"And maybe a leak here as well," Eyes said. "Comrade Androuët says that she was warned. She had packed her clothes and other belongings into the boat; she was not coming back. And now we have learned that someone called Helen Landry from France. The call was picked up by MSIE and reported immediately to the DSE, but the duty officer there neglected to tell Washington."

Eyes unfolded a white sheet of note paper. He read, "Telephone intercept, red list, cut off at fourteen point two seconds. Alert response to public telephone, Gare du Nord, four minutes approximately, no subject, no prints."

He read on in silence before he spoke again.

"The cash card was left in the telephone. The cash card has a number that has never been issued, and there is no cash balance assigned to it. It should not have made the telephone work, and yet it was used to call the United States."

The Russian interrupted. "The duty officer did not tell Washington? How is that possible?"

"We should ask the duty officer," Eyes said. "It appears that he was going on vacation. He is now in the south of France."

The Russian responded. "To begin, we must interrogate the duty officer in the DSE. Max, I make you responsible."

Max nodded affirmation.

The Russian shook his head, and in a rare display of temper he hammered his fist on the table. "Bungled! We had Landry in our hands."

The telephone rang on the Russian's desk. Valerie waited for an approving nod, then picked it up.

"Listening," she said. She listened. "Please wait."

Covering the mouthpiece with her hand, she looked first at the Russian and then at Max. "It is Morand, calling from MSIE," she said. She hesitated before she continued. "Daniel has been killed. So also has one of Morand's men, an agent from Lyon. They were just found in their car, in the Isère River."

Max's mouth opened but no words came. The Russian showed no reaction, reached to take the telephone from Valerie.

"Karel here. What happened?"

He listened.

"And Comrade Senac?"

He nodded at the answer.

When he put down the phone, he sat back in his chair, folded his hands on his lap, and stared at the wall above their heads.

"All at once," the Russian said, "we have lost a woman in the United States who took us two years to find, we have lost a man in Albertville, and MSIE has lost another. . . . We have no clues, nothing to tie these events together, but we must ask if there is not a thread between them.

"Morand will investigate in Albertville. Daniel reached the hotel where Comrade Senac spent the night as Annie Beaumont. . . . Daniel woke up the night clerk to know the room. That is the last we know. Comrade Senac was gone when the night clerk woke up this morning. Annie Beaumont has a reservation in Courchevel today, but she has not arrived there and Morand doubts that she will."

Eyes stood up, his eyes blinking behind his spectacles. The events were coming too fast for his systematic mind.

Valerie watched him leave the room, a figure bowed over by doubt and confusion.

The Russian growled at Max and Valerie. "Something is happening, and we do not know what it is."

ONLY the Star's faint green light, a soft glow off the screen, lit Landry's face and hands. He had been at the terminal since Chantal had left on her mission to Albertville—almost thirty hours. His body was adrift in the darkness, his mind locked to the screen.

It was too early for news, either from Chantal or about Helen. In the meantime, the minuet went on, the lines on the monitor scrolling out and vanishing in response to his fingers on the keys. Landry began to believe that he could crack the New State.

The Star could add fire to the conflict between the first secretary and the Russian.

Department 100 could be discredited, and the Russians would abandon their Russian.

Paccard could be eliminated.

Marcel Chabon was the question mark. If Chabon was willing, he could replace Paccard.

But first Chabon had to help Helen escape the DSE.

It would be hours before the Star could know Helen's fate. Landry tried to put his fear for her out of his mind.

Instead, he thought about the opening offered by the appearance of the new aide, Gentiane, in Department 100. Her recruitment was like a delicate strand of thread leading into the labyrinth. The Russian's staff had been a blank, but now it could be penetrated by following that thread.

Somewhere in France, almost surely in Paris, almost surely within the government, a woman had been removed from her job and given a new position. The woman would be dedicated, a party member. The change had been made within a narrow span of time. The Star could find her.

Fatigue weighed on him, forcing him to concentrate on the screen and forget the ache in his shoulders. His work was at a logical point to break off and sleep, but the identity of Gentiane was still locked inside the machine, and he would not sleep anyway until he knew Helen's fate. He stood up, stretched, and let his muscles creak into a new alignment.

Then he sat down and started the search.

There were so many women working in the government who had recently changed assignments. So many were party members. His mind wandered in circles, seeking definitions that could winnow the list down. Almost all had parents who were party members, had been members of Communist Youth, lived in or near Paris. And yet, the individual who had been selected to become Gentiane must have been special.

It was three hours later that Landry tried the Russian language

as the definition of his target. Only three names came up. Two
were interpreters in the Foreign Ministry, and both had been
transferred to Moscow.

The third was Valerie Clavel. Within five minutes, her dossier
confirmed her credentials: time in the eastern countries, well
approved by her superiors, and now she had been transferred out
of the Ministry of Education into a clerk's job at the Ministry of
Justice. It was not a logical career step, unless the clerk's job was
a cover for the Russian's security organization.

Her residence had not changed.

Landry nodded affirmation. As he committed Valerie Clavel's
dossier to his safekeeping files, he speculated. Her appointment
could be an accident of circumstance; she might be an innocent.
He wondered if Comrade Clavel was pretty. She was young.

His watch told him that he had to quit, and his eyelids started
to close as he sat in front of the monitor. With an effort of will,
he shook himself awake once more.

It was time to check again in the DSE files for Helen. His fingers took him to Helen Landry's dossier.

One word jumped off the screen at him.

>*SHOT*

Shot while trying to escape capture. In a boat—that was like
Helen, to escape in a boat. But she had not escaped.

They had killed her.

He scrolled down quickly, through the reporting references to
the substance of the tragedy.

He read and reread the words, prayed that the glowing epitaph
might somehow be erased and replaced.

The agent named Androuët, the same who had discovered
Helen, had shot her with a "silenced weapon," then verified his
kill.

Helen had tried to run. And now, she was dead.

Even after two years apart, they had been bound together, and
that tie had been fatal. If he had not warned her, if she had been
caught unaware ... would it have been better for her? Landry

tried to suppress the wave of guilt. Helen could never have lived as a captive, even if she had survived the interrogation. But she was gone now, and a part of his life had been scrubbed out.

At the bottom of the file, Landry found a cryptic note:

>*COMMUNICATION FROM MINISTER OF ECONOMY, SEE LANDRY ROBERT.*

In his own dossier, Landry saw that Chabon had lived up to his word. Chabon's call to Ebert had come only a short time before the agent's bullet had killed his wife.

He was swamped by sadness, but he knew sleep could not come before the whole discipline was complete.

He queried for René Leveque in the MSIE files. The screen flickered and then—surprise—a mass of data, recently entered.

If he had heard footsteps on the ladder, he would not have felt a greater surge of adrenalin. Reports, lists indexed to subject matter—Leveque's parents, his childhood, his diploma, his work, his superiors, all canvassed and cubbyholed. Landry did not need to look at the reports. They would all present the same hollow conclusion: René Leveque was a fiction. His alias was dead.

Flash, Flash, Flash.

They were looking for him—a search bulletin, complete with portrait. The picture would not help them much; it was different by intention from the picture and appearance of François Blanc.

He expected the same explosion of information when he keyed in the name of Chantal Senac.

Flash, Flash, Flash.

She would be picked up the moment she returned to her apartment. He pushed on a key and the computer told him the time. The train should have come in from Lyon with Corinne Delonnet on board twenty minutes ago.

She should soon be at the building on the rue de l'Espérance.

He wanted to leave the screen, but the screen was full of information, holding him. He scrolled down, knowing that he should move. There was not a moment to spare. An agent had seen her on the train to Lyon, MSIE had culled through the passenger list and had focussed on Annie Beaumont. An agent of Department 100 had been dispatched by plane to Lyon to arrest her.

She was so important the she merited an agent from Department 100. Daniel . . . who was that?

As he continued scrolling down the screen, a new format appeared and the letters changed style. It was a police report from Albertville.

A car found in the river and identified as an official vehicle assigned to the MSIE branch in Lyon. Pulled out—how long ago?—two hours. . . . This report had just come in.

Two men found in the car, one shot in the head, the other dead of unknown causes.

Chantal Senac had taken a room at the Hôtel de la Gare, but she had been gone by morning.

Where was she, then? With de Celigny? Or could she be in Paris, oblivious to the havoc behind her in Albertville? He could not wait.

As he stood up to go, a new entry appeared, letter by letter as an unknown hand tapped on a keyboard somewhere in MSIE:

>*S-E-N-A-C C-H-A-N-T-A-L-*
 S-B-1-1-2-8-4-5-

 R-E-P-O-R-T-D E-N-T-R-Y-

 1-1-2- R-U-E- D-E-L-E-S-P-E-R-A-N-C-E-

Her return was merely being reported. They were not there waiting for her. There might still be time.

Landry raced up the ladder as fast as his limp would take him.

OFFICER Théophile Loubel of MSIE put down the telephone and lifted himself from his chair. He was a very large man, and he moved his mass slowly. He needed to consult a file, and that meant walking to the computer monitor. He sighed. It was a small penance to move his bulk from its comfortable chair, but life was a penance for a man of size in a nation of critics. Nothing in the revolution had changed the French talent for wicked disapproval. He lumbered to the monitor on the other side of the room. Logically, there would have been a monitor next to each telephone, but no, here in MSIE, only the inspector had his own monitor, and the rest needed to share. It made him sulky each time he was compelled to walk away from his desk.

He keyed in the contact name and the search bulletin number and watched the Star's response come up on the screen.

Clear orders: the labyrinth wanted the woman detained. Loubel frowned. He did not relish the Russian's orders. They made everyone too self-conscious, too worried about making a mistake, and then mistakes multiplied like fleas on a dog.

Loubel flicked the keys with his fingers, his touch light and accurate. He was good at the computer. It would make sense to let him manipulate the Star for the others.

With meticulous care, he noted the woman's personal description and then called up the cross-reference for the man. He read the instructions in that file and thought about what he should do.

The police could be there in five minutes, but if the police were clumsy, if the woman was damaged, explanations would be required afterward. Loubel did not want to give explanations. He dreaded confrontations where they would think about his overweight and ignore his words, no matter how correct and blameless he might be. It would be better to have an MSIE team go to fetch her. The monitor showed him that the nearest team car was at the Gare de Lyon. That car was on a delivery for Section four, so an approval from the day officer in Section four would be needed.

He used the telephone beside the monitor.

There was a problem. The car at the Gare de Lyon was waiting for an arrival. Was the arrival someone important? Of course . . . a friend of the deputy minister for foreign trade. Yes, a very good friend, a woman, arriving from Cannes, they have been apart for a week. Of course she could not take a taxi, and a limousine from the ministry was out of the question, she was not his wife. The day officer added the last bit of information as though Loubel wanted to make a public display of the minister's liaison.

Loubel put down the phone and laboriously pencilled a note of the conversation, for eventual use if he should need to give an explanation. The next nearest car was passing the Porte d'Orleans. It might take twenty minutes, but if the woman had just returned to her apartment after a week away, it didn't seem likely that she would leave in the next half hour.

Loubel gave the dispatcher the particulars, and then he called the MSIE command officer to report on the action in progress, so the young lieutenant could call the Russian's staff, while Loubel's responsibilities were discharged in good order with no fuss. A man could be fat in France, and still do his job.

THE little van, a fifteen-year-old Citroën, badly painted, with mismatched dabs to cover the dents and scratches, took him across Paris with agonizing slowness. He needed to move at post-revolution speed, and if the crush of traffic was much less than it had been before, it was no less frustrating to be swept along at the mañana pace of the New State.

He tried to remember what she had said of her apartment. He knew she lived alone and that the room was up one flight of stairs.

He should ask the concierge, but she had been sure that the concierge was an informer.

What if MSIE was already there, ahead of him? They would be looking for Engineer Leveque.

He wished for a commando team with de Celigny in charge.

He rolled down Tolbiac, his senses at a peak. Where the rue de l'Espérance met Tolbiac, he slowly advanced across the intersection, looking up the empty street. There was a place to park just past the crossing, and he took it.

He left the little van with the doors unlocked, its keys under the seat, the identity papers for its owner hidden in a slit in the tattered upholstery.

Twenty steps back to the corner, then turn and walk to the building. It was taller than its neighbors, visible from the corner. No one on the street, no one in any of the cars parked along the curb, no van or truck that might conceal someone, no sign of any danger. He walked along the block, turning his head to see the numbers, as though seeking an address.

He entered, leaning on the heavy door to open it.

The concierge was there waiting for him, a tiny man, his eyes popping.

"Comrade Senac?" Landry asked. "Where?"

"You are fast!" the concierge replied. "I just called fifteen minutes ago. She is up the stairs here. On the first landing turn right, it is the only door."

"Go into your room. Don't let yourself be seen again."

"Yes, I understand . . ."

The little man turned to his door, reluctantly.

"Quick!"

The concierge went in and the door closed behind him.

Landry raced up the stairs, turned right, and softly rapped on the door.

He heard her move.

"Who is it?" Her voice was muffled.

"Leveque. Hurry."

The door opened. He stepped inside and kissed her, brushing her cheek. An embrace would take too long, and she sensed his urgency.

"The police will be here soon."

"I'm ready," she said, patting her hair. She smiled at him.

"We will go out together. The concierge thinks I am a policeman, and you should look terrified in case he peeks out his door. As soon as we are out of sight from his door, you must walk toward the Place d'Italie and wait at the first intersection. I'll go the other way and come around for you in my van. It would be bad if someone here should see you entering the van."

From the sidewalk, Landry checked to see if the concierge could be watching from a window, but the street-level windows were boarded over.

"Three minutes," Landry said. "I'll be there."

He watched her start out. Her walk to the crossing at the top of the street was not far, but was twice as long as his to the van. They should arrive at the top of the street at the same time. He walked as quickly as his limp would let him, down to Tolbiac. At the corner, a large white Peugeot turned off Tolbiac and onto the rue de l'Espérance. Three men, two in front, one in back. Not police, but tough . . . MSIE? He wanted to turn to see if Chantal was far enough away, but he did not dare.

The trip around the block was like a trip around the moon.

The rue de l'Espérance ended at a crossing of narrow streets in a small circle of pavement. There were no shops, just residential buildings. The place seemed empty as he drove into the circle and turned right toward the top of Chantal's street.

He applied the brakes, rolling to a stop at the curb by the corner. Trees and a kiosk on the curbside blocked a clear view. She was not there, but the white Peugeot was coming up the rue de l'Espérance toward him. They should see the van moving, it was not a normal place to stop. He engaged the gears and turned down the rue de L'Espérance.

There were still two men in the front seat of the Peugeot. The back seemed empty.

They did not have her, unless the third man was holding her in the building. He drove slowly down the rue de l'Espérance, looking. As he passed the building where she lived, discretion kept him moving. If she was not in the Peugeot she must be inside with the third man, but that seemed strange. They would have taken her away.

Slowly, he continued to the corner and turned again onto Tolbiac. His hands and feet directed the van without any conscious purpose, onward around the block, back to the rendezvous point.

He slowed again coming to the corner. She was there, beside the kiosk, stepping onto the street.

Now she was in the van.

"Hello," she said.

"You frightened me."

"Let me get out of sight," she said, squeezing between the seats and stretching out on the floor. "I heard their car, and I hid in a doorway until they left. I thought they would see me."

He had already started to turn down the rue de l'Espérance,

and he continued now, for the second time, past her building. He saw a man coming out of the building and identified him as the third of the team, left behind by the others.

She spoke, from behind him. "I hope you can tell me what is happening. I have been so scared."

"I am glad you are here."

Her hand reached out to touch his arm. He was glad, to the roots of his being.

"OPEN your eyes," he said, releasing her hand.

"Where am I?" She looked around the room. There was not much to see—it could all be taken in at a glance.

"You are a guest in another home of the well known Engineer Leveque."

"Where? ..."

"It is better if you do not know."

She sat on the bed and smoothed the blanket beside her with her hand.

"I have another place we can stay," he said. "More comfortable than this. I must make sure that it is still secure."

"This is where you really live, isn't it?"

He nodded.

"Then I would like to stay here, if you would let me. With you."

"The bed is very small for two."

"I will not take much space."

He was relieved. The last apartment should be saved as a last resort. But she would be a prisoner in this place. She could never show herself.

She continued. "And later, whenever it is possible, I would like to go back to Albertville, to find my son."

He thought about that. The risk of discovery had not passed. Events had moved so fast, the strings were starting to slip through his fingers. He needed to regain control.

"That will not be easy, it will take some preparation. Tell me about your trip."

She reached out her hand to his and pulled him down onto the bed, burying her face in the warmth of the hollow where his neck met his shoulder. She put her arms around him and held him for a moment, and then kissed him.

"Wait," she whispered. "We can talk later."

The hunger in her ignited him, drowning thought. He found her buttons and then found her with his hands and lips, remaking the union between them.

They slept, wrapped in each other's arms. Chantal woke and turned to fit her back against his chest. She dozed, conjuring images: she was in a train, sitting beside a madman holding a gun, praying that he would not shoot it. Half conscious, she squeezed her lover's arms around her and felt his warmth. A smile curved her lips, and she slipped away into a sleep without dreams.

8 Valerie Clavel leaned back in the comfortable seat of the limousine, disappointed that the questioning had not gone to the end. She had anticipated a "final interrogation," had been eager to break the fresh-faced young officer down into the shreds of his subconscious, just to see what was inside his fair head. He had made her angry at first, coming off the train in his vacation clothes, smug in his privileges, and then when she had seen his fear, her anger had changed to curiosity.

Eyes, as the director of Department 100 intelligence, had the same instinct to chew and pull and tear the questions down to the last morsel once the process had begun. But Max, the head of Action Branch, had stopped the car and put the young captain out on the curb.

"He was telling the truth," Max said. He was driving. He took the next right turn and steered the limousine with assurance back toward the edge of the Seine.

They were silent.

Max spoke again. "I will give you odds that every part of his story checks. There is no conspiracy. The vacation was planned, it was not arranged as an alibi. I think our young captain deserves a reprimand, but we should not kill him for his mistake. We need our friends in the DSE. We must keep them with us."

He stopped at a red light.

"Do you agree? I may be wrong. You should tell me what you think."

Valerie was thinking of the DSE captain as he would have appeared, prostrate under the lights, answering their questions, speaking in the flat tones of the already dead, remembering everything.

"I agree," Eyes said from the back seat. "He was not lying. We can only guess what else he might have told us."

"Good. And you, Comrade Gentiane. Agreed?"

"Of course," she said.

THE Russian was waiting for them in his office, but he stopped them before they could speak about their talk with the young captain.

"We have news of Comrade Senac," he said. "MSIE reported just after you left. She returned this afternoon to her apartment. MSIE's people responded to a call from the concierge, but they arrived too late. A man with a limp came to her house and took her out. The concierge thought it was a man from MSIE, but it was surely Leveque. This says to me that Leveque was not directly involved with the business in Albertville."

But it was not Leveque that he was thinking about. What had Chantal gotten into? Could it be that someone had cracked the cover of Arnaud Senac's death, made the connection between Chantal Senac and Karel of Department 100, was using Chantal Senac to attack him?

He knew he had been wrong, during those first years in Lille, not to share his secrets with her. He should have recruited her to work with him, but soon it had become impossible, all her friends were in the establishment. He had loved her. Did he still? He had to put the questions out of his mind. She was a fugitive; they would find her, and then justice would be done.

"Tell me about your talk with the captain," the Russian said.

Eyes spoke for them. There was no evidence that a plot had been cooked within the DSE. It was the wrong agency, in any case. If the government had decided to attack the labyrinth, they would have used MSIE. But MSIE had reported the phone call.

"I am more concerned about Comrade Senac's trip from Paris, and losing Daniel in Albertville," the Russian said. "This matter is still out of control and MSIE knows about it. We should discuss it in the security meeting."

Eyes responded, "I do not like to admit failures, it shows weakness."

The Russian overrode the objection. "We sent Daniel and he failed. We will make them feel more secure if we take the blame and acknowledge that we need their help. And then I think they will help us to understand what went wrong. It is delicate. Some of our colleagues may seek to take advantage. We can be sure that Paccard is looking for support against us from MSIE."

The Russian turned to face Eyes.

"My birds should sing to me, if some of our colleagues start to change sides," Eyes said. "Not all will sing, but a few. We will know."

"Be sure," the Russian said. "We must be sure."

THE meeting started promptly. They initiated the voiceprint identification, and the Russian settled into his chair as though it was a meeting like every other.

The Russian added and subtracted possibilities, the simple arithmetic of the possible and the impossible.

Whatever had occurred in the United States had nothing to do with Leonid Paccard.

The phone call to Helen Landry suggested someone working outside the government, not inside.

Landry's phone call to Marcel Chabon suggested a leak in Washington, but the DSE station in Washington had little influence or information.

Chantal's trip to Albertville could not be related to Helen Landry.

But one catastrophe on top of the other—making him weaker?

If there was a scheme, he was only seeing parts of it.

He looked around him at his colleagues. . . . Were they loyal to the revolution, to himself?

Their loyalty depended on the Russians. If these people

thought that the Russians were withdrawing support from Department 100, their loyalty would go up in smoke.

The first requirement was to clean up the matter of Daniel's disappearance before Paccard heard about it or the Russians started to ask questions.

Gousset, the head policeman, tapped on his microphone for their attention. The tap fed back a dry click, audible in the speakers that subtly amplified their voices. Heads turned. He gathered his breath.

"I have details on the autopsy that we performed today on the body of the agent from Department 100: he did not drown, he was dead before the vehicle went into the river. Also, he was not killed by the blow to his head. The blood to his brain was cut off—the work of someone who knows how to kill with his hands."

Gousset let the words sink in before continuing. "We are puzzled by the identity of Annie Beaumont, the alias used by Chantal Senac. There is no real Annie Beaumont who has lost her papers, the identity card and the cash card were not stolen. And yet, a valid cash card and an identity card were used to buy the ticket from Paris to Albertville. The night clerk saw the identity card when the woman checked into the hotel—and when he saw the picture of Chantal Senac on the search bulletin, he not only said that it was the same woman, but he thought it was the same picture. And the night clerk used her cash card for her payment. The transaction was perfectly normal. I do not believe that it is possible for anyone to forge these documents. This tells us that someone used the Star to create the documents—that someone has found a way to get around our controls."

The Russian's eyes met Morand's, saw the same reaction. The Russian gestured for Morand to say what they both understood.

Morand tapped his microphone for attention. "The cash card that was used for the telephone call to the United States was perfect. It had no cash balance, its owner had no name, and yet it was used to call outside France. We have examined it carefully and can find no evidence that it was a forgery. It was issued by the Star, like the false cards of Annie Beaumont."

Chantal! She filled the Russian's thoughts. Her trip was tied in with Helen Landry and so with Helen's husband, the American genius who had created the Star.

Had Landry somehow compromised the Star?

Impossible, if Landry was a fugitive in the United States.

The Russian forced his attention back to the meeting. He interrupted. "Who is here who understands the workings of the Star?"

The question was addressed to the room, and like most questions that bear a threat of recrimination, it had no answer.

"Comrade Morand," the Russian continued, "do you think it would be possible for someone with total knowledge of the system to break into the Star?"

"The Ministry of Communications will say that it is not possible. They would be frightened to admit otherwise."

"Then, you think that it is possible?"

"If a man could make it, a man can break it."

"Robert Landry could break into the Star, if he was in France."

Morand nodded agreement. He looked around the room, his chin out, as though inviting dissent.

"That is the only reasonable explanation," the Russian said. "That he is here, in France, using the Star."

Ebert interrupted. "But Comrade Chabon told me that Landry was in the United States."

"Landry was reading our files in the Star, here in France," the Russian answered. "He knew that we had found Helen Landry. He knew what you told your Washington branch to do. He may have known when I gave my approval."

Silence fell around the table.

Valerie gave words to the thought that they were sharing.

"It means that he could be . . . looking at our words. Listening to us. Now."

Around the table, the participants stared at the chromed mushroom stalks placed in front of each one of them, and one by one, hands reached out to cover the stalks, to stifle their own self-betrayal.

"Gentiane, go out and find someone who can turn off the recording device," the Russian said. His hand securely cupped over his microphone, he added, speaking almost to himself, "The friend of Chantal Senac, the engineer, Leveque, is Robert Landry."

Valerie left the room.

The Russian held tight to his self-control, his mind struggling with the notion of Chantal as a messenger to a killer. He knew such a mission was beyond his wife, and yet his agent was dead. What had she done? He let go the microphone and pressed his hand to his forehead. He wanted to call out to her. The sound came, like a breath between his lips . . . "Chantal."

No one heard. The others waited, hands extended to cover the microphones, as though they were observing an occult rite.

The Russian was attacked by self-recrimination. As Leveque, Landry had been in his hands. Betrayed by sentiment for his wife, by wanting to prove—to himself!—his generosity, he had protected Chantal's relationship with this other man. Now, they would have a devil of a time finding Landry. And with him, Chantal.

Who could say what Landry might do with the Star? The possibilities were frightening. If the man knew he was detected, he would fight back. Even minor sabotage could bring France to a halt. . . . Given time and thought, what havoc could he wreak?

They could not turn off the Star. The nation lived on it. Years would pass before they could replace the systems that depended on the Star's lightning speed and limitless memory. It would, in fact, be impossible to go back to the dark ages of paper and microfilm. The Star could not be turned off, and yet it could hardly be defended from the man who had created it. Anyone with a telephone could be in contact with the Star, and thousands were, daily, in order to do their jobs. To sequester the Star would be next to impossible, if Landry could break the security provisions without detection.

The Russian put his fingertips together and pressed them to the bridge of his nose, shutting out the rest of the group while he weighed the possibilities.

The race was on to solve the puzzle and find Landry. What could be made from Landry's call to Marcel Chabon? It had been made from France. The Russian imagined a line of attack if Landry should ever call Chabon again, but it was not to share with this group.

He put his hand tight on the microphone and broke the silence.

"There are no secrets, but this must be kept . . . secret. No one can know that the Star is not secure, or we will have a panic. Do not risk any leak. We are the only ones who know, it must stay among us."

Valerie returned. Her eyes asked what she had missed, but nobody spoke.

"The switches are all off," she said. "We can speak freely."

"We have much to discuss," the Russian said. "We must find Landry, wherever he is hiding."

ROBERT Landry and Chantal Senac stirred themselves awake.

He kissed her. She opened her eyes and smiled.

"I like it very much, sleeping here with you," she said, rolling lazily to face him.

He propped himself on an elbow and looked down at her. I love you, he thought. Your smile, and your delicate features, your way of looking straight at me as though my eyes were an open window. Your courage.

"Tell me about your trip," he asked.

Lying beside him, she began from the train station.

Landry listened. She described the shot outside her window, and Landry understood that Jacques de Celigny and the agent called Daniel had met . . . a chance and fatal encounter. She was clear and it hardly needed repeating, but he asked her every detail of the moments with Albert Gola, intent on knowing how Gola had reacted, whether he seemed stable, like a planner, like a leader. Albert Gola seemed strong and sure, she told him, a leader, but violent.

"Good," he acknowledged.

"Can I ask you about Noël?"

"Of course."

"How . . . how can we rescue him without injury to him and to us? Albert Gola said to tell you that you were a dreamer. What will your dreams lead us to? It could be a nightmare."

"He said I was a dreamer? Why?"

"He asked me what you intended, and I told him that I thought you wanted him to attack the government. It's true, isn't it?"

She knew that Gola had already attacked and killed, in front of her hotel.

"He said that you were a dreamer, but that you might have found the right man. It was not a comfort to me. Your dreams frighten me."

"We can only start with dreams. To rescue Noël, to live together in happiness with good friends, and with neighbors that you trust. To emerge from grayness. All dreams."

"But why you? You could be out of this . . . with your powerful friend."

"At first I wanted to stay with the Star, because I thought I could gather a resistance against the Russians. And then they did things that made me angry, so that even after the idea of resistance was finished, I wanted to hurt them. They killed or spoiled my friends, the men who worked with me here in France, and then I learned to hate. And there is something else—now. You once met my wife, Helen. They killed her, while you were in Albertville."

"Oh . . . I am sorry."

"They have been looking for me since the revolution. Looking for me, they found her. She tried to get away and they killed her . . . in the United States."

"You loved her?"

"Yes."

"And me? You must tell me . . . will you look at me and see her?"

"No, never."

"I remember her so strong and so beautiful. I cannot believe that any man would choose me after her. Robert Landry, I need you to tell me ten times an hour that you love me, so that I never let go my hope."

"I love you," he said. "My marriage was over before the revolution, and we have just begun. But Chantal . . . the main question is you. Why is Department 100 interested in you, so much that they would send an agent by plane from Paris to arrest you? A simple cleaning woman does not deserve such special effort. Who is Inspector Theron? Why is your son in Notre-Dame-de-Bellecombe and not really in Czechoslovakia or Poland?"

"I don't know," she said. "I have told you everything, and I don't know."

She pressed herself to him.

"I'm sorry," she said. "My head is empty of ideas. . . . I can only wait and maybe a nightmare will tell me."

THE pulley at the top of the long ladder squeaked. As she lowered her weight onto each new rung below her, the soft upward tension on the rope at her waist yielded. She thought of his hands, holding the rope at the bottom of the ladder. Without the rope she would have been terrified by the abyss below her.

After a while, she could not hear the pulley.

It was dark in the vertical shaft. Only a faint yellowish luminescence came from the bottom. The ladder was made of metal, and an occasional reflected glint off the rungs was her sole visual contact with reality.

The light at the bottom grew closer, and her hands' convulsive grip on the rungs relaxed.

At the bottom, he undid the loop and, grinning, kissed her on the lips.

"Come," he whispered, unaccustomed to speaking in the cave.

She followed him the few steps to the end of the grotto where the terminal was placed. A stack of books made a seat for her.

His fingers moved quickly on the keyboard, and her eyes hardly had time to register the display on the screen before it was replaced.

Landry called up the transcript of the security meeting. He identified the names of the participants on the screen: *Karel*, the "Russian" of present-day folklore; his assistant, *Gentiane*; *Morand*, the Minister of the Interior and directly in charge of

MSIE; *Ebert*, the director of the DSE, the man responsible for Helen's death; and the head policeman, *Gousset*.

Gousset began the meeting with a description of the death of Department 100's agent.

"You escaped from them twice, once in Albertville, and again in Paris—lucky," Landry breathed as the words of the meeting scrolled onto the screen.

But then, Morand connected the false cash cards, made the tie between Chantal Senac and the telephone call to Helen Landry—Landry felt his pulse quicken, his palms turning moist with sweat.

The other side had won a great advantage.

Ebert reminded the meeting that Chabon had said Landry was in the United States. Landry was struck with doubt: was Chabon compromised for giving false information?

Landry could anticipate the next conclusion, and he read on with fatalistic calm as the Russian drove to the end: Robert Landry was in France, and the Star was compromised.

>*GENTIANE/ "IT MEANS THAT HE COULD BE . . . LOOKING AT OUR WORDS. LISTENING TO US. NOW."*

The screen went blank, and then one more bit of text scrolled out. The letters appeared slowly, one by one behind Karel's name. . . . The voice processor had had difficulty in assimilating the sound:

>*KAREL/ "CHANTAL."*

The screen went blank again, and an underlined message rolled across the screen:

>*POWER INTERRUPTION—TERMINATE RECORD*

Landry leaned back from the screen, his palms flat on the table.

"They understand everything," Landry said, but then he felt that Chantal had gone rigid by his side, and he saw a look of sheer horror on her face.

"Karel," she stammered. "The Russian?"

"Yes."

"He said my name. At the end."

'You cost him an agent."

"'Chantal,' he said . . ." She put her arm around his waist and asked, "Do you love me?"

"Promise . . ."

"It is important for me, because I may be more dangerous to you than my love is worth, unless you love me as much."

She paused, as though hoping to be interrupted. Then she spoke in a voice so low that he almost could not hear.

"It could be my husband. . . ."

Tears welled up, and she brushed them with the back of her hand. Landry touched her cheek, waiting for her to go on.

"Arnaud spoke Russian. He had a collection of Russian authors in his library, all in the original. He had a shortwave radio, and he would listen to Russian broadcasts. But there is more that makes me suspect him: Arnaud knew everyone. He used to keep books full of notes about people."

She looked so vulnerable. He wanted to protect her in his arms.

"I escaped the fate of all my friends. Someone has looked out for me."

"Someone changed the records for your father and Monsieur Sussoy."

"Exactly . . ."

Now she let all her memory spill out into words. "Arnaud was often gone. He was always hunting. The dead game would be sent to him after his return, already dressed for the freezer, but that did not mean he was really the hunter. And the most important thing . . . There was social outrage in his nature. I learned to avoid some subjects with him. I can remember gossiping with friends about a banker who kept three women in three fabulous apartments, and another time, about a very rich man who had bought a fabulous speedboat that cost two thousand francs an hour to run, and both times Arnaud became so angry that he could not speak at all."

He embraced her and felt the wet tears on his shoulder. The

revelation filled in the gaps in his understanding like a flood pouring into a valley. He held her tight while she sobbed. When she pushed herself away, he reached out and touched her wet eyes with his fingertips, to brush the damp away.

"I'm sorry," she said.

"Many things would then be clear," Landry answered.

"I don't know so much about Arnaud's life before we were married. I know that he had a career disappointment in Paris, and that was why he was in Lille. Exile. He was angry about it, but when I asked him, he told me that it was better I should not know what had happened. He has had such a revenge, on all of us. On me. I knew him as a good man. A good father and a good husband. I lived with him."

"Your son was not transported to Czechoslovakia, but he wanted you to believe the boy was there."

"Yes ... He did that to us."

Enormous tears welled up again from Chantal's eyes, and she reached out to him. He held her while she cried for her husband and for her child, and her sorrow swept over him so that his own eyes started to fill.

All the pieces fit. Landry's mind shuffled facts and guesswork into new arrangements. Arnaud Senac was the Russian. Questions vanished, and new questions took their place.

They were in grave danger. The Russian had been so close, it was a miracle they had never been caught. The Russian was very close, even now.

Arnaud Senac would start now to tear through the web of false identities that the Star had made for Robert Landry.

"What are we going to do?" Chantal asked.

"Hide. They will be looking for us."

THIS time it was Mr. Jackson calling from the United States, but Marcel Chabon expected the same voice when he picked up the receiver.

"Chabon," he said.

"Thank you for trying to help," Landry said to him. "Your effort was wasted."

"What happened?"

"You do not know?"

"I am not in the security apparatus. They tell me nothing."

"Helen is dead. They killed her."

"I am sorry. Truly, Mr. Landry, I am sorry sometimes for what we do in the name of the New State."

"Marcel Chabon, I am not in the United States, as I told you. I am here in France, and this is now known to the security organizations. There is a manhunt starting now, to find me. You may be questioned for saying that I was in the United States. You may even be suspected of complicity."

"That seems likely."

"You can explain that I bounced my call to you from the satellite that we use to talk to the United States. It is impossible to trace the source back to France."

"Is that possible?"

"I did it," Landry answered, and then asked Chabon, "Do you know about the labyrinth? The man called the Russian?"

"I know what everyone knows, nothing but the name. Sometimes I doubt if this man exists."

"He exists. He is dangerous. Be careful."

"I am careful, Mr. Landry, which makes me wonder why I should be talking to you now. But . . . I must ask you. You have access to the Star?"

"I do."

"Do you trust me, Mr. Landry?"

The phone was silent for a second before the voice said, "I don't know. I would like to."

"I understand that the security services will be looking for you. If I could help you, I would. But I myself am in need of help now. I am in trouble with the State Factories. Do you think you could do some work for me, even while they are looking for you?"

Landry formulated the answer carefully. "Put your problem into writing and file it in the Star. Put in the following sequence of letters . . . write this down: X,S,X,R,Q,K. Don't use the letters for the name of the file. Use an old file name that will not attract attention. Do you have it?"

"Yes, but how will you know where to look for this file?"

"The Star will find that letter sequence in about five seconds. Good-bye, Marcel Chabon. I will tell you after I see your problem if I am able to help."

JACQUES de Celigny sat on the edge of his bed, rereading a neatly creased sheet of paper. It was a sad little document, recounting death and incarceration, but all his friends were not lost.

Charles Nagy, the man Jacques would choose first to help him, was working under guard on a State Collective near Nîmes. Nagy had been a cauldron of psychic energy, it was hard to imagine him under guard. Nagy had been with him in the same sector for how long, three years? No, four . . . and that would make him just thirty years old by now. Nagy had been fresh out of the university when he joined the police. De Celigny remembered Nagy moving down the street in Marseille like a flame spirit dancing off ignited alcohol, with bullets in the air and everyone else pinned down. It had been a good day for Nagy, that day in Marseille.

The list in his hands was a roster of policemen and rugby players—men he had learned to trust, independent, scornful of authority, wilful enough to fight back against the New State. Only two remained free. One was still working as a policeman in Paris. . . . De Celigny grinned at the idea that he might soon see little Maurice Thevenet, the ferret, a man to whom two and two could make five and five would be correct. . . . The other now worked in the rail system—Alphonse Euler, former detective, a keen, sceptical intelligence hidden behind a smile, the smile hidden behind an enormous walrus moustache. Could the New State have let this moustached demon loose at the controls of a train?

His men . . . his friends. Of the names he had supplied, eight were dead. Five, besides Nagy, were prisoners, including all three rugby players who were still living.

On the bed at his side, a train schedule lay open. He could travel. His wallet held a new identity card and a matching cash card.

It would be a small team, too small, but then ... He dreamed and wondered about the source, wherever or whoever it was, behind the woman who had come to Albertville. Under the earth in the Moreau garden there was a pair of submachine guns, ammunition, and a stout wooden box filled with plastic explosives and fuses that had been requisitioned for the DSE operative in charge of the office in Biarritz and were properly receipted.

He read, "rsvp: Directorate Public Information, attn: Mr. Dellon, 69440 Lyon —12N—6p 12 Apr."

His letter should go in the Faverge postbox between noon and six on the twelfth. Carefully, he drafted his reply. Before a new parcel could be sent, he would need to recruit the recipient. Already, Albert Gola had received enough material, and more might raise questions at the post office.

He would go first to Nîmes, to see how hard a shell they had put around Nagy.

CHANTAL cradled his head in her arms, hugging him close to her. He loved this soft pressure, feeling her warmth, letting her touch speak instead of words.

The bed was small, but together like this their space was less than the bed's; they were contained by it.

They had slept, and her eyes had opened first—his first waking notions were the smooth arms of Chantal, her cheek against his forehead.

"You are awake," she said. "You are pretending to sleep."

He looked at her, grinned, and shut his eyes.

"I love you," she said.

His eyes reopened.

"Tell me again," he said.

"I love you."

"I love your voice when you say that," he replied.

"When we are quiet and together like this, you fill me with happiness. After losing everything, missing Noël, I am happy because of you."

He nuzzled her.

"Now we know about Arnaud. Will you tell me about Helen? . . ."

He sat up. He kissed her.

Chantal asked, "How much did you love her?"

"She thought I didn't love her enough."

"So, did you?"

"Maybe not enough. I don't know how to measure it. It cuts me in two to think that she is dead—is that a sign of love? When we first met—it was in Canada, skiing—she was the only woman in the group that shared our helicopter. She seemed so graceful and easy in her gestures, so confident, so extraordinary. From the first day, I was focussed on her, listening to her, watching her move— sometimes making a little accident to touch her, just to see if she was real. She was nice, not inflated by her skill or her looks. She told me later that she felt as though my eyes were lasers that were drilling holes in her. . . ."

"I know that feeling," Chantal said. "I had it the first time I saw your eyes."

"I was not the only one who noticed her. She was like a magnet for men. If anyone flattered her or gave her a lot of attention, she would act surprised, as if she appreciated it but did not believe it was for her. So she made herself seem quite natural without encouraging anyone, and I thought that I was just one of the crowd. But then, toward the end of the week, she let me know that I was . . . chosen. And then I saw her in New York a week after we got back, and I rearranged my life so that I could see her all the time. I was just moving back to France then, to start work on the computer."

She stopped him by squeezing his head. "How did she let you know that you were chosen?"

"She had come to Canada with another girl, and she told the other girl not to come back to their room until ten, and then she came for me. . . . She invited me to her bed."

"There were two girls? I thought she was the only girl in the helicopter with you."

"We were the fast group. The other girl was not as expert, and she skied with a slower group."

"You were lovers from the first week?"

"It was a rapid courtship."

"Continue ..."

"I had been working for Parallel Technologies, in the States, for almost ten years. My childhood was spent in France. I had friends in the government and the banks here, and I was ready for a more important assignment from the company. I won the contract from the French government for the Star, and then it followed that I should be in charge of the project. Helen fit right in. She liked living with me, and she said that the French Alps had the best skiing in the world. So we moved to France, and about a year later we were married. It was a good life for us. She was accepted by a few of the fine French wives of Paris, and men liked her company. We had many invitations, and in the winter we spent every weekend skiing in the Alps.

"But after a year and a half, she started to complain that I was not paying attention to her, that all my focus was on the Star. I guess it was true. She said that I did not look at her the way I looked at her when we first met, and I guess that was true, too. She was not a complaining kind of woman, and she told me these things as though she was talking about the rain. She started going on weekends by herself ... well, in fact, I sent her on weekends by herself because I was buried in the work on the Star. It was fascinating, you know, to put a whole nation on a single computer. Parallel Technologies had some patents that had solved the big problems, so I never had doubts. I knew the machine was going to work long before we ever put it into operation. But the mass of detail was overwhelming. The connections were so complex, the security so heavy, that as I let my mind travel deeper and deeper into the maze of the Star, time would pass unnoticed. I can remember not knowing when I had last seen my wife. She found Guillaume. He was a painter. Guillaume was good looking and truly funny. He could make anyone laugh. You remember him? ... He was in St. Tropez."

"No ... there were so many people there."

"I will tell you about Guillaume. One of Helen's women friends had a husband who was famous for his mistresses. The husband had designs on Helen, and when Helen wouldn't play, the wife became a friend. The wife wanted Guillaume for her own lover, probably to get even with her husband. That didn't work, because she introduced Guillaume to Helen, and Guillaume decided that he wanted Helen instead. So then Guillaume and Helen started spending weekends together, and I confess that I was glad. She was on an adventure with her romantic French painter, and at first she was happy. But the liaison wasn't perfect. After a while, she complained to me that Guillaume was too distracted to be any good in bed, and when the three of us were together— understand that he was a charming man, whom I liked very much—she would start to sulk if Guillaume and I became too amused by our conversation."

"It does not sound like love."

"Maybe not. I would suffer if I thought you were with another man, and I never suffered with Helen over Guillaume."

"What happened then?"

"The so-called revolution ... I learned what would happen after the World Peace Agreement, from my company in the United States. I only half believed it, but their predictions gave me fear, and were reason enough for me to prepare to control the Star. I was proud of what I had done with the Star; I could not leave my work to be exploited by a bunch of apparatchiks. And I believed that I could make a difference here, more than any Frenchman. I prepared this place, by myself, in total secrecy. No one knew, not even my closest associates. I had no idea how savage the revolution would be when it came ... that my friends, all my colleagues, would be rounded up and interrogated. If they could have given me away it might have saved some of them. . . . If I had known what they were going through, I would have come out. But I did not know until it was over, too late. That was a terrible thing. In the meantime, the New State thought that I had left France with Helen. I gave Guillaume my passport, and the two of them left France together. You remember, at that time all nationals were supposed to be repatriated to their own hemisphere, and here were two Americans going home. We were not too dissimilar in physique and age, Guillaume and me, and I am sure the frontier police were more interested in Helen than they were in her "husband." Guillaume had friends in Venezuela. He could be there now—I think that in South America they are less serious about the World Peace Agreement than in the United States. Helen ran for cover; it was obvious that they would use her if they could, to grab me. Even I did not know where Helen was, until the DSE found her in Annapolis and I read their report. And I called her to warn her, and they killed her. That's the story."

"What do you want, Robert?"

"I want to hurt the people who did these things. I want to put them out of the government and get a better one. I was ready to give up when I met you, but since then there have been . . . discoveries. I think that I can see a way. And if that doesn't work, I will spoil the Star and let the country sink into chaos and pray that the end is better than what we have today. That's what I want. Can you share that?"

She nodded. Tears were streaming down her cheeks, and Landry tried to imagine why.

THE hill was long and steep. He stood up over the pedals and pulled on the handlebars, sweating despite the chill in the early morning air. Jacques de Celigny cursed his physical condition as he adjusted his effort to reach the top, tempering the pain in his chest from unaccustomed hard breathing. His body needed work, more than the factory or the restaurant could provide. If he was going to lead, he had to be strong. The bicycle was all right, old but oiled and maintained. He had rented it from the railway at the station in Nîmes. Simple pleasures were not dead in France; a man could still go bicycling on his vacation, to enjoy the country byroads.

His eyes fixed on the crest of the hill, and he started to count the slow rotation of the pedals, putting aside the temptation to stop and walk. At seventy-seven turns, he had reached the top. He dismounted and walked the bicycle into the tall grass beside the road. The dry grass crackled under his feet. It was still too early in April for the lush new growth of spring.

Canopies of umbrella pines spread over the narrow road, camouflaging the surface with a panoply of shadows. Not a car had passed in twenty minutes, and he could hear no one coming.

He left the bicycle behind a bush and walked slowly away, stopping often to listen and observe, pushing through brambles and evergreen shrubs. One hundred meters from the road, he came to a break in the terrain where the hill dropped away below his feet.

Below him, neatly ordered in rows of barracks, a prison camp was laid out within the confines of a high wire fence. Two parallel rows of fence, about four meters apart, surrounded the camp. Light towers were positioned at each corner and at twenty meter intervals. A high watchtower was set in the center of the camp.

De Celigny sat, careful to hide his face, in the shadows of a leafy plant.

He spent the late morning counting guards, and then counting the trucks as they came back for lunch. It seemed that there were four work groups. The camp was small, not more than one hundred inmates and a dozen guards. The fields were all outside the perimeter fence. A power line fed electricity into the camp, a heavy black umbilical cord suspended from a series of poles that marched out to the road passing by the entrance.

Nagy's rescue should not be difficult, despite the reluctance of de Celigny's secret friend to mount an escape effort. Before the revolution or after, it was always the same with headquarters, doubts and explanations. In the next letter de Celigny would explain that the value of Nagy exceeded by far the minimal risk of getting him out.

De Celigny returned to the road, mounted his bicycle, and descended the hill. He pedalled slowly past the camp, following the paved road, remembering the dirt tracks that led off to the sides. Twice he passed groups of laborers tending the fields. He returned past the camp and climbed the hill, pedalling to the top, suffering, before he could glide downhill to Nîmes. He felt serene, at peace. He returned the bicycle and caught the next train to Marseille.

His old friends would be as happy as he to see Nagy.

* * *

ON the train from Marseille to Paris, de Celigny presented his cards for a random security check without a qualm. The policeman was not looking for trouble, was not looking for anything at all except an end to a boring day on the train. The cards were returned without a glance at de Celigny's face.

"Merci," de Celigny said. His cards were perfect, issued by the government with his most recent Albert Gola photo, although the name on the cards was not Albert Gola. The card contained all the internal magnetics and fluorescent markings that defeated counterfeiting. Three more sets of cards were in his knapsack, wrapped inside waxed paper in a large ham sandwich, each set with a computer-generated photo-image of its intended recipient. A miracle.

Twenty minutes after his arrival in Paris at the Gare de Lyon, he was walking along the quai beside the canal, which once had led barges as far as the Place de la République, and then underground all the way to the Seine. The canal was placid and oily, a black, slick slash through the city streets. Maurice Thevenet was living on the rue de la Grange, just off the canal.

De Celigny found the address and then found a brasserie nearby. He went inside and took a table where he could watch Thevenet's front door.

Thevenet had remained a policeman, assigned to the tenth arrondissement, where he now lived. De Celigny assumed that his old friend had lost any position of trust, that his rank had been reduced to the lowest rung, where his background with the former regime could make no difference.

De Celigny wondered if Thevenet was still living with the same woman. He hoped not; he remembered a fiery tempered Niçoise, whose passion for Thevenet was matched only by her jealousy.

A beer came.

He inhaled the foam off the beer.

The police station was five blocks away. If the police still worked on the pre-revolution schedule, Thevenet should be signing out now.

The brasserie started to fill with men coming from their day's work. De Celigny's back was to the entry, and he wondered if he could move to keep both the entry and Thevenet's doorway in sight. It was uncomfortable to have people moving in and out without being able to see them, but he decided to stay where he was.

The door to Thevenet's apartment was clearly in view across the road, blocked from sight only when a truck or van passed. The building looked poor, with paint peeling off the wooden molding around the door and the windows. An iron grillwork over the windows had left streaks of rust on the paint below the sills.

He waited.

A heavy woman with a shopping bag came down the street and turned into Thevenet's building. It was not Thevenet's Niçoise.

A hand gripped his shoulder. De Celigny froze.

"Old friend, it is good to see you," a soft, hoarse voice said in his ear. "You know there have been circulars out for you?"

De Celigny's head did not move.

"You came here for me?" the voice said.

De Celigny nodded.

"Come across to my place, five minutes after me. Apartment six . . ."

The hand was gone, and a minute later de Celigny watched his friend cross the street.

The apartment was tiny. The building had settled during the decades since it was built, and the movement had pulled apart the seams of its walls, ceiling, and floor in long cracks and zigzag fissures. The space was chaotic but clean. Pots and pans hung on a rack over the sink that shared the living space. De Celigny recognized a group photo that hung under glass on the wall. It would have to be destroyed, because it had a good likeness of Jacques de Celigny and Maurice Thevenet together, and even of Alphonse Euler. It had been taken of their group after a commendation from the minister for breaking a heroin operation.

"Where is your woman?" de Celigny asked.

"She works from noon until midnight."

They sat facing across a rickety gray-painted table. Thevenet had not changed in the two years since the revolution. The eyes were still bright, the movements still quick. He was a small man, and even seated, his head barely came up to the height of de Celigny's shoulder.

"I thought they had you," Thevenet said. "There was a big hunt for you and then nothing, so I thought they had succeeded. Your wife? . . ."

"They killed her trying to find me."

"Children? . . ."

"Taken."

"And now?"

"I am the hunter."

Thevenet's fingers drummed the table. His hands were delicate but strong, the veins standing out on white skin.

De Celigny studied him, waiting for his friend's mind to work. Thevenet's mind was like a sponge in a bucket, sopping up all that was around it. Sometimes it took time. It was better to let it work.

"Who do you hunt?"

"The men who killed some of our friends and put others in prison."

"There were many, with Russian tanks behind."

"I am not alone."

De Celigny knew his words were true, but he still felt baffled by his unknown allies.

"I am here," Thevenet said, "because I told them everything I knew about you. They spent a long time with me, and I did not resist."

"Of course. There was no reason not to tell them."

Thevenet stared at his friend and drummed the table with his fingertips.

"You have been to Alphonse?"

De Celigny shook his head. "You are the first."

"I see Alphonse often, every two or three weeks. The railroad is driving him mad."

"And you? How goes your career in the police?"

Thevenet did not answer.

De Celigny waited. He could remember waiting ten minutes or more for Thevenet to answer a simple question, and once waiting overnight.

The answer came out, when it came, without a pause. "My life has been a penance. Each day has been a punishment for not refusing them when they questioned me. There was nothing to give them that they did not already know, and I wanted to stay alive, and I talked and talked. I have paid since then, like a man burning in hell. When I saw the back of your head, it was a relief ... as though you had come back to redeem me. I think I have been waiting for you. What can we do together?"

"Alphonse?"

"He will be glad. We speak about you often. I know how he feels."

De Celigny took the sandwich out of his bag and opened it on the table in front of him. The waxed paper was nearly the color of the cheese in the sandwich and was smeared with white mayonnaise.

Unwrapped, the cards lay like casino chips on the table, waiting for the wheel to spin.

Thevenet's likeness was good, making it easy to find his identity card and his cash card.

Thevenet whistled, inspecting the cards, turning them edgewise and tilting them against the light.

"They are real," de Celigny assured him. "Everything on them is real except the name. It seems that the cash card has an unlimited balance behind it. Don't ask me how I got them or who made them, because I don't know."

Thevenet reached out for the cards with the moustached photo-image. "Alphonse," he breathed. "Extraordinary."

Thevenet's fingertips rubbed over the cards, feeling their presence. "With these, we are free," he said.

De Celigny nodded. "Take these cards for Alphonse. We three should meet soon, over a weekend in the south of France, but first I must ask if you can receive some parcels."

"The south of France?"

De Celigny pushed out the last card and wiped off some mayonnaise with his thumb. Thevenet's eyes widened, and he smiled again, a big grin.

"Nagy!"

"We will have a reunion, in the south of France."

IT would be child's play to help Marcel Chabon. Landry was amused that this task was beyond the computer experts of the New State. Chabon needed a relocation plan for a single State Factory in Angers. A pilot project. To each worker in this factory, Chabon wanted to offer a choice of the available jobs in France, with transportation and relocation. Or, the option of staying in the State Factory. Many might stay if the conditions were decent and the alternatives were less attractive.

In either case, the poor souls who had been redeployed would recover a small measure of freedom. Many could start to find an outlet for their abilities. It was not dramatic, but Landry asked himself if this was not the first step on the road back. Because of Chabon.

But Chabon would never get far, with Paccard set against him and the Russian holding France in a grip of iron.

How did the Russians feel about Chabon? Would he be accepted to take over, if the others were out of his way? Landry had daydreamed this, but now he was gathering both the character of the man and the means to put him in charge.

He had to go up to the surface to telephone Chabon.

9 Marcel Chabon listened to the voice and exulted. The man who was now hunted by every policeman in France was at the end of the line, like a wary trout coming to the fly.

"It can be done," the voice told him. "Give me a week, maybe a little more."

"You mean you can give choices for each worker in the factory? You can make a relocation plan for the workers who choose to leave?"

"Yes."

"Can we replace those who leave the factory?"

"If the pay is adequate, there are many around Angers who might like the factory better than farming."

"So . . . you will do it."

"Yes. We should put some distance between the source in the Star and your own people who will need to implement the plan. The official source of my work will be a bureau of the Department of Health and Education, located in the valley of the Loire. But don't thank the minister of health; the bureau will not exist."

"Then I should thank you. . . ."

"I have a question for you: will Paccard let you do this?"

Chabon hesitated. "Let me think how I should answer. . . . Paccard is against whatever I do. Paccard will make some trouble. But my success is my defense. The Russians like what I do because France does not need to import anything from them. The Russians understand that our State Factories are inefficient, that we must change, and that I must be in charge. Do you see?"

"But if you go too far . . ."

"I must be careful, of course."

"If you lead the French too far toward a normal life, don't you fear the Russians' intervention? Or should I speak of the Russian, singular."

Chabon took a deep breath. Landry was following logic. The answer must be logical, to wind in the lure.

"You speak of fear, and you are right. But I have no alternative. . . . I can only continue."

"If I gave you an alternative, Marcel Chabon? If Comrade Paccard was eliminated and the Russian was discredited, would the Russians choose you?"

"I think they would have to choose me. There is no one else who can run the government and the military, no one else with the strength or the name, and they know that—it is why Paccard worries about me."

"Would you be ready . . . If I was to take the necessary measures?"

"I would need to meet you."

"We will never meet: You will need to meet someone else, whom I will send. But I must ask you now, because it has worried me ever since they made you a minister in their New State—why did you agree to work with them?"

"Because I was the only hope for France, and I still am. Now let me ask you the same question. Why are you, an American, doing this?"

"Because I want to hurt the men who have caused so much hurt. And because I would like my machine to do the good it was intended to do."

"Well, enough then. We are allies. What will happen next?"

"I need to make arrangements. In the meantime, I will work on the pilot release program for your State Factory."

VALERIE Clavel, "Gentiane" in the labyrinth, had just enough space to sit, between two terminals and their attached gray boxes, in the tiny room she called her office. There was not room for two, so Max stopped at her door and watched her until she looked up and saw him.

"Good afternoon, comrade," she said, her fingers hovering over the keys of her computer. She was glad to see him; he was not often in the labyrinth, and his presence comforted her.

"It is already evening, Comrade Gentiane," he corrected her. "The time goes fast. What progress with our search for Robert Landry and Chantal Senac?"

"In Paris, the search plan is set and working now. We should be engaged throughout France by tomorrow night."

"Compliments," Max said. "You spent last night here?"

She nodded, admitting to herself that she was tired. She had slept three hours on a cot in the cafeteria. "There is so much to do."

"How long will it be before we have been in every residence and workplace in France?"

She made a mental calculation.

"Two hundred days, with all the manpower that we can provide. The police are crying; they say that we have ended all their other work until the search is over."

She added, "Paris can be finished in thirty days. And some places, like the Muslim parts of Marseille, we may not do at all."

"That is too long. But that is not why I came. You must add two other fugitives to your list. A policeman named Thevenet and a former policeman named Euler. Both of them worked years ago in a small special operations team. Does the name of Jacques de Celigny mean anything to you? He was the leader of the team. Later he was elected as a mayor and as deputy to the National Assembly. De Celigny is on the list of people we would still like to find. If the search net is out, we can look for these men as well as Landry and Chantal Senac."

Valerie nodded wearily. It seemed so strange. Instead of taking her place in a well-ordered organization, she had stepped into a mess of loose ends. And now, one day at a time, she was spinning out the strands, trying to tie them together.

She looked at Max for reassurance. He was calm, even cheerful. But she wondered if they were not destined to fail. . . . And then, what would happen to Valerie Clavel?

"You are tired," Max said. "I will call Morand about de Celigny and bring you the details in the morning."

That was wrong. If she seemed tired, it was a weakness. "It is my job to coordinate the search, and I should call Morand. Thank you, comrade, I will be glad to do it."

"As you wish. Good hunting, comrade."

She was loading information from the Star onto a tape. It was her daily task to load the tape cassette into a slot in the Russian-made Model Z90 and let the Russian machine distribute the newly entered files within Department 100. In this way, the Star could safely be used to communicate with Department 100. There was no way for data in the Z90 to enter the Star.

Habit already moved her fingers. When the spooling on and off was complete, she read from the screen. It was mostly mundane, repetitive stuff. But not the next item. Her eyes widened. The comrade first secretary wanted to speak to the Russian.

The Russian did not meet with anyone outside of the labyrinth or the security meeting.

Ten minutes later she was in the Russian's office.

"There is a communication from the comrade first secretary," she said. "He demands to see you."

His big head lifted, and his eyes settled on hers.

"Tell me," he invited.

She recited the message verbatim.

"Please go to Eyes' office and ask him to come back here with you. I must call our friends at the embassy."

Eyes' office was not far from the Russian's, but the twists and turns of the labyrinth and a series of code-locked doors made an obstacle course of the trip. Why didn't the Russian telephone Eyes to come? Valerie put the question aside and obeyed.

The Russian was talking to the embassy, speaking in Russian, when Valerie and Eyes returned.

". . . Then we agree. You spoke to him once at the beginning of this affair, and you should not speak to him again. I will send someone to him."

He listened.

"Of course."

The Russian put down the receiver and quickly explained the

embassy's advice. "Our friends think that exile for Leonid may be too visible ... too destabilizing. They are concerned about the troubles we have suffered, and now they do not want unnecessary problems. We need to offer an alternative that is equally firm, but within normal procedures. An interrogation by a tribunal, a secret trial. Our friends do not want to be involved: This is for us to settle with Paccard."

"If Morand kept the secret, Paccard should not know about the leak in the Star," Eyes said, thoughtfully phrasing his words. "But everyone in France knows about the search for Landry. Paccard may think it is a good moment to measure our strength, when we have other more important concerns."

"Who should go?" the Russian asked.

Valerie sensed Eyes' eyes on her.

The Russian continued, regret in his voice. "Daniel would have been my choice...."

"I have no one who can represent you," Eyes said. "It is Gentiane's responsibility to act as your messenger."

The Russian nodded.

So, she thought, it comes so fast—my first task of great responsibility.

The Russian looked from her to Eyes and back again.

"Paccard might use her as a hostage for Leonid," Eyes added. "But I do not believe it is likely."

"She might simply fail to deliver a clear message," the Russian said. "Or she might fail to understand the response."

She interrupted. "Please let me do it. I will not disappoint you."

They did not answer, and she feared that she had spoken out of turn.

Eyes broke the silence.

"We can send someone from Action Branch with her."

"Which one?" the Russian asked.

Eyes said, "Kimba, if Max agrees."

The Russian frowned. "Kimba is not subtle."

"He will convey an unspoken message to Paccard, to balance Gentiane's youth."

The Russian looked at his aide and said, "We cannot let

you fail. We must prepare you for every possibility at the meeting."

They told her the history of the Paccard affair and made her repeat back the details: the two missing girls, presumed murdered; the man Mounier, erased; the way the investigation had foundered in a morass of supposition that only Leonid could explain.

The Russian ended with instructions to his aide. "Go send a message to the first secretary, Gentiane. Tell him that Department 100's representative will be in his office at ten o'clock in the morning. Then finish your work and come back. You will need to rehearse your role."

From her office, Valerie sent the message. She then called Hubert Morand, the minister of the interior, and asked him to add Jacques de Celigny, Alphonse Euler, and Maurice Thevenet to the search list. She completed her daily routine with a mixture of impatience to be finished and anticipation for the job ahead.

The Russian was waiting alone when Valerie came back to his office. They talked about Georges Paccard, the man she would confront. The Russian spoke of the first secretary with scorn—for his vanity, his ceremonies, his swelling bureaucracy of sycophants, his precious Parade Guards always on display. Paccard's only principle was the principle of power.

They discussed the tactics that Paccard might take, as bully, as suppliant, as insulted dignitary, as a friend of Moscow.

She repeated the message, and then the Russian played the role of Paccard. She answered easily, because the logic was simple: the purity of the revolution was more important than any man, the comrade first secretary needed to keep his good name above criticism for the sake of the revolution.

There was skill in the Russian's role playing. If he was not satisfied with her responses, he would push her for better words, so that she would react naturally under stress.

She could say nothing about force. But the threat of force should hover, unspoken.

When he was satisfied that she was ready, he asked her if she was hungry.

She wanted to go home and sleep, but she could not refuse any gesture from the Russian. She nodded.

"Come," he said.

He led the way through the door in the wall behind his desk. She had never been through that door. Following him, she stepped into a corridor lined with shiny steel plates, unpainted and welded at the seams. The corridor turned after thirty paces and ended at a blank steel door without hinges, locks, or handles. It opened with a squeak as they approached, and then they went through a series of steel doors, four in all, each opening and closing automatically.

Behind the last steel door was one panelled in rich dark wood, and he turned an ordinary knob to open it. She followed him inside.

Lights went on, although he did not touch a switch. She stood still, just over the threshold, while he walked toward the kitchen that opened off the main room to her right.

"Would you like an aperitif?"

"I have some excellent white wine, Corton Charlemagne from before the revolution."

"I would like that."

Fine Oriental rugs in dark red and blue covered the floor. On the walls was a tan canvaslike fabric. Old-fashioned gilt frames held antique engravings of game birds in flight, and an oil painting of hanging rabbits, pheasants, and quail. A dark brown leather couch faced a fireplace in the wall across the room, and Valerie caught herself wondering what convolutions and barriers led the chimney up from the flue to the ground above. An amply proportioned leather easy chair and two cushioned wooden chairs completed the seating. Against the walls there were two great dark chests of drawers and a bookcase with glass doors.

The wall to the left of the door was formed of vertical louvers, closed, their stark white out of keeping with the traditional decor. To the right, opposite the louvers, was a counter, with an opening that led into the small kitchen. She could see pots and pans hanging from hooks on the wall, the burnished copper gleaming.

A closed door, made of fine old wood, faced them in the opposite wall. She tried to guess whether the bedroom was behind the door or behind the louvers.

He came to her, extending a flute glass of vivid yellow wine.

"You cook for yourself?" she asked.

"I have no servants."

"Can I ask you about this place, and how you live?"

"Please."

She sipped the wine. It was delicious, a big taste in her mouth, unlike any liquid she had ever known.

"The corridor outside was built by Russians, no?"

"Yes."

"But, your apartment? It was not made by Russians."

He smiled and held up his two hands. "By this Russian Frenchman. I received some help from close friends."

"Do people come here?"

"Sometimes. Good friends in our organization."

"Women? . . . Forgive me."

"No. You are the first." He turned toward the kitchen. "I intend to make a salad and a venison steak. There is enough for two. Will that please you?"

"Very much."

"Do you like old Bordeaux wines? I have a fine old bottle of Lafite-Rothschild that I must open to let breathe."

"I know nothing of wine. You must teach me."

His head bent in acknowledgment.

"May I ask you about your life before the revolution?" she asked. Even a little knowledge could give her an advantage.

"I think it would be better to wait," he replied. "I will tell you that I have a wife and child. They both believe that I am dead. It was impossible for me to share my work with them. I miss them a great deal, but we should not speak of it."

He looked so sad, saying these words; she understood that he would be glad to find some comfort.

She said, "Then you are truly alone here."

"No," he answered. "I have my five companions. Turn around."

She followed his gaze and gasped. Five people were staring at her, immobile, accusing, from behind the opened louvers.

But they were not people. She saw that they were sculpted figures, larger than life size, their sightless eyes directed at her.

She had spilled some of the wine. She put the glass down on
the top of the bookshelf and turned to him, putting her arms on
his shoulders, and she gently leaned against his massive body.

"You frightened me."

He did not embrace her, but he did not push her away. His
arms held her waist, and he pulled his head back so that he could
see her face.

"These are the work of a friend who lived in Russia. They are
my companions, representing the people I serve. Each day I open
the wall and let them remind me."

"Who is your friend?"

"He took a wrong turn and died in a prison of the KGB. It is a
sad story."

She looked at the pieces behind the open louvers. Their eyes
were like dead lamps. In the center stood a gaunt man, his right
arm outstretched, with a woman leaning into him for support. A
girl was standing free, and two children stood beside the woman.
They were neither naked nor clothed, but outlined in an abstract
between the two, calling out in silent loneliness.

"He questioned the revolution's progress in Russia," she said.

"I am glad that I don't need to explain."

She embraced him, pulling her body against his.

He returned a pressure around her waist and then took his
hands away.

"I did not bring you here for this. I thought you would be hungry."

"I am," she said. She wanted to have him. She tried to think of
food. "But let me cook for you."

"I will do it. I like to cook."

She sat at the small table in the center of the kitchen and
watched him in silence. His hands were sure and strong, his
movements economical.

The venison was delicious, pink inside and pungent with
gamey flavor, graced by a few fresh green string beans. The wine
was extraordinary, its round, dark taste almost too strong for her,

but it matched the venison. It was a man's meal.

They finished the bottle with some heavy yellow cheese, Tomme de Savoie. Valerie wiped her lips with the linen napkin.

"I want to sleep with you," she said.

He looked down at the last of the wine in his glass.

"Some day, when the revolution is safe, I will be able to live again with my wife and son."

"Let me love you. You will not be the first that I have loved and lost."

He looked at her, his eyes steady and sad. "I am responsible for you."

"Yes."

"I might need to ask you to die for me."

She nodded.

"Or, not even ask."

"I understand."

She stood up. "Is this the bedroom?"

"Yes. . . . So, I am seduced."

He was gentle and efficient, without passion, and she worked to have him please her. The best time was after he had collapsed beside her, and she could press herself against his mass and warmth. She bathed in her victory and slept, her head against his shoulder.

They woke early. He scrambled eggs for her and made toast in an old-fashioned toaster with flat metal sides that folded away from the heating element. He gave her fresh oranges to squeeze for juice and had to show her how; in her family they had never squeezed fresh oranges. The coffee was hot and strong, with heavy cream floating at the top.

"You will corrupt me with toast and orange juice," she told him, smiling.

"We will not be corrupted if we can find a way for everyone to share."

She looked to see if he was serious. He was, but then he smiled at her.

"We should always be glad to enjoy simple pleasures. You have given me great pleasure, Valerie, even before this night."

He had used her real name. It could work well, she thought, with this strange man. He might even start to love her.

"Tell me about your lover in Moscow," he asked.

He was looking down at his plate.

"He was my lover, and then it ended."

"Did you love him?"

"I thought that I should, but no, I did not."

"Did you sleep with his friends?"

She thought her heart would stop. He knew, his connections had told him. It was a test.

"Yes," she said.

"How many?"

"At least two, but a third one came to me in a mask. He could have been one of the two."

"Were you frightened?"

"No, they wanted to possess me, not to hurt me."

He nodded.

"How did you know?" she asked. It was fair to ask, even if he would not say.

"They say it gives them more power over a female asset if there is more than one involved in the seduction. I think it is nothing more than perverse carnal lust. Who is your control?"

"A man calling himself Pyotr. It is not his name."

"You met him?"

"Twice. He is older, older than you by ten years. Very pale, thin, with thin gray hair that is white over the temples. He acts tough, without any politeness to me."

"How do you make contact?"

"Normally by telephone, on my way home from work, each sixth day."

"What have you told him of your new work."

She started to feel frightened.

"Everything."

"It is all right," the Russian said. "You should continue to tell him everything. I would like to speak with you before each call, to be sure that your messages to him are clear. You are in a game with some danger, and we should be careful to keep you safe."

She nodded. He had taken control of her life. Now she would need to win it back.

He carried the plates and cups to the kitchen sink, and returned to stand behind her. He put his hands on her shoulders and let them slide down to cup her breasts.

"Would you like to go back to bed?" he asked. "We have time before you go to see Paccard."

EYES was at the door, with the special agent who would accompany her to the first secretary.

Valerie understood why Kimba was not "subtle." He was over two meters tall, thick and round like a column, his arms folded akimbo over his chest. His eyes were lost in a fold of fatty tissue under densely matted black eyebrows. A scowl line creased his brow, and his fatty lips were drawn down in an expression of permanent dislike. Uncombed, his black hair had clotted together in places. Still, his attire was proper for a visit of state, a plain dark blue suit with a matching navy blue necktie neatly knotted under the clean white collar of his shirt. Only the heavy shoes distracted from his correct costume. Still, his size and his angry face outweighed all other impressions.

Kimba greeted Valerie with a smile that distorted his features into true ugliness, but he did not speak.

The Russian spoke. "We are sending Kimba with you as a symbol of our capacity to act. Normally, Kimba is a man of few words, and in this case, he should have nothing at all to say. His instructions are to ensure that you return safely here."

Eyes added, "In your discussion with the first secretary, you should look from time to time at Kimba. When you do, he will smile. For some reason, his smile makes people nervous."

Kimba smiled again, with horrific effect.

The Russian continued. "The show of force must be sufficient. We must not threaten, but the comrade first secretary must respond."

"Paccard will not make trouble even if he knows about our

problems," Eyes said, "unless my understanding of his personality is incorrect."

KIMBA led Valerie out of the labyrinth by a long passageway, through a pair of locked doors marked "Danger of Death" with skull-and-crossbones over another legend that said "High Voltage." A second door opened into a subterranean public garage. Their car, a small red Renault from before the revolution, was parked with many others. After a moment to change the license plate on the back, Kimba drove. His suit gave off a musty smell of camphor mixed with mildew. She welcomed the light of day as they emerged from the ramp to the surface, and she was surprised to see that they were at the Pont Marie, on the Right Bank, far from the labyrinth.

On this early April day, a mist shrouded the city, a veil of moisture hanging in the air, translucent, almost golden where the sun's rays had penetrated. Facing them, the soft light washed a muted harmony of color over rows of narrow house fronts on the picturesque island of St. Louis. These were once the most expensive residences in Paris.

They crossed the island to the Left Bank and drove along the Seine, past the cathedral of Notre-Dame, glowering in the mist, her bell towers lost in shards of gray cloud. They passed the kiosk that served as Valerie's normal entry point into the labyrinth, passed the Pont Neuf, and continued along the Seine, which was hardly visible through the stone balustrade that edged the river rampart. They turned toward the first secretary's residence, the Matignon Palace, tucked back in an austere maze of public buildings converted from private mansions of the eighteenth and nineteenth centuries. Valerie took a deep breath and tried to make her mind go blank. She was rehearsed, ready. Now her only foe was excitement, her best ally the calm that she was forcing on herself.

Ten minutes later, a Parade Guard raised the barrier that separated the rue de Varenne from the courtyard of the Matignon. They drove under the gatehouse arch, and the tires crunched on the fine pebbles in the courtyard. There was an arcade on either side, and the fine broad façade of the palace was directly ahead. High glass windows looked out on the courtyard, giving openness and light to the neoclassical mass of the building.

The high door was guarded by two more Parade Guards, in gleaming plated tunics and black pants with lavender stripes up the sides. Beyond the door, a male secretary awaited her.

While her presence was announced, Valerie gazed calmly at the giant portrait of Lenin on the wall behind the desk, flanked with portraits of Joux and the man she was about to meet, Paccard.

She was dressed for a formal meeting with the first secretary. Her tailored black suit buttoned up to the collar of a dark blue shirt; a red enamelled star set in gold was pinned to her lapel as the only touch of color. She wore no other jewelry. Her makeup was too discreet to be noticed, and her thick hair was pulled back tight into an austere chignon.

She felt taut, alert, but not nervous. Her skin was dry, and her lips were moist. She smiled at Kimba and watched the male secretary cringe as Kimba smiled back at her.

Another pair of Parade Guards came through a door to the left. They were big and hard looking, with submachine guns on slings over their shoulders.

"You will go with them," the male secretary said.

Valerie and Kimba followed.

In an anteroom, the guards stopped them and patted them down. Valerie relaxed under the touch of the guard's palms, even when he pressed into the cloth of her skirt between her knees. She wondered if Kimba carried a weapon, but he passed as clean.

A side door opened, and a colonel in dress uniform looked in at them. His face seemed made of wood, and there was a deep scar on his left cheek. He shut the door without speaking.

They were walked through a metal detector and into an elevator up to the floor above.

The first secretary was sitting behind his enormous antique desk, his back to the window that overlooked the palace gardens. He rose to his feet on seeing Valerie and came from behind the desk.

"Please wait outside," he told the guards.

He extended his hand, and Valerie took it. Faced with the man who was placed at the top of the party, she realized that she had underestimated him. He was both older and more alive than his official portrait. His features were active even in repose. Hardly hearing his greeting, she told herself: watch out.

"I decided to receive you alone," Paccard said. He glanced at Kimba, who smiled in response. Paccard showed no reaction to the smile, and again, Valerie cautioned herself. There was more to the man than she had been led to believe.

"Your bodyguard should wait outside," Paccard said.

"My instructions are to remain with my colleague at all times."

"You are frightened by me?" Paccard's expression claimed a small victory.

She refused to let him have it. "No, of course not. Kimba, you may wait outside."

They waited while the giant strode through the doors, which swung closed with a sepulchral thud.

"Would you care to sit down?"

She sat, facing the desk, primly crossing her legs.

The first secretary sat on the corner of his desk, so that he was looking directly down at Valerie, his face only a meter away from hers.

"Have you worked for Department 100 a long time, comrade?"

"My identity and all matters concerning Department 100 are protected, comrade first secretary. With all respect, I may not answer your question."

"You seem very young . . . to bear such a responsibility for your chief."

"He asked me to express his personal regret that policy does not permit him to be here."

"Of course. He is the man they call the Russian, no?"

"With all respect . . ."

"Of course, of course, you may not say. Well then, how may we discuss if you cannot speak?"

"I may speak. If the matter concerns Comrade Leonid Paccard, I have precise instruction. If the matter is something else, I will go back to Department 100 and return with instructions."

"What are your instructions?"

"The matter does concern Comrade Leonid Paccard?"

"It concerns the office of the first secretary."

Valerie waited for him to explain.

"My son's departure for Gabon is already starting to cause talk," Paccard said softly, as though to keep the words close between them. "Everybody in the government knows that Leonid is being punished, and since they do not know why, all sorts of rumors are flying. It is causing a loss of prestige for my office. Your actions are weakening the authority of my government."

"What is your proposal?" She put the words bluntly, as though to an equal.

"To drop the matter. Leonid has suffered enough over a minor matter that should never have involved your organization."

"We do not agree that it is a minor matter. My chief has already explained his concern. There can be no corruption here. Our people must not believe that some of us have special privilege above the law."

The first secretary laughed, a bitter, short bark. "The people will believe that, in any case, because it is true."

"The greatest security for the New State is in the ideals of the revolution. Our task is to preserve those ideals."

Paccard laughed again, and the bark burst from his throat like a belch. "You believe that?"

"Absolutely."

His head bent toward her, his expression intent.

"Listen, my dear, if we all practice perfect chastity, there will be no future for the human race."

"That is not a defense for Leonid. . . ."

He straightened up, as though she had slapped him.

"Forgive me, comrade first secretary. Let me return to the question about your son. We agree that your personal reputation and the strength of your office are vital to France. . . ."

"That is useful."

"We give you another proposal. Instead of an interrogation by our service, we suggest that Leonid submit to questioning by a tribunal. Let a tribunal determine what has happened to Mireille Dupont."

"What would the tribunal decide?"

"They would be told to judge fairly, based on what they might learn."

"Have we found any trace of the girls? Would you expose my son to a charge of murder?"

"Only if he was guilty. We presume that your son is innocent. If he will submit to the tribunal, we may soon be confirmed."

The first secretary's eyes narrowed as he turned over the possibilities.

"Who would select the tribunal?"

"The tribunal would be chosen in the usual way, by the normal rotation of the criminal court in Paris."

"The Russian would not choose them?"

"My department would only ensure the absence of . . . influences."

Paccard nodded. He bent his head again, to be close to the girl's.

"So, if there are no . . . influences, you will be satisfied when the tribunal absolves my son?"

"Of course."

"And when should this procedure take place?"

"As soon as the court's schedule permits. . . ."

"The hearings would be secret, of course."

"Yes."

"And if I refuse?"

"Exile . . . Gabon."

"And if I refuse that as well?"

"If you refuse to act, you take personal responsibility for Leonid's safety."

"Are you threatening his safety? Treason?"

She did not answer.

"I need some time to decide."

"My instructions are to return with your decision."

This was the moment. If she was simply sent home, she had failed. She would not leave without an answer.

The first secretary stood up from the desk and walked to his window. He remained for a moment with his back to her, and then he turned.

"The tribunal it is," he said.

She rose to her feet, smoothed her skirt, and bowed her head to her first secretary.

"I will report your decision," she said.

"Tell the Russian he is not the choice of the French Communist party, nor was he made first secretary by the Russians he serves. He should not add to his present difficulties, which are as well known to me as they are to the Russians."

"I will report your words."

She bowed again, turned, and walked to the door. She could not wait to report. Victory.

Paccard stepped to his desk and pushed a button to release the door.

As Valerie disappeared, Paccard's colonel of the Parade Guards materialized from the side door.

"It is done," the colonel said.

"And now they will come out," Paccard said. "Now they must come out."

VALERIE looked for Kimba outside the doors to the first secretary's office, but the marbled hall was vacant. Even the two guardsmen were gone. She went to the elevator and descended.

"Where is my colleague?" she demanded of the male secretary at the entrance.

"In your car. He waits for you."

She went out the door and down the steps. She could see Kimba's head, oddly enough in the passenger seat, oddly tilted, oddly still.

Too still.

She knew he was dead before she pulled open the door, and she braced herself, but all her self-control could not prepare her for the shock. They had broken his neck then put him in the seat, reclining the back of the seat so that his bulk would not fall forward. His great head had lolled off the headrest, dangling to the side like a boar's head in a butcher shop. The eyes stared up at the roof of the car with a sadly tired expression.

Her knees sagged. She gripped the open door while she regained her strength. She knew they were watching her; she could not yield.

She reached in, released the seat back, and let it fall all the way to the rear under the weight of the corpse, then took the head with both hands and put it on the headrest. The skin was still warm. She shut Kimba's eyes. She was angry now, furious, because she had failed.

Or, had she . . . ?

She slammed the door shut, wheeled on her heel, and went back into the Matignon. The Parade Guards at the entrance let her pass.

"Call the comrade first secretary," she told the male secretary.

"He is occupied."

"Call him. I must know if he intends to keep his agreement with me."

"Wait here."

The man stood up and walked away, through a door.

She was alone.

Three minutes, maybe more, passed as a fury of thoughts raged in her head. She would not, she could not go back to the labyrinth with a corpse and nothing clear.

A colonel came through the door, the same officer with the scarred cheek who had stared at them when they were waiting to see the first secretary.

"What do you wish?" he asked. His face twisted as he spoke, so that the right side could form the words without help from the left.

"I wish an explanation. . . . I wish a confirmation from the first secretary of his agreement with me."

"Your colleague fell on the steps. . . . We put him in the car for you."

"I must see the first secretary!"

"That won't be necessary. His agreement is firm. He will submit Leonid to a tribunal."

She stared at him.

"Tell your master," he went on, "that he should send no more of his thugs to the Matignon. . . ."

The colonel stepped forward and, without touching her, guided her out the door. When they were outside, he said, in a low voice, "I am Colonel Yves Morot. I question the plans of the first secretary. . . . Tell your master that if you had come alone, we would have sent your body to him, instead of that one. Be careful . . . we do not need a fight."

She drove by reflex, trying to balance the cadaver in the seat beside her against the words that had passed between her and the first secretary, as equals in power, and against the confession of the colonel, as an equal in collusion. She told herself that she had won what she came for and had found a crack in the armor of the Parade Guards. She had survived a brush with death. She had lost a man. It was a trade that she would accept at any time.

EYES stood in front of the Russian's desk, facing the Russian and Valerie. His perpetual scepticism had turned sour on his face. His shoulders sagged as round as his steel-rimmed glasses. His jowls squeezed full over his collar under the downward pressure of his chin.

His head was shaking slowly in disbelief.

Standing beside the Russian, her arms clasped tight to her chest, Valerie stared at the head of Intelligence Branch and was glad. It was he, not she, who had failed.

"Nothing in our analysis suggested such a reaction," Eyes said, still shaking his head. "We have two assets in the Parade Guard. . . . They report more emphasis on ceremony than on combat training. The first secretary himself has always been a politician. . . ."

"We squeezed him too hard, and he decided to bite," the Russian said.

"He is not soft," Valerie added, her voice low but under control. "We should not think he is weak."

The Russian put his palms down on the desk in front of him and studied the face of Eyes. What could be said about magic that did not work? Comrade Paccard had been painted as an accommodator, in love with his status, incompetent as an administrator, too narrow to anticipate events, too unsure to act. The Parade Guard was an ornament, all spotless uniforms and rigid posture on parade. But these supposed show puppets had killed one of his best men, in silence, without leaving a mark.

"Gentiane, please call Max," the Russian said. "We need his counsel."

Max normally worked outside the labyrinth. Valerie went to her cubicle and rang on the secure line that went straight to his desk.

He answered on the first ring. "Please wait," he said, and Valerie could hear him speaking to someone in his office, "... this call will be important; may I ask that we end our meeting? I think you understand your task ahead."

Seconds passed while Valerie imagined a civil servant gathering his papers and leaving Max's office.

"Go ahead," Max said into the phone.

"This is Gentiane," Valerie said. "Karel asks you to come."

"What happened?"

"Leonid Paccard will go before a tribunal. But we lost Kimba. They killed him."

Silence. Then, "I will be there in fifteen minutes."

He came into the Russian's office with his raincoat still on, and as he slipped it off his shoulders and shook away the drops, he looked into her eyes, seeking signs of shock or stress, she supposed. Valerie returned his gaze, tranquil. It was Eyes who had made the mistake.

"Repeat again what happened at the meeting," the Russian said.

For the second time, Valerie recounted the meeting, from the beginning to the finish in front of the Matignon Palace.

Max turned red. "They must pay," he said. "We must find out which of them killed Kimba, and then we must take those men. So they will know."

Max looked at the Russian for affirmation, but the Russian showed no expression at all, as though he had not heard.

"Find out," Max said to Eyes.

Eyes seemed pained. "I will try. Now I don't know if I trust our assets in the Parade Guards. Give me a day, maybe two, to find out which of them killed our man."

He clearly wanted to leave, and the Russian nodded.

At the door, Eyes paused. "My compliments on your courage, Comrade Gentiane, you have earned my respect."

"Thank you," she acknowledged.

They sat in silence for minutes after Eyes' departure. The Russian leaned back in his chair and looked up at the ceiling. When he spoke, it was into the air, as though he were alone.

"Living here, cut off, depending on the reports and opinions of people I hardly know, how can I be accurate? This failure is mine. I decided to send a second man, thinking that a reinforcement would make Gentiane more credible. That was a mistake. Gentiane should have gone alone, and the result would have been good."

Valerie started to interrupt him, but the Russian was continuing his monologue. "I think we would be wrong to start a vendetta. We are supposed to guard the security of the revolution, not tear it apart. If Leonid Paccard submits to the tribunal, we have won a small advance for the revolution."

"And if not?" Max was trying to contain his anger.

"If Leonid Paccard does not live up to his father's promise, there should be action."

Valerie started to speak. "There is more to report," she said. "The colonel who is responsible for the Parade Guards . . . he spoke to me, at the end. He said that they would have killed me if I had gone alone. The first secretary wanted them to kill somebody from the labyrinth."

She had their attention—the Russian and Max stared at her while she continued. "The colonel says that First Secretary Paccard intends to bring us into a fight."

Her eyes moved from face to face. The Russian's impassivity gave no clue to his thinking. Maybe he had no ideas. Max seemed at sea. Valerie wondered if they were strong enough, these two most powerful men in France, to survive a real fight.

The Russian was in a war, and he did not seem to understand.

She wondered who would win.

She wondered what it would mean for her.

THE woman's face mirrored his image of Marie Gaultier, but the great, pendulous breasts and muscular legs came surging up from the depths of primeval memory. Her silken skin pressed softly down on him, and he stirred onto his side, willing away his erection. Floating almost to the surface of wakefulness, he recalled the real Marie Gaultier, who had once shared his bed when he had just come out of the academy, until she had said that he was too strange and too quiet and had left him to live with a bartender. Often he dreamed of this lascivious Marie that he had never known, her body as ripe and smooth as a primitive fertility figure. Sometimes he would wake to an orgasm, and he would curse the creature for spoiling his perfect solitude. Now, he slipped back again into sleep, and when he started to dream again, he dreamed, as he did almost every night, of Jacques de Celigny.

The dream of Jacques de Celigny made him smile in his sleep. It was a dream of the best years, when he had first learned to understand his own gifts, before Jacques became a politician. In the dream, he was running ahead, finding his way out of sight of the enemy. Sometimes his pursuit would end in his enemy's bloody death, sometimes a death of quiet hands, and sometimes they would surrender, cowering under his gun, but they never escaped. De Celigny would come, moustache bristling in triumph, and shake his hand or squeeze his shoulder, filling him with joy.

This morning, when the prison guards came into the barracks with the loudspeaker to call them awake, the static-burred noise scraped him up to consciousness without a scrap of his dream intact. Charles Nagy rose and dressed with thirty-five other men in one of the steel-walled barracks buildings of State Farm Camp

241. He neatly folded the rough blanket on his cot and went out to take the communal breakfast of bread and hot broth.

Nagy always carried his tray to the same seat, at the end of a bench in the back of the building they used for meals. A sullen man named Jean-Marie always sat beside him. They never spoke. Nagy had resisted the pull of fellowship that bound the prisoners together. He hated the camp and everything about it, and he could not bear the sense of belonging there in any way.

All morning, they worked in ancient untilled fields to prepare the dense sod for planting. It was stupid work with primitive hoes and picks, tearing out the matted roots of the natural dry grass, hacking their way down to the sandy loam underneath. Machines could have done the work in a tenth the time, but there were no machines, and the labor was cheap.

The day was decent, brisk but not too cold. A man could keep warm by digging, and Nagy did not mind the exercise. His slender physique had always been stronger than it looked.

At noon, the bus came to take them back for lunch, the guards howling at the workers through loudspeakers: "Hurry up and board the bus."

Lunch was a soup of canned spinach and bits of pork.

Twenty minutes to eat, and the loudspeakers ordered them out, to line up for a head count before reboarding the buses.

Nagy knew the camp to the last strand of barbed wire, and he sensed something odd the moment he stepped out into open air.

Two steps, and he could see the reason. A van was stopped at the front gate, and three men were talking to the guard there. One of the men was holding papers out for the guard to read. The guard was shaking his head.

Nagy did not blink, but his blood pounded up into his temples.

The man with the papers was Jacques de Celigny. Maurice Thevenet was beside him, and on the other side of the van, half hidden, Nagy recognized the bulk and the moustache of Alphonse Euler.

As the head count ended and the prisoners started to file onto the bus, Jacques de Celigny folded his papers and yielded to the guard. State Farm Camp 241 was a vegetable farm; it raised no pigs, and therefore the document requisitioning a pig was in error, no matter if it did come from the prefect with an endorsement from the army.

Nagy rode out to the fields with the certainty that they had come for him. They had come to the gate to be seen, and they had known that he could do the rest. He could.

The prisoners marched from the bus, single file into the field, and picked up their hoes and picks where they had left them. Nagy worked now in a diagonal with his pick, and when he came to the edge of the field, he worked his way forward toward a stand of trees.

He knelt down, as though to wrestle with a stone, and looked for the guards. There were three. One stood by the bus, at the edge of the dirt road that had brought them from the camp. One stood at the far corner of the field. The third stood in the center. All carried submachine guns on shoulder slings, and the rules were clear: bullets for any prisoner outside the border of the field.

Nagy concentrated first on the guard by the bus. That one was fifty yards away and the most difficult to sense. Then, still crouching, Nagy turned to face the guard at the far corner. Finally, he looked right into the eyes of the guard in the center of the field.

And then, he stood up and walked away into the trees.

As soon as he was in the trees, he started to run in an easy loping gait that carried him swiftly away from the field.

De Celigny had come for him! He ran on a cloud, his feet floating over the lumps and holes in the forest floor.

They would miss him as soon as they counted heads again, and they did that often, at least every thirty minutes. It would take a little time to drive back to the camp, to organize a search. Enough time for him to make contact with his friends, to get away before the roads were blocked.

At the main road, he turned away from the camp and ran along the shoulder, listening for traffic. As he ran, he spied a man approaching on a bicycle.

He immediately recognized de Celigny as the rider, and he ran on until they met.

"Hello, Nagy." A big smile, and the moustache turned up with pleasure.

"Hello, Jacques."

"Go into the woods here. We will come back for you."

De Celigny pedalled away, and Nagy dove into the leafy undergrowth.

Fifteen minutes later, they were in the van, heading north on the narrow road that led into the desolate high country of the Causses. Alphonse Euler drove, with Thevenet in the right-hand seat. De Celigny sat behind with Nagy and the bicycle.

"They will call for help," Nagy said.

"We cut their power line. Do they have a radio that runs on batteries?"

"I don't think so. No, I am sure they do not."

"They will need to drive to a telephone. The nearest one is twenty minutes away. We have a good start. You did well, Nagy. We were sure that you had seen us at the camp, and we thought that you would come out to the road. And if you had not come, we would have gone in to bring you out. We were prepared for that."

"You have weapons?"

"We are well prepared. We even have a toy for you."

De Celigny beckoned, and Thevenet produced a stubby little pistol, an old Walther P.38. Nagy reached out and took it, extracted the clip to be sure it was loaded, put the clip back in, and then shoved the weapon into his waistband.

"Here is your new identity; if we are stopped you will need to show these." De Celigny gave him an identity card, a work permit, and a cash card. "And we have some clothes for you."

Nagy turned the card with his photo this way and that in his hand, trying to catch the changing light on his likeness.

"I am free."

"Well, we have some work for you. But you will enjoy it better than farming, I think."

They drove until it turned dark and then through the night, winding up a narrow road into the Causses, a series of plateaus north of Nîmes.

The Causses dwarfed anything in human scale. The ground there was desert dry because the limestone underneath was so porous that it would not hold water. Below, the downward flow of water from the surface had carved caverns and grottoes and sliced great canyons that divided the plateaus like slashes in the crust of a pie. The Causses had always been impossible to farm or graze because of the thirsty limestone substrate, a territory abandoned except for speleologists and the occasional romantic in search of isolation.

They sped across the high, barren flats and wound their way down into the plunging gorges, only to climb again, Euler cranking the wheel on the hairpins.

They passed through dark villages in the ravines, where the racing water flowing out of the caves and subterranean rivers made habitation possible. Dizzily they laced their way down and up, letting the motor scream on the flat heights to speed across a dozen kilometers, and then repeating the tire-squealing descent and tortuous climb.

After midnight, they took a side road to a place where de Celigny had waited, five years before, for ten fruitless days in hopes that a bank robber from Clermont-Ferrand would go to ground there. The bank robber had never come, had run to Spain and South America instead, but de Celigny had always remembered the place for its lonely beauty. There was a shed to hide the two cars that would replace their truck, and an abandoned farmhouse to provide shelter. On the way from Albertville, they had stopped here to be sure it was safe and had left the cars, water, and food.

De Celigny felt a smile tugging at the corners of his mouth. With Nagy at his side, the team was ready to work.

10

It was a time to be anxious, a day that might decide the future, for himself, for Chantal, possibly for France.... But he felt only anticipation.

Here in Albertville, at the foot of the French Alps, the air filled his lungs with a purity and freshness Paris never knew. The mid-morning sun, a disc of white gold, brilliant in the deep-blue sky, brought instant warmth, but in the shadows of the plantain trees the air was still cold. So he was walking through a checkerboard of temperatures, comfortably warm, refreshingly cool.

The city was an urban center for the surrounding mountains of the French Alps, at the confluence of the Arly and the Isère, fast-moving torrents that carry snowmelt out of the massifs of Mont Blanc, the Tarentaise, and the Vanoise.

Landry had come to Albertville because it was the home of Jacques de Celigny.

His cleanshaven jaw made him think of himself as Robert Landry, not as any of his other identities, always hidden behind a beard.

Eliminating the limp had been more troublesome than shaving the beard. He had adopted the limp at the time of his disappearance, thinking that his lameness would override any other identifying signs. Who would notice a small discrepancy in his cover when a malfunctioning leg was screaming for attention? But now it was hard for the muscles to shake off the hitching pull of the short step. He wanted to run, to force his legs into activity that would somehow erase two years of limping.

Even in Albertville, far from Paris, the flyers were posted in the shops and bistros. The bearded nonentity in the sketch of René

Leveque was hardly likely to betray Robert Landry, and the flyers mentioned his limp. The likeness of Chantal was much more accurate: a sharp observer could match the person to the picture. She would need to change the tint and length of her hair . . . if she ever surfaced from his cave under the rue Pouchkine.

The sunshine colored the close-pruned plantain trees in hues of olive and bronze. A gentle breeze blew down the valley, flicking the flags that lined the main thoroughfare through town, the Route Nationale that tied Chambéry and Grenoble in the south to points north, Megève, Annecy, and Geneva.

This was the road to Ugine, the next town north of Albertville. De Celigny should be working there now, in the mill.

Robert Landry walked with a long step, hiding his limp. The road from the train station led straight to a bridge over the Rhône. He stopped at the center of the span. It felt good to be alive, in sunshine, acting at last.

Across the river, in the Grande Place of a town called Conflans, there should be a bakery. He hoped that he could find it. Asking the way might create a dangerous recollection in some innocent's mind.

The road past the bridge paralleled the river, and then a sign, "Cité Médiévale," directed him up a steep hill. The main road continued straight, leading directly out of the town. Without hesitation, he turned at the arrow and followed the small road up a steep hill. At the top of the road, a concatenation of ancient slate-roofed houses perched on a cliff, backed into a verdant hillside. Snow-covered mountain walls towered in the distance behind the rooftops.

Feeling warm and out of breath from the climb, he turned through an arched gate set into a wall, then followed a narrow street of cobblestones between shops signed with the names of the old artisanat: vannerie, bourrellier, herboriste. Ancient Conflans had been renewed for tourists. He was a tourist and so should be invisible, although he wondered how much tourist trade was left after the revolution.

The Grande Place was a wedge in a bend of the cobblestone street, with umbrellaed tables set out in front of a small brasserie.

It was too early in the day for local trade, and the tables were empty.

Beside the brasserie, he found a narrow storefront with a painted loaf of bread on the sign outside, the bakery of the Grande Place.

It was empty, most of the shelves bare. Behind the counter, in a wooden rack, the ends of a dozen unsold loaves of bread stood vertically beneath the mandatory photographs of Comrades Paccard and Joux. A fading mountain scene topped a calendar, and a fresh white card announced the official price of bread. A sign over a small domed bell said, "Please ring."

He rang.

Immediately, a door behind the counter opened. The woman who stepped through it was tall and handsome, her head held high as she took him in.

"Comrade?"

"I am a friend of Albert Gola," he said. "You are Catherine Moreau?"

She looked at him, expressionless, as though she had not heard.

He waited.

"Who are you?" she asked.

"Monsieur Beretta."

"Albert is working now."

"I know. I will wait for him."

"Do you want to buy something here?"

"Lunch. Do you have a cheese tart? . . . Or a pastry with meat in it?"

She shook her head.

"What do you have that is not sweet? I have had no breakfast."

"I still have some bread. Perhaps you would like the rye?"

"All right."

"If you wish to make a sandwich, there is an épicerie two doors down the road."

"Thank you."

"You cannot wait here."

"In the brasserie next door . . . ?"

She gazed at him.

"Not there. . . . You can wait down below, by the river, at one of the cafés in Albertville."

"What is the name of the best one?"

"They are all the same."

"Then tell me the name of one of them."

"The Café Quatre Vallées."

"I will be there this afternoon. Please tell Albert that his old friend Pierre Beretta was looking for him, the friend who has been sending him small gifts in the mail. Tell him that I will be at the Quatre Vallées."

"May I have your cash card?"

He extracted the cash card from his wallet and gave it to her. She looked at it, turning it over, then turned and took a lumpy brown loaf from the rack, wrapped it in tissue paper, and gave it to him.

He waited while she passed the card through the reader, thanked her as he stuffed it back in his wallet, and left the bakery with the loaf in his hand, feeling her eyes on his back as he went out the door.

He went to the épicerie, bought a slice of pâté, and walked back down the hill from the medieval town. He paid attention to his stride, balancing his step.

He ate the sandwich sitting on the Albertville side of the Arly, his back to the Café Quatre Vallées.

He walked to the Bar Express, where Albert Gola worked at night, and drank a beer, sitting at the bar.

Replete with the sandwich and the beer, he walked to the south end of the town at the meeting of the Arly and the Isère. There, with the sun warming his back, he stayed staring down on the play of the waves, where the two currents flowed together, and wondered how Chantal was faring with the Star. He had left her with the MSIE files, foolproofed, so that she could call up the different dossiers but could not possibly trigger the alarms built into the system to warn of intrusions. He wondered if it made a difference now, since the other side knew that the Star was compromised.

His entry at the Café Quatre Vallées was two hours before

Jacques de Celigny should arrive. He had feared a hasty reaction to his arrival, and so he had come early, giving them plenty of time to approach him.

But when he opened the door of the café, goose bumps ran up his spine, a thrill of recognition. He knew the face from one of the electronic portraits on the identity cards. It was Nagy, waiting for him, watching with eyes that shimmered like ice in water as he came through the door.

Direct, he thought, no detours. He went to the bar, stood close beside Nagy.

"Good evening, Nagy. I am pleased to meet you." He spoke softly, and yet the words seemed to reverberate in the space between them.

"Monsieur Beretta?" The eyes danced.

Landry nodded.

"Have a beer. Wait here."

Nagy was gone, as though he had never been there.

Landry looked at the vacant space where Nagy had been standing. Nagy had done something to freeze his awareness while stepping away and walking out the door. It was legerdemain, a manipulation of the viewer's attention while rabbits and doves came from nowhere.

Landry asked for a beer, raising his voice to capture the attention of the barman, who was talking with a white-aproned waiter at the far end of the bar.

The bar was ten stools long, too big for the brasserie, but behind the bar a large mirror, its silver going gray in streaks, made the room seem larger than it was. Six tables and a jumble of chairs. Only one of the tables had a customer, a weatherworn man nursing a *pastis*.

It was good that Nagy had been waiting for him; Chantal had stayed until closing time at the Express, without a sign. He knew they would be suspicious of any stranger. They would need to look at him and decide that he was in fact the beneficent Monsieur Beretta, and a friend.

The beer came warm in the hands of the barman, who asked him if he was new to Conflans.

Could there be any connection between the barman and Albert Gola?

The moment to answer passed, and the barman shrugged and turned away. Not likely, Landry decided. This barman showed no signs of life beyond the motor functions of pouring, rinsing glasses, and working the cash card reader—a zombie of the New State.

Bright afternoon sunlight radiated into the Quatre Vallées, illuminating the barman's tired face, now turned to absorb the waiter's chatter about football. How many Frenchmen were as dead as this man? Would they rally if they had some room to breathe, could see a gleam of independence in the future?

The weathered customer at the table called the waiter, let his cash card be read to pay for his *pastis*. As he left, the swinging door displaced the patterns of light and shade.

A clattering, wheezing truck stopped outside, and two elderly farmers came in, their blue *tabliers* dotted with straw and streaked with mud. They asked for red wine in a carafe, mixed it with water, and talked about cows, letting the red liquid lie still in the glasses.

An old woman, carrying a parcel wrapped in brown paper, came in and joined them. They poured a third glass for her.

Four workmen, young and noisy, banged through the door and scraped chairs together to squeeze around a table, demanding beer.

A plump man with pink cheeks, wearing a tired dark blue business suit, came in to stand beside Landry at the bar. He asked for a glass of marc de Savoie, glanced at Landry, exchanged a glance with the barman. The barman gave a nervous shake of his head, almost like a tic, and raised his hands.

Landry's antennae vibrated with attention.

The man in the suit put his wallet away, and Landry understood that there would be no payment for the drink. Some sort of barter was going on, petty crime against the state.

The Quatre Vallées was filling up now as the factories and shops were closing for the day. Within ten minutes, the bar was lined with men, two deep. Landry felt constrained to buy another beer to pay for his place.

A push and a tug at his hip pocket, and he clapped a hand down to protect his wallet. He wheeled, looking for the culprit, but saw only the backs and necks of the men clustered behind him, a group drinking beer from bottles.

Yet under his fingers there was a small lump in his pocket. He reached in and fished out the crumpled paper that had just been placed there.

He turned back to the bar and spread the bit of scrap flat between cupped hands. "Leave at seven. Walk across bridge. Wait on Conflans side." Clear enough. He looked at his watch. Fifteen minutes to go.

They might have decided that they need not risk an intruder in their midst ... might have decided to kill him, alone on the far side of the bridge. He was prepared for that remote dark hazard.

Five minutes later he asked for the bill and was lucky to get his cash card back by seven. At exactly the hour, he walked out into the street and crossed it to the bridge. The sky had turned a hazy yellowish gray, monotone with the mountains. Long, soft shadows swept the valley.

The note had told him to wait on the other side, but when he was halfway across the bridge he heard the van. It slowed, stopped beside him, and the door opened on the right-hand side. Directly, he climbed in.

The driver was a medium-young man with a shaggy mass of hair that flowed over his ears and almost reached his collar. The right-hand seat was empty, and Landry sat down, conscious that someone was behind him in the back of the van.

A soft but resonant voice said, "Please come back here with me. We do not want you to know where we are going."

Landry turned and saw Nagy. He scrambled back between the seats and lay down, closing his eyes, not wanting to know anything more than he needed to know.

They drove in silence for half an hour. From the gear changes and the laboring motor, he knew that the van was climbing. In the last minutes, the van hammered its way along a bumpy track that banged his elbows and bruised his ribs. Then, peace. They stopped, the motor chuffed into silence.

"Stay still, Monsieur Beretta," Nagy said, the palm of his hand on Landry's shoulder, holding him down. "Go ahead, Pierre, as though you were alone."

Pierre went out, leaving the door open.

"In case we have more guests than we invited," Nagy said. "It is better to be sure."

Ten minutes passed.

Pierre returned. "He says to come."

"Let's go, then." Nagy said, removing his hand.

Landry clambered over the driver's seat and out the door. He stood for a moment, taking in the scene. The mountains were bathed in pink and purple from the last glow of the departed sun. In the valley, it was already dark. The lights of Albertville and Conflans twinkled in the shadows, and moving headlights traced the road south to Chambéry and north toward Ugine. The wind had disappeared; the air was cool and still.

Their van was parked under a massive rocky outcrop on the hillside. On its side panel, in faded red letters that were barely visible, the words *"Plomberie Tuyauterie"* proclaimed its trade.

"Come," Pierre said.

They walked up a narrow path between shoulders of rock, into a small clearing. A shepherd's stone hut was embedded squarely in the center of the clearing, the slate roof in ruins and some of the stones from the walls strewn on the grass.

They stepped down a rudimentary set of stone steps, and Landry understood that the floor had been dug out inside the hut. A half meter down, they went through a new wooden door. Walls and a roof had been constructed inside the original stonework. In the center of the single room, a kerosene lantern burned, its smoke curling up to a hole in the ceiling. The small space was filled with men in chairs, drawn up close around the lamp. Faces turned to look at him, foreheads, noses, and lips fantastic and grotesque, distorted by moving shadows as the lantern's flame flared from the gust of air that entered with them.

"Welcome, Monsieur Beretta."

The voice came from a corner of the room. He saw a moustache, eyes flashing, close-cropped curly black hair. It was de

Celigny. A submachine gun was cradled in his lap, and then Landry realized that all of the men had arms in their hands, all but Pierre, Nagy, and himself.

"Good evening," Landry replied. "This is a great day for me."

Pierre dragged an empty chair next to the lantern.

"Please sit down," de Celigny asked, his tone easy.

Landry sat.

"Do you know these men?"

Landry looked from face to face. "I think I do," he answered. "But not all."

"Please try to name them. It is a small game."

Landry understood that the game could be mortal. The small man facing him was easy. Landry pointed and said, "Maurice Thevenet."

He turned to find Nagy. "Charles Nagy."

He pointed at Pierre. "Pierre, the driver."

But there were three more men, all heavy set and about the same age, and any one of them could have been Alphonse Euler. Who were the others? The *garagiste* and the baker, surely.

"I am guessing now," Landry said, "but among these three men there must be Alphonse Euler, and the other two could then be Laurent Bellot and Henri Moreau. And of course, you are Jacques de Celigny, alive today as Albert Gola.... Do I win the game?"

"It is a passing score. And you, Monsieur Beretta, is it your face in a beard that we see on the walls of the town hall and the post office? Robert Landry, alias René Leveque?"

"It is me."

"The picture of you is very poor, but we give you a mark of honor if they are hunting you. Please tell us how you have supplied us with names and created new identity cards."

"I have the means to manipulate the Star."

"I know that Robert Landry gave us the Star. But we are still playing the game. How do you make it provide identity cards?"

"Your likenesses are in the Star's photo bank, and the Star can paste those into new identity cards. I can create a new personal file and a cash account. So, I can create new identities if I wish. I can divert mail using the procedure that postal clerks have at their disposal to correct errors, to redirect parcels and letters. These are examples, but I can control almost anything the Star controls, and that is almost everything that happens in France."

"What do you think, my friends," de Celigny challenged the others, "is this an agent of the New State?"

"He is what he says he is," Thevenet said.

"I am Euler," the man beside him announced.

"I am Laurent Bellot," the man closest to de Celigny said.

"I am Henri Moreau, the husband of Catherine." The last was the biggest man in the room, his size overwhelming his chair.

De Celigny spoke. "Your woman told me you might want to attack the government."

"It may be necessary."

"Why?"

"To have a better one," Landry answered.

"... Then we would like to hear what you have in mind."

Landry looked around the room. They were watching, waiting for him to tell them what magic he could perform.

"We can change the government. We can replace Paccard with a man the Russians will accept. He is in the government now, but he is a good man."

"Who?"

"All of us do not need to know his name. It is better, Jacques de Celigny, if I tell you what I think you need to know, and you can decide what to tell the others.

De Celigny glanced around the room. "What do you think, my friends? Should I continue this?"

Thevenet answered. "Yes. If you decide to help this man, I am with you."

No one else spoke, but the agreement was plain. Chairs squeaked and pulled on the rough wood floor as the men stood up. Each of them shook Landry's hand, and then the room was empty except for de Celigny and Landry.

"So," de Celigny said. "Who is your friend in the government?"

"The minister of the economy, Marcel Chabon."

De Celigny took a moment to digest this.

"I don't know anything about him," he said. "He was a civil servant, high up in the old government, no?"

"Yes. He was a technocrat with no politics. The Russians had worked with him and trusted him, and so they put him in charge of the economy because they thought he could make it work."

"He is a friend of yours?"

"I worked with him occasionally before the revolution. Now, I speak to him on the telephone. I know what he is doing and I believe in him. He can lead us to freedom. He seems to be ready for a coup d'état. . . . He says that if Paccard is dead, he is the only one who can run the government and command the military. I think that he is right. Except for him, the Russians have no one else to choose from."

Again, de Celigny was silent before he started to speak. "You have proven that you can make the Star do tricks, but the rest of what I hear is only hopes and dreams. You want to change the government, and so you find Minister Chabon. You want to eliminate Paccard and his friends, and so you find me. But you have no idea of real political power. Gorbachev gave away the Russian's power in 1989. Now that they are back in power with their German friends, they will never try it again. What can you show me that is different, to make me believe in you?"

"Nothing. You are right: we cannot throw the Russians out. But I don't ask for democracy. If we put Chabon in charge, recover our freedom by degrees, we will give hope to the people."

De Celigny stared at Landry without answering, and Landry tried to read the thoughts behind de Celigny's eyes. Had they come so far for nothing?

De Celigny spoke. "Tell me about the woman, Chantal Senac, whom I met as Annie Beaumont. Her likeness on the posters is better than yours."

"Unfortunately."

"When we met in Albertville, she spoke about my children and a child of her own. Her child is held by the government, like mine. She said that you can find my children, and her own."

"I know where they are."

"And then, can you and the woman find a place to keep the children safe?"

"No. I thought that here . . ."

"It is possible to hide the children, according to my friends. But do you intend that we should hide your woman as well? With her face posted on every public building in France."

"They will all be in hiding. She could care for the children." Landry was plucked by a twinge of anger. Did de Celigny think that the whole plan was intended to hide Chantal? "If you cannot keep her and her child, then we will find some other way."

"I did not say that, my friend. I am learning about your intentions."

"There is more that you should know. . . . The Russians have a secret organism in France. It is called Department 100, and it is run by a man who is known as 'the Russian.' You have heard the tales?"

De Celigny nodded.

"The Russian exists to ensure the security of the New State, to watch over the puppet government. There is a rift between Department 100 and the first secretary. If we create some friction between them, I believe we can damage the Russian beyond repair. We must eliminate him as well as Paccard, or Chabon's hands will be tied."

"We will do a great deal for Minister Chabon."

"Yes."

"How can I trust such a man?"

"I do not want to try to convince you. Let Marcel Chabon do that. Meet him."

"He will do that?"

"He wants to meet me. I will send you instead."

"So I get trapped, instead of you?"

"I will not risk my control of the Star, before or after Marcel Chabon comes to power, so I can never meet him. But you must meet him and decide, and I look to you to defend yourself."

De Celigny gazed at Landry.

"Will you do it?" Landry asked.

"Of course. It will be my pleasure to meet the minister of the economy."

So, it was done.

De Celigny occupied himself with the carcass of a thin chicken, splitting it in equal portions. They ate in silence and then halved a bar of Swiss chocolate, a luxury.

When the last mouthful of chocolate had disappeared, de Celigny began to speak, in measured words at first. "You are wrong in what you imagine. We can never withdraw from the Russians. Chabon will be another dictator like Paccard, and he will do as Moscow asks, like Paccard. If you think there is a happy middle between freedom and obedience, you are wrong . . . that is not how power works. And if the people hope to be free, they will soon learn the truth, that nothing has really changed."

Now the words started to come faster. "But I am going to help you, and you must know why. I want their blood. I mean the people who took my children and killed my wife. I want to kill many. More than the two who came for your woman in Albertville . . . as many as I can before I die. If it was my plan, I would start at the top and kill all of them, along with your Minister Chabon, and when the Russians replaced them, I would start again." De Celigny's voice cracked with passion. "I tell you now, so that you will understand me. If your plan works, then I will be glad. But if it does not work, then I will still be glad if I have acted."

"They killed my wife," Landry answered. "They destroyed my friends who worked with me on the Star. I understand you."

"Good. Then I wish you a tranquil sleep, Robert Landry. We will be awake before dawn, to get you out of here."

Landry tried to sleep, but he tossed and turned and wondered if he could control de Celigny. Landry wondered if Marcel Chabon would survive the meeting.

CHANTAL'S fingers were learning to move the cursor across the screen, from one part of MSIE's daily record to the other. There was now a dossier on the search for Chantal Senac and René Leveque/Robert Landry, and it was growing almost by the hour as the small army of police spread across Paris and France, looking for the fugitives.

The searchers had not turned up a single lead.

She had been alone for two days, and she wished Robert Landry would return. Every hour ticked by with the possibility that he was already captured or dead. She explored the MSIE files and wondered what she would do if he did not return. There was food hidden up above. Jars of *confit* nestled with tins of pâté and cans of fruits and vegetables, meat and fish, delicacies like olives and dried apricots, gathering dust in the warehouse along with the leaning stacks of old papers. There was enough to last for months. But without him, she might not last as long as the food.

Her bladder told her that it was time to go up to the toilet. She had to climb the ladder, and then she would put something to eat in her bag, to bring back down with her. She liked to stay down with the computer monitor, it gave her a feeling of security to be buried so far below ground.

To negotiate the climbs and descents, she wore a belt of Landry's with the rope looped through it, so that it would jam and catch her if she fell. The rope was a nuisance. It needed to be untangled and then fed through her belt every few steps. She promised herself that when her lover returned, she would stop using the rope and brave the abyss as he did, unsecured.

The toilet was in the back corner of the warehouse, on the opposite side from the sleeping room. Faithfully, she closed the trap door and tended the dust to be sure there was no discontinuity on the floor to mark the aperture.

She turned out the light and stepped out into the warehouse. René—no, Robert—had insisted that she find her way to the bathroom in the dark, brushing her fingers along the back wall until she came to the bathroom door. Lights had to be left out unless he was there to explain why they were on.

She found her way to the bathroom and opened the door. The facilities were too fine for an old warehouse: a sit-down toilet, a bidet, and a shower stall, connected to the little gas-fired hot water heater in the bedroom. The hot water took minutes to arrive, but it made the bathroom civilized beyond reason.

She sat in the darkness—and then went rigid. Someone was in the warehouse. Talking, so it could not be Landry.

Footsteps and voices, then a spear of light under the door. What sense of privacy had made her shut the door behind her, inside the empty warehouse?

The light vanished. A flashlight, they would be looking for the light switch. Light again, steady, a yellow line under the door with a soft intruding glow. The switch had been found.

She heard the footsteps and voices receding, then quiet. They were in the bedroom, looking for François Blanc. Then, again, voices, coming toward her . . . A shadow crossed the line of light under the door.

They were coming to the bathroom. Would it be safer to get up and squeeze behind the door, risking a noise, or safer to stay where she was, quiet? She was too frightened to move, she stayed, thankful that the open door would swing back against her knees. They would have to come all the way into the room to find her.

The knob rattled and turned, the door swung open. Light poured in from the outside, illuminating the sink and the shower stall. In a panic, she glanced without moving her head at the mirror over the sink, dreading that she would be looking into the eyes of a policeman. She saw the ceiling reflected in the glass. The mirror would not betray her.

"He lives well this Blanc, all the comforts of home." The voice was loud, almost beside her. Then a footfall sounded, a scrape and a bump. The bathroom door stayed open. "Where should we leave the notice?"

"Put it on his bed," a more distant voice answered. "He should find it on his bed."

Chantal felt a chill of recognition. The voice of arrogant authority belonged to the policeman who had interrogated her on the day she met Landry. She would never forget that boy with the thin moustache, pressing her to admit she was an impostor.

When they were gone, she remained frozen in place, terrified that they would come back and catch her before she could return to the safety of the cave.

Finally, she extended her hand and pushed the door shut.

She flushed and then washed in the dark, waiting for the hot water. They had seen nothing on their visit, nothing but an old warehouse full of papers. Their inspection meant that the warehouse was safe, and that was a blessing, a test that had been overcome in the house-to-house search for Leveque and Senac.

She opened the door. They had turned out the lights, and she felt her way back, her fingers brushing the cold bricks as she passed. What was the notice they had left?

She was halfway to the sleeping room when the warehouse door clattered and squeaked. The light came on, trapping her against the back wall, in plain view if they took two steps past the stacks of cartons. She was too far from the bathroom, she was caught. She put her back to the wall and waited for them.

Robert Landry, beardless, walked from behind a stack of cartons into sight, smiling.

She broke down in sobs, fell into his arms. "They were here, just now, looking for you . . ."

"I know. I saw them coming out the door. Where were you, the toilet?"

She nodded.

"Lucky they didn't find you. . . ."

She nodded again, sobbing in his arms. "In the room, they left some sort of note. I heard them."

"You must have been terrified."

"I was so scared they would find me and then wait here for you."

They disengaged from their embrace, and he led the way to the sleeping space. The notice was folded into a square, white with black lines, lying like an unexploded bomb on the bed.

He took it and read it. "It seems normal. They just want to see me at the police station, since I wasn't here to meet them when they came."

"The policeman has seen you before. He is the same one who came into the Café de la Poste when we first saw each other."

Landry raised his hand so that he could read the signature in the light. "Detective Louche. I remember the name."

"You can't go. He will remember you with a beard and ask why you shaved it off."

"I have to go, or they will surely come back here with some hard questions, harder than why I shaved my beard."

She squeezed him close to her. "I missed you. I don't think I can stand to worry about you any more. . . ."

He kissed her. He would have to go to the police, and if he did not survive the interview, it would be the last time in her arms. He loved her. He wanted to tell her about his trip and about the plan to make her foster mother of de Celigny's motherless children. For a long time, they stood, clinging to each other, seeking comfort from their love.

He could not tell her until he had come back from the police. It would not be fair to raise her hopes of seeing her child again, if the interview went badly.

THE Russian gazed at his computer monitor, impassive, his hands in his lap. He heard Valerie come in and spoke without turning his head.

"It is impossible to do our work without the Star. And we cannot be part of the Star without sharing our files with Robert Landry. An impossible situation, no?"

She knew the question was not meant for her. His mastery was at risk, and who could blame him for his preoccupation, in bed or in the office? But right now, he should be interested in what she had to say. She put her report on his desk.

"Do you know the name de Celigny?" she asked. "A policeman, before the revolution."

"Of course . . . He was a policeman who got into the news, then into politics. Attractive, well-meaning . . . and dangerous. We wanted him out of the way, but he was one of the few who moved faster than we did. . . . Have you found him in your search for Landry?"

"No. But two of his old police team disappeared from their jobs. And now, another one of de Celigny's team has escaped from a camp in Nîmes. Comrade Morand reported this. Morand thinks that de Celigny could be assembling his old friends."

"Maybe . . ." the Russian stared at her, letting the information fall into place. "It could explain the events in Albertville. Two men dead in a car, the work of a professional.... De Celigny could have done that."

It was Valerie's turn to stare as he continued.

"Landry must have used the Star to find de Celigny. Landry must have sent Chantal Senac to him. That is possible. Listen, Valerie ..."

She was startled by the use of her first name, which he never used except in his private rooms.

"... Ask Morand about the children. The wife of de Celigny died, but there were two children. We placed them in the home of loyal party members, near the town of Crozon on the coast of Brittany. If de Celigny has surfaced, we will need the children."

Valerie made notes.

"We should seek a way to inform de Celigny that we have them," the Russian continued.

She asked, "If de Celigny was able to find his friends, could he also find his children?"

The Russian cupped his chin in his hands and gazed at her, and Valerie realized that she had gained his full attention for the first time in days.

"Valerie, if Landry found de Celigny, he could surely find de Celigny's children.... Ask Morand to set up surveillance on the children."

Valerie thought about it. "Morand will complain. He is complaining already about the manpower that the search is taking."

"Ask him for two men, a covert surveillance to wait for de Celigny. Tell Morand that de Celigny killed his agent in Albertville."

"I will ask Morand. I will think of ways to communicate with de Celigny, on the radio or the television, a sort of public message."

"We cannot take much longer. Morand says that Georges Paccard knows about the search. Morand said that Paccard is almost incoherent, he is so upset about losing control of the Star." The Russian's jaw clamped tight. He knew it was possible that Morand had told Paccard, his nominal chief. The Russian tried to weigh his impression of Morand from his last telephone call. Was the man tipping over?

Valerie studied the still face of her chief and lover and calculated his chances.

SMOKE curled over the heads of the detectives of the eighth arrondissement, assembled to report on their search for Robert Landry and Chantal Senac. The room was noisy with the clack of fingers on keys. All over France, the morning was devoted to reporting. During the afternoons and late into the nights, they were out searching for the fugitives.

Detective Louche jabbed angrily at his computer's keyboard. The Star had failed him, deprived him of the credit that should belong to him.

The scene came back clearly in his mind. She had seemed strange, too fine to be cleaning offices. It had hit him at once, there in the café. He was good at reading people; it was his strength. There and then, in the café, he remembered thinking that something was wrong with her. She should have been the wife of some high party man, sleeping all day and going to parties at night, drinking vodka and eating caviar.

And now, when they were plowing all of France to turn up Chantal Senac, when he should be praised for his alertness, he was blamed for bungling the report.

The Star was blank. His daily reports were complete, seamless from the beginning to the end of the month of February, but there was not a word about Chantal Senac. He could remember reading the report into the Star from his notes, but of course he had not kept his notes, and now, according to the Star nothing had happened.

Inspector Groux remembered the encounter in the café. Groux had said to never mind about the Star, that everything in the report was already in the woman's official file, but then Groux had told all his detectives to pay more attention to the reporting procedure.

Louche did not understand why they wanted her. It was hard

to imagine her doing anything so harmful that they should search for her, house-to-house, all over France.

Detective Louche was filing the report of the day's search and wondering if once again the Star would turn on him and nullify his efforts. The Star supposedly never failed. That was why everyone blamed him: the Star was foolproof. If you made a mistake in the procedure it would stop you and make you start again, and then when you were finished, it would make you verify your work and would answer back that the file was saved in its memory.

No one had ever heard of the Star losing a police report. He hit the keys hard enough to give them pain.

His coffee cup was stuffed with cigarette butts, and he was only halfway through. He was coming now to the searches that were incomplete because the resident had been out. He had left a summons for each, politely inviting the recipient to come to the police station, not later than thirteen hundred hours the next day.

The problem was that many people worked at night, and so the nighttime search of residences was often in empty apartments.

The missing tenants would come straggling into the station to look at the wanted-persons bulletin and leave their statement.

It was eleven o'clock, and only two of the summoned comrades had come in. There were nine left to come. They would all arrive at lunchtime, just before the deadline. He would be lucky to get anything to eat before it was time to go out again.

An elderly patrolman walked into the detective's room, looked into the haze of smoke, and found Louche.

"Detective Louche, you have François Blanc, rue Pouchkine. Ready to see him?"

Louche reached for the stack of follow-up papers, turned the sheets until he came to the one for Blanc.

"Send him in."

The man who came in with the patrolman walked with a hesitance that betrayed his nervousness, but he did not limp. Part gone in the head, Louche concluded, seeing the blank eyes and the drooping mouth. A shy, thin man, cleanshaven, of course he could be René Leveque or Robert Landry for size and age, but that was the extent of it.

Louche did not get up. "You are . . . ?"

The man's head jerked to attention. "Comrade Blanc, François."

The words were hollow, as though repeated by rote, but the inversion of last and first names was correctly proletarian.

"Your papers . . ."

Landry stood at Louche's shoulder. They went through the routine of birthplace, birthdate, cash card number, employment, and family relations. To save time, Louche punched the answers directly into the computer and read the responses. The man's data were confirmed by the monitor. Then, together they looked at the photo-images on the wanted-persons bulletin, and Louche read the descriptions aloud.

The man was expressionless.

"Have you seen either of these people?"

"These people?" Landry pointed a shaky finger at the bulletin. "Yes."

"No."

"Who are your neighbors? Do any of them resemble these people?"

Landry shook his head.

"Do you have any friends in the neighborhood?"

"No."

"Where do you go to eat, to have a beer?"

"I eat in my warehouse."

"Always?"

Landry looked frightened, as though he was accused of something wrong, and nodded slowly.

"Where do you buy food?"

"The supermarket . . . rue de Courcelles."

It was the major supermarket of the area.

"You do not know anyone?"

"I care for my warehouse."

A retard, at best. Louche keyed the responses into the computer and then turned to François Blanc.

"If you see these people, you come back here and tell me, do you understand?"

"Oh, yes . . . I will tell you."

"You can go, Comrade Blanc. Take good care of your warehouse." Louche put Blanc's follow-up report in the completed stack without watching him go out the door. He tapped out the end-code for the report in the Star. That was the last of rue Pouchkine. He had found no one on rue Pouchkine or in the vicinity who had any recollection of a man with a limp or a beard, much less a woman like Chantal Senac. But the street was all back walls and garages; there had been no one to interview. One of the café owners four blocks away remembered a bearded man with a limp, but not any regular customer, and not recently. Even at the Café de la Poste, they claimed not to recognize Chantal Senac.

Eight more follow-ups to go.

The report on Chantal Senac might have been misfiled in the wrong report category. Could he have entered the wrong category code, put her into accidents or criminal investigations? Louche racked his memory, trying to call up the day, to register every detail of his activity. He put the Star out of his mind, tried to think of the events of the day, to restart the thought process. She had been sitting in the Café de la Poste. He had gone in with Detective Javel, leaving Groux outside. Slowly, like a cloud taking shape out of his subconscious, the scene formed in his mind. There had been others in the place, two men, no . . . three. He had been instantly aware that something was wrong about the woman, and so he had not paid much attention to the others in the café, but she had been sitting close to a bearded man . . . Leveque? He must have seen the man's papers. He would remember if they had said René Leveque or Robert Landry. Or, would he?

Something was stirring in the wells of his subconscious, something that was struggling to connect, but he could not raise it into awareness.

Wearily, he reached for the stack of reports. It was a bad business. One of the other detectives had been bitten in the leg by a watchdog and had shot the dog, killed it, blood everywhere. Louche hoped he would not encounter any vicious dogs. They frightened him. He hoped he would not encounter any vicious people. . . . The day before, a woman had claimed that the searchers took her diamond ring. She had become hysterical in the detectives' room while everyone turned around to listen and watch, and she had only calmed down when Louche threatened to throw her in jail. If the search was going to cover everybody in France, it meant seeing the crazies along with the sane. He would be glad when it was over.

11 A cold wind rolled off the Atlantic. It had been blowing hard out of the northwest for three days, building a swell that surged as high as the low cliffs at the ocean's edge, half a kilometer away. The sound of the waves came in with the wind, an undulating rumble under the rustle of the swaying leaves and branches. Comrade Hélène Pichette, bicycling home from the market, wore both a wool sweater and an oiled slicker jacket over her heavy wool dress. She had lived in Brittany all her life, and she knew the calendar: May did not mean that summer had come.

She pedalled up the road and complained to herself about the two men in her house. She suffered them because she had no choice, and because she had been promised payment. A fat extra bonus from the New State, plus the cost of their food, on top of her monthly allowance for the two boys, all would add to the growing balance in the cash card account.

The men had arrived after supper two nights before, and they were waiting for someone or something. She did not know, and they did not say. Long ago, she had learned not to ask why people came to stay. If she had complaints, she saved them for her husband, Paul.

She had complained about taking the boys, but Paul had insisted. It was for the revolution, he had said, and soon she had understood that the allowance from the New State outweighed the inconvenience. The children did not eat much, and the size of the Pichettes' cash account quickly mounted. Besides, they were not bad boys. They were easier to manage than her own two sons had been before they grew up and married.

Gusts of wind buffeted her as she pedalled, slowly, up the long drive toward the house that she had occupied for thirty-five years. Saturday, so the children would soon be home from their half day at school. They were starting to do better now at their studies, after so much trouble in the beginning. Missing their mother. There were plenty of children missing their mothers now, suffering for their parents' greed. She had never talked to the boys about their lives in Paris before they were orphaned by the revolution, and she knew almost nothing about their parents. Since the boys' arrival, Comrade Pichette had diligently maintained her ignorance, because she did not want to share their tragedy. She had fed them and gotten them proper clothes, and above all she had not permitted them to sulk and hide in their room, but had forced them out of the house to do chores and had kept them out to play in the cold and the wind. She knew the Brittany weather could take heads away from memories.

At first she had been the one to resist, but after the early weeks it was Paul who had not warmed to the children. He was the social philosopher, and for him they were capitalists, from birth and forever, no matter if both their parents were dead. If they ate well they ate too much, and if they did not eat they were unappreciative. For Paul, they could not do anything right.

They hated Paul, and he could feel it. For her own part, she was straight with them, and she thought they liked her well enough.

The end of her journey home was in sight. The road made a small bend past a rocky hillock where oak trees hid the house from the road. The macadam turned to small stones and dirt, and she grunted with the effort of making the pedals turn, thinking of the heavy wine bottles in the panniers. The men had asked for the wine. It was cheap Algerian red, but she had let the store bill her for expensive Bordeaux, and in return she had received a big bottle of detergent at no cost. The state would pay her extra for the wine, and the soap would pay her for the work of getting it home.

Home was in the center of a clearing, its unmowed grass still brown from the winter. Built by her husband's great-great-uncle, high and narrow, its walls of native stone, the house wore its age with rustic dignity, although the thatch on the roof had been replaced by fireproof asphalt tile. A cramped flight of stairs cut the house in the middle. The life of the household was in the kitchen, where everybody ate around a table that was as old as the walls. In the other half of the ground floor, a sitting room waited for important visitors who rarely came. That room was forbidden to any adult in working clothes, and to all children.

Two doors gave access from the outside, one in front at the foot of the stairs, one in back under the stairwell.

Comrade Pichette dismounted and walked the bicycle around to the back, where she leaned her steed against the wall and undid the buckles of one of the panniers.

She carried a plastic mesh bag full of groceries into the kitchen. Wind whistled through the closed windows, but the house itself was quiet, the children not yet home. The two men would be upstairs. They were always upstairs, had even asked for their meals upstairs until she had refused to carry them.

The men were lodged in the bedroom over the kitchen. The children slept in the attic, under the eaves. Her own bedroom was at the far end of the house, over the sitting room.

Water pipes groaned, a rasping echo to the wind. One of the men was running water up above. They all shared the bathroom under the stairwell on the second floor, the bathroom that Paul Pichette had installed with his own hands in the third year of their marriage, just before the birth of their second son.

She went back out to unload the other pannier, the one with the bottles.

As she stepped back in, the racket in the pipes quit with a wheeze, and planks overhead squeaked under footsteps. At some time after the turn of the century, Paul's grandfather had nailed ceilings below the cross-beams, but Paul had ripped out the decayed ceiling panels when he had put in new wiring for the electricity, and they had been pleased by the look of the old beams. They had left the beams uncovered, so that the floor above was now the ceiling below, and from the bedroom above you could hear every word spoken in the kitchen. She was glad that the sound did not pass the other way, because she did not want to hear the men.

She wondered what they did all day, besides eat and sleep and use the bathroom. Did they clean their guns? Play cards? What were they waiting for, and how long would they stay? Useless questions . . . She turned her thoughts to supper.

In the old days she and Paul had sat at the big table with visitors from Paris, men in the party, some of them tough and practical, some dreamers, all of them dedicated. Passionate talk had mapped out the inevitable triumph of the working class, the end of exploitation. Right at this table, they had kindled the first flames for strikes and marches, and for factory occupations in Brest. Paul had kept the faith, even when the proletariat slipped away into the camp of the social democrats and worse. But now that the Russians had finally put the clamp of destiny on the class struggle, she had to admit that it was not the revolution they had talked about.

So many sacrifices, things done without, while all of France was plunging into an orgy of materialism. She had not even dreamed of owning a car in those days. Instead, she had prized her bicycle as a symbol of freedom from the tyranny of the banks.

She did not regret the sacrifices. Paul and Hélène Pichette were better off than their neighbors now. What she regretted was that all the zeal had gone. And now, she had to share her house with potato-faced men from Paris who carried their politics in shoulder holsters.

The mesh shopping bag yielded a pair of fine sea bass, fresh from the morning's arrival in Crozon. The fish glistened as she laid them side-by-side on their paper wrapping. She spread the other purchases out on the counter, leeks to be steamed with white wine in the broth from the fish, a bag of beans, a dozen onions, and a bunch of shallots. Her giant bottle of detergent. Six eggs from the market. Their newfound affluence had allowed her to give up keeping chickens—she hated the foolish birds. She planted the liter bottles of red wine at the back of the counter, with a clump that she hoped they could hear in the room above, and, as if in response, the ceiling creaked.

The fish had dripped blood on the counter, and she turned on the tap in the sink to wet a towel. Absently, she dabbed the blood with the towel. It was not typical of the fish market; normally the fish were cleaned to perfection. At least it showed that the sea bass were truly fresh.

A splat of blood landed on her hand as she wielded the towel. She looked at the crimson spot, confused. Another drip landed on the counter, touching the edge of the wrapping paper beneath the fish, and then another.

She looked up. There was a small darkening between the floor-boards overhead, and then she saw a falling drop of blood and knew that the blood did not come from the fish.

She caught the scream in her throat; it came out as a croak of fear. She turned, slowly, dreading what she might see, but the room was empty. Quickly, she ran to the back door, her wind-breaker in hand from the hook by the door, and then outside.

The bicycle was gone.

If she tried to get away they would certainly stop her. Better to be in her house, locked in a room, but she dared not go up the stairs, and there were no locks on the rooms downstairs. She could telephone, not the police but Paul at the Mairie. Good luck that the telephone was in the kitchen, close by the back door. Her shaking fingers had pressed four numbers before she realized that the line was dead. Maybe it was better to run. She did not know whose blood it was, coming through the cracks in the floor, but someone surely was dead. The rag carpet up there would take liters to soak through. And no matter whose blood it was, there was murder in the house and the murderer had been running the water so she knew that he was there, now, and he surely knew that she was in the kitchen . . . and her bicycle was gone.

She almost cried out again as she remembered that the children were coming home. They were hers to protect. They would be walking up the road from the crossing where the bus stopped. She would go out the front door and run, get as far as she could, and if they killed her on the way there would be a body outside to warn the children. She put on her oiled jacket.

A gust pushed on the front door as she unlatched it, blowing her back into waiting hands, strong hands forcing her down, her arms pinned, and then her wrists were tied, round and round together. She was not dying, the hands were not hurting her, but her wrists and feet were tied together behind her and then there was a cloth over her eyes and another in her mouth, and the hands were dragging her into the sitting room. She heard the door close. She tried to move and could not, but if she was going to die, it was not now.

JACQUES de Celigny waited at the bend in the road, sitting between the rocks. He had seen the woman go by on her bicycle and hoped that all was well with Nagy and Thevenet, at the house.

He stood up when he saw the children, two small figures trudging up the road, their schoolbags slung on both shoulders like backpacks. Michel, the older, was a head taller than Jean-Pierre and a step in front. They both wore shiny nylon windbreakers and dark wool pants with canvas shoes, and they were talking, laughing. He stepped out into the road. They continued toward him, wary now, observing him.

As they came closer he could see that they were red-cheeked from the wind. His children. A lump formed in his throat.

He squatted down, to be at eye level, to be recognized. Held by suspense, he waited for their reaction. Two years was a long time in the life of a child.

Michel started to run to him. "Papa!"

Jean-Pierre was perplexed but followed his older brother. De Celigny laughed out loud with relief as he gathered them both into his arms, hugging them together.

Jean-Pierre started to cry.

Michel talked, a stream of words. They had thought he was dead, they had been taken to this house with a bad man and a woman, and the man would not speak to them at all and the woman, when she spoke, only told them what to do, what to eat, what to wear, and all the time, they thought he was dead, he and Mama. De Celigny had to break off the flow of words and lead them off the road.

"Is Mama with you?" Michel asked.

"No, she is truly dead. They killed her, and we must hide from them, if we want to live together."

The boys' eyes were big, looking at him.

"We are going to live together from now on, but we must hide," de Celigny said.

Michel nodded, and Jean-Pierre, rubbing his wet eyes with the back of his hand, nodded too. They understood hiding.

"We will travel to a new place. We must go now. We will not even go to the house."

"But will we leave all our clothes?" Michel asked.

"Someone will bring your things."

"Where are we going?"

"Far from here."

"Well," Michel said, putting his hand in his father's, "let's go."

"We must start by waiting."

Together they sat where de Celigny had waited, between the rocks by the road. They did not need to wait long. The minute hand on de Celigny's watch was just crossing the twelve mark when they heard the wheels of Laurent Bellot's pride, a Peugeot sedan, crunching up the road. The hardest part was done. Now they had a distant rendezvous to make.

Soon after sunset the children slept, Michel on the back seat and Jean-Pierre on the floor behind his father, his head cushioned by his folded windbreaker. De Celigny, too, went to sleep as the car droned on. Alphonse Euler, at the wheel, took the car onto the Paris-Nantes autoroute to fill the gas tank at an all-night gas station and left the autoroute at the next exit to drive east on tree-lined country roads.

Shortly after ten in the evening, the rising ground of the first soft hills of Burgundy lifted them into a bank of heavy clouds. Fog coated the windshield with film. Euler slowed, straining his eyes to see the road. It was time to change the Peugeot's plates and their identification cards, so he stopped at a farmer's side road and backed in. Before he started out again, he polished the windshield and scrubbed the windshield wiper blades. Any accident that stopped them would be fatal.

They continued across the heart of France. In the valleys where the fog was dense, Euler had to slow to a crawl, the engine growling in second gear. The hands on Euler's watch were invisible in the darkness, but he knew they were running very late. The headlights cast thin yellow spears no more than three or four meters ahead into the mist. Euler's senses started to play tricks on him; he felt the car climbing when they were rolling on the flat.

After an eternity, a sign marking the Paris-Lyon autoroute materialized above them. Euler drove another hundred meters, pulled over to the side of the road, and held his watch to the instrument panel. It was almost one in the morning. They had surely missed the meeting. He nudged de Celigny.

De Celigny's hand moved to the weapon under the seat. His eyes opened.

"We are just outside Chalons," Euler said, his voice a gentle rasp. "We are two hours late. She will have gone."

De Celigny flexed his shoulders to stretch away the sleep.

"She is there, or she is not."

Euler put the car in gear and cautiously started out. She was instructed to go back to Paris if they were unable to meet in Chalons. After putting de Celigny on the train, he would continue south, alone in the car with the two children. How to explain two young children alone with a single and much older man? And it would be difficult for Catherine to manage two children without help. Euler prayed the woman would still be there.

High streetlamps glowed above them now, their yellow light absorbed in the mist.

"It's thick, no?" Euler said. "We will soon pass a road sign facing the other direction. It marks one kilometer before the turn for the autoroute. We will pass it, go on to a rotary, and come back. There is a shelter there, just below the sign, to wait for the bus. She should be inside, if she is there."

Ahead they saw a dark rectangle above the road, silhouetted against the mist.

"That is the sign," Euler said. "The shelter is on our left."

Both of the men looked as they passed. The shelter was a simple pre-fabbed construction of glass and metal panels. It seemed empty.

"We must go back," Euler said.

"No," said de Celigny. "There is the gendarmerie, ten meters past the shelter."

Euler saw the gendarmes and thought quickly. They could have her and be waiting to see who else might come.

"Do you want to take them?" Euler asked. "If they are expecting us, it will be dangerous."

"If they were expecting us, they would not be parked where we could see them."

"We should take them, then?"

"We may have no choice," de Celigny said. "Here they come."

Euler looked in his rearview mirror. Headlights were swinging pencil-thin beams of light onto the road, and the blue light in the dome on the roof was flashing like a firefly.

Euler slowed and stopped at the edge of the road. Fifty meters ahead, where the road began a long curve, he could see the traffic circle, well lit under the streetlamps. He touched the butt of the Heckler & Koch.

The police car stopped twenty meters behind, and one man got out from the passenger side. His sidearm was buckled to his belt, but the distance was too great to move against the other gendarme.

"If it gets hot with this one, go in reverse and hit the gas," de Celigny whispered. "I'll shoot, you drive. Just get us where we can be sure of the driver."

Euler nodded. He rolled down his window.

"Papers," the gendarme demanded. He was young.

Euler extended the car's documents and their identity cards claiming residence in Lons-le-Saunier, to the east of Chalons.

The gendarme held a flashlight to the papers. "You have children here?"

"Sleeping, in the back."

The gendarme directed the flashlight's beam onto the back seat. He nodded.

"It is late for children to be out driving. Late for anyone, no?"

"We have been fishing, in the sea," Euler said. "We took the boys fishing."

"Which of you is the father?"

"I am," de Celigny replied.

"Where were you fishing?"

"Near Marseille, in Cassis."

"Did you catch any fish?"

"Nothing. We had bad luck. But the weather was good; it was good to be out on the sea."

"What was the name of your boat?"

"I do not remember," de Celigny said. "Do you remember?"

Euler shook his head.

"I have an uncle who runs a boat out of Cassis," the gendarme said. "It is called *Ange de Cassis*. Was it that one?"

"No, that I am sure," Euler answered.

"Too bad, he would have found you some fish."

"Next time, we will look for his boat. The *Ange de Cassis*?"

"Yes. His name is Gallotin, my uncle, Pierre Gallotin."

The gendarme gave the documents back to Euler. "Be careful on your way, it is very heavy fog."

"Thank you," Euler said. "We have been going slowly."

The gendarme started to walk back to the waiting car, but checked himself.

"You left the autoroute at Chalons-Nord? For Lons, you should have taken Chalons-Sud."

"I missed the turn."

"Well then, you must be more careful."

Turning on his heel, the gendarme strode away, his retreating silhouette pulsing blue in time with the flashing roof light.

De Celigny opened his door.

"What are you doing?" Euler asked.

"Going to make *pipi*. We need a reason to stay while they depart."

"She must have gone."

"She must, indeed."

De Celigny stood beside the car, his back to the road, his hands at his fly. The flashing blue light went dark, and the gendarme's car rolled past them, out onto the road. Euler waved at the gendarmes. The car drove to the circle, swung around, and returned past them. Euler watched in his mirror, his heart sinking as the red taillights turned off the road, three hundred meters back. They were resuming their vigil beside the bus stop shelter.

De Celigny sat down in the car and pulled the door shut.

"To be sure she is not there, we would need to kill them," Euler commented.

De Celigny nodded.

"It is not worth it," Euler continued. "Let her go back to Paris."

"Shit," de Celigny said.

"You want to take them out? With the two children in the car?"

"No. Drive."

Euler started the motor and engaged the gears. Carefully, he eased his way onto the road. The fog was thicker than before: the traffic circle ahead was only a faint glow.

"My God!" Euler exhaled, his eyes fixed on the road ahead.

Like a ghost, a form swathed in swirling mist appeared and as quickly disappeared into the dark as the headlights passed.

Euler hit the brakes, hard, sliding to a stop in the gravel on the shoulder.

She came from behind them, out of the heavy fog, and then she was in the car, arranging her feet to avoid the sleeping children, and Euler was driving again.

"We thought we had lost you," de Celigny said.

"I slipped out of the shelter when the police came to wait there. It seemed that the best chance was to meet you at the circle, like a hitchhiker, no?"

"And if we had been someone else?" Euler demanded.

"Two other men in a Peugeot? Well, I would have been a little drunk and told them I was waiting for my lover. My lover from Lons-le-Saunier."

De Celigny turned to look at her. In the darkness, she was barely visible, but she seemed different from his recollection, and he realized as the lights flashed in through the window that her eyes were heavy with mascara and her hair was now dyed dark. Of course, the woman of the posters could not travel without some effort at disguise. Now she seemed less like the friends of his wife, more independent—more interesting.

"The station is not far ahead," Euler said. "Are you ready?"

"Ready," de Celigny replied, his voice calm. He turned again in his seat. Half a day reunited, now to part again from the two boys. He would see them again, when . . . ? They were nearly visible in the shadows behind the back seat. He wanted to wake them, to give them a hug and a kiss. He wished he had talked to them more on the drive from Brittany. Now he had to struggle against the desire to stay in the car, to find a reason to break the plan and go with them to Albertville.

Instead, he forced himself to say good-bye.

"Good-night, madame," de Celigny said. "Take care of my sons. Good-night, Alphonse. I wish you a good trip."

"And the same to you, with a safe return," Euler responded. "I will stop here. The station is just three blocks ahead. Good-night."

De Celigny pulled the Beretta from under the seat, put it into his travel bag. He was out of the car before it had come to a full stop. The taillights of the Peugeot faded into fuzzy spots in the fog and then disappeared altogether.

He felt alone and free. His children were out of the enemy's hands. Hesitation was behind him.

As he walked slowly to the station to catch the train to Paris, he promised himself that when he was safely back with his children, he would see Chantal Senac again.

VALERIE was expected by the Russian, but she stopped at the open door and rapped on the doorpost.

Max and the Russian were sitting head to head on the Russian's side of the desk, their faces not more than a foot apart, their expressions matched in intensity.

They both looked up, and Valerie could see that each of them was erasing the conversation that she had interrupted, changing gears to speak now with her. She did not like them to have secret thoughts. What were they talking about . . . ? About her?

"How goes our hunt for Leveque-Landry?" The Russian seemed cordial, but Valerie felt the edge in the question.

"We have covered half of France," she said. "I feel that the searchers are starting to lose heart. We may not find him or the woman. Or Jacques de Celigny and his friends."

"So, we control our people with our computer, more completely than any government in history, and we are at the mercy of a man who controls our computer?"

No answer was required, and Valerie waited a few seconds before offering her question.

"What do you think Robert Landry wants? He has listened to our secret conversations, read our files, gathered a band of former policemen . . . Why? The answer might save us much work."

The two men looked at each other.

Max replied, "We were just discussing that . . . our failure to guess the man's motivation."

"What if he means no harm?" Valerie asked.

"With a man like de Celigny?" Max's response was quick. "He means harm. We can be sure of that."

The telephone rang, and the Russian picked up the receiver. He listened, expressionless.

"Both dead? . . . You have put blocks on the roads? . . . Yes, I know that there are already blocks on the roads. But do the gendarmes and police know that they are also looking for the children of Jacques de Celigny? . . . Thank you. Keep me advised."

The telephone clicked softly as the Russian's hand let it settle back into place.

"It was Comrade Gousset of the national police," the Russian said. "A neighbor went to visit the home in Brittany where the de Celigny children were in safekeeping. The neighbor found the woman who lives there bound and gagged. She was not harmed, but Comrade Morand's two men of MSIE, the men we sent to watch the children, were both dead. The children were gone. This is going very fast. They have anticipated our intentions, recovered the children, killed two more men . . ."

The Russian's gaze tracked across the wall above their heads and then he lowered it at Valerie. "You are right. The search has gone on too long, it will not succeed. We cannot even find de Celigny...."

"They are working together," Max said. "Landry in command of the Star, de Celigny outside, going where he will...."

The Russian's massive head turned to Valerie. "There is another child to watch. The boy named Noël Bazin in the little town of Notre-Dame-de-Bellecombe, near Megève. Put a watch on him, a better watch than we put on the de Celigny children."

He waited while she wrote his instructions.

The Russian continued. "Please tell Eyes in the Intelligence Branch what has happened. Ask him to call Morand at MSIE for the complete report. And ask him your question, ask him what he thinks Landry is trying to do."

Valerie looked from one face to the other. They were blank, waiting for her to leave, and she understood that the conversation she had interrupted would begin again as soon as she left.

"Should I close the door?" she asked.

The Russian nodded and she left, her back stiffer than normal.

"I don't know if she reports what I tell her to report," the Russian said.

"No need to take a chance," Max replied.

"So you think Landry might kill Paccard..."

"Yes."

"And then...?"

"It could make many things easier that are difficult at present."

"I agree, and now I ask myself if we should suppress the search for Landry and Chantal."

"No," Max answered. "They will never be found except by an accident, and it would raise questions."

"It is a dangerous game, Max. The Russians will question our control if Paccard is murdered."

"If we regain control as soon as Paccard is dead, the Russians will be content."

"And who will be our next first secretary?"

Max raised his eyebrows. "I thought you had already decided. Marcel Chabon is the only choice."

"WE need to cut off the Star," Eyes said. "Better to accept total chaos than let him create chaos at will."

Valerie grimaced before speaking. "We could not live without the Star."

"Landry is winning," Eyes spat out, as though it was her fault.

She spoke to their hopes. "We may find him still. The search is far from complete."

But with the death in Brittany of the two MSIE men that she had personally requested from Comrade Morand, her own hope was dead. Eyes was right. And what was the Russian plotting now with Max, in such secrecy that she could not know? Who was the other child, Noël Bazin? What did that mean?

The train of events could have mortal consequences. She searched her mind for a way out.

Pyotr might be interested in a true accounting. But how well placed was Pyotr? Did he have a superior in the KGB who was a confidant of the Russian? What if the Russian learned that she was making unrehearsed reports to Pyotr? A great risk, certain death. If she was to betray the Russian, even in the smallest way, she had to be sure of his downfall.

Eyes' eyes were still on her, and she was frightened for a moment that he could read her thoughts.

She said what was next in her mind. "I would like to go to my apartment for a day, to see if a few hours alone can clear my head. Will you tell the Russian?"

"Of course," Eyes replied, surprise on his face.

"I will call Morand, ask him for a guard on the Bazin child. . . . Do you know what that is about?"

Eyes shrugged. His own curiosity was stirred by this request of the Russian's, but he gave no hint of his interest.

"You will call me if there are any developments? I can be back in my office in twenty minutes if you need me."

"We will call you," Eyes said, "if there are any developments." His sour tone told of his certainty that there would be none.

On the telephone, Morand exploded with anger when she asked him to guard another child.

"You should tell the Russian that he asks very much from us," Morand said at last. "We do what we can, but we have limits, we have only so many men. . . ."

"He understands," she improvised. "He thanks you for your loyalty."

It took half an hour to straighten her desk and wend her way up through the maze to the Boulevard St. Michel.

As she walked to the *métro,* her thoughts turned on the Russian and what he would do if he knew that she had betrayed him. Images crystallized and vanished in split-second horrors: men dead in pools of blood, men with guns watching her as she walked, carrying fear so heavy that her legs were shaking under the load. Flashes of reason punctuated the nightmare, the how and where of bringing down the most secret man in France, but the real risks were more frightening than the fantasies. She was not sure that she could do it.

MARCEL Chabon lived alone in a big apartment that had belonged to a duke, in the Palais Royal facing the Louvre, where he kept his office. Wrapped in thought, he walked to work. The evening before, he had come back to the office after his secretary had gone and had found a message on his desk: Comrade Beringer had called and would call back in the morning at exactly nine.

Since Marcel Chabon did not know any Comrade Beringer, he assumed that it was a message from Landry. He had worried while cooking his supper and long after he should have been asleep that night: the object of a national manhunt was calling his office with no security, leaving messages like a common official for a colleague. The unexpected telephone calls from the United States were bad enough, and now calls from the unknown Beringer. What must his secretary think? She had been with him for so many years, through the revolution, but that meant nothing if MSIE pressed her for information.

As the last man to have contact with Robert Landry, he had received special attention in the manhunt. A delegation of MSIE, led by Minister Morand, had spent four hours in his office to understand, down to the last breath and comma, Landry's plea to help his wife. The MSIE group had gone away satisfied, Chabon thought. After all, he had met Landry before the revolution, who else would Landry have called? He had reported the entire conversation, as Landry had requested, to the head of the DSE, Director Ebert. There was nothing to hide in that. But Chabon knew that he was marked, he could not afford even an appearance of odd behavior.

His secretary was at her desk when he arrived.

"You saw the message, Comrade Chabon?" she asked. "He would not say what he wanted. Do you want to talk to him?"

"I think it has to do with a personal matter. You can put the call through."

He went into his office, turned on the computer, and read the electronic mail that had been distributed overnight by the Star. Many things called for his attention, none of them urgent. Chabon contemplated the telephone in front of him. The line was supposed to be secure, but if it was not? Chabon presumed MSIE could tap the untappable line and unscramble the scrambler. If Landry called again and said the wrong words, the affair could blow up, and a lifetime of work would be wasted.

The second hand on his watch was swinging through the twelve at nine o'clock when the light on Chabon's phone turned on. He let his secretary answer and let her buzz three times before he picked up the receiver.

Without preamble, the voice said, "Do you have a computer in your office? Is it turned on?"

"Yes," Chabon answered. "And yes."

"Then follow my instructions."

Chabon obeyed, tapping in a code, and saw a response on the screen.

>*SECURE LINK ESTABLISHED. THANK YOUR CALLER AND HANG UP.*

"Thank you," Chabon said into the phone. "Good-bye."

He put down the telephone. Could he trust that the Star was secure? He supposed so, if Landry was running it. The monitor went blank and then filled with writing. Chabon read a list of questions about the State Factory to be opened. There was a blank after each question. A cursor blinked at the beginning of the first blank, waiting for him to type a reply. Chabon thought a moment and then tapped the keys, watching his answer fill and overflow the blank, pushing the next question down the screen.

Chabon worked at Landry's questionnaire for half an hour, concentrating on the answers.

When he had filled in the last response, the screen went blank, and then a message appeared, letter by letter. Landry was typing it as Chabon watched.

>*GOOD. YOU WILL HAVE MY FIRST DATA OUTPUT IN FIVE DAYS.*

These words vanished.

>*DO YOU KNOW THE NAME JACQUES DE CELIGNY?*

Chabon typed "yes."

>*DE CELIGNY WILL SETTLE THE MATTER OF GEORGES PACCARD IF YOU WILL MEET HIM—WILL YOU MEET HIM?*

Chabon typed "yes, where and when?"

>*WE WILL ADVISE. AT FIVE PM THIS AFTERNOON, LOG INTO YOUR COMPUTER AND TYPE THIS CODE: MCRLM-CRLMCRL*

HAVE YOU NOTED THE TIME AND THE CODE? THIS COM-

*MUNICATION WILL DISAPPEAR AFTER YOU ACKNOWL-
EDGE.*

FUTURE COMMUNICATION WILL BE VIA THE STAR.

So, Chabon thought, Landry was not naive. They were finished
with the telephone, and they had provoked his secretary's curiosity for the last time.

Chabon jotted down the code and the time on separate pieces
of paper and typed "yes."

A sprayburst of light obliterated the message, and the screen
went blank.

The main risk of their communication was eliminated. Chabon
could think again about being named first secretary—a lifetime's
devotion fulfilled, under circumstances that he could never have
imagined. He could engineer the final rebirth of his dismembered
country.

But first, Chabon reflected, he would pass days more dangerous than any in his life. Paccard would go. And then he would
need to deal with the Russian and Department 100. He did not
have a solution for that, not yet, and it was much too dangerous
to ask for Landry's help.

THE windows of the Café de la Poste were gray with a film of city
dirt. It was as he remembered. Detective Louche stood on the far
side of the street, where he had led the woman, had asked her
questions and sensed her panic, even though her answers were
coherent.

The search for her was becoming a joke. Entering each and
every home in France was tiresome. It was no secret that some of
his colleagues were recording visits that had never taken place,
except in their imaginations while they were sipping *pastis*.

Detective Louche doubted that anyone would find her. Or her
lover, the bearded Landry/Leveque, or the brave de Celigny.
They were all fugitives from the same search, and Louche
assumed they were linked in union against the government.

Louche stood alone, spending the minutes allowed him for lunch, daydreaming success while the gray windows across the street reflected his dull stare.

Inside the Café de la Poste it was dark and cooler than on the sun-warmed street. The woman was behind the counter with the old useless cash register and the cash-card reader. The counterman, surely her husband, was taking a *croque-monsieur* from an electric grill. Did they remember him from that February day?

Three customers huddled close together at a table in the back. Workmen. There had been workmen in the back on that day.

The seats by the window were empty.

Louche tried to imagine her there.

"What do you wish, comrade?" It was the counterman. "Coffee, or tea? A beer?"

Louche shook his head, distracted, and again attempted to recreate the woman sitting there.

A bearded man had been sitting at the adjacent table. That could have been Leveque, of course, but Louche remembered nothing of him.

His mind's eye now filled in with the image of them both, sitting with their backs to the window in the dying light of a February afternoon. That was better.

Her hands had quivered in fishing through her sack of a handbag.

Louche forced the image of her hands out of his head and tried to remember the man. It was like concentrating on a blurred photograph. He'd had a beard. He could have been Landry/Leveque. But they had not seemed to be together.

Louche remembered asking if they were together.

The man had answered. What had he said? There had been surprise in his denial that he was with the woman to his right—that much came to memory—and the surprise had seemed natural even to Louche's acute sensitivities.

Louche could not recollect the man's identity card. Conjuring up the feel of it in his hand, the glint of the plastic surface under the light, the photograph and the computer-generated print, none of this could wrestle loose the man's name or employment.

He struggled to remember, and then he quit. His watch told him that he should be on his way to earn his daily bread.

"Nothing for today," Louche said to the counterman. "Good-bye."

"Good-bye, comrade."

Louche was halfway to the Champs-Élysées when the verbal exchange with the bearded man echoed into his mind as it had occurred:

"What are your hours of work?" he had demanded, sharply, as though the fellow had been malingering.

"Twenty-four hours. I lock up my warehouse when I go out to eat."

He had worked in a warehouse, then, and that in itself was unusual because there were not many warehouses near to the Arc de Triomphe.

Louche was eager to tell Groux, but why not find the warehouse first and give Groux a package? What if the man was Leveque? And if Leveque could be brought in, delivered single-handed by Detective Louche, while all France was being scoured in vain?

Louche almost broke into a run from his excitement. He could easily learn the warehouses within a kilometer radius from the Café de la Poste. Then, some days of observation, a few questions, and . . .

He thought of the warehouse on rue Pouchkine. It was so close, only a few hundred meters from the Café de la Poste.

The warehouseman had come into the station to make his report. Dullwitted, halfway from idiocy to intelligence. Clean shaven. Could he have been the same as the bearded man? Now, pride battled with reason in Louche's heart. He should have sensed a sham, that was his talent.

But the circumstances of the interview had been cluttered, the staff room crowded and busy, his lunch hour threatened. Louche admitted that he could have been fooled.

On impulse, he turned right on the Champs-Élysées and then right again, toward the rue Pouchkine. Procedures called for a report, for at least a three-man team to investigate, but this visit was only for reconnaissance, and how could he ask for a team without sharing his glory? He could always make up a story of coincidences to explain his violation of procedures.

In the rue Pouchkine, Louche extracted his automatic from its shoulder holster. He clicked a bullet into the chamber and reholstered the weapon. For a moment he hesitated, but then the opportunity to prove his true worth swept him on, to the door with the great old lock that he recalled needed a special pick. His fingers closed on his picks, ringed together and ready in the pocket of his jacket.

He tried the door. It was locked. A white button promised to ring inside for the warehouseman, but surprise would be better.

The large pick worked, more easily than the first time he had entered this warehouse.

Louche took the pistol in his right hand and gently pushed the door open with his left.

Inside, darkness. Louche put his hand out and found the light switch. In the light, the leaning stacks of cartons, the oblique rows, were as he remembered, but something was different. He felt a presence, an aura that had been absent before.

Quietly, his back to the wall, he sidestepped toward the small room in the far corner, where he had left the notice on the warehouseman's bed.

The room was empty, as it had been the first time. The warehouseman was not easy to find at home. Louche examined the room, pushing at the bedsheets with the muzzle of his pistol, wanting to search with both hands but too frightened to be unarmed. Louche felt no presence in this room, as though it was never occupied, and he was struck by the absence of any of the small litter or useless artifacts that most people accumulate in their living spaces. The storage area outside felt more occupied than this sleeping room.

Louche trusted his feelings. Could the man have been out there among the stacks of cartons, hiding in the dark?

He stepped back into the warehouse and stood there, listening, feeling for another human spirit. Where was he? In the toilet? Louche sidestepped again, along the back wall, his pistol raised.

The door to the toilet hung ajar. Louche pushed it open and stepped inside. It was empty.

Then, with a clang that split the silence like the crash of an axe, a bell sounded, as loud as a fire alarm. Silence followed, and then it rang again, two short bursts. The doorbell, Louche realized.

Louche's feet took him around the inside perimeter of the warehouse, his back to the wall, all the way to the door.

He turned out the light, opened the door a fraction, and stepped back, his pistol in both hands.

No one pushed on the door.

Slowly, he untwined the fingers of his left hand from the butt of the pistol, reached for the doorknob, seized it, and pulled hard, stepping forward as he did.

On the sidewalk outside, a short, moustached man stood a yard away, head cocked.

"Police," Louche said. "Hands over your head. Identify yourself."

"Charles Laitier, of Lons-le-Saunier," he answered, his hands elevated, like a bird's wings just before flight.

Louche stepped out into the street, feeling better in daylight. "What do you do here?"

"I have come to visit my friend François Blanc."

"He is not here."

"Then I will come back."

"No," Louche said. "Keep your hands up. Walk slowly to the wall. Place your hands high on it and lean against it. I think you understand, no? . . ."

"This is not justified," the man said, but he obeyed, his eyes on Louche's face.

Louche looked at the man spread-eagled against the wall, and exhilaration tingled his scalp. Could this be the other fugitive, de Celigny? The description fit perfectly. There was a weapon tucked in his belt, a bulge under his jacket marked the spot.

"Stand still or you are dead," Louche said. He approached, reached for the tail of de Celigny's jacket, and flipped it up over de Celigny's head. The pistol was there, and then it was in Louche's left hand. De Celigny remained stock still.

Louche looked up and down the street. He wished for help, some passerby to call the police station and ask for reinforcements, but there was no one. He stuffed de Celigny's Beretta in his belt.

"Step forward. Keep your hands above your head. We are going inside to wait for your friend's return."

The jacket still draped over his head, de Celigny responded, his movements deliberate.

He asked, his voice muffled from under the cloth, "Can you prove that you are police?"

"Silence! The proof is in my hand."

"I can't see." The raised hands came down to the covered head and lifted the jacket, then let it drop.

Louche was furious, but he could not come too close, and the transgression was too slight for him to kill. He felt a pang of fear and his resolution faltered, but now he had no choice.

"Inside, slow; I am right behind you."

De Celigny stepped over the threshold, and Louche closed the distance between them, then used his left hand to switch on the lights.

"Move," Louche said.

"Where?"

"To your friend's room."

"You will have to direct me."

Was it possible that de Celigny had never come to this place before?

Louche put his back to the door and swung it shut, leaning on it until the latch clicked.

"Turn to your left and follow the wall."

De Celigny walked with deliberate steps, and Louche followed four paces behind, his pistol raised. Every nerve alert, he felt again the aura of a presence in the stacks. How to flush him out? A plan formed, a safe way to diminish the risk. At the right place and moment, he would shoot de Celigny.

They reached the door of the small room. It seemed as good a place as any.

Louche felt the flesh of his finger compress against the trigger, but he could not complete the act without the appearance of struggle. He knew that Inspector Groux, the commissioners, even MSIE would be furious if they thought he had simply gunned down their quarry.

"Turn around," Louche commanded. "Face me."

As though reading Louche's mind, de Celigny remained facing the door.

"Turn!"

Louche quietly stepped forward into striking range, raising his weapon to club his victim.

Then he felt danger rushing toward the back of his own head, and this acuity killed him, because his reflexive evasion accelerated Nagy's strike.

Nagy cursed as the body fell.

De Celigny turned and looked down into the eyes of the corpse.

"Thank you. He was going to shoot me."

"He felt me coming. I am losing my silence." Nagy spoke like an aging runner admitting that he can no longer sprint.

"This is not the greeting I expected in this place. It cannot be so secret here if strangers with guns are answering the door. Who is this man? If he is really police, how can he be here alone?"

Nagy shook his head.

"It is Detective Louche," Robert Landry stated. He was standing in the doorway to his small room, the trap door open behind him. "I think I understand why he is here, and why he is alone. It is a shame he is dead, he could tell us himself."

"I did not intend to kill him, but he felt the blow coming and moved." Nagy frowned at the imperfect event.

Landry stepped forward and bent over the body, which was lying on its back, arms flung apart, the pistol still in one hand. "He was the detective who interviewed Chantal Senac last February, on the day I met her. I erased the Star's record of Louche's interview. Later, he came here and left a note for me. When I went to be interviewed at the police station in response to the summons, he did not recognize me. Something must have happened to make him remember. Bad luck for him."

"How could he be alone?" de Celigny asked. "The police never work alone."

"He let me slip through his fingers in the manhunt. Perhaps he was seeking redemption?"

"We must hope so," de Celigny replied.

They emptied a large cardboard carton, put Louche's body into it, and buried it under other cartons. Then they descended the ladder to the cave below, de Celigny and Nagy in the lead so that Landry could hide their traces in his room above. De Celigny and Nagy refused the rope and arrived at the bottom long before Landry.

De Celigny peered around the grotto, examined the single keyboard and the monitor with the bundle of cables leading away toward the Star's central installation.

"So this is it?" de Celigny asked. "You do everything from this hole in the ground?"

"Yes," Landry said. "This is all I need."

De Celigny sat down on a box of books. Nagy leaned on a wall behind him.

Landry began by talking about the division between Paccard in the government and the Russian in Department 100, and how the Russian could be discredited, weakened, and then destroyed. Then he talked about Chabon, once he became first secretary, opening the State Factories, loosening the bonds of central planning, allowing people to choose their work. Landry said that he imagined local elections, a free press, dismantling the internal security organization.

"You have talked about this with Chabon?" de Celigny asked.

"Not all . . . not yet."

"It is all theory then," de Celigny said.

"But I know what the man has done. Why would he change if he had real freedom to do what he wanted for France? When you meet him, ask him these questions and decide for yourself."

"I will. Let us hope that he has good answers. But Landry, something has been bothering me since we met in the mountains. You ask me to put my life at risk by meeting Chabon, but you do not trust him well enough to do the same. Is that not so?"

"It is not like that," Landry said. "We cannot replace my control of the Star. . . ."

"But I can be replaced. Right?"

Landry could not answer the logic.

"Give me some assurance, Landry," de Celigny continued. "I will meet Marcel Chabon, but first you must tell him how to find you."

"No . . . I can't."

"Then forget the meeting, forget your plan." De Celigny stood up. "Because if you do not give Chabon all your trust, then neither do I."

Landry saw his hopes vanishing. "Wait . . ."

He had lived so long now in the warm blanket of his secrecy. Could he give that up? . . . But he believed in Chabon.

"All right," Landry said. "I will do it."

Three hours later, Marcel Chabon received his instructions to meet Jacques de Celigny. He also received the address of Landry's warehouse.

12 At one-thirty in the afternoon, Louche's partner reported Louche absent. At that time, Louche was still walking toward the rue Pouchkine from the Champs-Élysées.

The report was the first of two concerning Louche's disappearance that scrolled down the screen of Robert Landry's monitor that night. The second was from Inspector Groux, requesting permission to divert three men to search for his lost detective.

As Landry read the electronic epitaph, his van was rolling slowly through the Bois de Boulogne with Maurice Thevenet at the wheel. It was midnight, and the first drops of rain from an oncoming cold front dappled the windshield. De Celigny, sitting in the back of the van beside the cardboard box, pondered the sound of the droplets hitting the metal roof. De Celigny wished that they did not need to unload the body.

The road through the Bois de Boulogne took them to a grimy area along the banks of the Seine, where the river separates the suburbs of St.-Germain-en-Laye from the city of Paris.

Thevenet drove to a vast, dark building, a food distribution center for the New State. The blank walls of the building towered over the neighboring warehouses for several blocks. The wet pavement of the parking lot gleamed under the streetlamps. There was not another vehicle in sight, moving or parked. Thevenet continued past the enormous building and returned again past the back of the structure.

"It is clear," Thevenet said. "Are you ready with the box?"

"Ready," de Celigny replied.

Lights out, they rolled to a stop one hundred meters from the warehouse. Nagy slipped out of the van, a hidden reinforcement in case of trouble.

Rolling again, they approached the back of the warehouse, where a row of tall disposal bins stood glistening in the rain.

De Celigny and Thevenet wrestled their cargo out of the van, up onto the edge of the first bin above their heads. The box rested there, like a great bird on a wire, and then rolled out of sight, into the garbage.

The sound of an engine broke the dull patter of the rain, and both men ducked back into the van. Lights shone, and a car passed.

As soon as the lights disappeared, Thevenet wheeled the van around and returned for Nagy. Their mission was about to begin.

THEY drove on the *périphérique*, the circle of highway around Paris, and left it to follow the autoroute north, under the wide bridge that carried the main runway of the Karl Marx Airport, and on, through a tempest of heavy raindrops, to the exit for Chantilly.

The narrow, high-crowned road past Chantilly wound up and down through low hills. Even in the rain, they could glimpse the silhouettes of fine houses, proud roofs and high chimneys, rising behind brick walls along the roadway. This was the land of the party's elite, fat cats in cream.

Thevenet drove confidently. He had been down this road five times at night; he could anticipate every bend and crest.

"What time is it?" Thevenet asked. "We are almost there."

"Ten minutes past one," de Celigny answered from behind him. "It is just the right time."

A stone wall by the roadside came into view. Thevenet turned out the headlights and stopped on the shoulder where the stone wall was replaced by a high wrought-iron fence.

"Here," he said. "I hope our friend in Paris is on schedule."

Thevenet picked up a large wire-cutter from beside his seat, attached it to his belt, and got out of the van. He stooped to find the aluminum ladder that had rested in the grass since his last tour of the countryside. The ladder went up on the side of the fence, and Thevenet climbed, the wire-cutter swinging and banging on the ladder rails.

Over his head was a cable containing the telephone wire from Leonid Paccard's house and an armed circuit set to trigger alarms in three locations: the Chantilly police station, the MSIE office at the airport, and the gendarmerie's barracks at Survilliers on the autoroute. The alarms were designed to sound if any part of the circuit was broken.

Thevenet reached up and cut the cable, letting the ends fall past his shoulders to the ground below.

In the police station, the MSIE office, and the gendarmerie barracks, nothing happened. Landry had spent hours learning how to disable the alarm system, and then how to de-program the backup alarm that would give warning if the system was disabled. From one A.M. onward, the elite of Chantilly were disconnected from surveillance, naked to aggression.

Thevenet climbed down the ladder, rung by rung, with the assurance of a craftsman at his work, as though it was normal to be working in the rain in the small hours of the morning outside the house of the first secretary's son.

"Where is Nagy?" he asked, returning to the van with the ladder.

"On his way to the gate," de Celigny answered. "Let's move."

They drove to the massive gate that interrupted the line of the wrought-iron fence. The gate was open, Nagy waiting inside.

He climbed into the right-hand seat, and they continued up the driveway to the house.

They stopped one hundred meters from the house and turned the van around to face the gate.

Nagy was out of the van before it stopped, running into the rain.

Thevenet carried the ladder to one wall of the house, laid it up to a window, and climbed. He tapped a pane loose, unlatched the clasp, pulled the window open, and disappeared inside.

De Celigny put the Beretta in his belt, went to the front door, and pressed the bell.

He waited, then rang again and took a step back into the driving rain.

Above, a light went on in the row of windows that cut across the mansard roof.

Another light, this one on the main floor, shone through the glass on either side of the door.

The door opened. The man behind it was unarmed, but he was large and unfriendly.

"Who are you?"

"I wish to speak to Leonid Paccard," de Celigny answered. "I have some information that will greatly interest him."

The man inside was a head taller than de Celigny, broad and muscular, with the stance and surliness of a paid bodyguard. "What is the information?"

"It is not for you."

"Then come back tomorrow. He is asleep."

"Go wake him up. Tell him that I have information about some merchandise. My information will not last through the night. He will be angry if it loses its value while he sleeps."

"What is your name?"

"Gabon, Comrade Gabon."

The door started to close.

"Can I wait inside? It is wet out here."

"Then be wet." The door swung shut.

De Celigny ran back to the van and took the Heckler & Koch machine pistol out of its scabbard under the right-hand seat.

As quickly, he ran to the back of the house, looking for the door where Nagy should have picked the lock.

Inside, the bodyguard marched up the stairs. His spoiled master would be angry to be interrupted with the new girl, but would be angrier if a business deal slipped away in the night. Who knows what kind of merchandise was offered in the middle of the night.

The girl woke first at the pounding on the door. Leonid was snoring beside her. Marina, Leonid's longtime mistress, was sleeping on the far side of Leonid. She too woke up from the pounding on the door.

Marina's head cleared quickly. She sat up and shouted at the door, "What is it?"

The voice was muffled behind the door. Marina turned on a light and got out of bed. She glanced down at Leonid, whose unconscious stupor was all too familiar. The new girl was wide-eyed, looking up from the sheets tucked under her chin. Adorable.

Marina walked to the door, unconscious of her nakedness, and spoke again, "What is it?"

She identified the voice of the bodyguard and pulled open the door.

It was not unusual for Marina to be seen naked: that was not the reason for the bodyguard's stunned expression.

"Comrade Gabon," he was able to say, but these were his last words. His knees buckled, and slowly he toppled forward into the room.

Marina looked into the hole of the long silencer on Nagy's pistol, where a faint wisp of smoke still curled.

"Quiet," Nagy said, his voice like velvet. "Back up, slowly. If you move too fast or speak, you are dead."

Marina obeyed, heart pounding.

Nagy followed her in, and then Thevenet came behind, his Walther P.38 in his hands.

The new girl screamed once and covered her head with the sheet.

Nagy spoke to Marina, "Why does he not wake up?"

"He drank a bottle of wine and took some pills before we came to bed."

"Wake him up."

"Are you going to kill him?"

"Is he worth keeping alive?"

They both looked at the sagging flesh of Leonid Paccard's torso, the open mouth and double chin. Marina shrugged. "He has done no harm."

"He is a disgrace to the revolution."

"You are going to kill him?"

"Not now. He will be more useful alive."

"Then . . ."

"Wake him. If he can't be made to walk, then you will need to carry him, you and your friend under the sheets."

"Giselle," Marina said. "Wake him up."

The sheets heaved as the new girl rocked Leonid Paccard's body.

"This is tiresome," Nagy said to Thevenet.

"Watch them," Thevenet replied. "I will wake him."

Thevenet stuffed his pistol into his belt. "Where is the bathroom?"

"There," Marina answered, pointing to a door.

Thevenet seized Leonid's ankle and pulled him onto the floor in a tumble of linen. The girl in the bed, stripped of her sheet, curled up and covered her head with her arms.

Thevenet dragged Leonid's nude body into the bathroom.

Reflex moved Leonid to struggle against the drenching cold of the shower even before the pain of consciousness started to penetrate his deadened brain. Thevenet held him, slapped him once, and then looked into the dull eyes of his quarry, who was now awake.

"Stand up," Thevenet commanded.

Obediently, Leonid stood. Thevenet stepped away and removed the pistol from his belt.

Leonid swayed and put a foot out to catch his balance.

His brain was half functioning now, still clouded, but aware. He understood the pistol and the man behind it.

"Step out of the shower," Thevenet said. "Do exactly as I say or I will kill you."

With Marina's help they dressed him. The two women helped him down the stairs, and then he walked, in short, staggering steps, out the front door and into the rainy night.

Nagy stopped at the door. "Tell the first secretary that we need his son to answer questions about events in Pontoise. He will understand."

Shivering, Marina and the new girl ran up the stairs, passing the bloodstained corpse of the bodyguard. The telephone in the bedroom was dead. They dressed and went to wake the maid, the cook, and the cook's husband, who served as handyman and gardener.

All three automobiles in the garage were immobilized, their gas lines and wiring cut. The handyman set out to call for help from the nearest neighbor, but he was stopped at the end of the driveway by Nagy and Thevenet. He passed the night bound hand and foot to a tree, while the four women waited in the house for help to come.

The Chantilly operation took less than twenty minutes. The van returned to Paris by the eastern link of the autoroute and continued south to the Porte de Vincennes. There they turned away from the city and drove to a small house, where a garage provided shelter for the van.

The day had begun well. Jacques de Celigny hoped that it would end as well.

Leonid was only an event. The meeting with Marcel Chabon would set the future.

At eight in the morning, neither First Secretary Paccard nor President Joux had received news of the kidnapping. But both were preoccupied by a single piece of paper that had been circulated during the night.

The sheet, an interministerial directive from Department 100, had not left Joux's knobby fingers since it had been given to him twenty minutes before. Alone in the back seat of the limousine, the president looked again at the paper. Gouts of water flew from his Moskva limousine as it raced toward the Matignon Palace. Its siren wailing in the deluge, a lone black car cleared the way as they crossed the river and passed the brooding mass of the Invalides.

At the Matignon, First Secretary Georges Paccard waited for his colleague. The same communication from Department 100 was centered on his desk. He was furious, because of the paper and because Joux had insisted on a meeting. He had no time for Joux.

The doors to Paccard's office were still closing when Joux asked the obvious question.

"Did you call the embassy?"

"My contact at the embassy knows nothing, but he said it was the Russian's right to send the document. The embassy will not intervene."

"So," Joux said. He felt the muscles contract in his jaw. Fear was crawling up his back, fear that he was about to lose his authority and with it his rank, and then even his freedom, and maybe his life.

The document was simple. At the top, it was marked, "Top Secret, For Ministers' Eyes Only." Three paragraphs followed.

The first explained that the integrity of the state had been compromised by a breach of the Star's systems.

The second stated that Department 100 was required to intervene, to restore security.

The third paragraph stated that, until resolution of the crisis, ministerial acts should be passed to Department 100 for review and approval.

The Russian had taken control of the government.

"What motive could the Russian have?" Joux asked.

"He is desperate," Paccard answered. "He is responsible for the loss of security in these last weeks. Two agents were lost in Albertville, and two more in Brittany. All France is turned upside down searching for a phantom. The Russian is trying to seize power before he loses what power he has. We must act now. Once the embassy loses their man, who else can they turn to but us?"

"Act, comrade? Do you intend to attack the embassy's representative in France?" Joux's voice quavered with horror at the idea of offending the Russians.

Paccard swept on, "MSIE will fight on our side, if Morand understands that his life depends on it."

A blue light blinked discreetly on Paccard's desk, and he reached for the telephone. He listened, and a new wave of rage and frustration contorted his features.

"Keep me informed. Spare no effort." Paccard slammed the receiver down. "My son has been kidnapped from his home in Chantilly."

"Incredible!" Joux exclaimed.

"The telephone lines were cut and the alarm system failed. There were two armed kidnappers. Leonid's bodyguard was killed."

Paccard glared at his colleague, as though daring him to argue. "The kidnappers wanted to ask Leonid questions about Pontoise, and the bodyguard died with the name 'Comrade Gabon' on his lips. We must counterattack, this is a provocation by the Russian. Are you with me?"

Joux refused to answer. He was almost as frightened of Paccard as he was of the Russians.

Paccard urged him. "The embassy cannot blame us if we attack. If you are not convinced now that we must act . . ."

Joux shrugged again and forced out the words. "You will not succeed. Let the embassy decide what to do."

Paccard's rage boiled so hot that he could not speak.

"What about Leonid?" Joux asked.

"They cannot keep him."

But as Paccard uttered the words, the meaning of what had happened struck a chord. They had kidnapped Leonid, out of his home. A symmetry formed in Paccard's mind, action to balance action. There could even be a way to divide the Russians in the embassy from their Russian in the labyrinth. With good luck he could do as Joux asked, let the Russians decide.

WHEN Russians came to visit from Moscow, Marcel Chabon would borrow a Moskva or Mercedes limousine and let his driver take the wheel while he sat in back with his guests. Chabon was no fool. He knew enough to flatter visitors. But at other times, Marcel Chabon drove while his driver sat in the right-hand seat. It was a small quirk of his character. So was the car he had chosen. Made in France by one of the State Factories, it was smaller by far than the limousines assigned to the other ministers. But as minister of the economy, Chabon liked to explain to his colleagues, it was important to test the output of his factories.

He often let the driver take an afternoon or an evening off, so that it was easy to go where he wished without being observed. This afternoon, he was alone in his car.

He did not know this part of Paris well, and the rain made it hard to see.

Chabon stopped the car at the western end of the Avenue Foch. The wide avenue was lined with trees, and an expanse of green grass separated its two roadways. The apartment buildings were clad in polished stone, with ornamental cornices and iron-work; once, in the recent past, an address here meant that the proprietor was rich.

He got out of the car, turned up the collar of his raincoat, and scooped an umbrella and hat from the ledge behind the rear seat.

An old building faced him from behind a high fence. He pushed the button that opened the wrought-iron gate, then walked through it and into the building. In the old days there would have been a doorman, but luxury apartment buildings like this had been cleaned out during redeployment. No doubt the former residents were working in the State Factories, his own unwilling employees.

He cocked his head as though perplexed, then went out onto the street and surveyed the adjacent buildings. An observer would have thought that he had mistaken the address.

He shook his head in a charade of exasperation, then put his hat on, opened the umbrella against the mist, and set out on foot, down the avenue, around the circle, and into the Bois de Boulogne. It would be a long walk, four kilometers, at least forty minutes, and he was glad for his rubber-soled shoes to keep his feet dry.

His route took him past a small lake. He stopped twice to iden-tify the correct fork of the road that would lead him to his desti-nation, a once exclusive club, with tennis courts, a pool, and a clubhouse. In the old days the club had been known as the place where one played polo in Paris.

With the revolution, it had been abandoned. The resonance of luxury and privilege had been too much for even the most cal-loused of the party elite.

The gateway from the road seemed almost anonymous, but a small sign still announced that the grounds were private and that nonmembers should desist from entry. The main building sat low and unpretentious, a one-story wooden structure with a covered terrace, the moldings of the doors and windows painted white and starting to go gray. A window was broken, perhaps from a child's rock.

Chabon walked around to the front of the clubhouse. A hedge, unpruned, blocked the view onto the polo field. He looked at his watch ... five minutes before the agreed time. His feet carried him past the clubhouse to a row of empty stables, their half doors opened in disarray. Behind that, a larger stable stood, its concave roof curving to the sky like an aerodrome.

What had become of the horses? There was no need for them now.

He walked on a gravel path beside the hedge as far as a lattice-work scoreboard, then turned back to a break in the hedge where he could pass through onto the polo field. It was enormous, filled with uncut grass and weeds.

His instructions were clear. He was to go to the middle of the field and wait.

The vegetation was up to his knees, sometimes higher, and heavy with water. He felt as though he was wading as he pushed through the grass.

When he got to the center, he stopped, telling himself that any half-decent marksman could kill him from the edge of the field.

He admitted that the uncomfortable weather suited the rendezvous. Who would venture out on a day like this, to an abandoned polo club on the outskirts of Paris?

Holding the umbrella low over his head, Chabon turned slowly, surveying the trees at the edge of the field. How long would it take for de Celigny to make the circuits around the outside of the grounds, to be sure that his visitor had come by himself?

The only sign of life was an occasional hissing of tires on the wet roads, distant in the Bois.

He turned, sweeping the field's limits. His eyes jumped over the clubhouse and then stopped. Something was different—a man's shape, outlined against the dark windows of the terrace, facing him. It was hard to see in the mist.

Chabon raised his free hand, and the man raised an arm, beckoning. Chabon cursed and started the walk back.

The door to the clubhouse yielded easily, and they went in. The wicker chairs had been stripped of their cushions; they sat low to the ground, their heads no higher than the seatbacks.

Jacques de Celigny took his pistol from his belt and put it on the floor between them.

Chabon said, "We both believe in France. . . ."

"That is a start," de Celigny replied. "But the question is, why should I believe in you?"

"Because, there is no one else, and I can do some good. Let me explain what I want."

Chabon began. "I have always understood that freedom is essential to a healthy economy, but I have also understood that uncontrolled capitalism is inherently unfair. I prefer a benign authority that shelters a free economy. I started working with the Russians during the first arms cutbacks in the eighties and the reforms after Gorbachev, and they found my ideas congenial. . . . This is the basis of the trust that they gave me."

"Go ahead."

"They still give me this trust. They have discouraged Paccard from sabotaging my programs and have protected me personally from Paccard. There is no one else they can count on, among all the ministers, to run the government. I can rebuild France as a healthy place where people can work in freedom, and I myself can keep the Russians happy. It is what they expect of me."

"You do not persuade me," de Celigny said. "The Russians made you part of the revolution here. I should kill you for that."

"I was head of a trade delegation in Moscow in late November of 2002, working out the details of a barter deal. They asked me if I would serve as a minister, in the event that there was a new government in France, It did not sound ominous at all. There was no reason to think that the government of France could be hostile to Russia, not after the World Peace Agreement, and it is always agreeable to be recognized."

Chabon smiled, as though mocking his own weakness of pride. The skin crinkled around his eyes, and he saw that de

Celigny was returning the smile. Would the meeting succeed, after all? Chabon continued, "I had no idea of the severity of the change."

Chabon saw the quick hardening in his companion's face and added, "I know about your wife and children. I am sorry."

"You say that you did not know what was coming?"

"I did not know."

De Celigny held Chabon's eyes until Chabon repeated, "I did not know."

"And if you replace Paccard? What is your idea of a better France?"

"There is much to do. Elimination of Russian influences in our intelligence services, our military, our production plans. Replacement of incompetence by talent and energy. A gradual process, so that they never feel it, until in the end we can make our own decisions. The Russians will not come back with their tanks if I am careful not to provoke them."

"And," de Celigny asked, "how would you manage the fate of those Frenchmen who went from house to house, who tore families apart, killed some and damaged others?"

Chabon turned the question in his mind.

"I say bury the past. There were all sorts of people engaged in that upheaval. Some were guilty of terrible crimes, others were only fulfilling their notion of social justice. There is no value in a purge, not now, or ever. You would only pile evil on top of evil. . . . I'm sorry."

De Celigny stared at him.

"All right," de Celigny said at last. "I will not argue with you, but God help the man who killed my wife, if I ever find him. . . . Let us continue. What do you intend for me, and for my group? How will we return to a normal life?"

"I will cancel the search for you. Your friend Landry is now planning to open the State Factories. You can easily join the movement of people back into society. Eventually I would like you to help me, if you agree."

"Agree? I ask these questions to hear your answers, but I have no hope for the future. I do not believe in you any more than I believe in Landry. But continue, comrade minister, can you suggest how I should kill Paccard?"

"We will kill Paccard together. Will you listen to my plan?"

De Celigny nodded, and Chabon knew that they could go forward until the next step. That would be enough.

FOR the first time in weeks, Valerie called Pyotr without a briefing from the Russian.

She explained that he was hearing the words of Valerie Clavel, no longer the Russian's words from her mouth

Her control listened without responding. When she was through, he told her to return to her work the next morning, but to be sure to call every day.

She hung up and stepped back from the enclosure that housed the public telephone of her corner bistro, The Heroes of the Revolution.

It was four in the afternoon, late for lunch, but the bistro's kitchen was willing. Valerie returned to her table beside the mist-blurred window.

An *andouillette* and a glass of rough red Italian wine awaited her, the *andouillette* in a bed of gravy-drenched macaroni. She ate slowly, enjoying every forkful. The rich offal sausage was an indulgent change from her daily fare in the labyrinth.

She felt the waiter's eyes on her. He would smell of garlic and sweat, and he would bore her with stupidities, but the idea of making love was not displeasing. Still, she scowled when she exchanged her cash card for the bill, and scowled again when he brought the cash card back to her.

The Heroes of the Revolution was only three short blocks from her apartment. She walked with her mind full of the Russian, buried in secrecy in the labyrinth, and of Robert Landry, wherever he was, playing a chorus of discord with the Star.

Just inside the door of her apartment, she stopped, sniffing. She never smoked, but tobacco smoke was in the air. Someone had been smoking in her apartment. How long had she been out? Not more than an hour and a half. Someone had been in the apartment recently. The concierge perhaps, the woman smoked constantly.

Hesitant, Valerie went to the wall closet to put away her umbrella.

"Be quiet, please," a soft male voice said from behind her.

She turned and looked into the eyes of a man with a pistol. He had been in her kitchen, waiting for her. In the doorway to her bedroom another man appeared, totally bald, his lips pulled back from his teeth by a manic smile.

"You will come with us," the man from the kitchen said.

"Who are you?"

"Turn around. We must be sure that you are not armed."

Her training was not sufficient, and her physical condition had been sapped by weeks underground. There was no chance for a sudden counterstrike. The men were professionals, holding their distance, covering each other. Slowly, she turned toward her closet.

"Hands on the wall, above the door . . . Thank you."

The frisk was thorough but gentle, the hands leaving a tingle of unfulfilled menace as they left her.

"You will be away for a few days. Would you like to take anything, such as toothpaste or a toothbrush, or any other necessities? We have a few minutes."

She understood that they were giving her leeway to use the remaining seconds to hide papers, to leave a message, baiting her to take them to whatever needed hiding.

"My kit, of course, to brush my teeth."

They followed her to the bathroom where she kept the toiletry kit. It had come with her from the labyrinth, and it was still zipped shut.

"That is all? . . . You wish to take some clothes?"

"That won't be necessary," she said. "Let's go."

EYES, the head of Department 100's Intelligence Branch, furiously wiped his glasses with his handkerchief. The Russian rarely came down to the intelligence offices. It was hard to think clearly with the Russian insisting on explanations.

There was far too much to explain.

—Earlier that day, a detective who once had questioned Chantal Senac had disappeared.

—The Russian's contact at the embassy had called to ask about a forged interministerial directive that had been circulated over the Russian's signature.

—Someone had kidnapped Leonid Paccard.

—Comrade Morand, the minister of the interior, had ordered the personnel of MSIE on alert at the request of the first secretary. Morand had reported this news without further comment, but he seemed to be sure that Leonid was held by Department 100. Who else would make a bad joke on Gabon, ask questions about Pontoise?

—And now, Gentiane had left the labyrinth for the first time in days and was somewhere up above in the streets of Paris, unaccounted for.

Eyes had gone out in the rain himself to look at Gentiane's apartment. He had noted the lingering smells of tobacco and sweat, the cigarette butts. The kidnappers had left their signs deliberately.

"Leonid is Landry's work," the Russian said. "De Celigny took him. The ministerial directive was a forgery by the Star. For Valerie, de Celigny again. . . . They are trying to cause a battle between the government and us. I will call the first secretary and explain this to him. What I do not understand is the detective. . . . Why has he vanished?"

"The detective," Eyes responded.

The two men's eyes locked, watching each other's minds at work.

"We must learn everything about the detective. Where he was when he disappeared, who last saw him, what he did the day before."

"We can obtain the detective's search list," Eyes stated. "Should we say nothing about Gentiane?"

"Nothing."

Eyes placed a call to Gousset at the National Police. Gousset was immediately available. Everyone engaged in the security of France was on call.

"Eyes, Department 100 Intelligence Branch . . . This detective that was reported missing . . . yes, Louche. Detective Louche . . ."

Gousset reviewed the action taken to retrace Louche's steps on the day he had disappeared, which had led to the determination that Detective Louche had used his lunch break to visit the Café de la Poste, where he had once interviewed Chantal Senac.

"What?" Eyes exclaimed.

And then the telephone line went dead.

Eyes rapped the telephone with his fingers. He looked up, exasperated. "The line is dead."

"Use another telephone," the Russian said.

The telephone in the next office was also dead. Within ten minutes, it was clear that all the telephones in Department 100 were dead.

Eyes went up to the street and took a department car. He would go to the Café de la Poste. But first he would go to Gousset, to hear the end of Gousset's report.

The driver turned on the radio. An electronic tone was playing out a tropical rhythm, in counterpoint to the beat of the windshield wipers. Eyes changed the station, but the next frequency was playing the same strange sound, a rhythm more than a melody. He spun the tuning dial. Every one of the state's six radio channels was emitting the same electronic tone.

Then the tone stopped, and Eyes heard a voice speaking with an odd accent.

"People of France, all broadcasting, and your communications by telephone, have been temporarily suspended for official restructuring. Please accept the regrets of your government for this inconvenience."

The voice transmission was repeated three times, and then the rhythmic tone resumed.

Eyes told the driver to return to the labyrinth. Gousset could wait. The Russian would need to know that Landry had lashed out at the radio and the telephones.

Before they had parked the car, Eyes heard the message two more times. It was, he was sure, the voice of Robert Landry.

VALERIE heard the snap of the light switch, and a wave of pain swept sleep away. She opened her eyes, afraid that she would see the bald man, afraid of what he would do to her. The walls were painted light green, as she remembered from the night before, before she had fainted for the last time. The paint on the ceiling had peeled off in long irregular flakes, so that the light of the naked bulb cast a kaleidoscope of shadows. The ceiling was very high, so it had to be an old building.

Except for her shoes, she was in her clothes, lying on her back on a bare mattress that smelled of mildew. She looked toward the sound of the switch and saw one of the men from the previous afternoon standing just inside the open door. He was middle-aged, of medium height, balding, neither thin nor plump, and his expression was as flat and dull as a brick. All his clothes—suit, shirt, and necktie, down to his heavy shoes—came from a State Factory. He was the good one, the one who had come when the bald man had tired and gone away, the one who asked her to tell the truth before the bald man killed her.

"Are you hungry?" he asked.

Her stomach was sore from the beating, and she did not think that she could eat, but she must eat. She nodded, and a sharp pain stabbed her neck so that she almost cried out. She tried to move, and her wrists came up short against a cord that was tied to the bed.

"Is he in the labyrinth?" the man asked.

"I don't know where he is. . . . not in the labyrinth. . . ."

"How do you know he is not there?"

"There was no plan . . . no talk at all about Leonid, no interest in Leonid, nothing to do with Leonid, and I know; I was there every minute. They could not have done anything to Leonid without my knowing that they were going to do it. . . . I swear to you . . ."

He left the room, the door closing behind him with a thud.

She shut her eyes and wished for oblivion. Every part of her hurt. Even the slightest effort brought agony. Pain ruled her, but then a clear cold sliver of reason pierced the wall of aches and bruises: they had lied. If the Russian was dead, then they had been in the labyrinth. If they had been in the labyrinth, they knew that Leonid was not there. If they had not been in the labyrinth, the Russian was alive. They had not been in the labyrinth.

Suddenly, rage filled her against the Russian. He was alive, still, but he had lost all control and subjected her to this torture. Whatever had happened to Leonid, the Russian had let it happen. . . . It was weakness.

She hated him.

She thought of the man who had beaten her. He had been precise in inflicting pain, so that she could die or recover without any signs but some bruises. Her injuries would all mend. His smile and the whites of his eyes forced themselves into her memory. She wondered if the mad sadist always worked with the placid brick-faced man. They made a good pair.

The door opened again. She kept her eyes shut, terrified of receiving more pain, wishing herself dead.

"She is still unconscious."

It was a new voice, half-recalled.

"No." That was the voice of the sadist.

"Leave us."

She heard the door close, and footsteps.

The bed creaked and sagged from the weight of her visitor. A hand touched her cheek.

She opened her eyes and looked up into the face of the comrade first secretary, Georges Paccard.

"I believe you," he said. "It is over. We do not have the chemicals here, and besides, we did not want to spoil you. But I needed to be sure, I do not apologize."

She stared at him.

"I thought the Russian had taken Leonid. I wanted to show the Russians in the embassy that your master has gone mad in his hunger to attack me. And now the Russian calls to tell me that he has not taken Leonid, that we are taunted by this man Landry who controls the Star. I believe the Russian tells the truth, because I believe you. Now, I ask your help . . ."

His eyes were cold, questing for a reaction. She waited.

"We cannot continue with the Russian gnawing at our power. We want to kill him, but we cannot find our way into the labyrinth. You can help us, or . . ."

She understood. She could agree to join Paccard, or be returned dead to the labyrinth as a real provocation to the Russian.

She would not die for the Russian.

"I must report to my control at the embassy."

"The embassy was controlling you while you were in Department 100?"

She nodded.

"What will you report?"

"That I wish to help you. My control must give permission. . . . But I will give you something now, before I talk to them."

"What is that?"

"Your colonel of the Parade Guards. He is not loyal to you. Don't trust him."

He reached out and started to untie her. She smelled tobacco in his clothes, and it smelled like salvation.

13 It was strange to Landry that Marcel Chabon wanted to be present at the event, and strangest of all that a technocrat's plan for assassination should seem workable, yet de Celigny had been convinced. He had come back sure of the plan and sure of Chabon. If de Celigny retained his doubts it was for the uncertain future of France, but even in this de Celigny had changed: his blind rage seemed to be tempered—revenge was impossible, let the past sleep.

Landry made mental lists of the hazards ahead—the gun would not fire, the bodyguards would sense a trap, a flat tire on the way to the restaurant . . . Well, they could allow time for a flat tire. His logical side said that no amount of preparation could forestall every risk.

Landry rechecked the reservation list for Taillevent. The best restaurants in Paris kept their reservations in the Star; it was easier and safer than the scrawled ledgers that had once served the purpose. Chabon had had no trouble getting his reservation. There were always tables reserved for members of the Communist party who were high officials. Since the remaining tables were fully booked, Landry had scrubbed two parties to make room for Jacques de Celigny.

He had reserved for de Celigny and Nagy a party of two, in the name of Claude Tribout, sports director of Lyon. Nagy could play the role of star athlete. In fact, that seemed much like his role.

So much for Paccard.

Landry turned to the continuing attack on the Russian. It seemed even more important for the future than the elimination of Paccard. The Russian must be feeling pressure now from the breaks in security. What could his masters think when radio and telephone communications were cut, when ministers were receiving false instructions on the Russian's authority, when the first secretary's son could be kidnapped and the Russian himself accused of the deed?

Whatever the Russian's masters thought, they would think again by the end of the evening.

Landry entered the military sector of the Star to verify the playback from his morning input. Amazing—every air squadron in France had acknowledged the secret mission. It said something for the state of discipline in the French Army of the Air. If only two or three units had taken the hook, he would have been satisfied.

Issuing the orders had been simplicity itself compared to redirecting the mail or creating false identity papers, and if this did not shake the Russians' confidence in the Russian, nothing would.

THE formation of eight Rafale fighters sped in the direction of Lille. Navigation lights extinguished, only their hot orange exhaust flames marked their passage through the dark sky. Paris had ordered them on an unusual training mission, to proceed to Lille in silence and blackout at supersonic speed, to arrive precisely seven thousand meters overhead at exactly midnight.

They were on altitude, on time, crossing over Lille.

The pilot of the last aircraft was the only one in the formation who saw the converging silhouettes. His reflexes saved him, pulling his Rafale up. In the space of a heartbeat, the sky flashed bright and then as quickly darkened. His vision dazzled, the pilot looked behind where shards of white-hot metal were tumbling in the night sky.

Someone in Paris had made a terrible mistake.

Directly ahead, a fresh burst of light, and then the shock of another explosion rocked him. The pilot rolled his Rafale upside down to see flames below. Upright again, he climbed for safety. Wing lights of other aircraft flicked on, filling the sky like a swarm of fireflies, and then another blinding midair collision eclipsed the other lights.

It was not just two squadrons on the exercise, or even three or four. There were hundreds of aircraft above Lille, all at seven thousand meters.

Where to go? Flight at supersonic speed had used up most of the fuel. Lille was impossible.

The pilot started a long glide, fumbling in the chart-box at his side for the radio facilities book. He dialled the frequency of Rouen into the radio direction finder.

The digital counters started to spin, and the needle tracked slowly around the dial in an aimless orbit. There was no directional signal on the frequency.

He tried Amiens, Le Havre, Caen, and they all failed him. He tried Paris. The needle spun, dumb.

No one would land in France tonight.

In a long arcing turn he climbed and pointed the nose east, to Belgium. Ahead, he saw brilliant pathways, the high intensity lamps on the Belgian autoroutes. But France was dark.

His fuel supply was already too low. As he approached Brussels he opened his dive brakes, dropping into the glide path, and at the last minute lowered his flaps and landing gear. The runway came up at two hundred and eighty kilometers an hour.

Only five hundred meters remained when the pilot saw the other aircraft descending on the glide path ahead of him. It was impossible to land. He pulled up with a curse.

When the turbine quit, he was ready. He levelled the wings and calmly pulled the ejector curtain down over his face. The rocket under his seat shot him out in a tumble of wind and noise. A crazy quilt of lights spun beneath him. Ahead, the trajectory of the dead Rafale ended in the last explosion of his night, with a puff of incandescent vapor.

His parachute opened only meters above the ground. A tile roof rushed up to meet his legs, and then shattering pain ripped through him as the impact broke his leg.

In his pain, he wondered what his plane had hit, and then he fainted.

He woke up in a hospital, listening to two men speaking Russian. When he opened his eyes, one of them bent over him and spoke.

"What has happened in France, flight lieutenant? Have you all gone mad?"

THE Russian stared at the computer monitor. After the failure of telephone communications in France, the computer was his link to the embassy, a voiceless Cyrillic script that scrolled across the screen in hitches and starts.

The writing stopped, and after a moment of thought the Russian tapped the keys, his own words appearing on the monitor.

Ten seconds passed, and then three words came back.

The Russian nodded. He turned in his chair and looked up at his colleagues. They sat erect, facing his desk, waiting in silence for the next blow to hit.

"Our friends console me with this farewell, 'You are responsible.'"

"What has happened?" Eyes asked. The intelligence chief was a bystander now—events were outrunning the information coming in to Intelligence Branch.

"All of our military aircraft took off on a mission ordered from Paris. Each squadron received the same orders, to arrive at midnight over Lille, in radio silence, with lights out, at the same altitude. Some crashed in midair, we don't know how many. There was a power failure on the ground. All the navigation aids went down, and the transmission channels were jammed, so no aircraft could land in France. Two aircraft made it to Belgium and one to Britain. We hope that other aircraft and pilots may be safe, but we don't know yet."

"What does the embassy say?" Max asked.

"It is a catastrophe."

They sat in silence.

"There is more," the Russian said. "All of the commissioned officers who were not on flight duty were ordered to Paris yesterday afternoon. So there was no one in any of the squadrons to ask or answer questions about their orders. . . . He is winning, you know."

The computer erupted in a shrill series of chirrups. The Russian looked at the monitor.

Suddenly, he cried, "Valerie, they have her! . . ."

More words spread across the screen, and the Russian's face hardened.

When the transmission stopped, he acknowledged with a single word, and the screen went black.

"So, First Secretary Comrade Paccard has Valerie, and the embassy has told him to give her back. You are instructed to go for her, my friend." He looked up at Max, his trusted head of Action Branch. "They say you must apologize to the first secretary, and he will return Valerie to you. It may be a trap, but you must go."

Max accepted with a nod.

"If you do not come back, I am sorry, but then I think we all will soon be dead."

"Of course." Max's voice was steady, his pudgy face calm.

"I wish you well."

The Russian stood up and walked around his desk. As Max rose, the Russian embraced him, thick arms wrapping over the rounded shoulders of his friend.

"I will bring her back," Max said, speaking into the Russian's ear. "Be at peace."

IT was not even eight, and the sun was still down behind the mountains, throwing out gray-gold streamers of light. Catherine Moreau would come at noon.

Today, they would go to Notre-Dame-de-Bellecombe . . . during school time, because Chantal could not risk seeing her son, being recognized, before they were ready. Not yet.

Chantal was standing in front of an abandoned shepherd's hut that had been dug out and finished inside, so that it seemed a ruin from the outside. It was her home now.

Already in the early morning, the boys were up above, out of sight exploring the rocks. Catherine had encouraged her to let them climb, saying that the risk of accident was less than the risk of the boys cooped up, getting restless and finding ways to make mischief.

Soon, she would climb up after them. What was true for the boys was equally true for her.

Seven quiet days had passed since Chantal had been delivered here. She could look out and up, let her gaze rest on infinity, and breathe deep. In the cool light of the morning, the mountains around her and the pine-washed air were a tonic. Already, some flex and bounce had come to her city-sapped muscles.

In her dreams, the good ones, she dreamed of waking up with her son in her arms and René Leveque standing beside her bed. When she was awake she daydreamed of René in bed, but when she slept, she dreamed of hugging her son.

Chantal picked her way though the rockfall behind the hut and started to climb up a cleft in the granite. She was slow, knowing that she needed to be careful. A twisted ankle or broken arm would be fatal.

The exercise satisfied her, the tug and haul of the climb building her strength, giving her an antidote to fear.

She settled her upward movements into a slow, pleasing rhythm, locating a foothold, placing a hand, pulling up, then again a foot, the other hand, and pull. It was not dangerous. The rocks were solid and the angle not steep. She quickly gained a vantage point where the gut below was blended into the surrounding rocks, invisible unless its location was known. The cleft narrowed, and she pulled herself almost straight up for a half a meter, until she was on a shelf.

Breathing hard, she turned and braced her feet, her back to a large flat slab. Around her, the mountains made a circle against the sky, a distant barrier against revolution and terror.

Her feet curled over the curve of the stone ledge, comfortable in rubber-soled canvas shoes with threadbare spots over the toes, a gift from Catherine. As she waited for her breath to return, the light of the sun descended to the rocks just above, and she felt a stir in the air, a rising warmth that made her think of taking off

the light wool sweater in blue and green birdsfoot checks that
Catherine had given her.

She turned to climb again. Yesterday she had followed the gully
that marked a seasonal watercourse, and she had not liked the
loose scree of shards under her feet. Now her eyes followed a
steeper route, on granite, hugging a rib that thrust upward toward
the sky.

Her destination was a small grass-filled flat, set against the
mountain wall, an oasis of vegetation where a family of marmots
lived in noisy disharmony. She would find her way up and still be
down in the hut before noon to meet Catherine.

Her nerves and her balance were steady, despite the height,
and this gave her a small vanity of self-confidence.

A sharp tick sounded above her, repeated, and then a flying
pebble bounded past her from above. A marmot, she thought. Or,
the boys. She climbed again, thinking that she was alone, and
then wondering if she was alone.

She thought she heard a voice.

Waiting for another sound, she clung to the rock, holding back
her breath to make quiet for her ears. A sigh of wind, a rough
bird's cry from a *choucas* wheeling in the sky overhead. . . . There
was no human sound.

She climbed again, hands and feet slowly moving her upward,
her lungs beginning to heave as the effort burned up her supply
of oxygen. She paused to recover her breath, and again she heard
a sound, a rock striking a rock, too loud to come from a marmot.
The boys? But why would they be so quiet?

She started up once more, dividing her attention between the
rocky spurs and the lip above her that marked the rim of the
grassy flat.

With a pull and a push, she was just beneath the lip. Halfway
up, there was a nice round boss of rock that would take her foot,
so that she could scramble over and onto the grass. She found a
fingerhold to balance her and put a foot up onto the boss.

Slowly, she pushed up until she could see over the lip. The
grassy flat was empty, its brilliant wildflowers nodding in the
breeze.

Her hand was over the edge when she asked herself where the marmots were. The last time she had been in this place, the marmots had made a cacophony of complaints about her arrival before scurrying into their burrows.

Then she was up, on her feet, marmots or no marmots. She looked at the sheer stone wall above her and saw nothing but a squadron of black *choucas*, turning in the purple sky. What had she heard?

She sat down in the grass among the flowers. Her higher vantage point revealed a high dark dome in the distance, gleaming with tints of gold from the sun rising behind it. Mont Blanc.

Footsteps, running, crashed behind her, and she wheeled in panic. Arms seized her as she turned, and then she melted in relief. It was little Jean-Pierre, his brother close behind.

"Surprise! We caught you!" Jean-Pierre squealed.

"We watched you climbing up," Michel said, an enormous grin spread across his freckled face. "Did we scare you?"

"Oh, yes, you did," Chantal said. She laughed, relief unwinding through her bones, and reached out to gather both boys close to her. She loved them, she thought: they made her miss Noël all the more.

They watched the rising sun turn the dome of Mont Blanc white, its ice and snow gleaming.

"I must go," Chantal said. "I must meet Catherine."

The boys came with her. In single file, they slid and jumped down the gully full of scree, and then down through the cleft in the rocks to their own small meadow.

Catherine was early, waiting for them with kisses, clothes, food.

The two women told the boys to be careful. They would return before sundown.

Catherine led the way, her back straight, her long legs stretching surely as she plunged down the path, and Chantal worked to keep up. Catherine owned a Deux Chevaux, an ancient vehicle that looked like a pair of bicycles, with extravagantly pleated curved sheet metal to connect the wheels and shelter the passengers. At the head of the stony track that led down into the valley, the Deux Chevaux was nestled between two huge rocks, its head-lights peering out like a frog from a pond.

They drove to Notre-Dame-de-Bellecombe, the Deux Chevaux leaning on the curves and groaning on the uphills, its panels squeaking wherever the screws and bolts had worked loose in the sheet metal. The motor ran well, thanks to the ministrations of Laurent Bellot, Catherine's brother.

Catherine had made inquiries of some people she knew in Notre-Dame-de-Bellecombe. Noël lived with a young widow named Isabelle Bazin, who had lost her own husband and son in a winter avalanche. No one except Isabelle Bazin understood how Noël had been delivered immediately after the revolution, and Isabelle was not given to sharing confidences.

The Deux Chevaux chugged up the hill, and the rooftops of Notre-Dame-de-Bellecombe appeared, outlined against the sky.

They motored through the town, a collection of chalets in new wood, with stores for the visitors—skiers in winter, hikers in summer. Some stone buildings predated the others at the original center of Notre-Dame-de-Bellecombe, among them a house built of granite blocks.

"It is the Bazin house," Catherine said. "Your son lives there."

A good house, Chantal thought, old and solid.

They drove up a few kilometers to the Col des Saisies, then stopped by the side of the road and admired the view. At the top of the col, a sign had been placed to mark the altitude. Fields stretched from the road to stands of pine trees—the pines extended back on a rising slope to rock walls that climbed to snow-drifted ridges. The great mountains were behind, towering above the ridges.

A boy should grow with a clear head and a strong body in such a place. Arnaud had chosen well.

They passed the house again on the way down.

"I will know it," Chantal said, "when I come back for Noël."

Chantal thought about Arnaud, with a tremor of apprehension. What would he do if Noël escaped?

As they left the town, they passed a small new chalet, built for seasonal rentals, close by the roadside. A man, one of three who took turns sitting beside the window, wrote down the license number of the Deux Chevaux. He had been writing down such numbers for a month, and this one was new to him, although it was clearly not a tourist car. It had come from the same region. He called the other house, the one at the far side of the town, and learned that the Deux Chevaux had gone up to the Col des Saisies. Two women. Could be . . . ?

At the end of the day, the number would be called in for verification.

"**WHAT** do you expect to do with *them*?" Max demanded.

He faced three hard men of the KGB, glaring at him like dogs at a caged rabbit.

They were in a low-ceilinged room under the embassy, standing on opposite sides of a conference table. Max spoke to the man at the end of the table, a slight, stooping figure in a tightly fitted black sharkskin suit. The man, known as Pavel, listened to the question and then gazed at Max, his eyes hardly visible under heavy eyelids.

"They will carry out the assignment," Pavel answered, after a pause.

"In his office?"

"Wherever they find him."

"He will be in his office. He never leaves except when he goes to his grotto to sleep."

"Then, in his office."

"It will be a mess. You know that he can blow up the labyrinth if he wishes."

Pavel bent his head in acknowledgment, letting silence hold Max's words. When he spoke, his tone was pensive, the words coming slowly as he put them into French.

"They will go in with the girl called Gentiane. They will be there to pass her over to him. So he will not doubt why they are there."

"He is not a fool. He will know why they are there, and he will kill them. I know him. If he sees that he is betrayed by Gentiane, that the end has come, he will end the life of the labyrinth. He is quick to understand things, he will make this calculation faster than you or I would do . . ."

Again, Pavel paused, weighing the truth of Max's assertions.

"Then what do you propose?"

"Let me do it."

Pavel put his fingertips on the edge of the table and bent his head to think in private.

"Leave us," he commanded, his head still bent. "Go outside, Wait there."

The three KGB men turned like soldiers and marched out of the room in step. The heavy wood door slammed behind the last of them.

"We are not convinced of your loyalty," Pavel stated.

Now it was Max's turn to let silence freeze the words.

Pavel continued. "You have worked with this man for decades. You have followed him. Why should we believe that you will kill him?"

Max nodded, his expression calm. "You should understand that my loyalty is to the revolution, and the Russian has failed the revolution. There is another reason, more personal. . . . If he knows that it is my finger on the trigger, he will suffer only because he has failed, but he will know that all of us can continue the work. If we let these men of yours kill him, he will suffer because he will think he has brought us all down. I want to spare him that. Do you understand . . . ?"

"Yes."

"I have never given you a moment to doubt my loyalty, in all these years."

"It is true."

"You and I have worked together as long as I have worked with him. From the time when your French was so bad you needed a book to find the words."

"I hoped in those days that you might learn Russian."

"I am not a linguist. . . ."

"How will you do it?"

"I will take the girl back to the labyrinth. I will stop in my office to get my automatic. When we go into his office, we will arrange that he should stand with his hands free, so that he cannot blow us up, and then I will kill him."

"The men must go with you."

"There is a place where they can wait, just outside the last barrier, where they cannot be seen by the video cameras that send a picture into his office."

"Yes."

"We can dispose of the body there. There is a furnace. The others do not need to know."

"Yes, that will be best. Now, there is another matter. I hope that you will understand this. His successor must speak Russian . . . And you are needed in your present functions."

"Eyes? He speaks—"

"We have chosen the girl."

"She is very young."

"But strong. We have recognized her exceptional qualities since she was in Russia. That is why we sent her to you."

Max extended his hand, and Pavel put out his own, a fragile web of tissue and bone.

Max went out through the door without looking back.

"Go in for your briefing," he told the men outside the door. "I will meet you upstairs."

PACCARD waited with Valerie at his side. She was in a simple navy blue skirt and a navy jacket over a white blouse, appropriate attire for the comrade first secretary's office. She stood just close enough to him to make her new alliance clear.

They were expecting him, but they held their places like actors waiting for a cue, until he was well into the large room. Then Valerie stepped forward, and the breaking light in her smile seemed as honest and warm as the rising sun.

"I am so glad . . . thank you for coming to get me."

She stepped forward, held out her arms, and embraced Max. She held him tight enough for him to notice the firmness of her breasts. When she released him, she smiled again.

"I was surprised to learn that you were one of us . . . serving the greater cause."

Her words were so stilted, he could not relate them to the still lingering warmth of her body. And then he was looking at Paccard's outstretched hand. And Paccard smiled at him, the first smile he had received from Paccard in two years.

"Let me say that I understand much more now," Paccard said. "I also am pleased to know that you have served . . . as we all have."

"We each have our duty to the revolution."

Valerie was still close to him, and when she spoke, her voice was low, so that the first secretary could not hear, ". . . no regrets?"

He answered in a normal tone. "I regret that a colleague has failed, and I compliment you on your new assignment. I promise you my support."

She embraced him again and whispered, "I will need your help, you have so much to teach me."

He imagined her in bed, and then put the image out of his mind. He had an incredibly difficult task ahead. Could he trust his composure, his speed and his accuracy? He would face a man who knew him better than anyone on earth. If he failed, everything would be lost. The Russian would look into his eyes and read his mind, and react with the speed of a ferret in a mousehole.

He put his hands on her upper arms and held her, face to face, looking into her eyes.

"You and I will go in alone together. I will complete the mission. It must be clean, if we slip he can blow up the labyrinth."

The first secretary interrupted them. "Please report to me when your assignment is finished."

Valerie turned to face him. "I will report, comrade first secretary."

Paccard stepped forward. "Good luck."

In the hall outside the office, the high heels of her shoes ringing on the marble, she took Max by the arm and murmured, "I have made a good friend of the first secretary. He will help us."

"He will help you, he will not help the Department."

"It is the same thing, now."

"Has he found his son? I thought he would speak about Leonid."

"If we don't have Leonid, then Leonid makes no difference. They thought we took Leonid. . . . They tortured me to be sure that we did not."

Max looked at her, but her face was blank.

She asked, "Did we have Leonid, and I did not know?"

"No . . . It was surely the work of Landry."

They were on the steps behind the embassy. They entered the waiting car, and Max told the driver to wait for another car to come.

A black Moskva limousine pulled up behind. The three KGB were squeezed together in the back seat, behind a lone staff driver.

Fifteen minutes later, they were in the first vestibule of the labyrinth. Max left Valerie with the three men. He moved quickly, first to the office of the concierge, where he filled out the forms to initiate the makeup of three temporary identification cards. Then, passing the barriers as fast as he could enter the codes, he went to his own office.

In his mind, the actions were fixed in sequence, and when the steel door closed behind him, his movements flowed with deliberate speed.

Jacket off, hung from a hook on the door.

In the side drawer of the desk, his Walther, removed from an ancient box with a peeling leatherette cover and threadbare velveteen cushions.

The clip out of the Walther, the firing mechanism checked, the clip examined.

The pistol in his belt.

A scabbard from the drawer that had held the pistol. Strapped to his right ankle.

A double-bladed knife in the scabbard.

He shook his left leg, looking to be sure that the cuff of his pants lay flat.

He ran through the sequence again in his mind, to be sure that nothing was forgotten, and then he was en route back to the KGB squad. The three identification tags were ready for him to pick up.

Valerie Clavel led their descent into the labyrinth. Two of the KGB followed in single file, followed by Max, followed by the last of the KGB. They walked in silence, passing each barrier in turn.

At the last barrier before the Russian's area, they stopped. "Wait here," Max said to the men.

Valerie and Max went through together and paused outside the Russian's door. They were in full view of the television eye over the door, and they only glanced at each other.

Max pressed a series of buttons on the button bank beside the door. They waited.

A green light over the door switched on, and the door clicked open.

Valerie took the knob and pulled.

The Russian was sitting behind his desk, a great smile across his face. As Valerie entered, he stood up and opened his arms, ignoring Max. Max stepped to the far corner of the office, taking station, noting that the Russian's hands were empty.

Max was concerned that the Russian should not move too close to Valerie, but she anticipated the danger and put up her hands.

"Stop. You have something to answer for, to me."

The Russian stopped. His smile vanished like a wave on a rock.

"I have been kidnapped and tortured, because of you."

The Russian stood stock still, his head cocked.

"You have failed in your duty to the revolution," Valerie continued.

"You are dismissed," Max said. The Walther was in his hand, its muzzle steady on the Russian's heart.

"No . . ." the Russian said, his eyes taking in the gun and returning to Valerie.

"Wait," Valerie commanded. "I wish to tell Comrade Karel that I have been appointed as his successor. My first act will be to bring in his wife—she is no secret to me."

Surprised by this, Max glanced at Valerie, and the moment's inattention launched the Russian. As the Russian leaped back toward his desk, Max's first bullet caught him in the chest, throwing him to the side. The second bullet entered his shoulder, knocking him down, and the last snapped his head back, cutting off a groan.

They looked at the body, and Max spoke. "Go get Pavel's men, they will need to report our success."

She stood for a moment, looking down at her lover.

"Go," he said. "They will become impatient."

She went.

As she returned past the last barrier, bringing the KGB with her, another shot hit their ears like a hammer blow and reverberated against the steel panels in the passageway.

The Russian was lying facedown. A black stain of blood grew on the carpet under his head.

"He was not dead," Max said. "He is now. He deserved to die without pain."

His left hand was covered with blood, and he rubbed it on his jacket, leaving an ugly smear.

"Good," one of the KGB men said. "What will you do with the body?"

"We have an incinerator large enough for such tasks," Max replied. "I will take care of it. What else should we do here?"

"Nothing," Valerie said. "Thank you, Comrade Max. This was not easy."

Max could not look at her without betraying his emotions. But his triumph was not complete. The hands on his wristwatch were vertical—exactly six o'clock in the evening. He would need to hurry.

14 Chantal had woken before sunrise and prayed that she would see Noël that day.

Laurent Bellot had driven with her to an overgrown cart track by the roadside. He had parked, and then she had followed him for four hours, up to a grassy ledge above the valley that separated them from Notre-Dame-de-Bellecombe. There they stopped to share a lunch of bread and cheese.

She was to continue alone on a hiker's path, down to the stream, where she would find a wooden bridge. She would climb the other side of the valley and enter the town, a hiker on an early summer vacation. Her hair and eyebrows had been re-dyed, a lustrous black, her identity changed to that of an unmarried secretary from Thionville named Marie Olivet. She wore a red kerchief around her forehead, walking shorts of sturdy cotton, a feathery brown-wool sweater over a T-shirt, wool socks, and her already beloved canvas shoes—Catherine's clothes. A well-worn nylon sack contained a rain parka in case of a shower.

From her reconnaissance with Catherine, the arrangement of the town was clear in her mind: the school, and the brasserie where she could take an afternoon cup of tea and observe Isabelle Bazin's small house, until the policemen came for the woman. Noël would be at school. When he came home at four, his own mother would be there instead of Isabelle Bazin.

Each time Chantal imagined this meeting, her heart would grow tight in her chest.

Her child had seen her likeness on the post office wall. He had known that the name on the posters was his own name. What had Isabelle Bazin told him about her? Could he resist the monstrous falsehoods of the New State?

What if he reacted in panic, started to shout and cry? It was a small town, where people would look out for their neighbors.

Laurent Bellot let her go with a gruff "good luck" and a bearlike embrace. She shouldered her knapsack and started out. A maze of scrub oak framed the opening to the path, at the end of the clearing. The path tracked level for ten meters and then turned down the side of the hill. The descent was slow, a gentle incline littered with branches and loose stones. She needed to crouch to pass under a low branch, and she scrambled over a fallen tree, but she continued without a pause, down into the valley. The sound of the water running over the stream bed told her that she was near the bottom.

The bridge was broken at the center. Chantal let herself down the near side, feeling the sway of the wood under her weight. At the bottom she jumped, slipped on the opposite side, and put a foot in the water, but then caught the planking in her hands and pulled herself to safety.

The path up to the village seemed steep. She was winded within minutes and stopped to catch her breath.

Voices and footsteps sounded from above.

She moved off the path into the undergrowth and squatted out of sight.

Two men went by, talking in loud voices about the troubles with the telephone. France was a deaf-mute, one of them said. They did not see her.

She waited for their noise to fade to silence and then returned to the path.

She walked into the town on the central street, until she came to a small side road marked "dead end." She turned to follow it and then set out across a field, to circle and reenter the town from below, where the brasserie and Isabelle Bazin's house were located.

Fifteen minutes later, she was seated beside a small round table at the brasserie. She could see the front door of the house, only twenty meters away, and she could see for fifty meters down the road coming into the town.

She had tea. The rising sun found its way above the rooftops, and its warmth steamed the morning dew off the street.

Out of sight down the road, Laurent Bellot approached, an alpinist's pack on his back. Inside the pack, a well-oiled MAT 49 machine pistol nestled in a heavy wool sweater with three fully loaded clips. Before he reached the spattering of chalets that marked the town itself, he turned into a cow field and started up toward a dense grove of pine trees.

Laurent dreaded his mission, but knew that if the worst came, it was necessary. Catherine, Henri, even Philippe, had voted unanimously. If Chantal risked capture by the government, she could not be allowed to survive for questioning. He would kill her for the sake of the rest.

In the trees, Laurent turned and slid the pack from his shoulders. He opened the top flap and sat down, his back to a stump, his legs extended in front of him. Eyes on the town, he let his fingers search the interior of the pack, sliding around the greasy metal of the weapon, to find a paper-wrapped parcel. He extracted the parcel, unwrapped it, and idly ripped off a mouthful of sausage.

In the brasserie, Chantal sipped her tea and waited for policemen to come.

They certainly would come. Robert Landry had never failed.

But what if they were delayed, or if Isabelle Bazin was out? Could they find her before Noël came home? And then, if Isabelle told a friend that she was leaving with the police, and if the friend came to her house to look out for Noël . . .

They had insisted, Laurent, Henri, and Catherine, that she quit the plan if it varied by the least fraction. Chantal understood. Her friends were risking their lives so that she could reclaim Noël.

Something moved, as sudden as the flap of a bird's wing, behind one of the windows of Isabelle Bazin's house. Isabelle, or someone, was at home.

A small blue van with a blue light on top, with "POLICE" lettered in white on the side, came around the bend in the road. It slowed and stopped short as it came to Isabelle Bazin's house.

Two policemen got out, short stout men in navy blue, with little red accents on their caps and their lapels. They carried holstered pistols on their wide leather belts.

The door was open. The first policeman entered, and the second, after a moment's pause, followed.

Chantal strained to see past the open door, but she could see only a black void behind the open door. After only a minute, two at most, one of the policemen came out, and then the woman, with the other policeman behind.

Chantal watched the woman try to turn and go back, but the policeman behind pushed her forward. It was Isabelle Bazin, but it was not the scene Chantal had expected. Isabelle Bazin was in a panic of loss. As the woman's face came into sunlight, Chantal saw, as sharp and clear as a razor's edge, that Noël's foster mother was desperate. Chantal remembered the night she had lost Noël.

The policemen were vigorous. While the first pulled her arms, the second gripped her waist and pushed Isabelle Bazin, struggling, into the back of the van. The van doors slammed behind her. In horror, Chantal watched the van make a half turn, reverse its direction, and disappear around the bend in the road.

The door of the house stood open. That was wrong. Isabelle should have locked it when she left, but the police had not given her time.

The police would keep Isabelle for a long time in the Megève station, waiting for instructions from Paris that would never come, giving Chantal time.

She was supposed to enter the house. She would enter, earlier than planned, and shut the door behind her.

It took moments to pay for the tea with her cash card, and then Chantal was out of the brasserie.

She started up the street, away from Isabelle Bazin's house and onto the side road that she had taken after first entering the town.

Hidden in the grove of pine trees, Laurent Bellot watched her. The police van had been ahead of schedule, and so was Chantal, but that was good, the danger was in delay.

Chantal approached the house from the back and quickly scanned for neighbors who might be watching. Not a person was in view, in the field or in the houses. She strode along the wall of the house, turned the corner, and stepped in through the open door, then swung the door shut and leaned back as though to seal it.

Carefully, keeping a distance from the windows, she walked forward to a place where the window light let her make out the hands on her watch. It was only three. Noël would not be home for an hour.

The house seemed full of the presence of its occupants, but Chantal did not feel like an intruder. She turned slowly in place, absorbing the home of her only son ... bright pictures of flowered mountainsides, the colors alive in the shadows ... a half dozen books strewn on a low bench that faced a massive couch with rumpled pillows. On the floor under the bench, the unfolded pages of an old newspaper waited to be discarded, and Chantal resisted her housekeeper's instinct to do just that. She took a step toward the kitchen.

In a small house down the road, two men had been spurred into action by the loudspeaker on the table between them. They had been listening for two weeks to radio transmissions from a set of microphones in Isabelle Bazin's house. They had heard the policemen come into the house, had heard them leave, had watched the police van drive down the road, returning to Megève. Now, one of the guardsmen was calling on a walky-talky to the other set of guards, planted in a similar vacation chalet on the road above the town.

The man pressed the receiver to his ear, his ugly face screwed up in a scowl as he listened.

"OK," he said. "Out." He switched the walky-talky onto standby and addressed his comrade. "They heard the same thing that we did. The police lifted Isabelle Bazin."

"The boy is still in the school?"

"That's what they say. . . ."

The man by the loudspeaker had not shaven in three days. "Listen!" His ear close to the loudspeaker, he raised his hand, as though to command attention. "There is someone inside the house. . . ."

His companion punched the transmit switch on the walky-talky. "Sounds in the house. Someone inside."

The response crackled back.

"Understood. . . . On our way."

In Isabelle's house, a broad doorless opening connected the living room to a kitchen in disarray. A shirt was hanging on the back of a high wooden chair. Cookbooks, and recipes handwritten on scraps of paper, shared space with pots and pans that had been washed and left on the kitchen counter. In the sink, a piece of beef was thawing. At this sign of affluence, Chantal realized that Arnaud Senac had provided means for the woman to take care of Noël. Their son.

Chantal went back to the living room and up creaking stairs to the second floor. The first bedroom was Isabelle's. The covers were pulled up over the bed, but it had not been made, and clothes were lying on the floor.

At the end of the short hallway past Isabelle's door, Chantal found Noël's room. The bed was made, the books arranged in neat rows on shelves, the clothes hanging on a bar. He had inherited Arnaud's sense of order. He had a small writing desk with a chair drawn up under it. The desk was bare except for a carved wooden bear with "Chamonix" on its base, three pencils, a writing pad, and a photograph in a thin wooden frame.

The photograph brought instant tears. Standing in front of some snowcapped peak, Noël's arm rested around Isabelle Bazin's waist, and they both were smiling.

As she stood looking at the photograph, Chantal begged Isabelle Bazin's forgiveness. The pencils felt like a magnet to her hand, begging her to leave a note, to tell Isabelle that Noël's real mother had come for her son.

Someday, if they survived, she would bring Noël back to Notre-Dame-de-Bellecombe. He would be grown and free, and she could meet Isabelle Bazin as a friend. Chantal thought of the police van on its way to Megève and grieved at Isabelle Bazin's pain. She turned to go downstairs.

Chantal paused at the foot of the stairs. She had a half hour to wait before her boy came home. She glanced at the living room window, where she must have seen Isabelle Bazin from the brasserie across the street.

Two men were in the street. Heavyset men, carrying heavy sacks on their backs. One turned to go into the brasserie, and the other started toward the house, disappearing out of her line of sight. Chantal ran to the back of the house. Wasn't there a door? There was, with an old-fashioned wrought-iron latch that rasped easily out of the catch, and then she was outdoors, running to the corner of the next house where she could put herself out of sight.

She ran into the field without looking back, in fear of seeing her pursuer.

Then she took a side step and made herself look back.

He was there, a hundred meters behind.

She ran. Ahead, a stand of pine trees was her only hope to hide. The soft grassy earth gave like a sponge under the impact of her feet.

As she reached the trees, she turned again. He had gained a third of the distance between them.

The crash of her feet on the undergrowth echoed in her ears.

She had to stop. She crouched down and clasped her racked ribs with her arms and tried to listen, but her breathing was too loud in her ears.

Then she heard a crackling beat of running steps coming toward her through the woods. Chantal started on her hands and knees at right angles to her first course, looking over her shoulder for a glimpse of the man who was coming for her. If he went far enough, she might double back behind him and escape after all.

She saw him, and immediately she stopped and lay down, squeezed against the ground. He went past, running without effort past the place where she had turned.

She tried to think. The grass was tall. She could crawl through the field and be invisible. She untied the red kerchief that held her hair and stuffed it under a knobby root. Then she set out, half running, half walking, as softly as she could, listening and looking, until she could see the field ahead, under the branches. She turned again to the left and ran through the pine trees, parallel to the edge of the field.

When she had reached the corner of the pines, she lay down again, gathering her breath and her strength.

The houses looked so far away, and even there she would not be safe.

Would she ever be safe, in the rest of her life?

She left the woods in a low crouch, trying to keep her back below the level of the grass.

"Stop there," a man's voice cried, not twenty meters away.

She ran and heard the snap of the weapon as it was armed.

The first bullet moved the grass in front of her. She kept running. She would let them kill her before she would let them catch her.

Then she heard steps behind her, quartering the angle of her path across the field, and she prayed for another shot to end the chase. Her lungs were screaming for air, and the man was near now, gaining fast.

The stock of his machine pistol swung in an arc and came down on her legs below her knees. She stumbled, hit the earth in a soft fall, and put her arms over her head.

"Get up," the man said. "We have been waiting for you."

She lay motionless.

"We can carry you. It would be better if you would walk."

A piercing whistle cut the air.

"My friend comes back now."

He laughed, a croaking sound that made her shudder inside.

She heard another voice, lower, interrupted by short snatches of breath—the first man. He had doubled back and come out of the woods as fast as he had gone in. "It is her?"

A rough hand dragged her arm away from her head. She looked up and saw an evil stare in a brute's face.

"It is the one," he said.

And then, his body leaped, and he started to fall, and as the other man turned to face the sound of gunshots, he also crumpled to the ground. There was blood on the grass, blood on Chantal's legs and her shirt, a splattering from the impact of the bullets on her captors.

"Chantal!"

She recognized the voice of Laurent Bellot and got to her knees. He was at the edge of the trees, his weapon still raised. "Come," he called.

She picked herself up and raced toward him, wishing that he would put down the gun.

He turned and disappeared into the pines before she reached him. She caught him ten meters in, putting a fresh clip in his machine pistol, his eyes steady on her.

"We will go down through the woods, below the town. I have the van there."

She followed his back. They stayed deep in the trees, away from the edge of the field, crunching softly on the needles and twigs underfoot.

The way was not hard. They jumped across a small stream, and once they had to slide down a steep wall of earth and rock, but in half an hour they turned back in the direction of the road. Laurent remained ahead, the machine pistol in his hand.

They continued for fifteen minutes, until they saw light through the branches. Laurent stopped and beckoned for her, and she came forward until she reached his side.

He whispered in her ear.

"Go ahead of me, very quietly in case they are waiting. If you see no one, you must go down the grading to the van. Then, look all around you, and be sure, be sure that you are alone. Then wave once ... like this ... and I will come, and we will leave this place."

She went, flinching each time she made a noise. At the end of the trees, she paused and looked in every direction, letting her eyes rest in place after place, to be sure that she would detect any movement. A bird flew. Another bird, moving in the corner of her eye. She waited and watched and let the minutes pass.

She plunged over the lip and rolled to the bottom. When she was down, she picked herself up and ran to Laurent's van, looking in it and under it. She surveyed the road above and below. She saw nothing but the road, a grassy bank, trees above, mountains in the background. It was a beautiful day.

She waved, once, as Laurent had told her.

He came quickly, the gun in his hand, from a place far to the right of her own descent.

The grade let him fly in long jumping steps, his arms outstretched for balance, and each jump seemed suspended in the air before he landed and took off again.

A burst of gunfire caught him in mid-leap, and he rolled over in the air, doing a somersault, coming down on his back and sliding to a stop on the slippery grass.

Another burst caught him in the grass, and Chantal knew that he was dead when the gun flew out of his hand.

She was sure that they would kill her if she went for the gun, so she went for it, running hard toward the black metallic object that lay a meter from Laurent's outstretched hand.

A man came out of the woods, above Laurent, another from the opposite side of the road, and they too raced to retrieve the gun of Laurent Bellot.

Heart pounding, praying for a bullet to end her anguish, she ran, and then her hand was on the gun, raising it, finding the trigger under her finger, trying to aim. She pulled the trigger and saw as she pulled that she would miss: the man was diving out of her sights, and Laurent's MAT 49 was spraying bullets into the air, its recoil slamming the grip back onto her, driving the barrel up until she had to let go the trigger, and they were on her with knees and fists, smothering her with their weight.

Her right hand was pinned around the gun, under the knee of one of the men.

Carefully, he pried her fingers off the grip and eased the pressure.

"Be calm, Comrade Senac," he said. "You have lost. There is nothing for you to do unless we wish it."

She looked at him for the first time and recoiled from his face. He was totally bald, and he was smiling at her with insane pleasure.

THE gray bellies of the clouds over Paris were streaked pink and orange by the setting sun. Nagy walked slowly down the Avenue de Friedland from the Arc de Triomphe, stopping to look up and down the broad avenue for men sitting in cars, delivery vans with windows covered, heads in windows. There were none of these. ... His feet took him past rue Lamennais on his right. Twenty meters from the corner, the sign marking the restaurant, "Taillevent," was barely visible, a discreet bit of light wrought iron.

When there had been restaurant guides in France, Taillevent had been perennially anointed among the eighteen or twenty best restaurants in the world. At Taillevent, the chef's fame was less than the renown of the restaurant, and this had saved both the chef and the restaurant. When the celebrity chefs had been redeployed, their restaurants faded into obscurity, while Taillevent prospered from the patronage of the New State.

For Nagy, the ritual pleasure of good eating was a discovery that he had made after leaving the academy, and then the revolution had ended that part of his education. The weight of the pistol tucked under his armpit was a distraction, but it did not take away his curiosity about the restaurant.

Paccard would be unprotected inside. Bodyguards were not privileged to eat in such a place. They would wait outside, where they would be the responsibility of Maurice Thevenet and Alphonse Euler. This part of the mission would take some time.

So, Paccard should not die until after the dessert. Nagy expected to have a good meal.

At the door, he looked down at his new State Factory charcoal gray suit of polyester and wool and his new black shoes with round polished tips. He was the first to arrive, to use all his senses for sniffing out danger. If he had to break off the engagement, he could just leave the restaurant before de Celigny arrived.

He stepped inside, into a carpeted room, a reception area. Crystal diffused the light, and polished wood glinted with somber reflections. The space was formal, simple, discreet but not cold.

"Comrade . . .?" The host was a young man with fiery pink skin that swelled smooth over round cheeks.

"I am to meet Comrade Tribout here, there should be a reservation in his name. . . ."

The young man consulted a printed list of names.

"Comrade Tribout, yes . . . at eight-thirty."

"I am early," Nagy said.

"Please come with me, your table is ready."

Nagy's nerve ends were alive, but there was nothing unexpected in the dining room ... just the decor and decorum of a great French restaurant.

He was one of the first arrivals of the evening. In the corner farthest from the door, a very heavy man, in a charcoal gray suit much like his own, was sitting with a blond woman. Her purple gown framed a white, ample bosom. She looked quite beautiful at first glance. With a second look, Nagy credited the masking softness of the light for making her more beautiful than she would be outside.

Another party was sitting at the side of the room, six men, speaking quietly in what Nagy presumed was Russian. He accepted them for being what they seemed, four distinguished visitors from Moscow being flattered by their two Russian-speaking hosts in France. Taillevent existed for such flattery.

His table was perfect, in the center, his seat facing the entry to the room ... He counted the empty chairs, not more than fifty, and he wondered which ones would be for the first secretary and his companion, the minister of the economy. There was another dining room adjacent. He hoped they would not be split off out of sight, but it seemed unlikely that they would be seated far from the entrance.

Nagy ordered a kir made with champagne. When it came, he watched the pink of the cassis lifting into the golden effervescence above. He would not drink, though he liked the taste of wine with food: he could not filter his reflexes through the gauze of alcohol, not tonight.

Two couples came in with loud greetings to the host, party members showing off for each other. Then, to their consternation, they were told that their reservation was not listed; the evening was fully booked. Nagy listened to the words floating into the dining room and admired the Star's work—Landry was a magician with the computer. He could do anything.

Now, waiters moved, and a table would be prepared upstairs, in the private dining room that was not, thanks be, booked for that night. The restaurant would always take care of such valued clients.

Another group arrived. One of them had a scar on his temple

that ran down onto his cheek—severed nerves had locked half his features. This man had a hardness that plucked Nagy's attention.

De Celigny arrived. He was Comrade Tribout, sports director of Lyon, celebrating—what?—with his best runner.

The man with the scar was seated at a table directly behind Nagy, and Nagy marked the spot, adding this detail to his plan— when the action began, de Celigny would kill Paccard while Nagy guarded de Celigny's back. Then de Celigny would lead the way to the entry area and cover the dining room while Nagy went through the door to the street.

"How long have you been waiting?" de Celigny asked.

"Ten minutes. Not long...."

Menus were placed in their hands, great creamy rectangles of the finest paper stock, and Nagy turned his attention to the choices that were spelled out in elegant copperplate.

"Has it changed since the last time you were here?" Nagy asked de Celigny.

De Celigny surveyed the list. "They have some of the old dishes—I remember the lamb with the black olives was good, for example. But it's easy for them to put dishes on the menu. It is harder for the kitchen to keep at the same level ... especially if the clientele can't tell the difference. We'll see ..."

De Celigny leaned forward and spoke softly. "Pay attention to the host. He used to be a waiter here, and there is a small chance that he might give my face the name of a former deputy in the National Assembly."

Nagy nodded and glanced down at the menu, looking for the lamb with black olives.

He scanned the menu and conjured up dreams, reading the names of the dishes: langoustines, a pastry of pâté, crayfish swimming in fresh vegetables, a whole kidney, and there was the lamb with black olives. He would try the lamb de Celigny said was good ... and then, to look at the desserts, a fantasy in excess.

The tables started to fill. Another group, three, found their reservation missing from the reservation list, and now the host's reaction was polished: yes, it was understood that their reservation was not recorded; the Star had failed already once this evening, and would they care to share the private dining room upstairs with the other party?

And then, the first secretary and prime minister of France, Georges Paccard.

Behind Paccard was the short, blocky figure of the minister of the economy, Marcel Chabon.

De Celigny's back was turned to the arrivals, and he asked Nagy a question with his eyes, so that Nagy could nod assent.

Both men wore dark suits and white shirts, but Paccard had the better tailor—his jacket snugged over his shoulders without a wrinkle. Chabon wore a plain State Factory wool-and-polyester suit, ordinary and anonymous.

They were taken to a table just inside the entry to the room. Chabon recognized someone in the Russian group and went to their table to speak, brushing de Celigny's shoulder as he passed. One and then all of the Russian group stood up, with much bumping of chairs, and came with Chabon to be presented to Paccard . . . smiles, two words in Russian from Paccard, which brought laughter.

Paccard stood politely while the Russian group flowed back to its table. Then his eyes swept the room, and Nagy saw a flicker of recognition in Paccard's expression. Recognition mixed with apprehension—something was wrong. For an instant, it appeared that Paccard was moving directly toward de Celigny, but Paccard continued, past Nagy's shoulder.

Nagy looked at de Celigny, who nodded an all's well. Behind his shoulder, Nagy heard Paccard's voice. "Colonel Morot, a pleasure to see that my staff can take the time to eat well . . ."

The response, dry, ". . . I have come here for many years, comrade first secretary. It is a habit I cannot break."

Nagy glanced over his shoulder. It was the man with the scar on his cheek, now sitting down. Georges Paccard turned to return to his companions. A mixture of anger and anxiety played across Paccard's face, and Nagy tried to imagine the cause. Would it make a difference?

Chabon's expression was neutrally cordial, as though nothing more was in his mind than an excellent meal in prestigious company.

Nagy ordered foie gras to begin, followed by the lamb. De Celigny asked for a shellfish salad followed by sweetbreads with a sauce of wild mushrooms, savory *morilles.*

"Do you want wine?" de Celigny asked.

"No, thanks," Nagy replied, touching the kir.

"Water then . . . a Badoit?"

"Please. That would be fine."

De Celigny spent some time looking at the wine card—some noble vintages were still in the cellar. But when the sommelier came to the table, de Celigny asked him to send Badoit.

"Have you thought about the future," de Celigny asked Nagy, "if all goes well?"

Nagy nodded. "I would like to be married."

De Celigny cocked his head, surprised. Nagy had always seemed happy to be free.

"Do you have a woman in mind?"

"No, but I will know her when I meet her."

A look of sorrow crossed de Celigny's face, but the moment passed.

The water came.

"To your wife, wherever you may find her," de Celigny toasted, raising the water, its light bubbles coating the glass. He was smiling now.

Nagy returned the smile and raised his glass of water.

The foie gras was presented as a rich little gray cushion, centered on a large white plate with a sprig of parsley as its only decoration. A tiny drop of blood signalled that it was perfectly cooked. Nagy ate it slowly, thinking that it was better than anything he had ever put in his mouth, so rich with flavor.

De Celigny carefully made forkfuls of fresh scallops and crisp greens from his salad, savoring each bite before preparing the next.

Nagy watched the two ministers at their table. What were they talking about?

The main dishes were served almost too quickly after the first course was cleared, as though to prove that the influence of the New State had improved the efficiency of the restaurant.

De Celigny pronounced his sweetbreads less than perfect, a little too well done. Cued by this criticism, Nagy wondered if his lamb had not also been too long over the flame, but the brown sauce was delicious.

After their first course, Paccard and Chabon joined in taking duck, with a bottle of Burgundy wine.

It was almost time for dessert.

The dinner plates vanished, and the waiter came back with the menus. De Celigny ordered a chocolate mousse. Nagy ordered a *tarte tatin*, the caramelized upside-down apple pie that had been invented by mistake in the distant history of French cooking.

Nagy tested himself, stretching his fingers, wiggling his toes. He rehearsed in his head the movement to rise and turn with the pistol in his hand. When he did it he would not think. Thinking was too slow.

The *tarte tatin*, magnificently browned and gleaming with dark crystallized sugar, was set in front of him, and he edged off a bite.

The ministers were finishing their duck.

The quiet outside told them that Thevenet and Euler must have done their work.

"Are you ready?" de Celigny asked.

Nagy nodded.

"Here we go."

De Celigny and Nagy together, as slowly as if they had simply finished their meal, backed their chairs away from the table and stood up. As de Celigny turned to Paccard, Nagy turned so that he was back to back with de Celigny.

Nagy looked for the man with the scar and felt the eyes before he saw the face. They were burning into him, but the man was frozen, immobilized by the pistol in Nagy's hand.

Nagy forced his eyes to move, to dance away from the scarred man and see the others, while his pistol held its aim. The guests were looking now, all of them, at de Celigny behind him.

No silencer ... The sound of the shot was stunning, then another, then two more. Nagy's ears were ringing, but he heard de Celigny....

"Out!"

Nagy moved, his feet backing in swift half steps, his eyes still on the people at the tables, on the man with the scar, not even seeing Paccard on the floor.

At the entrance to the dining room he turned to locate de Celigny. De Celigny was covering now for Nagy as Nagy went past into the reception area.

De Celigny glanced at Nagy and then staggered, spun by the impact of a bullet that came before the sound of the shot.

Nagy wheeled to shoot and saw the scarred man rolling out of sight, into the next room.

"Move out!" de Celigny gasped. His left hand was on his chest, and blood was coming now, flowing over his fingers and spreading a black stain on his jacket.

Nagy went through the door first and saw the squad massed across the street. He dove for the sidewalk, squeezing off a round, but no fire came back. Then de Celigny came through the door, and the darkness erupted in a sheet of flame from the muzzles of a dozen machine pistols.

Nagy rolled away as the street roared with the sound of the barrage. His ears were still ringing with the echo of the volley as he sprinted for the Avenue de Friedland, going for the spot where they had left the van. But the van was gone, its place taken by a black Fiat with rust coming through the fenders.

Where was the pursuit?

Nagy forced himself to stop. Where were they? He tried to feel them, but he was alone.

They could easily have killed him. Instead, they had waited for de Celigny. An ambush.

He started to move, as though he was being followed, planning his route into the *métro* underpass, under the Champs-Élysées, and up on the other side, then a quiet run into the residential territories of the sixteenth arrondissement. Then a wait, a long wait, and a return with many stops and switchbacks to be sure that he was not followed to the warehouse in the rue Pouchkine. It was only three hundred meters from the restaurant.

LANDRY did not like it, but there had been no other place. Leonid was in Landry's last refuge.

The little house in Vincennes had survived the manhunt—the police had entered for the door-to-door search, seen that there was no furniture or other sign of habitation on the single floor, and marked the place vacant, duly noted in the Star.

So Landry had given up his last best secret, the address on the rue du Donjon, next to the Château de Vincennes. The house had a garage of its own where the van could be hidden, and strangers were not remarkable in this area: many newcomers had arrived to replace the well-to-do who had been redeployed.

Most important, a trunk cable had been laid through Vincennes from the Star, in the early days when the installation was intended for the fields near Melun. The cable ran underneath the house. Landry could control the Star as easily from the house as he could from the cave under the Arc de Triomphe.

But now the place was Leonid's. To prepare, Euler had nailed thick insulation boards up on all the walls. The windows were already shuttered, like most of the household windows in France, but Euler had covered these on the inside, so that the interior of the house was sealed and soundproof.

Landry was pleased by the soundproofing but not by the pulley bolted into the bedroom ceiling, the hole cut in the wall between the bedroom and the living room, or the wire that ran over the pulley and through the hole.

When it was Leonid's feeding time, the wire was drawn tight and cleated. That meant that Leonid was standing immobilized under the pulley with his right wrist hoisted at arm's length above his head, so that the door could be unlocked and the food taken in.

The wire was connected to Leonid's wrist by a tight loop and a heavy clamp that had been squeezed shut with long-handled pliers.

Leonid cried out when Landry pulled the wire tight, and Landry winced. He did not like to inflict pain. Normally, it was the job of Euler and Thevenet to take care of the prisoner, but they were occupied with Paccard.

Landry pulled the stocking over his face, took the plate of cold spaghetti, and unlocked the door.

The room was bare except for a mattress on a metal-framed bed.

Leonid was dressed only in a shirt, and his eyes were bleary.

"Let me down," he begged, his voice rising as he spoke. "You are cutting my wrist. . . ."

It was true. Leonid's wrist had reddened from constant contact with the bare wire, and now the skin was turning dark and ugly where the wire squeezed into the flesh.

Landry put the plate on the bed and, without a word, went out and locked the door.

He stripped the stocking off his head and released the wire from the cleat.

Landry shuddered. It made him sick to keep a man imprisoned.

SLEEP was impossible before de Celigny returned. Landry descended the ladder to the bottom of his cave beneath the warehouse and went back to his seat in front of the monitor. He tapped a key and stared at the character that he had put on the screen.

He sensed a stirring above, and a rush of excitement seized him as he took the ten steps to the ladder. There was no sound of steps on the rungs, but someone was coming down.

The light of the cave caught the man's feet, then revealed him as he reached bottom and turned.

It was Nagy. Alone.

"They knew," he said.

Landry stared. The man was strangely calm.

"The others . . . ?" Landry asked

"De Celigny is dead. . . . Also, I think, Thevenet and Euler. There were a dozen men waiting for us outside the restaurant, and one inside. They knew we would be there, and they killed Jacques de Celigny." Flat, like announcing the arrival of a train.

"But you escaped and came here, you were not followed?"

A barely perceptible shake of the head.

Landry's hand extended to grasp Nagy's shoulder, but Nagy slipped away from it, as though recoiling from a snake.

"No," he said in the same flat tone. "Excuse me . . ."

He moved to the end of the tunnel, by the cable that joined to the Star, and sat down, his body heaving in silent sobs of anguish.

Landry did not move. He stood transfixed for minutes, seeing Nagy's sorrow and thinking of de Celigny, the brave man who had lost his life for a dream that was not his own. What had gone wrong?

When Nagy came to the table with the monitor, his face was calm again, his manner composed.

"You did not ask about Paccard," Nagy said. "They wanted us to kill Paccard. They did not try to protect him. Paccard is dead."

Immediately Landry understood. "Chabon?"

"We played this game for Chabon, but he did not play for us. . . ."

Landry could not believe it, but it was clear to Nagy. He must be as clear. They had been betrayed. Clear away all assumptions, start again. Chabon was the enemy.

"Listen, Nagy, we will need the apartment where we are keeping Leonid. Chabon knows where I am. It won't take long before he sends his men here. Go, now. Take Leonid somewhere and leave him. When you get back, I will be ready to move out."

"Why don't you come with me now?"

"I must prepare the Star. . . . It will not take long."

Nagy took the keys to the van and disappeared up the ladder.

Landry felt the hate rise, a bitter taste in the back of his throat. His trust was betrayed, and now how long would it take for Chabon's men to come? He needed to work fast.

IT was good to be in the safe haven of the labyrinth. In the shower, the jet of hot water pulsed from the shower head and beat against her skin, steaming away the caresses that she had endured from Comrade First Secretary Paccard that afternoon.

Her body had come to terms with the soreness that still lingered from the beating, but the first secretary's hands had left her with a crawling of the flesh that would need more than a shower to wash away.

Wrapping herself in a warm, thick towel, she could appreciate the luxury that came to the first secretary's mistress. That part was good. But now that she was securely in charge of the labyrinth, she could play Paccard like a fish on a line. She would never let him touch her again.

The telephone in the kitchen rang. It was almost eleven, and she asked herself what it could be at eleven in the evening.

Eyes was speaking to her. His calm was betrayed by a tremble in his voice. Paccard was dead, assassinated by Jacques de Celigny.

Eyes said that Marcel Chabon was the selection of the embassy to take over the government.

Valerie absorbed this news. So, patience and secrecy had won for Marcel Chabon. She wondered how she would manage the change.

Eyes completed his report. De Celigny had been killed by Parade Guards under the command of Colonel Yves Morot....
Now Valerie's head started to buzz with questions.

Valerie thanked her intelligence chief and asked to be notified of any developments.

"You received a radio message," Eyes said. "It came in from a mobile unit, calling from a town called Notre-Dame-de-Belle-combe. You are asked to respond."

She used the intercom for the radio contact. Her conversation was brief, and she was smiling before she signed off. Abruzzi frightened her still, but he pleased her very much. She had done well to keep him as her own.

Abruzzi had already covered two thirds of the distance to Paris. Chantal Senac would be in the labyrinth by midnight.

She went back to her old office, the cubbyhole where she knew how to manipulate the Star, and she turned on the switches. Carefully, she tapped in a message to Robert Landry.

15 Landry hoped he would have an hour or two before they came. His fingers were a blur on the keys, entering the commands that would transfer his control of the Star to the computer in Vincennes. When Nagy returned, he would be ready. The monitor glowed and flashed.

Landry tried to avoid thought of de Celigny or Chabon. He had wasted de Celigny's life, and he could not concentrate when he thought of Chabon's treachery.

The work took half an hour, and the computer told him it was half past eleven. Nagy should return by midnight. Landry scrolled through the MSIE files before closing down for the last time from his cave. The first reports of the assassination were just coming into MSIE's daily journal. And then Landry read a notice, inserted in MSIE's news, framed in a box outline so that it could not be missed.

It was addressed to him.

>*René LEVEQUE, Robert LANDRY*

Comrade Chantal SENAC was detained in the town of Notre-Dame-de-Bellecombe, carrying false identification in the name of Marie OLIVET of Thionville. Her interrogation commences at 0100 hours, with intention to learn your location. Your immediate surrender will avoid this necessity.

Commencing 0100 hours the interrogation of Chantal SENAC will be communicated to this file by voicewriter.

s/Gentiane, successor to Karel
Department 100

He stared wide-eyed at the Star's message. The labyrinth wanted to find him and so Chantal would be taken to the labyrinth.

Terror overflowed Landry. He felt powerless against forces that were stripping away his control.

What if they were lying? What if they did not have Chantal, if they had killed her? It made no difference for him, he could not abandon the chance that she was still alive.

The girl must have returned to replace the Russian. Landry bitterly recognized that if the Russian was gone, Chantal's last official protection had been stripped away.

The secret of his location had been kept by Chabon, but it made no difference. The game with the Star was over. Just knowing that Chantal's pain would be captured in the Star was enough to force him up to the surface.

He glanced at his watch—a little more than an hour before Chantal's interrogation would begin. In a panic, he realized that he could not save her if he was detained by Chabon.

There was no question of waiting for Nagy. Landry shut the machine down.

He would take nothing with him, no identification, no cash card, only what was necessary to save her. It was a small trade to give for her, he would give up his body and his mind.

As his steps took him up the long ladder, his thoughts were already far away. He prayed that they would let him see her. They might not.

For the first time in two years, he left his sleeping room without dusting the trap door or setting the thread on the threshold.

He moved quickly to the front of the warehouse. His hand reached out to the switch, and the warehouse went black. He turned the great knob, felt the latch release, and pushed on the door.

A powerful grip took him by the elbow and gently pushed him outside.

The silence of it made him think it was Nagy, returned already from Leonid, but the voice in his ear was too deep and rough to be Nagy.

"Be quiet, my friend, you must come with me."

He thought that he knew the voice, and he was surprised that the man had come himself.

THEY were in the street. When Landry tried to turn his head to see his captor, the pressure on his arm urged him forward. The man was a head shorter than Landry, his shape round and solid. A hat was crammed down on the man's temples. The muscles driving his fingers into Landry's arm suggested an athlete's brawn. They came up to the first road crossing, and Landry was propelled around the corner.

The sound of the engine preceded the car out of the depths of the side street, and the back door swung open even before the car stopped. Landry was pushed in head first and thrown back in the seat as the vehicle accelerated, then forward and sideways as it braked and accelerated again around the turn. The door slammed shut as an afterthought.

"Calm," the voice growled in his ear. "I am going to cover your eyes, and then you must get down so you cannot be seen."

The blindfold was a cloth sack of some kind, slipped loosely over his head.

"Down."

Landry obeyed.

A long engine-roaring straight made Landry guess that they were on the highway along the river. The hand steadied him, and the car stopped. Somewhere near the Seine?

"Move now, quickly," the voice said, close to his ear, and he was on his feet, the hand now on the other elbow, urging him forward, supporting him when he stumbled.

"Stop."

Landry stumbled to a halt.

"We are safe here, out of sight. I must know your name."

The sack was still over his head, and Landry raised his hand to lift it, but the grip on his arm restrained him.

"Your name. I must be sure you are the man I need."

"Robert Landry is my real name. I have other names."

"You were on the way to save a woman. What is her name?"

"Chantal Senac."

"Good . . . We will walk from here. Make as little noise as possible."

"I must help Chantal."

"You can, if we are lucky."

From half a step behind, the man guided him, using gentle pressure. Landry responded as best he could. They passed through several doors, pausing at each one, and finally they were in a narrow corridor, where Landry's elbows bumped each side as they walked. Their footsteps echoed, and Landry guessed that the walls and the floor were metal. At last they paused a long time, and Landry guessed that they had reached a series of doors. Hinges moaned, bearing great weight, and moaned again to close with a wheeze of air, making a seal behind them.

Then a latch clicked. The cloth hood rasped across his cheeks and nose, and he could see.

He looked into the face of Marcel Chabon.

"It is you."

"We are going to try to save Chantal Senac and destroy an enemy," Chabon said. "It depends on you."

They were in an apartment, simply furnished except for an extraordinary sculpture group in white plaster that filled the end of the room to Landry's left. Chabon left Landry by the door and went to an open kitchen section, separated from the living area by a counter. Chabon took a Smith & Wesson revolver from a drawer, checked to be sure that it was loaded.

"Do you know how to use this?" Chabon asked.

"I am not sure."

Chabon explained the pistol, showing how to aim and shoot straight with both hands. Landry's mind was racing ahead to Chantal, but Chabon forced patience, made Landry demonstrate what he had learned about the revolver.

Then Chabon explained what Landry had to do.

* * *

THE chill of the room seeped through her cotton blouse and walking shorts. She was seated in a canvas and metal folding chair, secured to the frame by wrappings of adhesive tape that held her wrists and ankles. To offset the chafe of the tape, she tensed and relaxed her muscles . . . her arms, then her legs, then her back and neck.

She prayed that the chemicals would bring oblivion. The room looked like a hospital's. Nothing could be hidden, not the smallest deception, under the white light that poured down from the translucent ceiling. The white tile floor, scrubbed and gleaming, reflected the ceiling and seemed to give off a light of its own. Apparatus of all sorts lined the spotless white walls, a battery of stainless steel implements and white enamel cabinets, and a row of cathode ray tubes that was surely intended to monitor her vital functions, to keep her on the edge of life as long as she was needed. A table like an operating table in a hospital was waiting ready for her. Pressure tanks were cradled in a small cart beside it, connected by a long coil of hose to the mask that would be placed over her nose and mouth.

They had said nothing to her. They had led her in from the limousine, taped her to the chair, and left her, as though all words should be saved for her interrogation.

Sadness filled her, for Catherine and for Henri, for de Celigny's children, because she would soon be submerged in the chemicals, and she would give up their names like a child reciting a lesson. She wondered if the interrogators would find, buried deep in her, any clue to Robert Landry. He had been careful to keep her from knowing the location of the warehouse. He could be lost in a trackless ocean for all she could tell them of his whereabouts.

The door opened, and a ruddy, brick-faced man looked in at her, made a sorrowful face, and disappeared. The door closed.

She wondered who he was.

Three men had brought her to Paris, a bald man with a high-pitched voice, and two thugs, brutal in their ugliness. They had handled her roughly, like an unwieldy parcel. Except for the bald man. She had caught his eyes, looking at her, and the dreaming expression on his face had sent gooseflesh up her spine.

The man who had opened the door had seemed normal, the first expressive face she had seen since Laurent Bellot's. A dim glow of hope soothed her fears. Maybe, she found herself thinking, it might not be so bad ... but then she braced her expectations for the reality of interrogation. The best to hope for was a void without pain, and with no return. Everyone knew that the drugs destroyed the brain, turning it into a mess of garbage.

The door opened again, and the same brick-faced man returned, carrying a clipboard in one hand and a ballpoint pen in the other. The pen was bright red, with a gold stylus, and he held it like a baton, between his thumb and his forefinger, point extended.

As he entered the room, he was reading the paper on the clipboard. His gaze lifted to her and then returned to the clipboard, matching the presence with the paper, and his eyes remained steadfast on the paper as he intoned, "Your name?"

"Marie Olivet."

He shook his head. "Your name, please."

"Marie Olivet ..."

"You must not try to lie; it will only cause you more pain."

He looked up from the paper, as though to apologize for bad news. She could see no threat in him.

"What difference does it make if I tell you my name?"

"None at all, but I must write what you say, on the report. It is a requirement."

He raised the red ballpoint pen and poised it over the clipboard. His parted lips and cocked head communicated eager expectance.

She did not speak. The idea of resistance was forming a wall of silence within her head. If she pushed back all conscious thoughts, willed them back, maybe the chemicals would burn out the wells of her subconscious before they gave up Henri and Catherine.

"I beg you," the man said. "Listen, I know this man who comes to question you. He is a sadist. I cannot stand to watch him when he is torturing his victims."

She stared at the tip of the ballpoint pen and pushed her consciousness into a blank. But then the pen wavered. Someone was coming.

Chantal heard the high-pitched voice before she saw, in the doorway, the bald man who had killed Laurent Bellot and brought her from Notre-Dame-de-Bellecombe.

"What does she say?"

"Nothing . . . she will not speak."

"Ah, very good. You may go now. Tell the others we are ready."

A young woman dressed in an austere black suit, a girl, swept into the room, an ethereal smile on her lips. What did it mean, a girl so young? Chantal asked herself. Confident strides brought the girl past the bald man to Chantal's side, so close that her thigh pressed on Chantal's shoulder. Without warning, fingers twined into Chantal's hair and snapped her head back. Chantal looked straight up into cold green eyes.

"Where is René Leveque?"

Chantal's wall of silence held the breath in her throat, but her body responded with a reflexive shudder. Then the grasp on her hair was gone, and the face was gone. She was looking at the white teeth of the bald man, and there were more people, a dozen at least, coming into the room.

"This place is bad for me," the bald man said, his voice a keening whine. "This place is cold."

"What would you prefer?" The voice came from the girl, behind Chantal. Her voice was airy and light, without any modulation.

"Any other room, but I cannot concentrate in this place. There is no feeling, the ghosts are dead in here. . . ." The man started to laugh, and the laughter soared an octave before he stopped.

The girl again, authority under her clear tone: "We must be connected to a voice processor . . . to send a live transcript to Robert Landry, René Leveque, or whatever she wants to call him. We communicate with him by the Star."

"The only connection is here?" The bald man had come close to Chantal, and he absently reached out a hand to caress her cheek. She recoiled in horror, and the hand withdrew.

"Eyes' office," she said. "We can go there."

"Thank you," the bald man said.

"Follow me."

The girl strode past Chantal, pushed past the men in the room, and was out the door. The bald man took one step, wrapped Chantal's hair around his hand, and jerked her backward, tipping the chair onto its back legs. He pulled. She shrieked from the tearing at her temples, and then she was moving, dragging in the chair, bumping out of the room, over the doorsill and down a corridor, the light dim after the brilliance of the interrogation room, the chair catching and resisting their passage. They were going fast, almost at a run. Her eyes could not focus on anything but a spinning, jolting continuum of light and dark, and her ears absorbed, over the scraping of the chair, the hammering of feet, the crowd that had been in the room, now following.

They are mad, Chantal thought, crazy. And they had not even begun.

They crossed another threshold, and then she was down on her back, still immobilized by the chair, on the floor of what she saw was an office. She looked up at legs and stomachs and, above that, faces, two that she already knew, the girl and the bald man, others that were strange—grotesque chins and nostrils, indifferent eyes, and some hungry eyes that were not indifferent.

A hard object pressed her temple. A shoe, she imagined, forming a toe's shape from its pressure. The high-pitched voice of the bald man cut through the noise of scuffling feet around her head.

"Do you think she knows where he is?" the voice was asking.

"I think not," the girl's answer came. "Her pain must make him come in."

"So, let us begin."

"No, not yet. We have ten minutes to wait until the appointed time. Pick her up."

Hands raised the chair, and Chantal found herself in a small, crowded office, beside a desk, looking across at the girl in the black suit. The girl's innocent smile floated across crimson lips.

"Listen to me," the girl said to her. "We think you do not know where he is. . . . We will ask you and ask you, over and over again. We expect you to tell us in your pain that you do not know where he is. Just remember this . . . If later we find out that you do know, if you later can tell us where to find René Leveque, you will live to see your son die in suffering. He is only one day away, your son, in Notre-Dame-de-Bellecombe."

The cruelty slashed Chantal's heart. She started to cry, great tears coming unbidden to her eyes and streaming down her cheeks.

"You cannot tell me where to find René Leveque?"

The silence still held her throat, but Chantal shook her head.

"Then, in a few moments I will ask Comrade Abruzzi to repeat the question. . . . Is the voice processor turned on?"

A mumble came in response. "Wait please, comrade, it seems to be on, but we are not sure. . . ."

Hands touched Chantal's neck, and she knew that it was the bald man.

His high voice commanded. "Undo her wrists and ankles; we will put her on the desk."

The tape tore at her wrists, and she tried to will herself to oblivion. Hands were pulling at the tape on her ankles, and she was suddenly free, rising, lifted out of her chair from behind by rough hands under her arms, onto her feet, and as her deadened legs buckled under her weight, the same hands pushed her forward, facedown on the desk.

"Hello? Here you are. I have been looking for you in the interrogation room. . . ."

It was a new voice, a voice with gravel in it and no trace of madness.

The girl spoke, and there was a shading to the airy tone, wariness. "We moved, Comrade Max. Comrade Abruzzi needed a place with more nerve and gristle than the interrogation room."

"I think I can save you some trouble. The man you seek has come in. Landry is here."

The room went still. Chantal raised her head and saw, at the edge of her vision where light blurred to gray, a short man with a paunch, standing at the door.

"So . . ." the girl cried, "the plan was a success!"

"Not perfectly. He came in with a gun, and he threatens suicide if we do not show him this woman. He fears that we have harmed her. We could have killed him, of course, but he is too valuable. What are your wishes, Comrade Gentiane? This is your department now, I do not interfere. . . ."

"Where is he?"

"In the interrogation room."

Hands still held Chantal, bent at the waist, with her chest and head on the desk, her feet on the floor. She struggled to see the man who had come in. René had surrendered to save her. She wished she was dead.

"Do you think he will cooperate?" the girl asked.

"I think he will kill himself if we do not grant him his wish. I should suggest that we comply, it can do no harm."

"Well, then," the girl said. "Let's go."

Chantal heard a soft, high-pitched exhalation, like air coming from a punctured bicycle tire, and knew that it was the bald man, moaning the escape of his prey.

Half-carried, half-walking, Chantal was led back down the corridor that had marked her headlong passage minutes earlier. They made a procession, the short, plump man—Max?—then the bald man, herself between two men, followed by the girl who was called Gentiane, and then the chorus of spear carriers, noisy in the wake of the parade. Chantal knew it was only a respite, not a reprieve. Once they had René, they would use her to coerce him, gorging their appetite for cruelty on both of their victims. If René knew their ways, he would kill himself without delay, while he still had freedom to do it.

The door was shut ahead of them.

The round, short man turned and spoke to the girl, Gentiane.

"In case he decides to shoot the first person through the door, it should be his woman, no?"

The girl nodded.

Chantal was pushed to the front, and then the round, short man, hardly glancing at her, was at the code buttons to unlock the door.

The door swung open, and she was shoved forward into the room. René was there, a gun in his hand, raised to his temple, the barrel pressed into his hair.

"Chantal," he said, but his eyes left her immediately, and Chantal was hurled to the floor, the weight of the round man on top of her.

Robert Landry pointed the revolver into the sea of faces in the doorway and pulled the trigger. The explosion filled the room, and then another drowned out the reverberation of the first. A scream of pain, and the door slammed.

Quiet ... The room was sealed in silence—the door was as soundproof against the shouts outside as it was made to be against cries of the victims within.

Then Landry was on his knees beside Chantal, gathering her into his arms, holding her as if he could squeeze her out of danger.

"Get up," the round man said. He picked up Landry's pistol and extended his free hand to help Chantal to her feet. "They cannot open the door, but there is a way around. Landry, did you kill the girl?"

"No," Landry responded to Marcel Chabon.

"Then we have a fight on our hands. I am going to send you back to your cave, Landry. We will talk when I am finished here."

They left the interrogation room by the back exit and then passed two doors that blocked the corridor. Chabon was deft, but each door took an agony of seconds before the lock yielded to the code procedure. On the far side of the second door they met a man with a heavy automatic weapon in his hands.

"How many men does she have?" Chabon asked.

"About fifteen still alive, comrade."

"Give me your weapon and take these two up to my driver," Chabon said to the armed man. He turned to Landry. "We will meet soon. We have work to do."

They parted where the corridor split. Five minutes and many doors later, Landry and Chantal saw streetlamps and the flash of passing headlights gleaming down into an open stairway, and then they were up on the street. They waited for an opening in the flow of traffic and crossed the road that parallels the Seine. On a side street, parked in a forbidden space, they found a nondescript Peugeot, which Landry recognized as the car that had brought him.

Their escort rapped on the window, and a head appeared on the passenger side. The driver had been down on the seat, out of sight, feigning sleep.

Landry and Chantal rode in the back seat. She collapsed into his arms, letting the knots of desperation come undone, shutting out the future.

They parked in the same alley where the car had waited for Chabon to bring Landry from his warehouse. The driver took Landry and Chantal to the warehouse door, followed them inside, and sent them through the trap door down to Landry's cave. Landry understood that they were under the driver's guard until Chabon wanted them.

At the bottom, Chantal put her head on Landry's shoulder, and he pressed his face into her hair, drawing strength from his love for her.

They stood a long time, in each other's arms, the physical contact stronger than words.

When she spoke, she held him still.

"Who is the man who saved me?" she asked. "Is he a friend?"

"No, he is not a friend," Landry answered and fought a wave of anger. "He is the new first secretary, Marcel Chabon."

"She called him Max," Chantal said.

"He is part of the labyrinth," Landry replied, remembering the deft movements of Chabon's fingers unlocking the doors. "It was all deception. He took me there because the girl could control me through you, so he wanted you out and hoped that I might kill the girl."

Mind-splitting rage filled him. "He was part of it, working for the Russians. Christmas of 2002 when the Russians came, takeover of the government, redeployment of our people. And I helped him to become first secretary."

"What will we do?"

"We are trapped. Even if we get out of here, they have your son."

And then they heard footsteps on the rungs of the ladder above, a light step. Chabon's driver?

Nagy appeared. At the bottom of the ladder, he stood quietly, absorbing the presence of Chantal without a word.

"There was no guard up above?" Landry asked.

"He is unconscious, and he will be quiet even after he wakes up."

"We can get out! But how did you get in here . . . ?"

"I was in the warehouse when you came in. This secret place is becoming well known."

"We can go to the house on the rue du Donjon. Where is Leonid?"

"He drank a whole bottle of Cognac and is sleeping in the street near the Place Pigalle."

"Noël," Chantal said. "We must protect him from them."

Landry looked at Nagy and knew what Nagy must do. "You have the van?"

"Three streets away."

"We will not be free if Chantal's child is in their hands. You must go now to Notre-Dame-de-Bellecombe, get him before they think of it."

MARCEL Chabon watched on the closed circuit video. The chase was nearly over. Like terriers after rats in the warren of passageways, the hunters of Action Branch tracked the men of Ugo Abruzzi and killed them by ones and twos. At the end, they had backed the last three into the kitchen for Intelligence Branch, where there was only a single door behind a corner. They were hard men, hard to kill. Chabon looked in vain for Abruzzi or Valerie. There was no sign of either—had they abandoned the labyrinth? It would be difficult for him if the girl ran to the embassy.

He called for tear gas. They would roll a canister into the kitchen and shoot the last three as the gas drove them out through the door.

Chabon estimated that they would be finished in an hour, and it would take another hour to get his men out. With or without

Valerie and Abruzzi, there was another task remaining before he could leave.

Chabon retreated to the deep security of the Russian's apartment.

At the end of the steel corridor, he had to search his memory for the code to enter.

The last latch clicked, and he stepped into the Russian's lair. Chabon had worked side by side with the Russian to finish the apartment, and he knew it well. He himself had put in the timing devices with wires leading into the cellars of the labyrinth.

He bowed in greeting to the tableau of white figures, standing in silence behind the open louvers at his left.

As the door closed behind him, the girl came out of the bedroom, a pistol in her hand.

Chabon stopped in mid-stride. Careless! He should have expected more of her; he knew her well enough. A strong character, she had not run.

She spoke. "Where is Landry?"

"I do not know. Gone back to ground."

"It makes no difference if you know. I do not need your help. Chantal Senac will do anything for her son, and Landry will follow. Ugo Abruzzi is on his way back to Notre-Dame-de-Bellecombe. This time he will bring Noël to me, and I will have Landry." Her clear voice carried in the apartment. "The embassy will be surprised to learn about your game to become first secretary and, now, to destroy me."

The ambition in her face twisted and turned in the air between them, and he tried to imagine what marvelous towers were building in her head.

"You will have to kill me," Chabon said. "I will not leave this place with you."

She shook her head.

"You must live to answer many questions."

Chabon stepped back, and as though drawn after him, she took a step forward into the room, raising the weapon in her hand.

"Stop," she said. "I will not kill you, but I can turn your knees into jelly. I think you would prefer to walk."

He took another step back and felt the counter top against the small of his back. He remembered the Russian on his knees, carving the floor with the tip of a pocketknife, and he bowed his head to find the small *x* that marked exact center in the room. He stepped sideways to be exactly over it.

"Come," she said. "Enough of this."

The temptation to look up almost overpowered him, but he feared that she would read his eyes. He raised his right hand to his forehead, as though he was faint, put his heel on the *x*, and started to sway, thinking that she would shoot him before he could complete his charade. As he fell forward, his left hand reached for the counter top to catch himself, and his fingers found the switch underneath.

Three rounds smashed her before she heard the sound of the machine guns. The sound followed her death like the roar of a train, an impact of decibels that echoed the impact of a thousand bullets on the walls. Chabon held himself motionless until the volley was over, and then, as the echoes rang into silence, he blinked away the storm of light and fury that he had turned loose. In front of him, in a cloud of plaster dust, the shattered tableau of sculpture dangled in shards from steel armatures underneath. Bolted to the armatures, littered now with splinters and bits of plaster, the guns were exposed, their magazines exhausted. The guns had been aimed to cover every sector of the room except the narrow capsule of air space that hovered over the *x* on the floor. The Russian's own hands had created the white figures to commemorate an ideal world that had never existed on this earth, and to provide a last defense should a siege end in this room. Chabon had thought it was a quirk of the Russian's imagination.

He left Valerie's shattered corpse in a spreading pool of blood.

He thought about Ugo Abruzzi, en route like a falcon launched from its master's wrist.

Chabon knew that he needed the boy to make Landry work for him. But even more, he needed Abruzzi dead. The man knew too much about the night's events, about the minister of the economy who was also Max inside the labyrinth.

The doors clicked shut behind him with the oily smoothness of precision machinery. Chabon returned to the Russian's office and entered a code to open a metal cabinet on the wall. He pulled a red lever inside the cabinet and heard the siren that told the people in the labyrinth to evacuate.

The telephones were still dead. The police would have to radio the order for a car from Megève to pick up Noël Senac and arrest a bald man if he should appear in Notre-Dame-de-Bellecombe.

MARCEL Chabon identified himself to the duty lieutenant at the National Police headquarters and explained that he was acting as first secretary following Paccard's death. The duty lieutenant knew about Paccard's assassination, but he knew nothing about Chabon's new status and had no instructions. With all respect for the minister of the economy, the police in Megève could not be ordered on a mission without approval from the director.

Director Gousset had gone home very late, after he had reviewed the reports of the assassination. The duty lieutenant was reluctant to call his director, but Chabon insisted with veiled threats.

Now Chabon regretted the total secrecy of Action Branch. He did not know Gousset, the director of the National Police. He would have to argue for help while Abruzzi was on his way to Notre-Dame-de-Bellecombe.

Gousset refused point-blank until he had referred to authority.

"Authority?" Chabon demanded. "I am the authority."

The voice on the line was burred with irritation. "I mean Department 100, comrade minister, if that means anything to you."

Chabon bit his lip to keep from crying out in frustration. He could not reveal his role in the labyrinth without betraying himself. "I know about Department 100, comrade director," he said.

Gousset continued. He could only communicate with Department 100 via the Star, because the telephones were not working. He would have to return from his home to use the Star's terminals at national headquarters.

The floor trembled under Chabon's feet. A picture fell off the wall of the duty office and crashed onto the floor. The duty lieutenant grasped his desk in fear of another earthquake shock, but Chabon understood the tremor. It meant that there was no more Department 100. The explosives would have ripped open the labyrinth, and the waters of the Seine would be filling it now.

Gousset would never have an answer from Department 100. Chabon clenched his fists. Would he have to leave Abruzzi at large, with all that Abruzzi knew? Would he have to explain to Landry that Chantal Senac's son was a hostage?

Chabon accepted reality: only the embassy could tell Gousset to obey. There might still be time, if Pyotr would cooperate at four o'clock in the morning.

The radio in the duty office crackled into life. A patrol car reported an explosion in the vicinity of the Île de la Cité.

16 Isabelle Bazin walked with Noël from their house to the door of the school. Sturdy and straight-backed, she was hardly taller than he. Her round face was framed by thick, close-cropped black hair, while he was fair, his hair a flowing blond crown. She kissed him good-bye, hugged him, and waited to watch him go. He turned to smile at her before he disappeared inside.

She was terrified for herself and even more for the boy. She did not want to leave him.

Yesterday, that terrible day, Noël had found the doors open when he came home from school, and she could only explain the front door, not the back. Who had been in her house to leave the back door open? The same one who had killed two men in the field behind her house while she had been in the Megève police station?

Two years before, Noël had come to her like a mystery, a golden child full of sadness and love. Fate had just struck at her with wrenching cruelty: her husband and their three-year-old child had died, crushed by a freak snowslide. Noël had been like a miracle, a gift in compensation for her loss, and with him a full cash account and a comforting presence, a voice on the telephone, promising shelter. But if the shelter was stripped away, Noël might be taken from her as suddenly as he had appeared.

Noël's mother had been on the posters. She knew that, because Noël had told her that his true family name was Senac, and that was the name of the wanted woman. Isabelle had worried even then, while respecting the boy's silence about the posters. And now?

Wednesday, the eleventh of May. In five more Wednesdays

school would be finished, and she would have six weeks of free-dom with Noël. She dreamed of a way to go far from Notre-Dame-de-Bellecombe, to places where Noël Bazin and his new mother could travel without a history. But there was no escape from the New State. The Star could find them in an instant, no matter where they travelled in France.

The school was five hundred meters from her house, and Isa-belle walked slowly home, thinking of Noël. He did well in all his courses, the best in his class, but of all the courses, he did best in Russian. His teacher said that he should surely win a high place in the government someday.

The curve of the road brought her house into view. She noticed a large black Moskva sedan with Paris plates and tinted windows, parked in front of the brasserie across the road from her house. What did that mean?

As she approached the door, she made herself think of what they should eat for lunch.

She opened the door to her house, and a shiver ran over the backs of her legs, climbing up her spine in a rush of gooseflesh. Reflex made her draw the door shut, and she stepped back, won-dering what it was that she had sensed.

Whatever it was, she started to cry. Her home, the place of her earliest memories, had changed, and she could not say why.

She drew a deep breath against the tension and told herself that it was normal to be distraught after the false arrest and the shootings. Isabelle took two steps away and started to walk to the back of the house. She snatched a glance at the windows and saw nothing more than a passing reflection of herself and the morning sky, but the walls seemed ominous, as though bulging with some horror.

A wrought-iron handle held the latch to the back door. She put her hand on the lever, felt the latch release, and put some weight against the door to swing it open. It creaked, as it always did. Inside, the house was quiet. She put one foot on the doorsill, listening. And then a wave of fear swept her again, and she withdrew her foot, pulled the door shut, and nearly ran down the steps.

She would come back with a friend, though she could not imag-ine what story she would tell.

As she walked up the road, the growl of a vehicle behind her made her turn. A gray van was coming up the grade, and she stepped to the side of the road to let it pass. But it slowed and stopped in front of her house. As she waited, it started again with a cough and drove by her. Her eyes met the eyes of the driver as he passed. A strange young man with eyes like clouds . . .

The van stopped at a wide part of the road ahead, and the driver emerged onto the road. He was looking at her, waiting for her, and she walked toward him.

"You are Isabelle Bazin," he said to her when she was a meter away. His voice seemed to come from a faraway place inside her own mind.

"Who are you?"

"I come from the mother of your adopted son."

"Chantal Senac?"

A nod. "Some people may try to take the boy. They want him as hostage, to make sure of his mother."

She stared at him, hypnotized by the cloudlike eyes.

"But, who are you? . . ."

"It is not important. . . . I offer you rescue. Do you believe me?"

Someone was waiting in her house. This man had come to save her. She wanted to believe him.

"Yes."

"That is your house, behind us on the road?"

"Yes. I must tell you something. I think someone is in my house now."

He thought for a moment. "If you think so, I think you can be sure of it. Where is the boy?"

"In school."

"Can you go into the school and take him out?"

"I can. I will."

His body swung back into the driver's seat, and he looked down from the van.

"Get him out of school. I will turn around above the town and pick you up on my return. When I stop, don't delay, just get into the van with the boy."

He was gone. She stood at the roadside until the van disappeared, and then started toward the school, wondering what excuse she would give to get Noël out.

NAGY drove out of the town, watching Isabelle Bazin framed in the outside mirror.

As he looked for a wide place to turn around, he wondered what the future would bring without Jacques de Celigny, and again he conjured up his last sight of his best friend, dead outside the restaurant. A few moments later, he snapped his attention back to Isabelle Bazin and decided she had had enough time to get her son out of school.

Nagy stopped by a driveway and backed the van into it. He rechecked his weapons, the rapid-fire Heckler & Koch that Jacques de Celigny had given him, the little Beretta pistol, and his knife, free in the scabbard on his wrist. Once he had used them as deftly as his own hands or his feet, faster than thought. Now, he was less sure, and he prayed that he would not need to fight. Thieves' luck, he had not encountered a roadblock since leaving Paris, and he had found the Moreau's stone house in Conflans still safe. Catherine Moreau had said yes, they would find a way; she would take Isabelle Bazin and the child

Who was inside Isabelle Bazin's house?

He put the Beretta in his belt and took his foot off the brake. Anxiety tugged at him: had he made an error to leave Isabelle Bazin behind in the town?

ISABELLE had just started toward the school when she heard a motor behind her and stepped off the road to let the vehicle pass. It was the Moskva from Paris, and it continued until it reached the school. There she saw it stop and saw a man get out with a pistol in his hand. He walked through the front door of the school.

Isabelle started to run, but before she had covered half the ground, she saw the man come back through the door, pulling Noël behind him.

He pushed Noël into the car and ran around to the driver's side. The car lurched forward, accelerating toward her.

She stopped, transfixed, in the center of the road, until her reflexes took her out of the way. The car blew past her in a gust of dirt and exhaust. On her knees, she turned to watch it disappear, carrying Noël away.

She looked desperately for the van and saw it coming down the road to the school. She got to her feet and broke into a run, begging the young man to see her. The van accelerated, skidded to a stop beside her, and she climbed in.

"A man with a gun took him down the road," she said.

They were already moving, loose stones clattering under the chassis, the engine wailing in protest. The old van swayed on the first turn, its tires at the limit of adhesion.

Downhill, it could go as fast as the skill of the driver and the bends of the road would allow. She had never imagined going so fast. And yet he seemed calm, his hands loose on the wheel, his head upright, eyes steady. Only the movement of his feet and his right hand on the gearshift lever betrayed their speed.

They had driven for perhaps three minutes when he spoke.

"How long were you there before I came?"

She thought before she responded. "Seconds . . ."

"Then maybe we will catch him. He will not expect pursuit. There was just one man?"

"With a pistol."

He nodded.

She asked, "Do you have a pistol?"

He nodded again.

The road ran straight for half a kilometer along a graded slope. At its far end, a black automobile disappeared around the next bend. They had both seen it: the car that had come from Paris for Noël Senac.

"His machine is comfortable but not fast on the turns," the man said to her. "We can catch him."

"And then?"

"We will try to save the boy. . . ."

The van's motor screamed, nearly bursting with the speed of the straightaway.

Now Isabelle's thoughts were churning. "What if he threatens to kill Noël?"

"He will not. The boy is worth nothing to them dead. They want him as a hostage."

At the end of the straight road they pitched into a sharp turn, coming up hard on a bump.

"What will you do?"

"We will hit the Moskva from behind. You will be surprised to see how hard it is to control a car when it has been knocked from the rear."

"And then? . . ."

He did not reply.

"I beg you to save my boy."

"I will try."

Briefly they were climbing, and the van's small motor agonized until they crested the rise and accelerated down again.

"What does the road do next, after this turn?" he asked.

"It turns again to the left."

"And then?"

"Straight, to join the Route Nationale."

"We will catch him there."

The van rocked around the first bend, swayed, and leaned again around the second, accelerating into the straight. The black car was there, three hundred meters ahead.

But coming up the hill from the fork off the main road, just passing the stop sign, was a small blue bus with a blue light on the roof, a police vehicle. It turned abruptly into the downhill lane, backed, and quickly moved forward, blocking the road. The Moskva's brakes locked and the tires shredded rubber onto the asphalt. The back of the Moskva swung into the grass. The car lurched sideways across the road, swerved back, and slid nose-on into the bus.

They slowed gradually and rolled up behind the Moskva. A policeman was on the road behind the blue bus. Another was in the bus, motionless. There was no movement in the car.

She heard, "Get out and hide, wait until you see me. . . ."

He was gone, and she was opening the door, was out of the van and running to Noël in the crashed car ahead.

She heard her friend's voice telling her to stop, but she could not. She pulled open the door of the car, reached for Noël. A hand seized her wrist, and she looked up into the face of a bald man, his yellow teeth set in an insane grin as he pulled her over Noël so that she was halfway into the car.

In his other hand he had a pistol. He aimed it out the window on his side and fired once. She heard a cry of pain and saw the surprised face of a man outside. She recognized him as he fell—one of the policemen who had taken her to Megève.

Noël did not move. Was he dead?

Now the bald man was pushing her, and they were all three out of the car, huddled on the asphalt. The bald man pushed her shoulders against the road with his knee and brought the hilt of the pistol down hard on her temple. The impact exploded like a cannon inside her head, a shower of sparks and then gray.

She could hear him as though he was on another planet, his high-pitched voice piercing the ache in her brain.

"Come out, come out. Let me see you, or they die, both of them. . . ."

Quiet.

The weight of the bald man left her. She tried to raise her head, but it was too heavy with aching, and she could not.

His voice again, calling to her friend . . . and then she heard a reply from far away.

"He is worth nothing dead. . . . Give him up and you can go safe. . . ."

Close by, she heard the bald man grunt and felt a tug beneath her. He was taking Noël.

Isabelle rolled onto her elbows and struggled to lift herself. She succeeded in raising her head, and then she crawled after them, around the front of the police bus. She saw the bald man opening the door of the bus while the boy lay on the pavement beside him. A shot crashed, inside the bus. He had shot the other policeman, he was killing everyone. She crawled toward them, her head splitting with pain.

The bald man was in the driver's seat of the bus now, and its starter was chattering. The motor caught and ran, and he was back on the ground, taking Noël by the arms, lifting him.

There was a roar of gunfire, a hammering of bullets on metal, breaking glass. Hot water showered her shoulders, and she heard air escaping the tires of the bus. Her friend was killing the bus, cutting off the bald man's escape.

The bald man crouched beside the bus, the boy in his arms. For a moment, his crazed eyes met hers, and she could feel death very close, but then they both heard a motor's sound.

An ancient Citroën Deux Chevaux was laboring up the road toward them.

"Listen," the bald man said. "I will leave you here dead, or you will come with me in that car. Will you come with me and the boy?"

She nodded.

"Then lie still now, as though you were hurt."

As he jammed his pistol into the back of his waistband and ran to greet the oncoming car, she crawled forward to Noël. A huge bump swelled the boy's forehead, but he was breathing and alive. He moaned.

The little Citroën rolled to a stop twenty meters from the wreck. A woman was driving, her head visible in the window.

The bald man ran toward the car, waving his arms, as if the victim of an accident, but when he was close, he showed his pistol. He made the woman get out of the car, took her keys, and came back for the boy, his pistol up, ready, looking for the young man who was somewhere out in the grass.

As he came closer, he said to Isabelle, "You first, get into the car, so he will not start shooting at it. Quickly, or you are dead."

She managed to put her weight over her feet and stumbled toward the car. The woman was back beside the car now, taking something from the back seat.

Isabelle opened the passenger's side door of the Citroën as the woman moved away from the other side.

The bald man held Noël with one arm, was backing toward them, his pistol raised to face his invisible adversary.

She saw her friend then, rising from the grass behind the police bus, and in the same moment the bald man reacted. He wheeled smoothly, still holding Noël against his chest, and fired. The young man fell backward, his weapon flew into the air, and he disappeared into the grass.

The bald man let Noël slide onto the road and advanced toward the grass, knees bent, his pistol extended in both his hands in front of him, his lips pulled back over his teeth in a terrible smile.

The crack of a shot stunned Isabelle. The bald man slowly toppled to the ground. His pistol discharged, bucking against dead hands, and then he was still.

The woman beside the Citroën raised the barrel of her rifle and slowly walked forward to where the bald man lay.

Hands to her head, Isabelle stared. The woman was tall, with thick brown hair falling to her shoulders, and she had the confident stride of a *montagnarde*. She leaned over the body of the bald man and pushed at his shoulder with the gun barrel.

Satisfied, she walked into the grass. Isabelle climbed out of the car and ran to Noël.

Isabelle held the boy close, feeling his breath and warmth in her arms.

"Is he all right?"

"Yes."

Now the woman and the young man were standing over her. He was holding one hand to his shoulder, blood seeping through the fingers. The woman spoke.

"Isabelle Bazin, my name is Catherine Moreau. I think you have already met Charles Nagy."

Kneeling beside her, he gently put his fingertips on Noël's forehead, and Noël's eyes opened. Nagy looked up into her eyes and grinned.

"Hello," Nagy said.

He put his hand on Noël's wrist and waited, feeling the pulse.

"He will be all right."

His hand left Noël's wrist and reached up to touch his fingers to her cheek.

"And you?" he asked.

She nodded and put her hand over his, holding his fingers against her cheek.

"Let us go with Catherine," he said.

MARCEL Chabon marched into the Matignon and dismissed his Parade Guard escort at the door of the elevator. He was grim. On his first day as first secretary, his first official duty had been a meeting with President Joux. The meeting had only made clear the president's weakness and greed, and he was only one of many. Now that Chabon was able to deal with the weaklings, he wondered if his anger was sufficient to weed out all of them.

The Parade Guards outside his office opened the door for him to pass.

A white paper was centered on the desk, reflecting the midday light from the windows. The paper carried a bold red stamp at the top, big enough to read upside down.

URGENT.

Chabon took the paper and read.

The report from Megève was succinct. One policeman shot dead, another seriously injured; an unidentified man, totally bald, also shot dead, found on the road beside a Moskva sedan from the Ministry of Industry, Section of State Factory Controls. The car had been one of the labyrinth's. The bald man was surely Abruzzi.

Marcel Chabon wanted to rejoice in Abruzzi's death, but a new mystery submerged this victory.

Where was the boy and his foster mother?

Chabon studied the report. Abruzzi had abducted Noël Bazin from his school. Abruzzi was dead, and the boy was missing. There was no trace of Isabelle Bazin.

The dead policemen had been going to fetch the boy. Gousset had finally yielded, when the embassy had commanded him to obey.

Ugo Abruzzi had gone for the boy as well, and had got him, snatched him from the school. Someone had killed Abruzzi.

The only choice was the last man of de Celigny's group, Charles Nagy. Nagy had gone straight to Notre-Dame-de-Bellecombe for the boy.

The battle for the Star was not yet over.

Chabon had no more Action Branch, no staff at all except for the sycophants he had inherited from Paccard. Despite his title, he was alone. He counted on the Star as his weapon against the bureaucracy, but to wield the power of the Star, he needed power over Landry. The boy was important. Chabon reminded himself that Landry was dangerous. Landry could never be allowed to talk about Marcel Chabon's role in the last day of the labyrinth.

Chabon picked up the telephone from its onyx receptacle and keyed for the receptionist.

"Listen, I have need for my car. It is still assigned to the Ministry of the Economy, a new Peugeot from one of our State Factories. I will drive it myself. Do you understand . . . ? Have the car brought into the courtyard and left there with the keys. . . . I will not need a chauffeur."

He listened to the frightened voice of the receptionist asking if an escort was required.

"No, thank you. I wish to go alone."

It was completely abnormal for the first secretary to travel unescorted. He could not get away with such aberrant behavior for more than a day or two.

TWICE in twenty-four hours, Marcel Chabon had come to park on the short, dark side street that opened onto the rue Pouchkine.

Chabon walked to the corner, then down the rue Pouchkine to the warehouse door. He used the key that he had kept and let himself in. Darkness? Strange, what was his driver doing in the dark? Now his nerve ends were tingling, and he could feel a glow of sweat. He groped until he found the light switch on the wall and bathed the warehouse in dim light.

Chabon walked to the back of the warehouse, to the little sleeping room in the corner, and opened the door. Again, he searched for the light switch.

The trap door was shut.

Where was the driver?

Chabon warily turned back from the door and surveyed the sagging columns of paper boxes, the cobwebbed ceiling, the dust and mildew. He walked back into the shadows of the warehouse, pausing between steps to listen to the sound of stillness.

He heard the driver before he saw him, a soft rasping of breath lost in the rows, and he let the sound lead him part of the way. Then he backed up and made a circuit, coming into the rows from the other side, every sense alert, like a tiger approaching a tethered goat.

The man was sleeping, his hands and feet bound with tape, a gag in his mouth, his knees taped to one of the steel columns that supported the ceiling. Chabon had the wrists untied before his driver's head stirred awake.

Chabon removed the gag.

"Who did this?" he asked.

"I never saw him," came the answer. "Forgive me, comrade."

"How did he come in?"

"He was already here, hiding."

Chabon helped the driver to his feet.

"Wait by the door," he said.

He went to the little sleeping room and opened the trap door.

He lowered himself onto the ladder and started down. The light above faded into a glow and then into total darkness.

When the bottom finally met his feet, he held the ladder for balance. The darkness was as vast as space itself, as dense as the core of his brain.

His hands moved from the ladder to the walls, and he felt his way around the cave, his senses reduced to the weight on his feet and the rock under his fingertips, systematically sweeping up and down on the rough, damp stone, looking for a wire that would lead to a switch that could illuminate the cave. When he thought that he had touched every part of the walls, he searched the air above his head, turning slowly, a blind and clumsy dervish with arms extended above his head. He found the bulb by contact and reached to the switch above the bulb.

The cave was empty.

Chabon left the light on. He commenced the long climb back to the top. On the way, he decided that he could not let Landry survive out of control.

THE telephone clicked off line, and the chairman of Parallel Technologies immediately rolled the tape back to the start of the conversation. He was excited. What a coincidence, what a chance. He listened again, first to the woman asking him to speak to Marcel Chabon, the new first secretary of the French Communist party, prime minister of France, and then to the man himself, asking for help. The accent was heavy but the English was precise: France offered money and Robert Landry, in return for technical assistance with the French national computer. How much money? Any reasonable amount, said the voice.

And Landry? Did he want to come home?

Yes, the voice said. If it can be arranged.

The chairman listened to his own voice on the tape, explaining the difficulties. He was forbidden to transfer computer technology to the other half of the world. But his caller reminded him that no new technology was needed, only maintenance for an existing machine.

The chairman thought that this distinction might make the deal possible. To be verified . . . It was all to be verified, including the identity of his caller.

He had to know if this was the stroke of fortune he had been praying for. When Parallel Technologies should have been ready to collect the final payment for the Japanese project, his brightest kids were stumped. They were risking late penalties instead of finishing in triumph. But with Landry back, they had a fighting chance.

The caller suggested that the French ambassador in Washington could give *bona fides*. That reduced the chance of a hoax to near zero. The chairman agreed to call back after clearing the legal obstacles with the United States government.

The caller asked if there were experts on Parallel Technologies' staff who could understand Landry's work. Of course there were, the chairman responded, knowing that it was not totally true. He had at least three bright kids who could manipulate the French machine, but not one of them could match Landry's intellect.

The chairman listened to himself asking about Landry's well-being. The voice said that Landry was a fugitive from the security forces of France and that his departure would be a matter of life or death. The voice refused to elaborate on Landry's situation and abruptly said good-bye. The recording ended with a hiss of blank tape.

It would not be simple to get Landry out of France, that was clear, even with the new first secretary of the Communist party on his side.

He asked his secretary to place a call to the French Embassy.

In the house on the rue du Donjon, Landry's metal chair had a cushion, and a gooseneck lamp illuminated the keyboard. A wall-to-wall carpet lay soft under his feet. These new amenities did nothing to soften the end of his hopes.

Landry hit the keys with short, sharp strokes, carving out a safe life for the fugitives in Albertville, for Chantal, for himself: new names with family histories, cash cards, a provenance for children who would have to go to school.

When he was through, he would return to his plan of three months before and ruin the Star. It was defeat, but he was defeated already. France might rise again from chaos, but he would not let the New State use his machine to govern.

Chantal was out with the van, shopping for food in the markets of Vincennes. While Landry worked with the Star, her absence ticked away in the back of his head.

Her new identity and cash card had given her confidence to come and go from the house on the rue du Donjon. Landry hoped not too much confidence, but it was necessary that the neighbors see normal activity in and out, now that the place was occupied.

He heard the key turn in the lock and immediately stood up. There was a big smile on her face, and he felt the same tremor of response that he had experienced the first time he had seen her, in the Café de la Poste.

"We have a post card from Nagy," she said. "They are safe. With Catherine."

It was a card from the Haute-Tarentaise, a tourist greeting. *"Beautiful weather, wish you were here."* Under an illegible signature, Nagy had scribbled, *"We will be with mother."*

A knot of worry turned in Landry's heart as he thought of Noël and wondered how to create a new life with this woman and her son.

"What are you doing?" she murmured.

"I am making new identification cards for Noël and for Isabelle Bazin."

She looked at the screen, and he saw his own anxiety reflected in her eyes. She placed her hands on the nape of his neck and pulled his lips down to hers, kissed him with enough intensity to make his body stir.

"I think of my son and feel as though half of me is gone," she said, "and then I look at you, and I ask myself how we are going to live. This is madness, you know. . . ."

He embraced her gently, resting his cheek against her hair. She was tense in his arms, and he held her a long time before the tension eased.

She said, "You told me about your wife . . . how she lost you to the Star. . . . Will I lose you to the Star?"

The tips of his fingers rested at the hollow where her buttocks swelled out from the base of her spine. He felt the muscles harden as she waited for him to speak.

He answered. "The machine is nothing compared to you. I am going to spoil it for the New State, and then it will be over between me and the machine."

The taut muscles relaxed.

A wave of emotion for her swept his thoughts. He recalled how different it had been with Helen. She had been like a female Everest, a challenge with dozens of routes to decipher. He still remembered the sense of victory when she decided to yield. . . . But with time the barriers had lost their interest, he had wearied of being a Sherpa of love, and fatigue had come into their life, as unwanted as a street beggar and no less insistent.

With Chantal there were no barriers. They rode together at the front of the roller coaster, side by side, mind and body.

She spoke to him, her words muffled in the hollow of his shoulder. "I worry so about Noël. What if she won't give him up? I want to see him, and yet I dread the moment. . . . What if he blames me for deserting him?"

"You must go there," Landry said. "It should be all right."

He did not know if it would be all right. And if Noël came back with her, he was not sure how they would manage to give the boy a decent life.

And he wondered what Nagy wanted to do. Chantal would have to ask him.

17 Minister of the Interior Morand sat in a two-hundred-year-old chair, a meter distant from the vast desk of the first secretary. He stared at Marcel Chabon on the far side of the desk and tried to imagine his new chief's intentions.

Morand had expected vague formalities from the technocrat who had been minister of economic affairs. Instead, Chabon had asked for a computer terminal with direct read-and-write access to MSIE's secret files.

Morand shifted position, leaned forward in his chair, and scratched his head. "Comrade first secretary, let me be clear. . . . You want the machine here, in this office?"

"Yes. Here. And there is more. Please explain the security to me. . . . You have passwords?"

"Of course . . ."

"Explain how they work, please."

"It is complicated."

Chabon nodded patiently.

Morand explained, "The information of MSIE is divided into separately secure compartments. Within each compartment, a series of passwords is needed, each with different limits. Each password needs to be matched with the user's secret number. We change the passwords and also the user numbers every week, on Sunday night at midnight. I make up the list at random, out of my head, on Sunday afternoon. And then I give the list to your technician, and on Monday morning I personally give the passwords and user numbers to the department heads."

"Tell your technician to come to me," Chabon commanded. "The terminal in my office must have access to all the MSIE files, with passwords and a user number that I enter myself. I want to set up a special compartment of information that allows entry only by me, from the terminal here. Tell the technician that he must show me how to enter my own password and number, so that even he will not know them."

"May I ask the first secretary what he has in mind?"

Chabon replied solemnly, "You may ask, but I will not tell you."

Morand bowed his head.

Chabon relished being able to command from the top, for the first time, after so many years of juggling his way through the maze of the French bureaucracy. "Another request, comrade minister. End the search for Robert Landry and Chantal Senac. Remove the bulletins from the walls of the post offices and the police stations."

"Should we close that file as well?"

"For the moment, yes. I would like my computer installed by noon tomorrow."

"If we can do it in that time . . ."

"Please be sure that you can."

Morand shook his head. It was a mystery what Chabon wanted from the computer, and even more a mystery why they should give up the search for Robert Landry, who was so important that France had been turned upside down to find him.

They shook hands, and Chabon accompanied his minister to the door. Morand wished him luck, and Chabon watched him walk away before he turned back to his desk.

With a little good fortune, he thought that he would regain control of the Star.

It took three days and the combined efforts of the Ministry of the Interior and the Ministry of Communications to put a computer terminal in the first secretary's office, and it took three more days for the MSIE technician to debug the system of access codes, so that the first secretary could use the computer.

Chabon's first entry in his private MSIE file was a week after the date of his request.

*   *   *

CHANTAL concentrated on climbing, pushing back her anxiety about meeting Isabelle Bazin and her reunion with Noël.

She was alone, wearing Catherine's shoes and the hiker's clothes she had worn on the day of her capture.

She had come with Catherine Moreau in the Deux Chevaux to a shady covert at the edge of the valley, where a torrent had cut a slash in the descending wooded flanks of the mountain. There Catherine had stopped the car, kissed Chantal, and sent her on foot, to climb up to the rendezvous.

Chantal scrambled upward, following the watercourse, breathing deeply and stretching the muscles that had been idle since Notre-Dame-de-Bellecombe.

The top of the gully led her onto a path that would take her to the refuge. She continued up into familiar ground.

The roof of the hut huddled into the surrounding rocks, almost lost in its rocky surroundings. The rocks were silent except for the whisper of the wind.

She opened the door and went inside, down over the board that served as a sill and into the single room that was dug out of the rocky ground. Clothes were neatly hung on the walls, and there was a loaf of bread on the table, dimly visible by the sunlight that filtered in from the door.

She returned to the rocky patch outside and sat down to wait in the sunshine.

She felt Nagy before she saw him, ten meters away.

"Nagy . . . where are the others? My son . . .?"

"He is here. What do you intend, Chantal Senac?"

"I have an identity card for Noël and a new cash card for Isabelle Bazin. A message for you. . . ."

"Do you want to take Noël away?"

Chantal walked toward him, picking her way over the tumbled stones. He waited for her, as immobile as the slab he was standing on.

"Yes," she said. "He is my son."

"Wait here."

Nagy was gone without a sound, so quickly that she could not see the way he had taken.

Chantal heard the crunch and grit of approaching footsteps on the rocky scree. Isabelle was coming toward her from the place where Nagy had disappeared. Chantal saw a pale face framed in black hair, and from the dark hours in Notre-Dame-de-Bellecombe, Chantal remembered the sturdy figure, the upright posture.

Isabelle stopped once and then continued, her hand out, her eyes full of questions.

Their hands met.

Isabelle was crying, and now Chantal felt tears overflowing onto her own cheeks.

"We thought that you were dead," Isabelle said. "When Noël came, I never thought that you would come for him. I love him."

"Isabelle, for two years I prayed to God that someone would love him and take care of him, wherever he had been sent. My prayers were answered. I feel as much love for you as you have given to him."

Isabelle wiped her eyes. "Charles has gone to get him."

"Did he ever speak of me?"

Isabelle hesitated before answering, as though she wanted to be careful. "No. I think he could not stand the memory of losing you. . . . At first he surely thought that you were dead, as I did. But this spring, when your picture was on all the walls, he never said anything to me. I could tell that he knew it was you. He may have thought that you abandoned him. That would have hurt him more than thinking you were gone."

A spear of panic lanced through Chantal. Would she be rejected by her son?

Then she heard his feet on the rocks and turned to see him running toward her. She was on her knees and he was in her arms, bigger now than the child of her memory, a young man with a broad forehead and a straight nose, with weight in his shoulders that suggested the mass of Arnaud's body.

He let her go for a moment and then held her again. The sensitivity in his expression belied the beginnings of a hard, strong jaw.

"Come, let's go into the refuge," Chantal said, her eyes so full of tears that she could not take a step until she had wiped them clear.

At the entrance, Isabelle hesitated, as though not wanting to intrude, but Chantal put an arm around her waist and brought her in with them.

In the hut, Noël told about his despair, the end of happiness, when they had said that his mother was dead.

He told her how much he loved Isabelle Bazin.

She asked him about school, and he replied that he was the best in his class in all the examinations, but that the children of the town were still faster than he in the ski races. He spoke clearly, older than his twelve years, and she felt that he was full of purpose like his father, but he was more gentle than she remembered Arnaud—as gentle as Landry.

Then she told him about his father, how his father had been at the heart of the revolution when the Russians came, how he had taken charge of all France from a secret labyrinth under Paris. She said that Arnaud had believed in something more important than Chantal or Noël Senac. When Noël asked what that could be, she simply said that she could not explain it. It hurt, as she was speaking, to think how Arnaud had betrayed them. She said the Arnaud was dead.

She told Noël that she was living with a man she loved, and that she expected to live with that man for the rest of her life.

She said that the man would love Noël as his own son. In all this, Isabelle listened in silence.

Noël asked her, "Do you want me to go with you?"

"Yes," Chantal said.

Noël looked at Isabelle and then at the floor. He did not answer, and Chantal's heart sank.

Then the door opened, and Nagy asked permission to come in. With Nagy, scrambling down the steps, came Michel and little Jean-Pierre de Celigny, into Chantal's arms with a big three-way embrace that chased away her fear.

Later, she gave Isabelle the cash card that would have a permanent recorded balance of fifteen thousand francs, no matter how much she drew on the account.

And she handed Nagy the envelope from Landry that had been folded twice to fit into the bottom of her bag. She had begged Landry to give her a message in writing, so that she would not need to know it. Nagy frightened her.

Noël's future was never mentioned, and Chantal feared the moment of decision. He was even more precious now than in her long journey in time without him.

They slept that night on cotton mattresses that had been stacked against the walls of the hut. Nagy and Isabelle curled up together in a corner, and Chantal realized that a new identity card would be needed to provide for a man in Isabelle's house. Noël slept beside her, and when she put out her hand, he squeezed her fingers.

She did not sleep well, but in the morning Noël waked her. As though the dawn had brought the answer to the questions she had slept with, Noël asked her if he could ever come back to see Isabelle. She wiped away the cottony mist of sleep and she said yes, if it was possible.

They ate bread and cheese for breakfast, and they talked about the art of living in the mountains.

When it was time to leave, Chantal caught Isabelle staring at her.

"We will find our way back here, Noël and I," Chantal said, wondering if Landry could make it possible.

Sober-faced, arms around her neck, on tiptoes, Noël kissed Isabelle good-bye.

Michel and Jean-Pierre hugged Chantal and would not let go until she gently pushed them away.

Isabelle kissed her, leaving her cheek damp, but then Isabelle crouched down beside Michel and Jean-Pierre and put her arms around them, squeezing them to her. Chantal understood that Isabelle would be rich with love, even without Noël.

Nagy brushed his cheek against hers in farewell.

"Tell Landry that I say yes," Nagy said, and Chantal felt a chill.

She walked with Noël to the big rocks that bordered the hut's clearing. They turned to wave at Isabelle, Nagy, and the two boys, and Chantal wondered how soon she would see Nagy again.

Catherine picked them up where the road crossed the bottom of the watercourse, in the same place where Chantal had started out the day before.

THE clock in his head ticked away the last hours of her absence. Would she come back with Noël? They should be getting off the train in the next half hour, taking the *métro* and then the bus to Vincennes.

He wondered what Nagy had told her.

Questions buzzed in his head. Why had the search for Robert Landry and Chantal Senac been stopped? Were they trying to lull him while they launched an attack unknown to the computer? Landry had expected more pressure from Chabon, not less. But the New State was behaving as if the Star was once again secure: the security services spelled out their suspects, their investigations, even their intentions.

Landry keyed in the codes for MSIE as the beginning of his check procedure. After months of looking at the same array, where only the code letters and user numbers changed, he immediately recognized a change in the pattern. Someone had added a section of files and assigned a new set of codes.

Landry tapped in the codes and examined the directory of files. There was only one file listed. Its title was simply: *Message–1.*

Landry opened the file and read. It was brief, and it was addressed to him.

> *Comrade Robert Landry*

With all my heart I hope you will believe that my purpose is the same as yours, to win our country back from the Russians.

I still need your help. Will you give me the information that you started to develop for the pilot release project? There are many who will be grateful.

This file is for your eyes and mine only with passwords that were known only to me until you discovered them. I pray that you are reading this—and for your answer.

Marcel Chabon

It was incredible. Landry reread the message, wondering what he should do.

Landry knew that silence was the most powerful weapon. He could make Chabon suffer in doubt, wondering how the Star might strike against him.

The screen was like a magnet, drawing the answer out of him.

He wrote the text of his reply a half-dozen times before he entered it in Chabon's *Message-1*, below Chabon's words.

>*First Secretary Marcel Chabon*

I do not believe your plans for a new France, because of my wife Helen, killed, my friends at Parallel Technologies, Saccard, Blum, Guérin, Millet, Lamey, and Barneau, all destroyed without pity, and my friends de Celigny, Euler, and Thevenet, betrayed while assuring your succession.

I will help you to open the State Factories because refusal would be cruel. Do not ask for more.

You are no different now from what you have always been.

I do not trust you.

Landry

He verified the integrity of the characters and registered the file, leaving the message on the screen. It was done.

She was home at just the moment when his mental clock was ready to send shrill alarms. She came through the door with the boy, and in the first moment, Landry knew that he would like Noël. The boy came to him to be embraced, a kiss on both cheeks.

"They have called off the search for us," Landry said. "And Chabon sent a message. It is on the screen, with my answer."

"What does he say after all his murders?"

"You must read it yourself. I hope you agree with my answer."

CHABON looked at Landry's reply with a thrill of anticipation. The link was made: it was half of what he needed.

His next message was ready in his head and only needed to be put into the computer. Chabon typed and read over his words. They were almost all true. Chabon named the file *Message-2* and consigned it to the Star.

LANDRY had followed an electronic path back through the Star to the monitor on Chabon's desk, so that he was watching as Chabon composed the message, the letters filling the screen with a confident rhythm.

>*Comrade Landry*

Thank you for offering the work that you started. I ask you to continue your help despite your reasons to hate me.

Your wife should not have died—would not have died if we had known where to find you.

We needed you to show us how to manage the Star. I share responsibility for the hunt for you, but not for the shot that killed your wife, or the interrogation of your colleagues. I regret these events as I regret other mishaps in these confused times. If we had been able to find you, it would have saved your wife and your friends.

I also regret the loss of de Celigny, Euler, and Thevenet on the night that Georges Paccard died. The colonel in charge of the Parade Guards was in the restaurant with his chauffeur and bodyguard outside—an unforeseen hazard that cost de Celigny his life.

Let me try to persuade you by my hope for this country.

I want only fairness for all the people. Long ago I gave up the communist religion—it does not work except to put limits on unrestrained greed. But I believed in the Russian side because there was no better hope for fairness in the West. When the Russians came, I was glad.

We started with the terror that you have blamed us for, to be sure that France would never fall back. We were severe enough to convince the Russians, but we tried to limit the suffering.

The Russians gave us Paccard and a bureaucracy to control production and consumption. But I also had enough power to keep the political committees out of the factories, out of the banks, out of the laboratories.

You, Landry, you are the model worker—driven by what you can do, not by what you can gain—I have already provided shelter for people like you. They are many, and they are starting to work.

I have no fear of rebellion, not after two-and-a-half years—and finally I am able to eliminate the excesses of greed and gain that so enraged Arnaud Senac.

Achievement can be permitted but excess and self-indulgence are forbidden. Can you object to that?

By now you surely know that I have stopped the search for you and for Chantal Senac. I do not ask for your trust. You can work in secret.

Help me, Landry. How can you refuse?

Marcel Chabon

Landry typed his answer without stopping to think.

First Secretary

You will crush all dissent—how can you speak of freedom

from the Russians when you will replace their dictatorship with your own?

You can find the necessary information to begin the pilot release project by entering the following code in the Ministry of the Economy's daily record: XXBBS1e231

Our communication has ended.

Landry

THAT evening, Chabon received the call he had hoped for, from the chairman of Parallel Technologies. The United States government would approve a maintenance service for the French national computer. Chabon and the chairman agreed on a schedule.

It was the other half of the plan. Chabon sent a new message to Landry.

>*Comrade Landry*

I acknowledge with gratitude your instructions concerning the pilot release project.

Now, I give you some good news: Parallel Technologies asks your return to the United States. They have offered a man who can manage the Star in your place.

I offer you passage out of France, if you do not wish to stay.

The chairman of Parallel Technologies is coming in three days. You should return to the United States in his jet. You may go with Chantal Senac and her son, if they are now with you.

Do you accept?

Marcel Chabon.

Chabon expected to wait for the answer.

*   *   *

THE boy watched Landry as he showed how to move through the vast reaches of the Star. But then Landry came to Chabon's new message, and his mind left Noël. Landry called for Chantal and waited while she scrolled back the screen and reread the words.

He had put the possibility out of his mind since that morning meeting so long ago in Cleveland.

Landry turned to the boy. "Noël, would you like to go to the United States to live?"

Noël thought for a moment and asked, "Would Isabelle be able to visit us?"

"Things would need to change, but we would try. Will you go?"

"Yes," Noël said.

Landry imagined waking up each day without fear of discovery, with Chantal as his wife and the boy as his son.

"Would they let us live in peace?" Chantal asked. "They killed your wife in the United States."

Landry weighed what he could expect from Chabon, and the answer was as true as it had been hours before . . . *I do not trust you.*

He asked Chantal, "Will you go to the United States?"

"Yes, if you think we should."

He knew how it should be done.

IT was no more than a noise, an invisible dot against the light of the setting sun, streaking east toward Paris. The plane had flown nonstop from New York. There were three in the crew—pilot, copilot, and steward. Two passengers.

Crossing the coastline they plunged into a thick bank of clouds and picked up Paris radar control.

Fifteen minutes later, the little jet taxied slowly past ranks of wide-bodies at Karl Marx Airport. The letters *PT*, bold in red, straddled the luminescent gray and green of the fuselage—*P* for "Parallel," *T* for "Technologies."

Customs officers came on board, stooping in the tubelike chamber of the passenger compartment. The chairman received them seated in his easy chair. He had nothing to declare, not even a briefcase. His companion, an olive-complexioned young man with a mass of dark curls on his head, opened an attaché case to reveal a tiny computer. It was their only baggage.

An official Moskva limousine waited just five meters from the plane, a black beetle beside a landed swallow. Overhead, the darkening sky was steel gray and hard with threatening moisture.

The chairman led his companion from the aircraft to the car. He took the right corner of the back seat and settled into the soft velvet upholstery, his shoulder against the wood-panelled door. The younger man sat in the opposite corner. He started to speak, but the chairman put a finger to his lips.

Windshield wipers rhythmically stroked away the wet as the limousine took them on a fifteen-minute trip outside the perimeter of the airport, to a hotel that was too big for the narrow road. A junior manager carrying an umbrella greeted them in the parking lot and led the two visitors directly through the lobby to an elevator. They were lifted to the top floor, where the manager left them at an open door.

Their transatlantic journey ended in a suite overlooking farm fields that were disappearing in somber twilight.

The thick carpet, the carved wood furniture, stained off-white, and the heavy chintz curtains predated the change of regime. The chairman went from the sitting room into the bedroom. A pink and white comforter lay flat on the bed, matching framed prints of pink and white flowers on the walls. The bathroom was tiled white. Thick pink towels hung from a bar, the name of the hotel etched in the velour. New soap and shampoo waited fresh in cardboard boxes.

His inspection complete, he returned to the sitting room. He had stayed in a hundred suites like this, except for the two portrait photographs that hung between the windows. The chairman supposed that he was looking at Marcel Chabon's picture, but he did not know which one it was. He sat down, his back to the window view and the photographs.

Again the young man started to speak, and the chairman silenced him by cocking a hand to his ear and shaking his head.

They waited.

Half an hour later, the telephone rang. The chairman picked up the receiver and listened, a smile growing on his face.

"Robert!" he exclaimed. "Yes, it is really me, here in France."

The chairman nodded to his companion, then frowned and hesitated before he spoke into the receiver. "I remember that we celebrated in the bar of the . . . Brown Palace Hotel. Right? . . . Of course, you have to be careful, I understand."

The smile returned as the chairman put down the telephone. It did not leave his hand before it rang again.

"Hello? . . . Yes, that was him. He is on his way," the chairman responded. "Yes, I have his replacement here with me."

Hardly a minute had passed before a knock sounded and a key rattled in the lock. The door opened, and a round-shouldered man entered. He advanced into the center of the room.

"You are the chairman of Parallel Technologies? I am Marcel Chabon, prime minister of France and first secretary of the Communist party."

The chairman held out his hand and was surprised by the strength in Chabon's grip.

"Let me present Danny Perso," the chairman said. "Danny can make your computer dance if you want."

Chabon took Danny Perso's hand, and the chairman wished that Perso was ten years older.

"We wait then, for the guest of honor," Chabon said, and he sat down in the easy chair opposite the chairman's.

"Have you reviewed the draft contract?" the chairman asked.

"Our Ministry of Communications is reviewing it," Chabon answered. "We see no obvious problems."

"Then we should begin very soon," the chairman said.

The door opened and Robert Landry entered.

He stood just inside the door and surveyed the room.

"Robert!" the chairman greeted him, getting up from his chair.

"Hello," Landry said. "Wait, I must check the next room."

Landry strode into the bedroom, shutting the door behind him. Moments later he reappeared and, only then, went to shake hands with the chairman and Danny Perso.

Up to this moment Landry had ignored Chabon, but now he

turned to the first secretary. "You guarantee our safe conduct?" he asked in English.

"Yes."

"The jet can go at any time?" Landry asked the chairman.

"Yes."

"Do we have anything to discuss here?" Landry asked.

"No," the chairman said.

"Then I will call Chantal and have her come with her boy."

Landry dialled, listened, and said, "We can leave. Come."

"Let's go," Landry said. "She will meet us on the way to the airport."

"On the road?" Chabon asked.

"Yes."

"Where should I tell your driver to stop?"

"I will tell him where to stop."

Chabon nodded slowly. He looked up at the chairman.

"I have changed my mind," Chabon said to the chairman. "Mr. Perso seems very young. I am not convinced that he is capable of replacing Robert Landry. And if Robert Landry has sabotaged the Star, I fear that only Robert Landry will be able to undo the harm."

"What is that supposed to mean?" the chairman asked.

"He means that the deal is off," Landry said.

"But you said safe conduct!" the chairman shouted at Chabon.

Like ice, Chabon answered, "Words have no value when the fate of a nation is at stake. You will go back to the United States. I think Landry will help me if his woman and her boy are in our custody, and I would rather have his help than Mr. Perso's."

The chairman was red with fury. He took a step toward Chabon, but stopped when he saw the blade that flashed in Chabon's hand.

"Do not stretch my hospitality," Chabon said. "In any case, I am not alone. Others in this hotel are listening for trouble."

"My God," the chairman said. He looked at Landry, who was rooted in place. "I'm sorry, Robert."

"I am not surprised," Landry said. "He just wanted to get

me out of hiding. It was worth a try, but now you should go. There is nothing more for you to do here, and he will not let you stay."

Chabon took the telephone off its cradle with his free hand and put it on the table. He dialled three numbers and then raised the telephone to his ear. His eyes never left the three men in the room with him, and the hand that held the knife never quavered. He asked for an escort to come to the room.

The manager came through the door within seconds. "Please come with me," he said to the chairman and Danny Perso.

Landry held out his hand. "Thanks. We tried."

The chairman took Landry's hand in silence and then faced Chabon. "You will hear from me again."

"I will add you to my list of worries," Chabon said.

Alone with Chabon, Landry said, "You have won. What next?"

"We will need to pick up the woman. Easier if you come with us . . . to avoid an unnecessary panic."

"I agree."

Chabon reached again for the telephone, but Landry said, "Please wait. Before we go, I am desperate to take a pee."

He stepped quickly into the bedroom, and Chabon followed through the door, two steps behind, as Landry wanted him to.

Nagy's fingers struck true to the target, and Chabon died noticing that the window was open. He did not even moan.

Nagy's arms were tight around Chabon's round chest before his knees stated to buckle. Nagy lowered the body quietly to the ground.

Landry ran water into the sink and then flushed, for the microphones.

"I'm ready," Landry said. "Let's go."

Nagy took his Heckler & Koch machine pistol from the floor beside the door and followed Landry through the sitting room, into the corridor outside. The passageway was empty. They took the emergency stairway, Nagy leading the way with the machine pistol ready in front of him.

They stopped in front of the exit door at the bottom of the stairs. Nagy passed over the keys to the van. "The van is parked at the end of the lot nearest the road. Walk there slowly, get in, and start the motor. When I hear the motor, I will come."

"Where are they?"

Nagy did not answer.

Landry opened the door and stepped outside. It was almost dark.

"Stop," a voice said. "Who is that?"

"I work here," Landry said. "Who are you?"

"Wait there. Don't move."

Chabon's sentry was alone, posted at the corner of the building.

Landry placed himself a meter from the open door and prayed that the sentry would come close enough for Nagy.

The man stood a head taller than Landry. He came forward but stopped too far from the door. A weapon was in his hand, pointed at Landry.

"Identification," he said.

Landry reached into his pocket, put his fingers on his wallet.

"Shit," Landry said. "I left my wallet in my desk. I must go back."

"Wait," the sentry said, but Landry was already leading him to his death, stepping into the open doorway with the sentry close behind.

Nagy's extended fingers struck again, and this time his victim fell as though pole-axed.

"Go," Nagy said.

Landry's heart was beating like a snare drum. He went out the door, turned, and walked into the parking lot. A large blue bus with wire mesh over the windows was parked in front of the hotel entrance. Chabon's reinforcements had not been far behind. But Chabon had not known that Nagy was a guest in the hotel.

Landry located the van and walked to it, wondering how far he could go before men would pour out of the bus in pursuit. Each step was a small victory.

In the van, Landry put the key in the ignition and heard the rumble of the faithful motor. The bus stayed quiet.

He saw Nagy coming, a slight shadow moving without haste from the corner of the building.

They were rolling. Landry turned the van onto the main road to the airport.

"We have an hour and a half," Landry said. "It should be enough."

THE guards with black snub-nosed automatic weapons outnumbered the passengers in the departure area of Karl Marx Airport. Chantal clutched Noël's hand and prayed that she could control her shaking knees, hold her arm steady as she handed over their passports. What if they were asked questions? What if Landry had made a mistake with the documents?

They waited at the registration desk, presented their tickets to a severe-looking black woman, were assigned adjacent seats. The woman wished them an unsmiling bon voyage.

Signs led them to a stark chairless area facing a row of glassed-in cubicles. Only one of the cubicles was occupied, and there a line of passengers had formed. The narrow passageway past the cubicle marked the only way out of France.

Chantal and Noël took their place in line behind a florid-faced man. He was sweating, mopping his forehead with a patterned handkerchief, and he made Chantal think of the stickiness in her own armpits. She stared at the cubicle. When the officer inspected a set of papers, only the peak of his white cap was visible above the walls of the cubicle, and she could not see his face.

The line advanced slowly. Chantal held Noël's hand tight in her own.

Just beyond the cubicle, where the path led into the waiting area, a pair of guards lounged, with weapons hung on their shoulders.

The florid-faced man reached the cubicle. He passed a packet of documents through the small hole in the glass partition.

Chantal could not hear the officer's question, but she could see the florid man's alarm. He leaned close to the hole and started to speak, too rapidly. Chantal could not make out the words, but she saw that his explanation was not succeeding.

Then the officer stood up, signalled to the waiting guards, and opened the door in the back of the cubicle. The officer gestured for the florid man to follow and led the way to a blank gray door in the wall. They went through and the door closed.

The guards came and stood in the pathway, weapons ready.

Chantal felt totally exposed, next in line, facing the guards at five meters.

She forced herself to breathe slowly, to stay still, to keep her body from going tense.

The officer returned alone to his cubicle and gestured to Chantal to step forward.

She made her hand steady as she gave him the passports and the authorizing documents. She was Corinne Blanchard, an official of the Ministry of Health and Education, on her way to a conference on Third World education. She was escorting her nephew, the son of the commercial secretary of the French Consulate in New York, who was going to visit his father during the school vacation. Her papers included visas, approvals from the Foreign Ministry, and a letter from the Ministry of Finance authorizing her to change money. She had an approval from her senior at the ministry and from the minister himself. Noël had a letter from the consul and a document stating that he was entitled to his vacation after a year in good standing.

The officer took the whole package, hardly glancing at her. His head bent as he started to read. Occasionally his shoulder and head would move in a way that made Chantal think he was seeking information from the Star.

He raised himself to look over the partition at Noël and then looked up at her as he settled back into his seat. His black eyebrows met over his nose, which made him look as if he was scowling.

"Tickets and boarding passes?"

She fumbled as she extracted the tickets from her satchel, and she told herself to slow down.

He took the tickets.

And then, the whole mass of papers was coming back through the hole in the glass.

"Thank you," she said.

The officer waved her by and looked for the passenger behind her.

She gripped Noël's hand and squeezed with a sweat-damp palm. He looked up at her for reassurance, and she knew that he had been as scared as she.

They were early, and many seats were empty in the waiting area. Landry came through the formalities twenty minutes later. He did not acknowledge her or Noël.

"**Who?**" the chairman demanded. He had in the United States for only twelve hours and had just arrived in his office at Parallel Technologies headquarters in Cleveland.

His secretary told him again that Mr. Landry was on the telephone.

They met five hours later in the secure room where they had held their last meeting.

"I thought I would never see you again," the chairman said.

"But here I am," Landry said. "We need help. Chabon is dead. But our entry was illegal. All our documents are forged."

The chairman reassured him. The same people in Washington who had given him approval to go to France had just heard the results of the trip. They would find a way to provide shelter.

"I have a document here," Landry said. "It's another forgery, but Chantal agrees to it. It's a French certificate that says she's married to an American national. In case anyone wants to know."

The chairman grinned.

"So," he said. "Tell me what you did with the machine."

Landry told him that the bureaucrats in France would now have to contend with a computer gone berserk. The chairman listened, fascinated, as Landry described the interacting viruses that would attack the Star. The Star would become sick, recover, die, and come back from the dead. There would always be hope that the Star could be cured without the need to start over from zero.

"And can it be cured?" the chairman asked.

"No."

"The hardware is corrupted?"

"Yes."

"So the whole machine needs to be replaced. A three-year project . . ."

"If you are thinking of sending Danny Perso back to France, don't. Let their government sink."

"Anyhow, I couldn't get approval to sell a new machine to the Russian side."

"Do you have work for me?"

"If you don't mind working on the Japanese project. We're in trouble, and we need you."

PARALLEL Technologies loaned a new Oldsmobile to Landry. He took Chantal and Noël to a restaurant that specialized in lobster and steak.

They ordered "surf and turf" and talked about learning English and living in a house with grass around it. It seemed so normal to Landry, as though France was on another planet.

"What will happen to Isabelle?" Noël asked.

"Isabelle can go back to Notre-Dame-de-Bellecombe," Landry replied. "The Star has given a new identity to Nagy and the de Celigny children, so that they can live with Isabelle. Isabelle will have cash, and Charles Nagy will have work. The whole area of the Savoie will be spared most of the Star's problems. And if we can hope, Europe may change again, and we will go back and forth across the Atlantic . . . like the old days."

"What will happen to us?" Chantal asked.

"We will be safe," Landry said. "We can begin again, as people should, together and free."

"But . . ." She started to argue, weighing this new freedom against the fear she had left behind.

"I know," Landry answered her, his mind already at work. "Be patient. There may still be ways."